SWEET MUFFIN RANCH

Willow River Press is an imprint of Between the Lines Publishing. The Willow River Press name and logo are trademarks of Between the Lines Publishing.

Cover design by Suzanne Johnson

Between the Lines Publishing
1769 Lexington Ave N, Ste 286
Roseville MN 55113
btwnthelines.com

First Published: September 2023

ISBN: (Paperback) 978-1-958901-43-4

ISBN: (Ebook) 978-1-958901-44-1

Library of Congress Control Number: 2023940973

SWEET MUFFIN RANCH

Matthew Blasi

A Note from the Author: *Sweet Muffin Ranch* unequivocally takes an anti-dog fighting stance. One of the novel's central premises is that kindness and compassion toward animals is *absolutely crucial*, and that dog fighting is, in the words of the protagonist, something that can neither be stomached nor forgiven. I recognize the complex economic and cultural practices that help to perpetuate animal cruelty, including but not limited to dog fighting, and encourage those with knowledge of the activity to speak out and contact law enforcement and animal protection services. More information can be found at the following resources:

Stand Up for Pits: https://standupforpits.us/dog-fighting/

American Society for the Prevention of Cruelty to Animals:
https://www.aspca.org/investigations-rescue/dogfighting

The Humane Society of the United States:
https://www.humanesociety.org/resources/take-action-stop-animal-fighting

To Mom. Gone, but never forgotten.
You would have loved this book

Part I:
The Ranch

Chapter 1

Gene Temmens came home on a rickety bus. Over the twenty-hour trip he talked up the driver and brought the man's mood around from cold and distant to warm and friendly—close, even. He got the guy to loan him ten bucks, share a sandwich, and agree to drop him close to home. He also got the guy to talk, and in so doing, became privy to the driver's many woes, foremost of which was the driver's ex-wife, a woman who had accosted a member of their lawn maintenance staff into rough, and to quote the driver, "unforgiving coitus."

"Seven great years," said the driver. "I never strayed."

"Not once?" said Gene.

"Never. Now what I got? A bad back. A brother with rickets."

"Least you got this job," said Gene. He smacked an empty seat for emphasis.

"I would take her back," said the driver. "Even after all that. If she just asked."

"What are the odds?" asked Gene. But really, he didn't care, and all that prompted him to ask was boredom. The man's tragic arc as a one-sided betrayal, the resilient lover adrift on the highway, stuck behind the wheel with an aching spine, so on and so forth, it sounded made-up, like an inferior version of the kind of story Gene would tell to move someone to pity, and he'd tell it for better profit than boring a customer to tears.

"Not good," said the driver. "But I would in a heartbeat. This the way?"

Gene perked up when he saw familiar overgrown foliage outside the window. "Just follow that dirt road."

It was a detour of some significance that Gene had gotten the man to undertake, several miles outside the designated bus station and a mile from home where the road turned to dirt and gravel and the woods sprang up thick. But the few other passengers, those not asleep in their seats, hadn't noticed, and when the driver finally stopped the bus he shook Gene's hand, smiling like they were the best of friends.

"Never told me your troubles," said the driver.

"Few and far between," said Gene. It was a lie, of course. He had plenty of troubles. That's why he'd come home to regroup, maybe borrow some money, and figure out what to do next. But he wasn't going to tell any of that to the driver. Instead, he shook the man's hand, stepped down onto the dirt road, and stretched his cramped legs. The bus pulled away in a cloud of dust. Gene ran his tongue along his teeth and spat. His mouth was gritty, dry. He was sandpaper, inside and out.

It was a woody patch he cut through on the outskirts of Columbia, South Carolina. Big beards of Spanish moss draped the willow oaks, and frilly sassafras grew wild and sweet-smelling. In a culvert choked with dandelion weeds and plastic milk jugs, two turkey vultures were picking apart a possum. They plunged their hooked beaks into bloated pink innards and tore off long, bleeding shreds amid a thickening cloud of black flies. They returned Gene's stare with their own, black-balled, and unwavering, never ceasing their feast. Just beyond them was a dirt road winding through the trees, up and around the hill.

Home, thought Gene. Though it sure as hell didn't feel that way. Until a day ago, home had been Big John Bull's Dog Rescue in Austin. It had been a legitimate job—a rarity for Gene; a bizarre pit stop at the end of four years ping-ponging across the country in search of … well, that was the thing. He couldn't recall with any legitimate precision *what* he'd once left home for—what he was supposed to find or accomplish. Years ago, all he'd known was that Columbia was not for him. Being the state capital, it wasn't a small city, and it wasn't a city lacking jobs, people, or opportunities. On the contrary, it had been growing; a booming Southern metropolis approaching Charleston in size and density and already outpacing it in political importance. It was also deeply *weird*. Kudzu-draped forests and brambly rock foothills clawed at the edges of the streets, and longtime residents, to say nothing of the tourists, often found it difficult to distinguish between country and city. That was, Gene had to admit, its charm. Columbia was a place unlike any other, teetering on the brink of being overtaken by the wilderness it daily beat back with highways eternally under construction. Gated housing communities sprang up beside shotgun shacks dating back to the Civil War, luxury apartment buildings rose above boarded up bungalows, and on the outskirts, right where Gene had grown up, there lived whole communities of folk smart or savvy or dumb enough to have bought up crumbling mansions and ruined estates that better resembled museum displays of a bygone era. It was a city with fine universities whose students and faculty alike gathered in the off-hours to pack the bars, united in their disdain of the tourists who seemed unable and unwilling to locate the charm so apparent to residents.

But five years ago, all that charm had worn off. Gene had gotten tired of the few friends he'd kept from high school, of the bars he frequented, the paint-by-numbers romantic dalliances that never went anywhere for any real stretch of time. His interests had always lain elsewhere—namely in carving out some niche of his own. Nine-to-fives weren't for him. College wasn't for him. His calling was elsewhere, and his talents lay in suckering people into outlandish ideas. Grift, cons, he didn't care what anyone called it. Money wasn't the point. The point boiled down to a nebulous idea of hitting some long-shot odds that seemed, on the surface, impossible to pull off and yet would promise some fabulous and substantial reward. He lived for the feeling that whatever ridiculous enterprise he was presently engaged in, a scarcely educated country bumpkin could, and often did, outsmart everyone around him. The rich, the brilliant, the powerful, it didn't matter. The point, Gene maintained, was about *punching up*. And then getting paid for his troubles.

Gene had the wits for it. He had charm, natural charisma, and just enough looks to pull it off—dusty black hair, delicate eyelashes, long in the frame. The quick, crooked smile, that's what had gotten him out of more than a few jams. To that end, he'd spent an uneventful year in Colorado conning the ski bunnies, a few months in Philadelphia selling timeshares that didn't exist, and a few more in the Everglades where he'd helped a friend, Don Lettuce, gather funds to build an elaborate alligator hotel—a wild and untested idea wherein clients would aid in the tending, grooming, and feeding of a large and temperamental herd of savage reptiles. The whole thing, from the design of the gator pens and hotel layout to the structuring of fees and charges had been made up on the spot halfway through a night of drinking not one but two bottles of Old Grandad 114. It was ridiculous but that hardly mattered. Lettuce considered Gene's ideas to be strokes of genius and set to work acquiring land, renovating a building, and generally soaking every last dime he owned into what Gene considered a doomed and ridiculous venture.

As for Gene, he rounded up a group of wealthy investors, a pack of absolute dullards who had made millions investing in tech startups and smart cars, and skimmed heavily off their substantial buy-ins before he left Florida. It floated him for a year wherein he'd roamed: Tampa, Miami, Houston, New Orleans, and then Austin, where the money finally gave out. It was the moths in his pocket that made the job and free room and board in a shed off the back of Big John's rescue appealing to the youngest Temmens. But it was Big John himself who sealed the deal; a trusting one-eyed dogcatcher who rescued strays and whispered them into new and docile creatures ready for adoption.

On the interview, he'd given Gene the tour, asked him about his experience. Gene had none and was plain about it. Sure, his family had always had dogs, and sure, he'd done his fair share of training them in the most rudimentary ways—but professional experience? Nada. He told Big John about his sole volunteering stint for an animal shelter in Columbia, a position he held for a month until he learned what happened to the dogs who couldn't get adopted. Something about passing by the empty cages on his shift, cages in which sad, friendly dogs had once stared out at him through chain-link, got under his skin in a big, bad way. He quit one day without warning, without explanation, and even though he had told himself he was being ridiculous, the images of those bare concrete cages haunted him. And something about the way Big John looked at Gene told him the man knew it all without Gene having to say a word.

They'd wound their way across Big John's sprawling compound, most of which were large, open-air enclosures with shaded overhangs and long benches packed with snoozing dogs. Then Big John hit him with the big one: "Why this job?"

Gene had expected the question. What he hadn't expected was the blurry, smeary sadness it dredged out of him. The pay was decent, and the included room and board sweetened the deal, but that was only half the answer. The other half was a tangled shoestring of feelings he wasn't ready to pick apart. Not in front of Big John.

But he didn't have to. Big John led him to an enclosure where dogs not yet fully rehabilitated ran in snarling packs. He suggested Gene step inside, feel things out. Then they'd both know if he was right for the job.

Gene eyed the dogs who eyed him back "You want me to go in there?" he asked.

"Sure do," said Big John.

"Hope you got good insurance."

"Enough. Get in."

"This how all your job interviews go? I'm not getting in there."

"Dogs got to decide," said Big John.

"Decide what?"

"Whether you got the job or not."

The whole time Big John had stared into the enclosure, hands on the chain link, a knowing look in his eye. Gene had nearly walked out of Big John's then and there. He didn't like having to prove himself, especially considering the low pay on offer, and he sure as shit didn't like feeling that Big John could read him the way *he* read others. Plus, there was the whole setup, the chain link enclosure, the dogs, the sounds of their barking and whining and their nails clicking on the concrete. The whole thing gave him bad vibes. He felt like his older brother, Rich, a man haunted by (the literal, he claimed) ghosts of his horrific wartime exploits, afraid to probe at the edges of his memory and experience for fear of what lurked just out of reach. Put simply, there were things in a man that he would only ever struggle to explain, and Gene wasn't interested in sussing them out in front of a stranger.

That's what he told himself, anyway. But thinking back as trudged up the dirt road, drawing ever nearer home, he could admit that was only half true. Thing was, there was part of him that wasn't getting bad vibes, but in fact, an eerie yet comforting sense of familiarity. The way the dogs looked at him, looked *through* him, it rattled his bones. They, like Big John, seemed to know something about him, something deep and true, at a glance. And his interest was piqued, both by Big John's peculiar demeanor and the fact that the man seemed entirely confident about asking an unqualified stranger to enter an enclosure with untrained, possibly hostile dogs. It was the kind of stupid gamble Gene couldn't refuse.

He opened the gate and went in, not pausing when the big pit bulls and thick-coated mutts grunted and growled. What little he'd learned from his long-ago shelter job came back to him: stay calm, no sudden moves, and avoid eye contact. He stood rooted to the spots, eyes trained on the far end of the enclosure while the dogs closed in and got a good sniff. One dog, a large, thick-necked mutt with a meatball for a head, ambled slowly over, a gray mass at the periphery of Gene's vision, grunting and chuffing in the back of its throat.

"That's good," he heard Big John say. "Easy now."

Gene couldn't have replied if he'd wanted to. His tongue was pasted to the roof of his mouth. He felt sick and elated all at the same time. He felt the dog's cold snout brush his fingers and he looked down at the dog's enormous face, saw the mishmash of old scars all over his jowls. A thick white line of uneven fur looped the dog's neck where some restraint, a rope or chain, had dug into the animal for God knew how long.

"Bait dog," said Big John.

Gene said nothing. He knew a little bit about what dog fighting entailed—growing up in the South provided plenty of that—and he deplored the so-called sport with every fiber of his being. To extract pleasure from rich, gullible yokels willing to invest in outlandish schemes? That was one thing. To take sick pleasure in hurting animals? That was something else. Something Gene couldn't stomach or forgive.

"Rescued him last year," continued Big John. "Took him a while to get comfortable but look at him now. An absolute mush."

The dog began to lick Gene's hand, a gentle plea for attention. Gene squatted down, let the dog get a good, long sniff, and ran his hand over the animal's scarred, knobby head. Content, the dog turned and went back to its spot across the enclosure. Gene watched him go, watched his sad waddling walk. The other dogs paid him no mind. They ran amok, barking and playing and sniffing at Gene.

After a little while, Gene turned and went back through the gate. He was sweating through his shirt and the brim of his hat.

"You got it," said Big John.

"The job?" said Gene.

"That too," Big John said with a smile.

And that was it. Gene began his year-long apprenticeship to the dog whisperer of Austin. Big John Bull was a man more at peace with dogs than other people. It didn't matter the creature's past or temperament, if they'd chewed people, destroyed property, or were deemed too far gone to ever be rehomed; wild or broken, they all came to heel for Big John. The ones that could be adopted, Big John found them homes. The ones that couldn't lived out the rest of their lives in Big John's shelter, cared for until old age took them in the dogcatcher's loving arms. There was a strict no-kill policy at Big John's because it was a shelter, a rescue, and not, in Big John's own words, a fucking dog prison.

Gene had expected that first-day feeling to wear off, that sense of comfort at being around the dogs, that trepidation every time he saw an empty crate or saw a dog loaded into a car and driven off to its new home. But those feelings never abated, and neither did the confusion they stirred in him. Rather than think about it, he applied himself to learning what Big John had to teach him, which was more or less everything that could be taught about the ways of canines, how to soothe them, train them, and how to lead a pack. In short order, Gene mastered Big John's three basics of becoming a man among dogs: the walk, the leash, the loving calm. To Gene's surprise, it came naturally. Big John, on the other hand, was not surprised.

"Some folks just have it," he told Gene one night after the shelter was closed up and the dogs fed and bedded down. They sat in the parking lot under a fair, open sky, passing a fifth of bourbon back and forth. The day's heat radiated up from the blacktop and cooked the men as they stewed in liquor.

"What's the 'it,'" Gene asked. "Patience?"

Big John shook his head. "You can buy that at the Dollar Store. I'm talking about the dog star."

"The what?"

"You heard me. It's in there," Big John said, and directed a finger at the middle of his breastbone. "Way down deep."

"Best tell your doctor," said Gene.

"Very funny. But it's true. It doesn't go out. And if you got it, you got it."

"What if it does go out?"

"It don't."

"But what if it does?"

Big John took a swig on the pint and passed it Gene's way. "Then I guess you're well and truly fucked."

There passed between them a long moment of silence in which they passed the bottle, eyes on the sky. In times like those, Gene had always expected Big John to probe into his past, to suss out Gene's secret history, and in such times, Gene had fervently hoped such questions would never come. Being around Big John made Gene feel that his years on the road, his grifts and cons, had been the machinations of a child, an idiot set loose in the world to commit idiotic deeds. Had Big John asked him, Gene would have had to face his own smallness. But Big John didn't ask—not then, not ever. The man seemed content with the *now*, the shelter, the dogs, the time when night swept over the sky and the day's work was behind them until the next day began.

"Bring the bottle," said Big John as he rose from his creaking lawn chair." "Let's go read poetry to the dogs. They need education and art."

Off they went to read poetry to the dogs—Keats, Shelley, racy Byron. The animals issued howls of approval that spurred them to new literary heights. They tested poets against the dogs, and whoever failed to thrill the animals was deemed unworthy and dismissed. Billy Collins, for example, was much beloved by the dogs, but Ezra Pound succeeded only in driving them to boredom and their chew toys. And when the dogs were at last asleep in their pens, the two men retied to the porch to listen to mosquitoes crisping in the bug lamp, finish the bottle, and talk about the future. Big John wanted to expand the shelter. He wanted to save more dogs, give them better lives. And he wanted Gene to get certified, take the courses, get the piece of paper that would tell the whole world that Gene had the credentials and training to do the job as good as anyone. Gene told the man he was out of his mind—no way was he going to fork over money to get something that wasn't legally required (and since when had he cared about legal requirements?). But Big John silenced him by offering to pay for the whole thing, the classes, the supplies, everything. He knew the folks who taught the course, and what's more, he knew Gene would actually enjoy it, a certainty that Gene himself thought was ridiculous—until Big John was proved right. Gene took the courses. What's more, he *enjoyed* them, and by the end of his first year in Austin, he had the piece of paper and a sense of accomplishment he had never before felt outside of convincing rich idiots to pony up for an outlandish scheme.

By then, Gene knew the score. Big John wanted Gene to stay indefinitely. He never said it, but he didn't have to. And in those moments, Gene came to respect and admire Big John Bull. It was rare that he met a person who could teach him something. Rarer still to make a genuine friend.

If only Gene had kept out of trouble. Over the course of the year, he'd gotten friendly with a trio of loquacious bookies—Loke, Roy, and Malak. For a while, the tips he had been getting on college and pro sports games had been impeccable, so he began borrowing to make bets. It was risky, sure, but after the wild gamble that had been Don Lettuce's alligator hotel, Gene felt he could pull off anything. And that's when things went sour. He sank a hundred grand of the Texans' money into a long-shot college football game that was, according to his sources, a done deal. But disaster visited in many forms. In the first half, his team's quarterback was sacked by a three-hundred-pound senior, a hit that broke the kid's collar bone in two places. Two plays later, the team lost an offensive tackle to a concussion and their star receiver pulled a hamstring. The backups played like terrified adolescents and were subsequently flattened by the opposing team.

Gene panicked. With no hope of paying back the Texans and knowing the terrifying lengths they'd go to extract their due compensation, he decided to flee. He caught Big John at dawn while the man was opening the rescue and sprang the news.

"Leaving," said Big John. "Here? Now?"

"I got to," said Gene.

The look of crushing disappointment on Big John's face said everything. He stuck a finger under his eye patch and rubbed the puckered skin where his eye used to be. "In bad, ain't you?" he asked.

"Put it this way. If someone comes looking, you don't know me, never did," Gene said. "I'm sorry."

"What about them fellers?" Big John said. He swept his good eye over the packs of dogs gathering for their breakfast.

Guilt burnt Gene's cheeks. It crushed him to leave the dogs, the kennel, the place where he'd found some measure of peace for a year. Aside from the fun and games with the Texans, he'd kept his nose clean and his head down.

Looking at the dogs, he could admit what until that moment he would never have dared to let himself think: He belonged there. It felt like home in a way Columbia never had. But it was too late and if he didn't leave, he'd only pull Big John into his problems.

"I don't know what to tell you," said Gene. He shook the man's hand.

Big John nodded sadly. "I guess that's so," he said.

"Take care."

"Remember that dog star."

"Sure," Gene wanted to say. But he didn't say anything. Big John's stupid poetry about dog stars and magic lights. Absolute nonsense. But it stuck with Gene, rode with him all the way from Texas to South Carolina, and remained there in his brain, as irritating as a pebble in his shoe as he rounded the final bend in the road and climbed the drive to the Temmens estate.

There he paused, taken aback. What had once been a well-kept country estate had gone to seed. The three-story house was all torn screens and peeling paint, a broken window round the side covered by weather-grayed plywood. Roof shingles littered the waist-high weeds, the grass hardly less imposing save for a narrow path beside which the old push mower sat rusting. Gene hiked around to the side lot and found his car—a '99 Mitsubishi Lancer. Little remained but a badly rusted purple husk devoid of tires, glass of any kind, and seats. The car sat on blocks while beside it his mother's aging Datsun wore a fine sheen of pollen and bird droppings. Rusted tools lay strewn about, remnants of some forgotten repair project—likely Rich's, and as with all of Rich's projects, abandoned part way. Gene rapped the dented, rusted hood of the car and went back around front to stare up at the sagging eaves and the bowed floorboards of the porch. A window air conditioning unit buzzed somewhere along the periphery of the house, its noise barely audible over the uproar of crickets and cicadas. Out beyond the house, Gene saw the peach orchard, once the family's pride, in similar disarray. Rotting peaches peppered the many piles of rotting leaves. The whole place stunk like mildew and sour fruit.

Gene shook his head. They'd never been rich, his family—hell, they'd never really been *comfortable*--but they'd gotten by. His parents, Mattie and Dale, had done their best to keep the place up. Or had it always looked this way and Gene had simply forgotten? Had five years away from home tarnished his memory? He hiked through the weeds and climbed the porch steps, testing them with his foot to make sure they'd hold his weight. Before he'd made the last step, the front door swung open to reveal his mother, silver hair braided over her shoulder. She wore a loose-fitting housedress and perforated rubber shoes. Her face, more heavily lined than Gene remembered, still had its bronze tint, and her dark eyes were still sharp and wily. Mattie came from folks in Louisiana, a mix of Choctaw, Mexican, and Irish—a blend Dale matched with his family full of Cajuns and Creoles.

"Gene?" she said with an appraising tilt of her head.

"Mother," he intoned. "Yard needs work."

Mattie slapped the screen door. "First thing out your mouth is sass."

"I was going for 'tried and true."

Gene wrapped his arms around her, careful not to snag the plastic hose that looped around her ears and under her nostrils, connected to an oxygen tank on the other end. Three years ago, her chronic bronchitis matured into full-blown emphysema, the sum value of twenty years of cigarettes, annual bouts of pneumonia, and a career working in a chemical plant. Reluctantly, Mattie had quit the cigarettes for the gum, then the patches until they made her sick. So did the pain pills the respiratory specialist prescribed. But Mattie had an answer for that and had taken to growing a rather heady breed of marijuana out back. From the plants she harvested heavily-furred buds, dried and ground them, and encased the fragrant green powder in gel capsules—her space pills, as she called them. She smelled faintly of dried buds, menthol, shampoo, and the licorice chews she indulged in throughout the day.

"How you feeling?" Gene asked. "Why's the house look like shit?"

"Tried and true was right," said Mattie. "I'm fine, thanks for asking, but you won't be if you keep on. You hungry?"

"Thirsty," said Gene. "Where's Rich?"

Gene went directly to the liquor cabinet. The homecoming was making him anxious. There were memories around every corner, under every creaking floorboard, and if most of them were good, they only served to remind him that the house had never felt like the kind of home that Big John's had been. He needed a drink. Two drinks. Three.

"Rich is at the Days Inn," said Mattie. "Don't say nothing about the librarian."

"The what?" asked Gene.

"He bit her."

"That's a new one. What for?"

"You know his bad brain. And the ghosts."

The ghosts, Gene mused. Rich's explanation for everything. And what was the explanation for the house's condition? The depleted liquor cabinet? He found a bottle whose label declared itself whiskey, but its contents had been replaced by an amber liquid in which floated slices of puckered peach. He recognized it as his brother's frequent experiments in home distillation. The first few batches had brought out sweats, seizures, and incredible bouts of vomiting. Later batches had only slightly tempered the effects.

"Why didn't you call and let me know you were coming?" asked Mattie.

"Spur of the moment," said Gene. "What about Dad?"

"What about him? It's him that's responsible for this mess."

"Back gambling?"

Mattie and her tank ambled by, headed for the bag of licorice chews sitting on the dining room table. Mother and son were already locked into the old rhythms. Soon they'd be jawing about the past, then about the more recent past, and that was a topic Gene didn't want to get into. He sniffed at the peach brandy, hoping his brother had refined the recipe.

"Had it licked a while," said Mattie. "Then he got in deep with a bad fellow, some crazy that keeps calling here, saying nastiness. I've been making do with my disability, sold some furniture, sold your car."

"Parts of it," said Gene.

"The good parts. Be a dear and reach me that magazine and roll it up. That's a good boy."

Too late, Gene realized his error. Now armed, Mattie began to swat him with the magazine, pursuing him through the hall and up the stairs where she finally halted, wheezing hard and purple in the face.

"We hardly heard from you," she gasped. "Now you just turn up asking about the house like you give two whoops? I know you, boy. What kind of trouble you in?"

"Put that down and we can talk."

"I asked you a question. Don't lie and don't give me that face. Get within striking distance or fess up."

Gene retreated another step. He could spin a yarn about wanting to come home, check on his folk, but of all the people he could lie to with ease, Mattie was not among them. He braced himself and decided to give it a try: "I'm fine, okay? I just wanted to see how y'all are doing."

"There's phones for that," wheezed Mattie. "Counting that as half a lie."

"And borrow a little money."

Mattie winced. "Why can't the apple fall far?" she said and rapped the magazine against the railing. "You got your father's bad blood and not a damn dime between us. And I know what you ain't saying. You're in trouble. You're always in trouble."

"Look," Gene began, feeling suddenly foolish and small, a child before his angry mother. But Mattie waved away whatever he had to say and retreated into the living room. There she fell into the overstuffed recliner and put her feet up, taking the oxygen in big sucking breaths. The veins in her temples stood out with the effort. Gene waited until she'd relinquished the magazine in an unspoken cease-fire before he went into the kitchen, wet a washcloth, and applied it to his mother's forehead.

Mattie's gaze remained fixed on him. "Suppose I missed you?" she said.

"Supposed I missed you, too," he said.

"I'm supposing."

"I'm home now," said Gene.

Mattie snorted. "Question is for how long," she said.

"A little while," said Gene. "Don't get philosophical."

"I'll philosophical your face. Get my air machine. Then get out a while. I got to settle, think about things. So do you, I'll bet."

He did as she requested, uncoiling the hoses from the much-larger oxygen-producing machine that sat in the corner, and bringing them to her. The battle for air had tinted her face pale blue. Something about her in the chair, about the look of relief on her face when Gene switched on the machine and Mattie got a good lungful under the clear plastic mask kicked Gene in the stomach. She was right. He needed to get out for a while. He needed to think.

He found the keys to the Datsun hanging from a hook beside the door and found a spare bottle of whiskey on the porch. Only it, too, had been supplanted by the peach brandy.

Gene made it halfway to town before he pulled over to test Rich's latest batch. Sweet up front, pure napalm on the back end. Dangerous. But not wholly unpleasant. He sipped the brandy while he plotted out his day's trajectory. Rich had to come through with a little money. Rich or Dad. But from what Mattie had told him, neither was likely.

This town, this place, Gene thought. He was stuck in it.

The peach brandy fueled his rage. It also filled his bladder to bursting. He relieved himself on a tree and took evil delight when his stream destroyed the delicate webbing of a banana spider. Evacuating his bladder helped him to think. He would find Rich and see if he could spare a few bucks, but what difference would a few bucks make? Gene would have to get back on the road before long, certainly before the Texans figured out where he'd gone. Loke, Malak, and Roy didn't fuck around. They'd cave in his knees, take everything he owned. And when they realized he didn't own much, they'd start looking around for other things to take, other people to injure. Gene had to be long gone before that.

Sudden braying shook him from reverie. From the trees darted ten or twelve hardscrabble dogs, a loud, frantic pack that descended on the Datsun. They nosed about the tires before marking their territory, not a single collar among them. By the looks of it, they were a pack, some of them with ribs showing through the skin, all of them too lean. Gene zipped up and turned to get a better look. Not feral. Just hungry. Lost. He tried a low, friendly whistle, something he'd used at Big John's to test out whether or not new dogs had been housebroken or trained. The dogs bunched up right quick, ears pricked, tails lowered. A few of them barked and gave low growls. Not good. He kept his gaze on the trees just behind them, where he could see if the dogs made any sudden movements without making direct eye contact and waited until the barking had settled down. A pack of strays could be dangerous. Left to their own devices, dogs sometimes reverted to their baser instincts. He might know how to handle them, but other passersby might look for all intents and purposes like a threat. Whatever their temperament, he couldn't allow himself to be seen as vulnerable. Pissing on what was probably their territory could be taken as an act of aggression. He had to level the playing field—and fast.

Gene had just decided on trying his luck with a few commands when another bout of braying erupted from the woods. Another group of dogs emerged from the trees. A split pack, much larger than he'd imagined. The dogs convened and he identified the leader, a calm mutt spotted in brown and black. Bit of rat terrier, maybe, bit of coon hound. The dog took one look at him, eased back, and turned the pack into the woods. In a flash the dogs were gone. Columbia had always had a problem with strays, particularly in the poorer outlying areas, and it seemed to have gotten worse in his absence.

He was further ruminating on the dogs, his happier times, when the mosquitoes gathered in a whining cloud and drove him back to the car and the reality of his predicament. Spiders, mosquitoes, and stray dogs were the least of his concerns. A man could go for a walk, step on a rattlesnake, and meet his maker. Cottonmouths were known to wriggle aboard small fishing dinghies and assault sportsmen. Black widow spiders, brown recluses, killer bees, and blood-sucking swarms—the South was flush with flora and fauna that existed for no other purpose than to terrorize and kill. And speaking of getting killed, he needed a plan, action, and money or the Texans would find him and make the wildlife look tame in comparison. Dale, his father, was always good for a roll of twenties, and his older brother Rich had his vet pay, his disability. Between them he might scrape together a few hundred—enough to decide what to do next.

Gene drove back to the dirt road and aimed the car toward town proper. He had his plan now, yes, but he couldn't get his mind off the dogs. He imagined them hungry, covered in fleas. In his mind he saw them running through the woods and over the hills–to grandmother's house! Oh ho, the brandy was taking hold! In his mind's eye he saw the dogs and wondered: What if one of them had a thorn in his paw? What if they had ticks? What if some drunk redneck who *wasn't* Gene got the fright and took it into his mind to drive out there and *shoot* the dogs?

"Quit it," Gene said aloud. He was making himself sick. Him and the brandy both.

And anyways, he was finding the road strange in its dimensions. The Datsun kept angling itself to the road's shoulder, refusing to cooperate. Nor would the law as he was pulled over on a stretch with too much sun. The cop seemed an odd sort, plain clothed and without lights or sirens, much less a police vehicle. Just waving through the window and grinning like an idiot.

"This car's got attitude," Gene said when he managed to roll the window down. He tried not to squint so hard but his eyes, like the car, refused to comply.

"Gene?" said the man. "Holy, it *is* you!"

Gene blinked through a brandy haze. He cursed Rich's brew for its terrifying potency. The man opening Gene's door and trying to pull him from the car seemed familiar. Some dork in a straw hat, a raggedy t-shirt, and cargo shorts pulled too high. But the face, the young angular face, that Gene recognized. Not a cop at all! It was his old friend, James—all stick legs and bony knees and big stupid grin.

"How the hell are you, buddy?" said James.

"Drunk," said Gene.

"Then you probably shouldn't drive. Had no idea you were coming home."

"Unexpected," said Gene. He shielded his eyes from the sun's glare. "Just here to check on my folks and Rich," he said. "Anyway, I had the road. I could sort of see it."

"That Rich's brandy?"

"None other," said Gene. "Listen, you seen any dogs running around out here?"

"Tons," said James. "My girl says the whole city is bad with them."

"Your girl? Look at you."

"Not exactly my girl. Laura. She works for animal control."

Even in his brandy-fueled haze, Gene detected a great deal to unpack in James's talk about a 'Laura.' He shelved that for when he was sober and focused instead on what he could manage in his compromised state. "Animal control?" Gene scoffed. "That's cops for dogs."

"It's a job, Gene."

"I'm gone five minutes and everything goes to hell and you're dating a dog cop."

"Five years ain't five minutes," James said and waved his hand in front of his nose. "Christ, you smell like rotten fruit. Where you headed? I'll give you a ride."

"I'm good at driving."

"Not right now."

"No," Gene admitted, corking the brandy. "Not right now."

Gene sized up his friend. On James's face was the old, soft smile. James, always gullible, always trusting, always the scapegoat. For James was a rube, the pliable sort who could be convinced either under duress or liquor to go about nearly any tomfoolery. He'd also been a hopeless romantic—still was, by the sound of it—whose aptitude for talking to members of the opposite sex bordered on shamefully inept. James the ever-loving, never-loved; James the inept. Precisely what Gene needed. He climbed into the man's car.

"The Days Inn," said Gene. "Or whatever hovel where Rich is staying. We can come back for the Datsun later."

"Fine by me. Just don't have any more of that for a bit, yeah?"

"Don't plan to. But take it easy on the brakes."

James talked as he drove, telling Gene of his failed careers in catering, tuxedo rental, stand-up comedy. Gene feigned surprise. He loved the man, he did, but James had always been oblivious to his dearth of talents, and every enterprise was doomed by virtue of his participation. Cursed, some would call it. But Gene knew better. The man refused to acknowledge his faults, fooled himself into thinking he was the most skilled, the most qualified for every damn idea that lodged in his brain. And when it didn't work, the blame had to lie elsewhere. But one thing James always had was a little money socked away. And Gene was about to ask James for a loan, just a little something for old time's sake, when the man began dour talk of his recent job hunts, his dwindling savings. That last brought forth a sour belch from Gene's innards. It wasn't just wildlife out to harm a man. It was evaporating jobs, crumbling city economies. Big tech firms threatening to swoop in, build skyscrapers, and hire thousands of people, only for everything to go up in smoke. Rich folk fled the city and built sprawling, hideous mansions on the outskirts. Others fled to Charleston, Savannah, and Asheville. The city's water system was (still) in serious disrepair, boil advisories on the regular.

While James talked, Gene looked out the window at the city. Most of the places he remembered were shuttered—the bars, the restaurants, the low-income apartment complexes with their molded brick facades and cracked sidewalks. As they drove further from the city's center, the roadside weeds grew taller, choked with garbage, and here and there crosses wreathed in flowers marked the spots where people had met their end in sudden, wrenching collisions. In the parking lot of a Walgreens a homeless man sat baking in the sun, shirtless and visibly drunk, hugging a Redbox stand. The man's attitude of rapt submission seemed fitting testament to a city that would just as soon forget the people and neighborhoods like him.

At the Days Inn, James dropped Gene beside the front office, then swapped phone numbers and invited him to grab drinks later.

"More drinks," said Gene, shaking the bottle of peach brandy. "Sure, why not?"

"I'll invite Laura. And bring Rich."

Gene snorted. They both knew Rich was as likely to join them for a night on the town as he was to re-enlist, but that was James for you. Polite to the last. Gene slapped the hood and James drove off, leaving Gene to wonder, just for a moment, how he would retrieve the Datsun. But he already knew.

Rich was sitting outside his room and nurturing a plant. This consisted of holding a jelly jar within which a potato was putting down roots into brown water. Gene recognized his brother at once with his long hair and beard, his many tattoos, his glazed and meek expression. He appeared a dazed hippie in his sandals and beach shorts, his soiled white t-shirt. Gene found another chair outside an adjacent door, pulled it over, and sat down across from his brother. Rich looked up and blinked.

"Mom called ahead," he said.

"Figured," said Gene. "Happy to see me?"

"Plenty," said Rich.

Gene reconsidered his earlier statement and took a heavy pull on the brandy. "Spit it out," he said.

Rich shrugged. "You're back," he said matter-of-factly.

"Who could resist this view?" He could see through the open door into Rich's motel room, a cramped shoebox with a bed and dresser strewn with clothes, empty takeout cartons, and empty jelly jars ready for the potatoes scattered on the floor. The TV was muted, turned to daytime courtroom shows, the kind where people tried to explain to an exasperated judge why they stole their lover's lawnmower. The sight sobered him considerably. "We still doing it?" he asked.

"Doing what?"

"This," said Gene. "Our old routine. Arguing." Last time they'd been together, he and Rich had argued about everything—Rich's prospects, Gene's leaving, the ghosts. Christ, the list went on and on. Mainly they fought about who was going to stay and take care of Mattie and Dale, and Gene had won that one by hitting the road.

Rich looked at the bottle in Gene's hands, then reached across with his long, tattooed arm and took it. "This mine?"

"One of them. You pour out perfectly good whiskey or you drink it first?"

Rich took a long pull on the peach brandy, then sat back and smiled contentedly. "Good batch."

"Absolutely horrid," said Gene. "I got more questions."

"Welcome home."

"What the hell *happened*?"

"A lot of things," said Rich "Mom's breathing is bad. And getting worse. I was going to stay with her but I couldn't. Or she couldn't. Too much noise. And dad's dad but more so. He's in deep."

"To whom?"

"Hollis Lerne."

Gene racked his brandy-soaked brain. Hollis Lerne. Hollis Lerne? "Pawn broker? Has a shop or two across town?"

"That's the one."

"Does a little loan sharking? He's a blip, a chump."

"Not no more," said Rich. "He's bad news. Front page."

Gene very much doubted that, but he didn't come to argue about their father and his gambling debts. The only story Gene could recall about Hollis Lerne went as such: Hollis Lerne was a mild-mannered proprietor of a handful of dilapidated pawn shops with a reputation for minor loan sharking. Customers and borrowers alike walked all over him. A year into the pawn business, a man entered the store wearing little more than a raincoat and tennis shoes and carrying an unloaded small-caliber pistol. He proceeded to make much show of the weapon, scaring Lerne stiff. The man went on about how the postal system was reading his mail, poisoning his oatmeal, and watching him while he slept. Then he put the pistol on the glass counter and asked in a level, steady voice, "How much?"

Word on the street was that Lerne bought the pistol for market value, dollar to the dime. And there were other stories, too, all revolving around Lerne being little more than a door mat. Lerne was nothing to worry about. And anyway, he hadn't come to the Days Inn, drunk on peach brandy, to talk about a wet rag loan shark. He had other, far more menacing loan sharks to worry about. But first, he needed to make small talk, set his brother at ease. Rich was stubborn, and if he sniffed out Gene's ulterior motive too early, he would dig in his heels and become obstinate for no other reason than he could. Then no amount of smooth-talking would win him over.

"What's this about you biting a librarian?" asked Gene.

Rich winced, took back the bottle. "Don't want to talk about it."

"Ghosts tell you to do that?"

"She was mad. I got banned."

"Who needs books? You got daytime TV and plenty of it."

Rich stared at his knobby toes. "I felt bad."

"Send flowers, toothpaste," said Gene. He pressed no further because doing so would inevitably lead to a discussion about Rich's ghosts, apparitions that had haunted him ever since coming home from the war. General family consensus was that it was PTSD, nothing more. The only upswing in his brother's condition was his pliability, his ease of influence, upon which Gene was preparing to get to work. But first, a drink, a refreshment. The peach brandy was too warm.

Gene ducked into Rich's room, scrounged a clean-enough plastic cup from the bathroom, then started looking for ice. "Anyway," he said, "I get home and Mom's zonked on space pills and the house looks like shit. You take apart my Lancer?"

Outside, Rich held his tuber, staring off across the parking lot, lips moving almost imperceptibly under his beard. The goddamn ghosts.

"Hey," Gene barked. "Astronaut man. Ice. Frozen water. Where is it?" He tossed aside a pile of dirty clothes only to find an even dirtier pile. On the nightstand were Rich's medications in a dozen or so orange plastic pill bottles. "You still taking these? And you still seeing your therapist?"

"Now and again," Rich said from the doorway. He had quit mumbling to himself, or to the ghosts, and was starting to perk up.

Gene knew when Rich was lying, but he also knew not to press his brother too hard. He was trying to soften him up, after all, not raise his hackles. Though, looking around at the terrific disaster that was Rich's room, he began to suspect that Rich wasn't going to produce much in the way of funds.

"Keep going," said Gene. "Good for your brain. And speaking of brains, I need to cool mine down. Where the hell's the ice bucket?"

He emerged into the too-bright sunlight and took the bottle. Rich looked up, eyes bright, with a strange and secretive smile spread across his face.

"Got something to show you," said Rich.

"Don't take your shirt off," said Gene. He felt like his brain was starting to pickle. Rich led him to the parking lot where he presented what looked to Gene like a dilapidated ice cream truck crudely painted in dull gray. A stink of sweat and rotting upholstery wafted out of the filthy windows, and a glance inside revealed an interior as coarse as the exterior, empty but for two slashed-up seats, the gear shift, and a rusted iron ring posing as a steering wheel.

"It's my business truck," Rich said proudly.

"What business?" said Gene.

"I don't know yet. I was thinking something with the land, the orchard. Maybe delivering peaches."

Gene looked from his brother to the truck. Rich was kidding. He *had* to be kidding. "You don't got a business," he said.

"Not yet," said Rich. "But I want one."

"And I wanted some damn ice for five minutes now. You know those peaches got worms, right?"

"I'm serious."

"So am I! You telling me this motel doesn't have an ice machine? Never mind, I'll find it myself."

Rich grabbed his arm. "Think about it," he said.

"Think about what?" asked Gene. He picked a handful of bird feathers from the front grill to distract himself from a meltdown. Rich did this. He got a dumb idea into his head, some ridiculous notion that had no basis in reality, and chased after it for a few weeks, maybe a couple of months, until it fell apart. In the past, it had been opening a restaurant despite never having worked in one, or even being able to cook, or even knowing how to hire people who knew how to cook, and anyway not having a palette more sophisticated than a possum on codeine. Before that, it had been a house painting business wherein, again, he had no experience painting houses and could scarcely identify a paint brush from a skill saw. The list went on and on. The plants, the tubers in the jars, that was the only thing Rich ever stuck with, and only then at the behest of the therapist. That and the damned ghosts.

Then Gene had an idea. "You buy this outright?" he asked. "What's it worth?"

Too late, Gene realized his mistake. He'd moved too fast. A change came over Rich's face, first as he looked at his decrepit truck, then as he peered at Gene.

"I get it," he said. "The old routine. You want money, right?"

Gene scoffed in what he hoped was a convincing manner. "That's not the routine."

"Sure is," said Rich. "I know you."

"I'm just inquiring how my older brother is spending his hard-earned government money. And maybe wondering why you bought something that looks like it used to be full of dead bodies. What did you get it for? Two grand? Three?"

"Does Mom know? Or did you lie?" asked Rich.

"Slander. Here I am, trying to connect with my older brother, and what does he hurl in my face?"

"I don't got it. Everything went into the truck. But maybe if you come work for me—"

"Jesus," said Gene. "Work for you? Work *for* you?"

"With me, then. Truck's paid off. All I need is an idea and that's where you come in. You're the idea man. We could do it together, you know?"

Gene pressed his palms into his eyes. In a minute, he was going to say some rather unkind things to his idiot brother and then they'd be back to fighting, just like always, and Gene would be in the same place he was at that exact moment: screwed. Bad idea. He took some deep breaths while Rich pelted him with talk about some nonexistent business, telling him again and again that he *had* to do something, and that if he had to do it on his own, it wasn't going to work. Nothing he ever did on his own ever worked. He didn't have the necessary creativity. But Gene did. Gene felt the anger stick in his throat.

"What *it?"* Gene barked. "There's no *it,* no business. It's just you and a jalopy."

"I told you," Rich said. "That's where you come in. You're the idea man."

"Here's an idea," said Gene. "Insure it. Then light it on fire."

"I'm serious," said Rich.

"So am I. Now please get me some damn ice before my head explodes, all right?"

While Rich went to fetch the ice, Gene tried to reign in his temper. He hated the very thought that he was supposed to fix whatever dumb idea his brother was trying to hatch. But he hated even more his brother's pleading tone. He knew Rich meant it. The man was crazy enough to imagine that whatever this *thing* was that he needed, he genuinely believed they could pull it off together, much as he genuinely believed that the rusting hulk parked in front of the Days Inn was the proper vehicle for the job. It was nuts. And it wasn't getting Gene anywhere. That left Dale, their father.

"Put a damn pin in it," Gene said when Rich returned with the bucket of ice. "Does this thing run?"

Rich had brought a handkerchief and packed it with ice. "Mostly," he said, and Gene was relieved to see Rich had cooled off and taken the hint.

"Great," said Gene. "Take me to see Dad."

"Now?" said Rich. "You sure?"

"Good a time as any," said Gene. He accepted the peace offering that was the ice-packed handkerchief and applied it to his head. The boil in his skull subsided. So, too, did his expectations.

Mattie wandered the yard ripe with evening sun, happy her youngest boy had at last come home. She didn't dwell on the fact that Gene was likely only looking to scrounge some money before he got up to God knows whatever he was going to get up to. Her youngest was *home*. That's what counted. Now she had to figure out how to keep him there.

In high spirits, she went out to the orchard, keeping care of the oxygen hose's proclivity to snag on roots and brambles, and called out to the snobby peacocks. They were a mated pair that had shown up one day, all bright plumage and dirty looks, to saunter about the place with an air of continuous disapproval. In her years before the full-time oxygen, she had often coaxed the animals to issue forth and feed on crumbs, sometimes directly from her hand. She didn't even mind their stink-eye. But now they avoided her, startled by the hose, the tank. To her they turned their rumps, plumage spread. She took it as a sign, an omen. Disaster to come. That, too, she must find a way to thwart.

Mattie wanted her family, damn it. She wanted them close by and happy—or as close to happy as they'd let themselves be. She wanted them to be better than they were. Whole. Her health was bad, and her animals distrusted her but she had her boys, and anyway she didn't much trust them not to make messes of their lives without her there to guide them, right? Her in her old age, in her twilight years, it would be good to have her boys close at hand. And was it too much to ask that they stick around, listen some?

"My *boys*," she told the flora and fauna. Hours ago, just after Gene had left, she had taken two of her space pills. Now she was completely and utterly stoned.

Her mind was moving, though. Always did once she got high. So here was another thing: It was time to get back on the horse, clean the place up. She'd let it go what with her failing health and Dale's shenanigans and the total lack of money, but that was over. Wasn't there supplies in the barn? Boards, nails, paint? Didn't she have two good hands? She was ashamed of the paint peeling from the house, the broken window she'd left boarded up, the air conditioners threatening to guillotine the windowsills on which they rested. She hated to see the weeds so high, the orchard a mess, and the fence reduced to a handful of slumped and rotting rails. She hated, absolutely *hated*, to let Gene see his home in such disrepair because *she* had let it fall into such a state. Her and Dale, anyway. And the less said about her errant husband the better. So yes, time to get back on the horse. In her youth she'd been good with a hammer and nails. She had a green thumb that had faded to pale mint. But first, the birds, their loyalty.

"I know how to win you," she said to the peacocks. They had finally appeared from the orchard.

Mattie dug about her housecoat for her space pills. A simple thing to make such medicine. Much cheaper and more effective than most of her prescriptions, half of which she couldn't afford anyway. She swallowed one more to hold at bay the pain in her chest, then offered some to the peacocks. They gobbled them up, one apiece, and strutted about the weeds. Just like her boys, Mattie thought. So greedy.

There in the last of the day's light Mattie sat on the back porch and watched the peacocks get weird. They rubbed on the fence, then each other, dazed on feelings. That was all right, Mattie figured. Let them be into feelings. Mattie was, too. That third pill had nuked all the pain behind her ribs and left her placid. She was in her serene state, at peace with her wheezing condition. But peace with her family was a whole different thing. The key, she felt, was to get Gene interested in something. Get that boy's hands in a project and he'd forget to look the other way. Question was, what project? Fixing up the house, perhaps. There was always Rich and his recent talk of a business of some kind, though Mattie wasn't sure what kind of business could be run from such a decrepit truck other than dental villainy. No matter, she told the peacocks. She'd figure it out. She always did.

When the peacocks had retired to the barn and Mattie felt her stomach growl, she went back in the house, intent on fixing dinner and listening to records. Maybe when Gene came home, she would share her good feelings, offer him a few space pills, and see if he relaxed. She intended to enlist his aid in the restoration of the house, the orchard, and the barn. She intended to steer him toward helping Rich with, well, whatever it was Rich was trying to accomplish. In short, she intended to undo years of distance and the fractious family nature and instill in her boys—*her boys*—a sense of duty and warmth. With the help of the space pills, she couldn't fail.

In the kitchen, the phone was ringing, and had been for a while, she realized. She went for it, hoping it would be Gene. By now he was surely with Rich. She would tell them both to come home for dinner. Just think of it! Almost the whole family gathered about the table, eating their meager fare! She picked up the phone, jubilant, wondering what she could scrounge from the fridge.

"Where y'all at?" she said. "I'm fixing dinner."

"Yoo-hoo, halloo," said the voice.

Mattie's breath caught in her throat. It was the nasty voice, the one who hunted Dale. Through the phone there came a kind of gleeful panting that cut right through her lovely high and threw her back down to the pain in her chest.

"What we cooking, little miss?" asked the voice. "Greens? Chicken? Cold potato salad? Is your fair husband joining us for the meal?"

"Watch yourself," said Mattie, hating the dryness in her mouth. "My boy is home."

"That's lovely. Family and all. He aim to pay old Dale's debts?"

"It ain't no business of yours."

"Trust me when I say it is. Now, you'd tell an old friend if you'd seen or heard from Dale, wouldn't you?"

Despite herself, Mattie was afraid. It wasn't what the man said as much as *how* it sounded. All the man's words came out like a riddle, like questions to which he already knew the answer. And there was a weight to his voice despite the high cracked pitch. He knew things.

Mattie swallowed the lump in her throat and said, "Keep on. I'm loading the shotgun."

But the dial tone buzzed in her ear.

It was always the same, that voice. It didn't matter how many times she told the voice Dale didn't live there no more. It kept calling. And it was getting needier, more insistent. Stranger.

Chapter 2

Dale was in poor disguise, losing hand and mouth at the poker table. He cursed and swore under his mustache, a very real one, and scratched at the canvas boat hat he wore, a lucky find among the weeds. Dusted and straightened it made a very fine hat, a perfect fit. The cards, on the other hand, were anything but. He had to get it in gear, and soon, or he'd be out of the game, a crucial one as he had wagered his last cash reserve. Many months ago, he'd been ousted from his home and marital bed, exiled by his wife for gambling away practically all their money. Now he was struggling to win it back, dollar by dollar—he, Dale Temmens, once the best card player in Columbia and surrounding environs, reduced to fighting it out at the low-stakes tables in Andre's. The shame! The indignity! Those were bad enough. Worse was the day's losing streak, one among many, in which he was in the hole by several hundred dollars.

"Check," said the player across from him.

Two others folded.

Dale adjusted his dark sunglasses. It was down to him and the man who had checked, and Dale was bristling because the man had barely glanced at him all day. Instead, the man had kept his eyes on the cards, his face expressionless, while Dale had lost pot after pot after pot in spectacular fashion. He told himself that the man across the table didn't realize who he was playing, that he was too young to have heard of the great Dale Temmens. There wasn't a swamp poker player in Columbia that he hadn't taken for a ride. Folks used to line up to play him and take a whooping, practically an honor in those parts, and practically a bygone conclusion soon as Dale settled down at a table. But somewhere along the way his great talent had begun to fade, finally vanishing altogether during the fateful game that had resulted in his exile. Some skinny card shark from Minneapolis with heavy cigarette wrinkles about his face had suckered him, hand after hand, until Dale had to borrow a stake. And who should be sitting there but Hollis Lerne, a local loan shark and man of ill repute, known by many for his stiff borrowing terms and dire treatment of people who didn't pay. Under other circumstances Dale would have known better. But then and there, he wasn't thinking clearly. He'd been sure he could take the kid, clean the place out.

He'd been wrong.

Not a single game had gone his way since then. It was as if the deal with Lerne had cursed him.

In the shack, no breath stirred. Andre's was a well-known secret to poker aficionados in Columbia, consisting of a dingy, though heavily decorated, wooden building jutting off the back of Andre's Crab Shack—a seafood restaurant that prided itself on cheap crabs and surly service. Andre's was where Columbia's card cutters got their start or broke their luck and cashed out for good, a place in which loan sharks, scum like Hollis Lerne, hovered behind the tables, ready and willing to stake a player in the hopes of making a return, a place where anyone could get liquor or crab claws or even fresh, cold coleslaw brought to the table, wet napkins included, so as not to interrupt a game. It was the kind of place where special buckets were set under tables for players to urinate. It was, in the end, the kind of place where local legends lived or died, held aloft or cast down. Cheating was a rarity at Andre's because the proprietor himself, Andre, was almost always on hand, a massive Bowie knife sheathed at his side, and flanked by thugs who would just as soon crack a skull as a smile.

Not that Dale had ever cheated. He counted cards, sure, but that was fair game provided you had the brains to do it. And Dale had, in his prime, been the best card counter he'd ever met. But now? Sweat streaked down Dale's back and sides and soaked into his hat. He looked at his cards. By Dale's count, the man couldn't have better than two pair. But he'd thought the same thing three games back and look what happened.

The player across the table sighed and went all in. It was sudden. Dale smelled a bluff. He pushed his remaining chips into the middle, confident for the first time in a long time. He had him, Dale did. No question. Nothing better than two pair. He was certain.

The dealer called for the cards. Dale slapped down his three of a kind. The other player casually unloaded a flush.

Dale sat in a daze while the table cleared and cashed out. Had he miscounted? Was it a mistake? A simple blunder? Over and over in his mind, he went back and recounted, but after one or two loops he'd lost his place. He looked around at the other tables, saw the other players with their eyes on their cards. He felt they were pointedly refusing to look at him, to acknowledge who he was, who he had been. He wanted to rise up, angry, and demand another game, but he was broke—flat broke—and no one, not even other loan sharks, would stake him. Not with his outstanding debt to Hollis Lerne.

Dale rose and was almost to the door when Andre stopped him with a word. "Wait."

Dale regarded the man where he sat atop a pickle barrel, slowly and carefully carving up an apple with the enormous Bowie knife. Andre hewed a slice of apple and slid it between his teeth.

"What happened there?" Andre asked as he chewed.

"I had him," Dale blurted. He felt caught between the truth and a lie. He *had* had him, hadn't he? Or had he been wrong the whole time, the game lost long before Dale laid down his final hand?

"All you had was dirt," said Andre. "And that's getting kind of familiar, don't you think?"

"Andre, it's *me*. I'm the best."

"Not no more," said Andre. He turned the knife blade around, laid the tip against Dale's shirt, and stared hard into his eyes. Of course, Dale didn't bother trying to move out of the way. Even if he had, the goons flanking Andre would have returned him to his spot. Dale refused to be further humiliated.

"That kind of thrashing, it's bad for business," said Andre.

"My money's just as green as yours," said Dale.

"You don't got money," said Andre. "What you got is a bad count and a heap of debt to Hollis Lerne. You think everyone don't know that? I hear them talk. You ain't paid the man back and now you in here losing hand and fist. What's that say about me I let you dig your own grave? That's Hollis Lerne we talking about. How would he feel if I called him up, told him come collect? Grateful, I bet. Might even cut *me* a little slice of the take."

To accentuate the threat, Andre bounced the tip of the knife on Dale's collar bone. Dale knew that whatever loyalties they'd once shared, loyalties borne on the many years of Dale's tremendous successes, they had been exhausted. If Dale was cast out from Andre's, all hopes of regaining his lost fortune and graces were gone. He swallowed the knot in his throat along with a heap of pride and nodded.

"All right," he said.

"All right what?" asked Andre.

"I won't lose again."

"Not sure you can help it," Andre said as he freed the blade from Dale's chest. "Last chance, Temmens."

Dale backed out to the porch and gulped the night air, wishing it was cold and refreshing. Instead, it was hot like the inside of an oven, and the sweat continued to trickle down his sides. The unthinkable was fast becoming reality. If he lost Andre's, he lost everything—the wife, the fortune, the legacy—all for good. He had to dig deep, figure out where he'd gone wrong, where he was *still* going wrong, and he had to turn it around. And he had to do it before Lerne found him.

Amid consideration of such dark possibilities two hecklers approached. It was the way they moved toward him, with purpose in their steps, which frightened him. Lerne and his goon, likely come to collect. Dale's gaze darted about, looking for an escape. He could go over the railing, hope to God he didn't bust his ankle, and flee into the woods. But then they were on him, hands upon his shoulder and Dale heard one of them call him "Dad."

He looked up. Not Lerne. They were his sons, Gene and Rich, and for a long moment all he could do was stand there, shaky with relief.

"Good Christ," said Dale, "I thought you were someone else." They were talking then, asking him questions or answering questions he hadn't asked, but Dale couldn't hear them over the erratic roar of his own heart in his ears. Close call. A damn close call.

Dale snatched the bottle from Gene's hand, took a long, hard pull, and swallowed the liquor. He gestured with the bottle, let out a tremendous belch, and led his sons from the porch toward the culvert where they wouldn't be as easily spotted.

"Nice to see you, too," said Gene. "And what happened back there? That sucker wasn't bluffing. You had to know that."

Dale rounded on them, flushed with shame. "You saw that?"

"Wish I hadn't. What the hell were you thinking?"

"I lost count," Dale said by way of explanation.

"Since when?"

Dale shoved the bottle back into his youngest's hands. The mouth on that one. Gene had always been the talker, and often to his own detriment. Rich, on the other hand, had always been quiet, even before he'd gone overseas and gotten hooked up with his ghosts. Dale looked at Rich standing behind his younger brother, meek and cowed, and at Gene with the bottle in hand, red in the eyes but still sharp—sharp enough, anyway, to critique his old man's performance. He threw his arms around them both, hugged them close, and was grateful when they let him hold on just a little too long.

"Little rusty is all," he said. "I'm working on it."

"That's not what I heard," said Gene. "Mom says you owe Hollis Lerne."

"Your mother didn't say that," said Dale. "Your brother did. And sure, I owe him. For now. But I'm working it out. And as you can see, that's why I'm in disguise." He motioned to the boat hat, the old and tattered clothes that stank of sweat and fire smoke. His gaze darted from his sons to the shack, then out to the parking lot. He was looking for the silver Mercedes Kompressor, Lerne's favorite vehicle, and growing increasingly nervous.

"Look, never mind that," Dale said as he led them further into the culvert. "When did you get back? What's the occasion?"

In between glances at the parking lot, Dale watched his youngest son closely, noting the harried and cagey look in the boy's eyes. It was a look no one but his gambling father would recognize. Gene was in trouble. That much was obvious. What wasn't obvious was what kind and how much. Little else would explain his son's sudden and unannounced homecoming, much less showing up at Andre's with Rich in tow. Little else would explain such an impromptu homecoming unless Gene needed something, and Dale was sure he already knew what.

Gene looked prepared to deliver some story or other, probably something he'd rehearsed on the way over—or more likely, something he'd made up on the spot. If the boy had gone into honest sales, he would have made a killing.

"Let me stop you there," Dale cut in. "I'm broke. But I can help if it's money you need."

"How?" said Gene. "Play cards? Dig ourselves out fifty bucks at a time?"

"All I need is a stake, even a small one."

"That ain't a good idea," said Rich. "Mom would kill us."

"Your mother ain't killing anybody," said Dale. "Least no one but me if I don't earn back what I lost."

Gene rubbed his eyes. "That's not really what I had in mind."

"Me neither," said Dale. "Can't we just catch up a while? But not here. In fact, it's well past time I get on."

Gene's eyes narrowed. "Where you staying?"

Dale pointed off into the woods, saw the exasperation sink onto his youngest's face. The brothers exchanged knowing looks.

"Why not stay with Rich?" said Gene.

"Can't risk it," said Dale. "What if Lerne hurts him to get at me? Besides, I got a kind of place. I hate to cut it short, but I got to get on. You can come with me if you want."

But they didn't. They knew without prompting Dale for further details that whatever he meant by "place" was going to require explanation, and then processing on their part to make heads or tails out of what was going on, why their elderly father was wearing a trashy boat hat, why he was so scared of Hollis Lerne, why he was living in a car full of racoons, etcetera. And Dale was willing to explain! He was willing to tell them everything, but they had already turned, Gene mumbling something about catching up with him tomorrow, and Rich waving goodbye in his odd, forlorn manner. Dale watched his sons trudge up the culvert and across the parking lot toward what looked like a death trap on wheels, an ice cream truck for the criminally insane. As he watched his boys drive off, he couldn't shake the feeling that he'd failed them somehow, that he'd let them down. Dale's heart sank. It was getting to be a habit.

In a funk of despair, Dale set off for his abode. He lived in a decrepit pistachio-green Ford Fairmont set a few miles back in the woods. The car, like many peripherals of Dale's life, was a storied artifact of Columbia's history of ne'er-do-wells and miscreants. It was said that the car's former owner, a gruff Scottish hick named Flem Colly, had famously won the car in a titanic poker match circa 1974 against Andre himself, then a notoriously vicious player who was said to gouge the table with his knife as he lost hands. The match was said to have lasted ten hours, a vicious and prolonged war of attrition in which neither man would leave the heavily-scarred table to relieve their aching bladders—the very game that inspired Andre to institute the bucket option. The two players were well matched, near equals, and the final hands of the last game hung on a thread. Flem won on a bluff, a play of great daring. The pot was massive and included the car, which was new at the time.

To celebrate, Flem drove about town, casting dollar bills into the wind. That night he declared to the sky that no pleasure would be denied. He purchased a case of liquor and a guitar he couldn't play. At some point, he picked up from the bus station a Norwegian who spoke no English, a beautiful young man who may have been selling his body. They drove to the woods and drank, talked, and made sweet, very sweaty love, until Flem's body failed him. Then Flem began to serenade the man, terribly and without pitch. The liquor drove him to bad music. The Norwegian withdrew, aghast. Then he returned and clubbed Flem with the instrument.

When Flem woke, he was nude and in great pain. His clothes and money were gone. So too were the keys to the Ford. Humbled and chastised by his own nudity, the previous night's debauchery haunted him. He did not know how to hotwire the car, and anyway, he no longer wanted any part of it. He walked home, naked and delirious with a hangover and likely a minor concussion and was further humbled. The next day he returned and pushed the car into a ditch and forsook Norwegians and gambling and liquor and the flesh of men. That last one he retracted three years later when he ran off to Miami with a young hirsute Polack. The last anyone heard, Flem had opened a gambling addiction center and was living a quiet married life. A framed photograph hung in Andre's shack: Flem and his husband in tropical attire, tanned and furred amid a backdrop of palms.

Dale arrived at the car with the day's last light smeared red across the sky. To others, it may have seemed the car bore a dark lineage. Dale didn't mind. Fact was, the roof didn't leak, none of the glass was broken, and down in the ditch the shade from the trees was good and cool. He climbed in back and dined on a pack of mixed nuts, savoring tender cashews, his favorite, and pondering Gene's return. He knew his son well enough to know the boy's appearance was sudden for a reason. Gene was in trouble, that much was obvious. Less obvious was the *scope.*

"Takes after me," Dale said aloud to no one. But he wasn't completely alone. Ever since he had come to occupy the car, a family of friendly and curious raccoons had taken up residence in the tree directly above. They appeared now, climbing down the branches, and waited on the hood for Dale to throw them the raisins he detested. The raccoons were very polite, never bothered him while he slept, never tried to get in the car unless it was raining, never did mischief. Dale, in turn, always shared his meager fare with them. They respected him, the raccoons. They recognized his kind spirit.

His boys, on the other hand, disregarded him. Even in his current state, he was still their father. Who was he that his boys could treat him as such?

He stood and checked himself in the side mirrors, peering back at his own disguised visage. Hollis Lerne would never recognize him in such garb. He barely recognized himself.

Hollis Lerne sat naked on one of his many sofas, menacing a kneeling and blindfolded woman with a small caliber pistol. He had many sofas because he had many houses. Two in Columbia, one in Winnsboro, one in Lexington, and a few more scattered about. All polished tile, steam-cleaned carpets, gleaming stone countertops. He told this to the woman.

He said, "I got houses, immaculate."

"I bet, sugar."

"You don't even know."

There with a woman's lips swallowing him whole, Lerne contemplated himself. He was a thin man, said to resemble a young Randy Travis, the famed country singer, the one in the heyday before the police picked him up for all those driving infractions. Such was the resemblance that he had often imagined the man was his secret father, his mother a far-flung consort. He'd pictured his mother lying awake in bed, young and smoking unfiltered cigarettes as she awaited the arrival of Mr. Travis. Then a flash of headlights across the wall. A window opening.

"Close it," his mother would say to hide her excitement. "You're letting the air out."

"That ain't all," the crooner would say, already at work on his belt, his boots.

Lerne glanced down at the woman pleasuring him. She couldn't see the barrel of the pistol aimed at her head, but he could. It excited him. But the more he looked at the woman, the more his memory began to churn. Lerne remembered his mother only vaguely. He'd never much known her as he was orphaned at an early age when both parents died in a horrific boathouse accident. The accident was that there were a lot of gasoline cans in there, not all with their lids screwed on tight, and his mother was smoking. She was careless with the ash, with life in general. His father was probably there just to argue, their constant pastime. His mother retreated into cigarettes. His father retreated into nature shows and animal television.

By eighteen he'd saved enough from his many menial jobs to acquire a pawn shop, a meager strip mall storefront on the main drag. From there he worked up the pawn business and started loan sharking out of the back office, obstructed by his own meek ways. For Lerne had no talent for violence. He couldn't even bring himself to outsource it. That is, until he met Kinsey West.

West was a balding and paunchy puke from the suburbs, the kind of freak who wears boat shoes every month of the year. He'd come to Lerne and borrowed thousands, then defaulted for months, crawling to the shop and weeping openly in front of customers about his starving children, his husk of a wife, his lack of gainful employment. He had ulcers, West did. Ulcers in his guts, his ears. If only Lerne would give him more time, just a few months more—and so forth. This went on until the day Lerne, who had himself developed ulcers and a trembling disposition, decided to take vacation aboard a casino steamer. A little gambling, some drinks on the deck. A Creole jazz band played outstanding ragtime in the bar. It seemed the very thing to restore a man. Lerne dressed for the occasion in fine rose linen, a dapper straw hat. He appeared in the mirror as a true man of leisure, a Southerner, landed and with business interests. He drew about him an aura of mystery, spoke slowly and with eyes half-lidded in pleasure. To others, he wanted to be seen, respected, and a little feared. He wanted them to look at him and recognize that whatever he did for a living, he *did it* and then some. He ordered a Long Island iced tea and wandered the tables aloof and relaxed, peering at the gamblers. It was then that he saw West betting at. Lerne believed himself mistaken. Another look told him otherwise. There could be no mistake. It was West in the traitorous flesh, losing hand over fist and enjoying every moment.

Waves of nausea broke over Lerne. He fled to the ship's railing and retched green bile. He made plans to return to the deck, turn a serving tray into a weapon, and make violence on West's face! But fear churned in Lerne's gut, brought up more of the green stuff until he couldn't stand. In the end he had to be scuttled ashore, wretched in a little rowboat. West watched from the railing. He didn't know the limp pile of sweat-soaked linen was a person.

A week later, West skipped town with his mistress, most of his debt unpaid. Meanwhile Lerne was laid up, wracked with fever. West was scum, that was true. But he had also acted as a mirror, showing Lerne the painful minutia of his flaws. He was spineless, Lerne was. Weak. Undeserving of respect. Lerne behold himself in his own entirety, and all it took to make that happen was for Kinsey West to borrow money from him and piss it away at dice.

What did that say about Lerne? Never mind that no one feared or respected him. What did it say about *who* and *what* he was? Nothing good, Lerne surmised. And he surmised no further. He knew what he had to do. When at last he regained vigor, the first thing he did was hire Llewellyn, a man of few words and even fewer moral scruples, to be his enforcer. Lerne sent him after West, but the trail had gone cold. To make up for it, Lerne tightened the screws on his businesses, and hired clerks to work at the pawn shop. He also ramped up the loan sharking business, a surprisingly easy endeavor what with the strong underground gambling scene in Columbia. He sank money into real estate, wore only the finest natural fabrics tailored to size. He purchased his silver Mercedes Kompressor, practically his trademark, believing the vehicle to be an impeccable combination of luxury and sport performance. People would look upon him and see a vested Southern gentleman, a dynasty of one.

People began to fear and respect him, particularly when they failed to pay him on time, and he sent Llewellyn to drill a hole in their fingernails. But now, years after the fact, all Lerne saw when he looked in the mirror was the weak and mewling creature upon whom Kinsey West had trod. Nothing, he had begun to realize, was truly his save *fear.* That galled him, spurred him to approach his underworld contacts in the hopes that new criminal enterprises would engender some new feelings. The only thing he had warmed to of late had been a new joint venture with a fat Spaniard named Marco, a Charleston-based smuggler who dabbled in great evils, things to make even grizzled criminals blanch. They were to meet in a few days' time to discuss terms. An expansion of his criminal ways, Lerne hoped, new vistas. That would be the thing to reinvigorate him, the impetus for growth. The very thought excited him. He felt himself swell in the back of the woman's mouth, approaching climax. Yes, he thought, what he needed was something new, something he'd never before tried or tasted. The limits pushed, and finally, eclipsed.

The impulse took hold. He decided to start then and there via the most radical means accessible. What Lerne did was raise the pistol over the woman's head and fire. There was a puff of plaster from the wall across the room. The woman shrieked and fell back through the glass coffee table.

A surge of delight coursed through Lerne. He came in ropey spurts and struggled to his feet. There was glass between his toes, and a new tang on the tongue.

The woman cast aside the blindfold and crawled from the wreckage, bits of glass stuck in her rump, little trickles of blood running down the backs of her thighs.

"I didn't sign up for no shooting gig," she said.

"Yes, you did," said Lerne. "With all them monies I gave you."

"You got to tell a girl things."

"Get up. I can fix you."

He took from his sizable collection of pharmaceuticals several hefty pills—tranquilizers, mostly, and dropped them down the woman's mouth. To wash it down he provided Navy strength rum. It was a good cocktail, a mixture he relished on sleepless nights when his ulcers raged. Then he wrapped her in a towel, called Llewellyn, and sent the woman to wait on the back porch.

Lerne went over to inspect the bullet hole, a perfectly round O with bits of plaster scorched at the edges. Simply having cool, smooth metal involved felt, for lack of a better term, *right*. But something about the implementation felt all wrong. The gun intruded on itself, all noise and smoke. It stole some of Lerne's pleasure. He turned back to his sofa, saw the broken glass, the ruined coffee table, and the dime-sized drops of blood on the fine white carpet. New ideas, imperfectly formed, began to simmer.

He put these new ideas aside to shower, dress, and comb his big hair. He had business at his pawn shop, suckers to see at the card shack. Plus, a drive would do him good. Later he would stop for a burger and a few drinks at the bar and ruminate on these emerging ideas. The very thing to top off a productive afternoon.

As he emerged from his wardrobe, he saw through the glass patio door that Llewellyn had arrived. The henchman was guiding the woman around the side, and Lerne noticed little rivulets of blood had dried on the backs of her legs. He went out to them, intrigued by something he could not yet put his finger on.

The woman was foggy in the eyes. "What did you give me?" she slurred.

"Good medicine," said Lerne.

"Is my face on?"

Lerne bent close, aroused. He touched where a fleck of dried blood was stuck to her cheek. Was there no better way, he wondered? Something more intimate?

By the time Rich dropped him at the Datsun, Gene had had enough of the day to know he didn't want no part of the night. One disappointment after another, no sign of slowing down. But he rallied and drove to Hopper's Bar & Grill because he'd told James he would and because he needed to eat anyway, and what could one or two more whiskeys hurt? The peach brandy had left him parched and the scene with Dale had left him shockingly sober. He'd almost forgotten that James's love interest would be there, and that she worked for animal control. So, when he found them at the bar, he disguised his confusion by ordering a burger and whiskey—three shots in fact—on him.

Gene wasn't sure what he had expected from Laura. James's newest fixation? That much he knew. Worked for animal control? That, too, he knew. And it sickened him. Animal control varied from state to state, even city to city, but back in Texas he and Big John fought them daily to get dogs out of kill shelters—or worse—and into the rescue. He could count on one hand the number of times animal control had proven to be the better option even if that hand had no fingers. So, what had he expected? Not much. Another city worker punching the clock, cashing the checks, and doing as little as possible.

But Laura Gomez wasn't what he expected. She'd come right from work, green animal control jumper bunched around her waist, curly hair pinned to the top of her head, and a confident, knowing smile that hit him like a brick in the face. She oozed charm in a way few could, and carried herself with an easy, wordless grace Gene had only seen in the very best poker players. She was smart, funny, and Gene discovered about an hour into their drinks, learned about a great many things. Very learned. Her mother had taught Spanish in high school and her father was a mechanic on big planes for the Air Force. They moved for his job all the time, taking with them their large pack of dogs and acquiring new ones everywhere they went. Dallas, Tampa, Boulder, San Francisco—the list went on. She'd traveled a bit after college, worked as a bartender, then as a hotel manager, then as a used car salesperson, and at a dozen other jobs that failed to satisfy. Around that time, Laura decided to go back to school. She got into the graduate sociology program at Boston University and had been in the freezing north a few years when her family moved to Columbia. A year later, the cancer took her father. Two years later, her mother was shot outside a gas station. "Wrong place, wrong time," the cops told Laura, who that same night, packed her entire meager apartment in Boston and drove to Columbia to care for her deceased mother's dogs. The family pack had thinned over the years. All that remained were elderly rescues, a handful of sad, confused pit bulls who never quite got over their owner's death. She stayed in her mother's old apartment caring for the dogs while they fell off, one by one, until she was by herself. She had the dogs cremated, then stole into the cemetery at night and buried the little decorative urns beside her mother's grave.

"After that," she said, "I just stayed."

"Why?" asked Gene. His burger was gone, and he was bone tired, but he couldn't pull himself away.

"Why stay?"

"I meant why sociology. But sure, the staying part. Let's do that one."

"Easier than picking up again," she said. "My program director called me a few times from Boston, asked when I was coming back. Told him I was taking a leave, maybe indefinitely."

"So, you just dropped out of school?"

"Graduate school," Laura corrected him. "And not quite. But that is what someone who's never been would say."

Gene paused, picking apart her wisecrack. Anyone else had said it, he would have been sure it was a jab at his upbringing or the fact that he'd never gone very far in school. But there was something else about the way she had said it, as if she were inviting him to think about his own life, put it in perspective, and look at it from a different angle. At the same time, she was poking fun at herself, hinting that the road to and through graduate school wasn't what she, or maybe anyone else, expected—and not in a good way.

"Ever think about going back?" Gene asked.

Laura shrugged. "Sure. All the time."

"But you don't."

"But I don't," she said with a tired smile. "You get stuck in a place sometimes or a place gets stuck in you. Not sure which in this case. And anyway, the job pays pretty good and I got benefits. And I get to be around dogs again. Cops for dogs, right?"

Gene sucked his teeth. A place gets stuck in you. It sure as shit did. He thought of Big John, of his mother, of brother Rich, of his father. What did she mean by 'place?' Where was that for Gene? Then he shook it off. He was sentimental on whiskey. "James talks," he said.

"And talks and talks," said Laura. "But you don't quite have it right. I keep them out of kill shelters. I also get to adopt."

"You bring them home?"

"When I can," said Laura. She tightened the sleeves of the jumper around her waist and asked, "I look like a cop to you?"

"More like a janitor. College-educated janitor."

"All grad students are."

There was something about her Gene couldn't put his finger on, something raw and honest that disarmed him. If she'd been a boring dog cop, or just plain boring, or even just plain he could have said he'd called it. But she wasn't. Talking with her was like talking with Big John. Energizing.

James returned with drinks and in short order did what James always did: got sloppy. Two beers later he was trying to feed the juke box his keys, inquiring as to why the machine would not eat his perfectly good money. Gene could see the shape of his evening before him. It consisted of letting Laura drive James home so she could hold his hair while he knelt before the toilet bowl while he, Gene, went home to a house with hot, tepid air. Mattie would be asleep in her chair, snoring lightly, the oxygen machine hissing in the corner. Inwardly, Gene groaned.

They got the tabs sorted and together Gene and Laura steered James into the parking lot. At once he fell into the front seat of his car and began snoring.

"His tolerance hasn't changed since high school," said Gene.

Laura nodded, but Gene could tell she was already working around to something else. "What did he say?" she asked.

"About?"

"Us."

Gene slapped the hood of the car. There it was. And in plain English. "Loud and clear," he said.

"But is it to him?"

"Only his lawyer and Jesus know."

"Neither answer the phone."

"None of my business. What I can say about my friend is that his delusions are his own and wholly. But I do believe he communicated the nature of your relationship."

"Friendship," Laura said matter-of-factly.

"He didn't exactly use that term, mind you. But he also didn't *not* say that."

"Paints a picture," said Laura. She was gazing down at the sleeping, snoring form of James. He was face down in the back seat, spindly legs sticking out the door. She dug in his pocket and produced his keys. "It's complicated," she said. "Or was. We had a thing."

"Still none of my business," said Gene, hands up. "But if you're in a telling mood."

"He's still holding out hope. I guess that much is obvious. But we ended as friends. Good ones. I keep hoping that last part wins the day, you know?"

Gene nodded. He went to the Datsun, got the last of the peach brandy, and returned. Laura was sitting on the trunk watching the parking lot clear out. She took the bottle when Gene offered it, knocked back a slug of the liquor, and grimaced.

"My brother's invention," said Gene. "Feels as bad as it tastes."

"You related to Mr. Clean?"

"Close. You want to hear a story about ol' corkscrew and me?"

"If it's embarrassing."

"All good stories are," said Gene. Then he obliged her with the story about the drunken night when he and James, ages seventeen and eighteen respectively, drank Mad Dog, three pints each, and dared one another to greater and more terrifying feats of bravery. First, they had leapt from trees, then streaked downtown, nude and brazen, both meager adventures. The final straw came when James had dared Gene to fetch a hammer and apply it to the melons growing in Farmer Jacob's field. Gene shuddered. Farmer Jacob had long been known to harbor bizarre feelings for his crops. But the gauntlet had been thrown and the Mad Dog lent them outlandish bravery. He accepted the mission, fetched two hammers from the barn, and with James at his side, set off for Farmer Jacob's field. There within the wobbly beams of their flashlights they discovered true horror, for the watermelons had been dressed in little outfits, pink dresses and black clerical attire, a suit with a little red tie. Some were prettied with suggestive makeup. One wore a blonde and curly wig.

To the boys in their drunken states this seemed some grave affront to man, God, nature, you name it. It could not be tolerated. They applied their hammers to the farmer's crops, smashing all those ripe orbs, venting great rage before the drink laid them out, powerfully asleep.

Gene woke at first light, crazed with thirst and skull pain. He crawled to a sprinkler head and tore it off, gulping warm and brackish water. Thus hidden, he beheld Farmer Jacob appear: an old man in overalls, glistening black waders, and armed with a shotgun. The man roved among the ruins of his crop, tears standing in his eyes. At one point he fell among his wasted melons, calling them by names.

"Oh, Otis," he called. "Mabel, Warren!"

For a while, Gene explained, he lay there with the sprinkler quietly gurgling under his hands, terrified that if he made so much as a peep the man would open fire with the shotgun.

Then his partner in crime groaned and sat up. They saw each other at the same time, James and the crazed farmer. The former appeared a ghoul, layered in the flesh of melons, hammer still in hand. The latter rose, shrieking, and blasted a spray of buckshot over James's head. James scurried into the crops. Jacob struggled to reload the shotgun, still weeping, until the effort seemed too much.

As for Gene, he stayed put, too terrified to move. He watched the man get right down into the worst of it. By the time the old man was down on his belly, Gene had had enough. He ran over, snatched up the shotgun, and threw away the shells. All the while the farmer only peered up, sodden and broken.

"This is sickness," said Gene.

"Help me," the old man said. "I got to have them."

"You got them all right."

Laura passed back the bottle, nearly empty, and belched. "I would need two pints of Mad Dog on top of whatever brand of paint thinner you got in this bottle before I believe that story."

Gene nudged the snoring James with the toe of his boot. "True, every word. Ask him when he wakes up."

"Friendly bet?"

They shook. Gene said, "I'm broke."

"Me too," said Laura.

"Then what's the pot?"

"A bottle of the poison your brother distills. What's the moral of the story? Don't drink Mad Dog."

"That and the farmer's a weirdo. Something like that. I was trying to talk around how weird Columbia is, or maybe how weird it is to be back home."

"Didn't miss it?"

Gene took longer than he wanted before he answered. "Can't say I did."

"That's because you're not the type to miss anything."

"You wound me."

"Impossible. I'm not a dollar bill. Or a gussied-up melon."

Gene shivered. Maybe *that* was the moral of the story, because think about it: What right in heaven or hell did two idiot boys have in drinking three pints of Mad Dog brand flavored port wine, arming themselves with hammers, and descending on some weirdo's watermelon patch only to find, to their complete and nauseating horror, that the owner of said melons had gussied them up, had developed serious and disgusting affections for his sun-ripened fruits? What was the moral in *that?* What point was to be found in their desecration of his weird melon patch, their complete and utter obliteration of beloved Otis, Mabel, and Warren?

Gene didn't want those answers. Nobody wanted those answers.

In the distance police sirens wailed, then the blast of a firetruck's horn. One of the bar's patrons urinated on his own passenger door, a fist held aloft, and chanted, "Fuck Craig!" Who was Craig? A specific Craig? The Every Craig? Did he have it coming? It was not Craig's car being moistened unless, God help them all, the man with his dick in his hands *was* Craig. In time the potential Craig drove off, hands unwashed, and the bottle was, of course, empty. By then, so was the parking lot. There was just James's buzzing snore, the occasional raspy passing of a car on the road, and their own small sounds, the little insignificant gurgle of living and sitting on the trunk of a car at night in a parking lot where everyone, including them, should have long ago fled.

"Welcome home," said Laura.

But they didn't flee. Not for a while. Not until James farted in his sleep and broke the noisome silence.

When Rich arrived at the swamp, he was still no closer to an answer. His business idea was vague at best. His resources were scant. He knew he would have to use what was available—the barn, the orchard, the land, and the truck—and he knew he wanted to work with his hands, about the only thing of which he'd ever been much good. He imagined it—whatever *it* would be—would be an endeavor for good, a project that would earn some money, yes, but that would also make their lives better. It would bring them together, the brothers Temmens, maybe even Mattie and, if he could blunt his mother's wrath, Dale, and make them feel like a family again. More importantly, it would make Rich feel like he belonged to something, anything, except the noise in his head. But the ghosts gathered to call him a fool. No one would go into business with him, a brain-damaged buffoon.

"That ain't so," he told the ghosts. "Gene will help."

Help? said the ghosts. Were they talking about the same person?

"Y'all don't know my brother," said Rich.

Oh, said the ghosts. They begged to differ. Because the Gene Temmens they knew? He couldn't care less. And Rich was as useless as his potatoes. Why not forget that nonsense and get back to violence?

"Stop!"

A few bottles of that vile peach slop you brew, the ghosts went on. A few rags, a lighter. All he had to do was go into town, find someone sleeping on the street, and start cooking.

Rich fled the vehicle, and the taunting ghosts. He had to clear his head, take stock. Out by the water the mosquitoes descended in a humming swarm. Rich edged away, drinking from a bottle of his peach brandy until a proper warmth blanketed his brain. It was dark. The ghosts trailed along, nattering. Their hunger for violence was powerful, constant. What had happened was this: It was the war and Rich was serving in the Army for a reason he couldn't remember. He was infantry, just a grunt, and they were in some heavy fighting outside a village whose name he no longer recalled. They were rattled from gunfire, flak—the JTAC most of all. He called in a napalm strike and fudged the coordinates. The whole thing came in too close, blew everyone off their feet. The ground under them was concussed to shit. When the smoke cleared, Rich saw everything and everybody was ruined. People fused to their vehicles, bodies melted, lidless eyes jellied in the sockets. Then the ghosts got up out of the people and started complaining.

Rich was raving when they found him. He spent a month in the Army hospital, and six more in psych. He was discharged and shipped home, the ghosts in tow. He was changed, aimless. He had developed a terrible aversion to weapons, to violence. But the ghosts wanted nothing else.

At home, his arguments with his incorporeal companions scared Mattie and Dale. He took a room at the Days Inn to minimize their exposure and try to get his head on straight. At the behest of his therapist, he grew potatoes in jars, a cultivation of small vegetal life, and pondered his meteoric downfall. Who was the JTAC who called in the bad coordinates? Was he a devil? A moron? A devil in a moron's meatsuit? Meanwhile, the ghosts maintained steady pressure. They wanted violence, bloodshed. They wanted Rich to suffer as they had suffered. At last, he succumbed, bit a librarian. She asked if he needed help in the stacks. Down came his teeth. There were marks on her slim wrist and shame in Rich's heart. He waited for the police and made no additional fuss. Only his vet status saved him from extended jail time. But Rich knew it was a matter of time before he succumbed once more, before he did something even stupider. He had to get his act together, put himself to work. That alone might give him back a part of himself.

Rich went into the trees and took off his shirt. It was late and still hot, and he was sweating buckets. It was time to feel the night air, to get inspired. If he was going to get Gene interested, it ought to be a business where his brother could employ his talents. Rich made a list. Gene was good at talking, gambling, and falling down. He was also good with animals—that much Rich knew about Gene's time in Austin from their brief conversation when he'd driven his brother to find Dale.

Come to think of it, Gene had always been good with animals—or at least patient with them in a way he could rarely muster towards people. For instance, when they were just boys, maybe all of seven or eight, they'd found a stray dog taking refuge in what they called the cookhouse, a concrete shack perched on the edge of their peach grove where ancient machinery pointed to the estate's distant use as a small canning and processing station. The dog had been all out of sorts, nothing but skin and bones, and foaming at the mouth. It had gotten itself under one of the old desks at which the boys frequently played Gene's favorite game, "I'm the Boss Until There's a Union."

A word had come into Rich's young mind, barely eleven years of age. *Rabies.* He'd recalled seeing the VHS tapes in grammar school. A boy was forever walking home when a foaming dog darted from the bushes and bit him. In the hospital, the doctors jabbed the boy's stomach with long needles. The look of pain on the boy's face was exquisite, made comical by the doctor hovering above him and jabbering platitudes.

"Ow, oh, arrgh!" the boy in the video cried.

"Vitamin C is found in citrus fruits, did you know?" said the doctor, and in went the foot-long sticker.

Back then, in the cookhouse, Rich didn't want no part of getting his face ripped off. He didn't want either of them getting rabies and getting jabbed with foot-long needles. He didn't want either of them being the sad, sick, crying boy on the doctor's table. He did not, at eleven years of age, want to be the poster child of *stupid*.

He dragged Gene from the cookhouse and ran off to get Dale who locked the dog in the cookhouse and called animal control. The city boys came and led the dog away. The whole time the dog whined and whimpered, and Gene cried his eyes out. He kept on crying for days. But what Rich remembered most clearly was the dog's curious attitude as it was led away, likely to be put down. It didn't fight or bite or even growl, and Rich had the distinct impression—remembered clear as day—that the dog knew he was sick, knew what was coming was for the best.

Anyway, Rich figured, Gene probably didn't remember it. But if Gene's stories about Austin were to be believed he had a knack for dealing with animals. It would be familiar to Gene, something with which he could quickly and easily get involved. Animals, Rich decided. Their business would be about animals.

Animals? said the ghosts. We want *combat.*

"Ain't your business," Rich said.

Well, why the hell not? said the ghosts. We deserve one. Let's start a face-stomping business. Let's go into dental.

Just then, clamor arose from the trees. Moments later, a pack of dogs appeared, barreling toward Rich, howling and barking. At first the pack seemed a hallucination, a side-effect of the liquor. Rich hesitated, a mistake. Before he could react, they were on him, a Doberman nipping his heels, and a boxer scrambling up onto his shoulders, knocking him to the ground and chewing him about the hind quarters. He thrashed, splashing himself and the dogs with brandy, with the result that he was dragged about like a rope toy until he broke free and ran. The dogs gave chase, barking. In desperation Rich threw the bottle, a distraction. The dogs stopped to lap up its gurgling contents. Rich fled into the truck. Within minutes, the liquor had taken hold of the dogs. They fell into the dirt, wet everything in sight, and spent a while howling, just howling. Finally, the drunken assemblage tottered off and vanished into the trees.

Rich couldn't bring himself to blame the dogs. They were just pets allowed to run wild when what they needed was the same as what Rich needed. They needed guidance, rules, and routines. Stability. People might even adopt such dogs, give them good homes. All it would take would be some land, enough space, a shelter and—?

Rich stared after the animals, a knot of hope tightening in his chest.

Don't get any ideas, said the ghosts. Be realistic.

"That's what I'm doing."

Look, you're just one guy.

"But what if it wasn't just one guy?" Rich said. "What if it was two guys helping those dogs? Two guys with a truck?"

Chapter 3

Gene woke to a blast of tepid water. He tried to shy away from the source, shield himself with his arms, and received another blast in the face. His immobility struck him as odd. He looked about and found he was lying in one of the old horse troughs, a holdover from the days when the place had been a small working cannery and livestock was abundant. Mattie stood before him, glaring in disapproval, the nozzle of the hose trained on him. Behind her, an orb of riotous pain, the sun, hammering him with hard, unyielding light.

"Get up," she said.

"Why are you wetting me?" said Gene. "What time is it?"

"Time to get back on the horse."

"What horse?"

Another blast propelled him from the trough. He scrambled for the house and Mattie's jets of water followed, pelting him in the back. His mind reeled to piece together some legible sequence of events. They'd dropped off James, and then Gene came home feeling strange and unsettled. Then his mistake: Instead of going to bed, he rummaged around in the cookhouse until he found another bottle of peach brandy. There in the cookhouse, sitting in the ancient, creaking office chair and watching curtains of spider webs shiver in the breeze, he treated himself to a libation or three. A nightcap to settle his nerves. He had almost, *almost* forgotten how the peach brandy snuck up on you, how it ushered you gently into a warm, inviting buzz, while it pickled the brain, rotted the senses, and finally drove out all reason. For example, sometime between the hours of two and four in the morning, he had gotten the idea in his head that the horse trough would be an improvement over the ancient chair. Thus, he relocated. Thus, he despaired.

Now in flight, he burst into the house, dripping wet, while his mother's invectives smacked the back of his aching, swollen brain. There were other things to note. He had passed a tall ladder propped against the side of the house and the porch was cluttered with long-disused tools, fresh boards, paint, and pitch. Lengths of orange power cord snaked between his feet, disappearing through the screen door, and vanishing somewhere in the yard. From outside there emanated, God help him, the growl of a *power tool*.

He navigated to the kitchen where he rummaged in the cabinets, desperate for painkillers. His skull, sweet Jesus on a popsicle stick, had become a barbed and dangerous crucible. He needed pills and quiet and a lie-down. He needed *silence* and *fresh, clean water* or he was going to fucking *die*.

Then the screen door banged open, and Mattie appeared, mobile oxygen tank at her side, in the doorway to the kitchen. She was armed with a nail gun.

"Aspirin? Where?" said Gene. "Don't shoot."

Mattie fetched the pills from the cupboard and threw the bottle at him. "Where it's supposed to be," she said. "Why were you in the trough?"

"I don't remember."

"You smell like an onion with herpes."

"Please," Gene whimpered. "I beg you. No more talking."

"Your brother called," Mattie barked as she went behind Gene, slamming the cabinets he'd torn open in his frantic search for pills. "He says you won't help with his business idea."

"He doesn't have an idea! He has a hobo van! And for the love of God, stop banging things!"

"It's a truck."

"It's nothing."

"It's more than what you got, which is just a headache. And you know he needs something. You're his brother. It's your job to look out for him."

Gene made it to the window and squinted at the abject disaster that had overtaken the yard. Saw horses dredged up from who knew where, tools everywhere, a—was it a generator?—kind of growling *thing* that occasionally belched black smoke and seemed moments away from lighting off above the trees. Across the orchard and down the dirt road he saw the barn doors had been thrown open and all manner of junk had been piled on the lawn. All of it accomplished, somehow, by an elderly lunatic on oxygen.

Why, Gene wondered as he swallowed painkillers and drank a glass of water, was he kin to crazy people? Nor could he discern what they wanted from him because his brain was clearly not working. Why was the phone ringing and ringing and why wouldn't his mother answer the damn thing and spare him? He blinked and saw she was gone. Then he spotted her through the window. She was outside, oxygen hose trailing, attempting to ascend a ladder. He heard the nail gun and felt as if the matter between his ears would squeeze out.

Maybe, he thought in his suffering, hair of the dog would do the trick. Just a nip. There had to be a bottle *somewhere.* But the thought of even a taste of peach brandy made his empty, puckered stomach lurch. He had been home—what? Two days? And already he was destroyed. This could not go on. Tomorrow, he thought, maybe the day after, he would grab his bag and leave for someplace, any place where a man could suffer without being intruded upon by power tools or someone menacing him with a goddamn hose. And someplace without a ringing phone!

He wrenched himself from the sink, picked up the phone, and slammed it back into its cradle. Likely Rich, calling to chew his ear off. From outside came the sound of the nail gun. Then hammering. The machine on the lawn burped a plume of black smoke. He would shower quickly, and then take the keys to the Datsun and go into town where he could die in peace. But the phone was ringing again, and he could not delay. Forget the shower. The hosing Mattie had given him would have to suffice. He patted his pockets, turned in circles. Where were the Datsun keys? The cookhouse? Still in the car? In his mind he retraced his last wobbling steps from the prior evening. He went out to the trough, searching in vain. Likewise, the keys weren't in the cookhouse. The Datsun was not where he left it, parked instead beside the house. That meant only one thing.

At the base of the ladder, he peered up at where his mother was trying to pry some of the rotted eaves loose from the porch overhang and cursed the sun. "The keys," he said.

"What keys?" Mattie barked. A chunk of rotted wood fell into the weeds beside the ladder.

"I'm not playing," said Gene. "I'm sick. I need medicine."

"What you need is direction. Get up on this ladder. Better yet, go get the other ladder from the barn. Too much of this wood done rotted out."

"Forget it," Gene snapped. "I'll walk."

"If you won't help me," Mattie cried, "at least help Rich. It's all he's asking."

"Get down before you fall," said Gene.

In response another rotted piece of wood fell into the weeds. There was, Gene knew, only so much a man in the throes of a vicious peach brandy hangover could take, and he had reached his limit. He set off, disgruntled, and hadn't made it across the yard before Rich's truck ambled up the drive and skidded to a halt. From it his brother emerged, dogs affixed to his person in every conceivable manner. Two mottled gray mutts had him by his shirt sleeves and were pulling him in opposite directions, forcing the man into a violent spin while twin terriers, one on each leg, coupled with his shins. Rich crumpled in the assault, a look of abject terror on his face.

Gene was prepared to delight in his brother's predicament, when he saw three of the dogs release his brother and turn on each other. They bared their fangs. An honest to God dog fight was about to erupt and Rich was smack in the middle of it.

Gene rushed in, checked two of them with his knees, and hoisted the pack leader—the brown and black spotted mutt—by the scruff of the neck. If that didn't work, he was prepared to flip the dog over, hold him down until the dog tired himself out. The danger then was the other dogs; if his contact hadn't knocked them out of fight mode, everybody was going to the Emergency Room.

But as quick as it had come, the dog's rage evaporated. Held aloft in Gene's arms, the dog calmed and began to whimper. Gene turned to the pack, looked them dead in the eyes, and told them in no uncertain terms that he was in charge. The old pack leader was firmly in hand. The new boss was presiding.

All the fight went out of the dogs. They backed up, tails cautiously wagging, while Rich got to his feet. Gene set the dog down and calmly gathered the leashes into his hand. A few feet away, Rich had plastered himself against the side of his truck.

"What's the story?" asked Gene.

"Our business," Rich said.

"Cut the crap. Where'd you get them?"

"The woods, a bunch in town, all over. I been at it since last night."

"Well, put them back," said Gene. He led the dogs to the back of the truck, pulled open the doors, and paused, sure as he'd ever been that what he saw before him was a hallucination. For there stood a young billy goat of cream and tan hues, calmly nibbling a piece of insulation from the wall.

"You stole a goat," said Gene.

"I didn't steal anything! He was in the road."

"This is a farm crime. You got to put him back."

"Gene, we got the barn, the whole orchard. This is it, our business! It's animals!"

Gene stared at his older brother. If the pain in his head was less severe, if he wasn't worried it would startle the dogs and possibly cause another fight, if he wasn't concerned that his brother had stolen someone's goat and would soon face very real legal repercussions, Gene would have throttled the man. As it was, all he could do for several long moments, moments in which his headache threatened to shatter his skull was glare at Rich and try to keep his eyes focused.

"We could train them, adopt them out," Rich was saying. "People are always looking for pets."

"Designer breeds, maybe," said Gene. "You have any idea how hard it is to find a home for a mutt? How about a pit bull?"

"That's why we train them!"

"Nobody cares, Rich. There's celebrity trainers on TV. Everyone thinks they got the stuff. And who the hell am I? No one. Get it through your thick head. This ain't a business. It's a lawsuit in the making."

"Just stop for a second and think. A Temmens Brothers dog—it'll *mean* something. Look what you just did. You could teach me."

Teach him? Gene took a breath, about to fire back, tell his brother he was off his rocker, that there was nothing he could teach *anyone* that would shore up whatever mid-summer snowstorm masqueraded as his brother's mind, that there was no money to be made in dogs.

But what was the point? His brother's mind was made up—that was apparent by the look in his eye. Hopeless. All of them.

He gave Rich the leashes and turned to go. But not before he crouched beside the black and brown spotted mutt to give the dog a scratch behind the ears. The former pack leader licked his hand in apology, gave an embarrassed sneeze. That was all right. Gene knew the feeling.

Rich was in the barn loft, clearing space. He was sweaty and hot. And he was not to be deterred.

His first two days of work had passed in a rush of acquiring dogs, buying up cages and food bowls and leashes and all manner of dog-rescuing implements, and clearing out space in the barn where the dogs could stay. What he—*they*, the dogs and his family alike—needed was the fence fixed up, the water troughs scrubbed clean, and pens built for training. They needed time and space. Lots and lots of space. And between the barn, the orchard, and the land around the house, they just might have the space part covered.

Rich peered through a hole in a floorboard. Below, Mattie groomed the dogs, talking to them in a steady stream of babble. She was a little bit high on the space pills and sucking hard on the oxygen, but the dogs couldn't get enough of her brushing, her pets, and the treats that kept materializing from her pockets. Rich's heart was glad. His mother, at least, had bought in on the endeavor that lay before them. Dale was still M.I.A., and Gene, when he deigned to poke his head in, said nothing. He simply watched, frowning if Mattie babied the dogs too much or if Rich poured them too much feed.

But until there was money, a real shot at success, Rich knew he wouldn't be able to get Gene on board. And so, he worked, listening with pleasure to Mattie below while she cooed at the dogs and generally got them worked up over their own selves.

"Y'all just the sweetest muffins," she told the dogs as she brushed their glossy, freshly shampooed coats. "Every one of you."

"Gene said not to get them worked up," said Rich.

"He ain't here. He's out for mischief. Then in the cookhouse all damn night. The boy reeks like peach liquor."

And so on. Even glad for her company, Rich was fast approaching capacity when he uncovered an unfamiliar bundle, a Confederate flag so molded it was more black than blue and red. Mattie and Dale didn't truck with that flag or its fans—none of the Temmens did.

He remained there, frozen over the bundle, until Mattie startled him: "Everything all right?"

"We ever own a flag?" Rich asked.

"A flag?"

"The racist one."

From beneath him, he heard Mattie snort. "Of course not. Must have been the old owners. Put it with the rest of the trash where it belongs."

"Okay," said Rich. But he waited until he heard Mattie shuffle out of the barn before he touched it. Mold, yes, and bits of rotted fabric falling from where his fingers grazed the bulging ends. Rich shivered. There was something bad about the thing, something beyond vile pageantry. He felt the ghosts suddenly close in on him.

Slowly he unwrapped it to reveal a collection of Civil War ball loaders and a lone repeater with a sheathed cavalry saber, all looking worse for wear but, seemingly, intact.

Trickles of sweat ran from his armpits. To Rich, weapons represented all that was bad, the embodiment of that terrible conflict amid which he'd been irreparably damaged. The ghosts, on the other hand, were thrilled.

Go on, load up, they said. This is what we've been waiting for. Now it's here. Go on. Make us happy.

Rich covered the weapons. The less he saw, the better. They had to go. But where? And how? Calm down, he told himself. Think. They were old, that much he knew. Maybe cheap replicas, maybe antiques. Might be worth something and loathe as he was to sell implements of war, they needed the money. At least they'd go toward a good cause.

He waited until Mattie had wandered off to argue with the peacocks before he tossed the bundle into the truck and drove into town. To his disappointment, the antique dealers were closed. In growing desperation, he drove to the closest pawn shop still open, the sign blinking *Gold, Guns, Antiques.* There was something about the store, something he knew he ought to remember, but his mind was too fraught with terror and ghost banter. He selected from the bundle one of what he considered a middling specimen, a ball loader with a barely tarnished stock, and entered the shop.

The pawn broker looked up from a magazine and frowned.

"It ain't loaded," said Rich.

"Wouldn't worry if it was," said the broker. "You rob a museum?"

"Found them in the barn."

"What else is in there? Suit of armor? Mummy?"

"I got a bunch of these, the real deal. How much?"

"Let's see her."

Rich was all too happy to lay the rifle on the glass counter beneath which handguns of all varieties rested in states of high polish and gloss. In a case behind the broker were shotguns, an M16 with a telescope sight, an AK 74U in bright orange wood and charcoal metal. He backed from the counter, struggling to tamp down the swelling fear, and was cringing near the electric guitars when a twangy new voice broke in behind him.

"What's this stuff? Old-timey guns?"

Rich turned and felt his heart stick in his throat. Hollis Lerne leaned on the glass counter beside the broker, a toothpick jiggling about in his mouth, a sly look on his face. He knew the man from Dale's descriptions and the man's uncanny resemblance to famed country singer Randy Travis, the big hair, wide eyes, bright teeth. Against the backdrop of guns and ammunition, the man was a terrible and outlandish sight to behold. Then Rich realized what he had done. *Guns, Gold, Antiques.* It was Lerne's store!

Lerne took the rifle from the broker, turned it end over, sighted down the barrel at Rich. "I know you," he said around the toothpick. "I know your daddy, too."

Rich felt cold sweat pooling under his arms. The ghosts were nattering in his ears, but he couldn't hear them over his own pounding heart. He'd made a terrible mistake.

"Just this one?" Lerne asked. He was looking the rifle over, impressed. "Been a while since we had any stock like this. Color me interested, young Temmens."

Rich couldn't think, couldn't breathe. He wanted to turn and run but he couldn't move. "Not for sale," he managed to gasp.

Lerne lowered the rifle, then leaned in with a hand to his ear. He grinned. "Say again?"

"I changed my mind," said Rich. "Not for sale. I want to go elsewhere."

"Not for sale?" said Lerne. He directed a wink and a grin at his clerk, then turned back to Rich, still grinning, more a showing of teeth than an actual smile. "Everything is for sale."

"Not them," said Rich.

"Them," said Lerne, and he directed a comically fake look at his clerk. "There's more of these here beauties? Maybe out in that monstrous vehicle of yours?"

Rich took an involuntary step back, almost toppled into a rack of guitars and dusty amplifiers. When he righted himself, Lerne was practically on top of him, no longer smiling.

"Richard, ain't it?" said Lerne. His gaze held Rich. "You know me. Me and your daddy got history. And you came here, my, my. Let's go and see."

Lerne was close, very close, much shorter and smaller than him, a gangly, wicked apparition in baby blue seersucker. But with unsettling gentleness he took Rich's arm and led him to the truck, threw open the doors, drew back the faded flag, and whistled at the weapons. Rich could only stand in mute terror while Lerne ran his long, meticulously groomed hands over the flag, the weapons. Every move the man made seemed calculated, deliberate, as if he were holding back some terrible power that was constantly threatening to leap out of him and rip apart the world. Gene was wrong. Lerne wasn't a chump. He was dangerous—far more dangerous than any of them had guessed—and now he had Rich, held him powerless without having to lift a finger. Soon Lerne would take him into the back office of the pawn shop and employ brutal, unorthodox methods to learn Dale's whereabouts. And when he got what he wanted, he would turn all his attention to Rich. He would hurt him. Bad.

Then a change came over Lerne. His hand twitched and froze above the pile. A sound rose from him, a strange exhalation that made Rich's skin crawl. His hand lowered to the pile and uncovered the saber still in its scabbard.

"What's *this?*" said Lerne.

Rich watched, horrified, as the man withdrew the saber from its sheath. The blade had been broken a foot from the hilt but fairly gleamed with neither rust nor decay. Lerne turned it over in his hands, a look approaching reverence stamped on his face.

"How much?" said Lerne.

"A grand," Rich blurted between his teeth. "Two grand. Three."

Before the absurdity of what had come out of his mouth had fully sunken in, Lerne ushered the sword into the store, engaged his clerk in brief conversation, and sent the man into the back office. A moment later, the clerk reappeared with an envelope, and in an instant Lerne was once more at Rich's side and handing him three thousand dollars in crisp, clean cash.

"He'll buy the rest," Lerne said and motioned offhandedly toward the shop.

Rich swallowed the ice-cold ball of fear that had lodged in this throat. He had to get away from Lerne and the weapons, but the cash in his hand gave him pause. What if he never got another opportunity like this? How much more would Lerne give him? Five thousand? Ten? His thoughts raced ahead and imagined all the good that kind of money could do for his business, for his family, for the dogs. But his eyes, his stupid eyes wouldn't budge from Lerne, and as he stood there, dumbly taking inventory of his dire situation, he saw the saber was still in Lerne's hands. So, too, was the awful look on the man's face. He had connected with the weapon in a way Rich could not, would not, understand.

No, Rich decided. It didn't matter how much money Lerne would offer. He had to get out and *fast*.

One last thought sprung up in Rich's mind, a long shot. "What about my pop?" he said.

Lerne came to, looked at Rich as if seeing him for the first time. "What about him?"

"Can I put it toward his debt?" Rich motioned toward the rifles, the flag, the whole awful scene.

But Lerne's smile had returned, cruel. "These fine treasures ain't a drop in that bucket," he said. "Tell your old man to come see me. Right quick. And tell him if I catch him out and about without a thought in his head of paying me back, well, old son, I'm inclined to take it personally."

With that, the man climbed into a silver Mercedes Kompressor and sped away. Rich stared after it, his insides cold and puckered. What had he just witnessed? The ghosts crowded close, triumphant.

That man, they said, would eat you alive. He'll eat your daddy for sure. He could swallow the whole world. We like him.

A sudden thump jolted Rich. He turned, saw the broker standing at the window. The man was motioning for Rich to bring in the rest.

Free of Lerne's spell, Rich slammed shut the doors of the truck, jumped in the driver's seat, and cranked the ignition. With the ghosts wailing in his ears, he drove at breakneck speed to the edge of town, practically weeping in fright. How could he get rid of the weapons? Would they float if he threw them in a lake? Would they burn?

Don't you dare, said the ghosts. Go back and trade them in for a proper gun. Bullets are cheap.

"I'll burn them," Rich threatened.

Just try, said the ghosts. Just as likely to light yourself. Then they'll arrest you and put you in a dark hole with us, real cozy.

A hole, thought Rich. That was it. He drove as deep in the woods as the truck would allow, and hiked further still until he could no longer hear the city noise. There he dug a hole, deep and wide, and cast within in the weapons in their shitty, faded wrapper. He worked with furious energy, the sweat dripping from the end of his nose and matted lengths of his beard. Behind him the ghosts howled and screeched in outrage. Rich covered his ears and shut his eyes, and with the dark came again the image of Lerne with the saber, his cruel smile, his flashing eyes.

Lerne went to the Spaniard's house to discuss a joint venture, something which had been in the works for some time. Marco, a wad of blubber with an oiled beard and drowsy brown eyes, said he was looking to expand out of Charleston, head west across the state. He'd heard of Lerne, knew him to be a keen self-made man. He wanted to talk about a partnership, an opportunity to invest. They were sitting on the back porch, the green and sloping vista of the manicured lawn before them, drinking fine single malt scotch from crystal goblets, very expensive stuff. Small talk, they made. Chit-chat. Then Marco turned to the matter at hand. "Dogs," he said.

"Dogs?" asked Lerne.

"Yes. To fight."

Lerne sat up, intrigued. He listened as the fat Spaniard went on about wanting to expand his small dog fighting ring, a profitable personal hobby that he'd cultivated into a thriving business in Charleston. Already he had scouted locations, lined up interested fighters. What he could not so easily secure were bait dogs: animals to be used as practice dummies for the champs. That, Marco explained, was the hard part. A man couldn't clear out a pet store or the local shelters without attracting some attention these days. There were always the tried and true methods of scouring the classifieds for dogs being given away, picking up strays, all of which was time consuming and far from a sure thing. The cops had begun to use such avenues to set up stings. No, what he needed was something from outside Charleston, and he needed the dogs well-trained, obedient. He needed a legitimate method of acquisition and distribution. If Lerne could only help with that, Marco would offer him a significant cut.

To Lerne, who had never before seen a dog fight, it was at once a dazzling and terrifying prospect. Of course, he knew of dog fighters. Who in the South didn't? But the sport had gone deep underground. There were too many nosy individuals, too many animal rights groups, too many concerned citizens, who as far as Lerne was concerned, could get fucked with barbed wire if they stood between him and making a profit. The only thing that had kept him from the business of dog fights was the simple fact that he had hated and feared dogs ever since one had bitten him as a child, a shrieking and maddened Boston Terrier that had escaped someone's yard seemingly for the sole purpose of savaging young Hollis. Lerne had been walking home from school, a small and quiet boy of seven, when the dog had squeezed from a hole in a fence.

"Hey, Spot, hey, Rush, whatever is your name," Lerne had said. "I'm very gentle and your friend."

In response, the dog sank its teeth into Lerne's leg. The pain was otherworldly. Nothing he did dislodged the animal. It remained tethered and gnawing for some time, for three blocks in fact, until Lerne climbed the steps of his own porch, bleeding from the calf and terrified out of his mind, where his father pried off the dog.

"What did you do to it?" his father bellowed, weeping at both his son's injury and the snapping animal he gently placed over the fence.

This was several months before the boathouse accident. His mother and father were fighting, and his father was often very emotional, staying up late to watch National Geographic and weep at the plight of rhinoceroses.

Lerne had explained to his father that he wasn't to blame. The dog just came at him, all teeth, all fury. Pop Lerne didn't listen. At the hospital little Hollis took ten stitches. The doctor reeked of ether and wobbled, jabbing at

Lerne's leg with the needle and thread. Little dots of blood welled up and turned into rivulets. The whole time his father went on about the horrors of elephants being hunted for their tusks. Blasted them from jeeps, the hunters did, Pop Lerne told the whole room. Killed those lumbering aspects of the divine for some white bone. A crime almost without equal.

"Is this about Mom?" Lerne asked when they returned home.

"A diminishing rain forest," his father said. "Think about it. Where will the animals go?"

"Dad, can I watch TV with you but maybe not an animal show?"

His father had ducked into the fridge and emerged with a beer. "Here's a new game. Let's be silent in different rooms."

Ever since then, Lerne had been terrified of dogs, their snapping jaws, their fangs, their traitorous hearts. They lived to pounce and bite and kill, the filthy things, unless—*unless*—someone got them first. Lerne hated dogs. He hated them because of the pain they'd caused him and the fear they roused in him. He hated animals in general for the sympathies they had produced in his father, the likes of which he, with his gnawed leg, had failed to cultivate. So many folks walked about as if the animal they housed and fed wouldn't or couldn't rip them apart given the slightest provocation. To Lerne, dogs represented all that was awful about people, their weaknesses, their vulgarity, their willful stupidity. As such, the idea of engaging in Marco's scheme to use the animals for brutal sport made him giddy. He started talking, almost automatically, telling Marco the many ways he could help with the man's enterprise, how he could front the money for building a pit, find additional locations, and even provide shelter for the dogs until they were summoned. And he knew people, lots of people. Columbia was *his* town. He'd make sure no one interfered.

"My friend," said Marco, very pleased. "We make good business."

"Very good by the sound," said Lerne.

"And these terms? You agree?"

"Let's say I provide more, build kennels, breed them, supply an endless bounty. You will see fit to offer more, yes?"

Marco smiled. They shook hands.

Business concluded, the Spaniard went on about his dogs, their lineages, their victories. Lerne only half listened. He was already running the numbers.

If what Marco was saying was true—and he had every reason to believe it was—he stood to make more money on dog fights than any of his other enterprises such as gambling, pawn stores, the small prostitution ring over which he lorded, or just plain beating debtors, like Dale Temmens, to a pulp. Besides, supplying the man with dogs would pose little problem. Columbia was overrun with strays and animal control was laughably inept. What had Llewellyn been telling him of the Temmens boy and his so-called business? A dog rescue? The oaf who'd sold him the saber, Rich, had been seen about town, rounding up strays, beating animal control to the punch. And what of young Gene Temmens, recently returned to town? Word on the street was he'd worked at a rescue out west with some kind of dog expert. A simple thing to control those boys. Lerne had their daddy by the noose. They would fall in line.

Lerne promised to be in touch with Marco soon, very soon. He made ready to leave but the Spaniard presented him with a gift, a black Labrador with a good and glossy coat. Lerne recoiled in terror, panting.

"Is it for hitting?" he said.

The fat Spaniard looked puzzled. "For house," he said. "A pet."

"How wonderful."

With great reluctance and a pounding heart, Lerne took the thing's leash and led it to the car. Once alone on the driveway he stuffed the dog into the trunk with much kicking and swearing, an act that nearly paralyzed him with terror. Only a nip from his flask salvaged his frayed nerves. All during the drive back to Columbia, the creature yelped and banged about. Lerne was drenched in cold sweat and approaching a serious fit, the flask nearly empty, when Llewellyn called with good news.

"Boss, I think I found it," said the henchman.

"Old Dale's hiding place?"

"Looks like it."

"The directions," said Lerne. "Then wait. I won't be long."

He hung up and drained the last of his flask. How opportune, the discovery of Dale's hiding place. It afforded him a chance to try his hand at some of the new violence. And he had options aplenty. He slid a hand down toward his pistol, then paused. Ever since he had touched the saber, he had begun to change. Lerne had never been much for knives and up-close combat, but something about the broken, disgraced saber had spurred his imagination.

He had begun to envision himself using it as a tool of intimidation, something to wear on his hip as he entered, swaggering, into some debtor's abode.

"Got my money?" he would say.

"Help, no, aiee!" the debtor would say.

And Lerne would draw the broken blade, oblivious to the debtor's cries, and advance upon the person.

What came next? His mind reeled with delicious possibilities.

That, too, was new. He had been outsourcing his violence to Llewellyn for years, confident in the man's ruthlessness. Sometimes Llewellyn showed him pictures of what he did to outstanding debtors, and sometimes Lerne turned away, his stomach curdled, reluctant to look at the bloody, tortured scenes that flicked by on the henchman's phone. But ever since he'd gotten ahold of the saber, other thoughts intruded. It was true that Kinsey West had been the last debtor to disrespect him so completely and publicly—the last since Dale Temmens. But did people respect him? Was he looked upon and thought of in a manner befitting his station and ambition? Did he not own many houses? Several legitimate and illegitimate businesses? Had he not redeemed himself? Could they not know him?

Did he know *himself*?

A wave of anger and resentment broke over him as he drove. Its source was indeterminate. Of late, he thought more and more of carving someone's flesh with the tip of the broken blade, a jagged and uneven thing, and when such fantasies arose, he could not imagine turning aside. No. He would watch the carving even as he did it. He would observe every detail, take in every bleeding wound the blade made in flesh, and memorize the victim's tormented cries for—what else?—posterity. In such fantasies, he was not then who he had once been. He was someone else, a new man. The man he was becoming.

He reached under the seat where sat the saber, newly polished and oiled, and caressed the scabbard. For what was a gun? A crude machine. Loud, fast, and easy. You could stand a great length away and squeeze the dull trigger and watch some puke fall over with a hole in their face. What did it mean? Lerne scoffed. But a blade, now, that had purpose written all over it. No disguising what it was made for. No prettying it up. Which was precisely why he had of late purchased additional weapons, enamored with the simple grace of a medieval broadsword, a Venetian Renaissance stiletto. Already he had designated a secret room in his house for his growing collection. A museum, he told himself. A treasury of sharp things.

It was late in the afternoon when he arrived at the spot, a dirt road deep in the woods. Llewellyn's black Cadillac was parked on the shoulder. The henchman approached, mopping his sweating forehead.

"Boss," said Llewellyn. "Something's howling in your trunk."

"Which way?" said Lerne.

Llewellyn pointed. "Straight through and down," he said.

"Open my trunk and put the creature in your car. I won't be long."

"You're going alone?"

Lerne smiled and climbed from the car. "First time for everything," he said.

Soon he found it: a pistachio-green Ford Fairmont raucously tilted into a ditch. There were clothes piled up in the back glass, and on the seats. Lerne crept forward, joyous tingles dancing down his spine.

"Yoo-hoo, halloo," Lerne called.

The doors were unlocked. Lerne popped the trunk, the hood. The former held more clothes and bric-a-brac. The latter contained only the ruined engine. Lerne checked under the seats, got on his knees and peered under the car. No Dale. Lerne rose in frustration, tried in vain to wipe the mud from his knees. How could the old man elude him so? How could he fail to be spotted in town? At the card shack? Thought he was clever, did he?

Lerne drove his boot heel through a taillight, tore the bulb and socket free and flung it into the woods. He put a stone through the back glass and scattered the man's possessions, cut the clothes to shreds, slashed the seats. Still his rage would not abate. Dale Temmens was old, weak, and feeble. A gambler who had lost the touch and thus had lost everything, even his own home. Broke, homeless, and on the run. Yet he evaded Lerne at every turn.

No more, Lerne decided. Columbia was *his*. He would leave a message for old Dale. Let him and everyone else who ever crossed him what fruits such treachery would bear. To that end he whirled about, looking for an outlet, and spied a raccoon perched in the branches above the car. The animal pricked its ears when Lerne produced some chewing gum and waved it in offering.

"You tell old Dale," Lerne said as the animal began to descend. He unsheathed the saber. "Tell him we said *hello*."

Dale traipsed from place to place, looking for someone, anyone, to stake him. He went to the country hardware store where small time gamblers were known to play sweaty cards in the back office, too afraid to try the real hustlers at Andre's. He went to the auto shops where greasy mechanics and body repair guys sanded gray blotches of filler from bumpers and fenders, and they wouldn't so much as give him the time of day. He even hitched a ride way out to the Walmart in Pine Acres where the stock managers maintained a careful sports pool and held late-night poker games in the stockroom while they waited for the deliveries. All to no avail. At each place he was told there were no stakes to be had. Dale Temmens had been a legend. But folks were wise to his recent losses, his crushing defeats, and they could smell the stink of failure about him. No one wanted to back a loser.

Dale hitched a ride back, ruminating on what else he had learned in his travels. Namely that his youngest, Gene, had been out looking for loans as well. And the boy, like his father, was getting nowhere fast, turned down due to Dale's bad credit. That would do little, Dale knew, to improve the boy's mood. But Gene's fickle moods were the least of Dale's concerns. He'd been suspicious of Gene's return, knowing that little would willingly bring the boy back to the homestead he'd fled except trouble. The need for money only confirmed it: Gene was in hot water. The only questions were what kind and how hot.

Not for the first time, Dale regretted how he'd raised his boys, Gene in particular. Rich couldn't help it if he'd gotten his brains rattled in a war—a war Dale had vehemently disagreed with, much as he'd vehemently tried to dissuade Rich from enlisting. Rich had been young, yes, and flush with the stupidity that a still-developing brain brought to the table, but there was also a sad kind of desperation about it. His brother, Gene, had always garnered the lion's share of attention, not the least for the trouble into which he was constantly getting. Rich had always been quieter, shyer, more obedient, but also larger, more physically imposing. He'd tried his hand at all manner of sports and even played as a second stringer on the high school football team, but his athletic prowess was as spotty as his conviction to the sport, and by the time the season was over, so was Rich. Dale had always maintained that Rich joining the Army had been one part getting away from home and seeing the world, and one part proving to himself (and maybe everyone else) that it wasn't just his younger brother who could get into trouble. And what had he gotten for it? A head full of ghosts that chewed his mind.

Meanwhile, what kind of influence had Dale been on Gene? All the gambling, the cards, the constant scrambling for the next big payoff—what else explained the boy's character? If Gene was in trouble—and Dale felt for sure he was—then Dale was, in part, to blame. He'd set the pace. Provided the template.

Once back in Columbia, Dale pushed aside thoughts of his boys and hiked out to the last possible resort. By day, Sloane Gully ran a bar, the Downward Slope. On the side, he'd developed a reputation as a stake man known to back long shot odds despite their record. The only problem was his rates—he took seventy five percent, no exceptions. More if the gambler ticked him off. And Gully was famous for dealing harshly with those who failed to pay back their stakes. Not as bad as Lerne had become, Dale thought, but plenty harsh all the same. More than a few of the hacks he saw now and again at Andre's walked with a permanent limp thanks to Gully.

At the Slope, Dale stopped in the parking lot to check his disguise. He was in his black *Holy Diver* shirt, a faded and threadbare keepsake from his concert-going days, and jeans with missing knees. The neon tennis shoes had been salvaged from a shoe store Dumpster. Atop his head was the soiled canvas hat. Beneath it, a blonde wig with a rangy ponytail trailing down his back. He adjusted the dark sunglasses over his face, smoothed his mustache, and looked about for Lerne's signature silver Kompressor. Unlikely to meet the man in such a dive, but Dale would take no chances.

Within the cool dark of the bar the Allman Brothers droned from dust-feathered speakers. Dale had never understood why anyone would debase their ears with the Allmans when Ronnie van Zant and company had done pretty much the best you could in four albums. There was no accounting for taste. Dale shot a glance toward the jukebox and confirmed his suspicions. A bevvy of too-young men had gathered about the machine, plastic beer cups in hand, to pour over what they no doubt considered essential Southern rock. College kids, likely on a jaunt from the condos their parents paid for, there to see what real rednecks did on their days off. Dale made his way to the bar, ordered a beer, and waited until Gully emerged from the back. He waived at the man and grinned when the proprietor's only reply was a blank and unfamiliar stare. Gully came over and leaned on the bar beside him.

"Help you?" he asked.

"Don't recognize me?" said Dale. He tipped back the hat and wig, pushed the sunglasses down the bridge of his nose. Gully leaned in, squinting, then arched his eyebrows.

"Not bad," said the man. "Fooled me."

"More than you is the idea." Dale reset his disguise and drained the last of his beer. "He ain't here, is he?"

"Who? Lerne? Hell no. He don't come here."

"Another beer, then, and a little conversation."

"You got money?"

Dale stared at the man behind his dark sunglasses. "Gully, it's *me.*"

"You indeed," Gully said as he reached over the bar, took two beers from the cooler, and set them on the bar. "Dale Temmens. Course, that name ain't what it used to be, is it? That's why you're here."

"Can't a man stop in and say hello to old friends?"

"Old associates," Gully corrected. "And can't old associates just tell it like it is? You ain't taking me to prom, now, is you?"

Dale opened his bottle and took a long swig. Cold beer was just what he needed after a long day hitchhiking in the heat. Gully's tone was another matter entirely. "I know what folks say," Dale told him. "But I'm still me."

"Not according to recent losses."

"Everyone hits a speed bump."

"Speed bump?" Gully laughed and held his hand up to Dale's brow. "About yay high? Ain't no shame, though. You getting up there. Good a time as any to retire."

"Sure," said Dale as he swallowed his pride. "That's the plan. But first I got to pay back what I owe."

Gully was nodding along, the look in his eyes getting darker and darker. "How much and by when?"

"Whatever and yesterday," said Dale. He took a sip from his beer, a thrill of relief going through him. Gully would stake him. He'd get into a game, take it to the suckers at Andre's, and avenge his own defeats. He was back on the horse, sabers up!

"I appreciate it," said Dale. "And don't worry. I'm going to win. I can feel it."

"Hope so," said Gully. "But the terms are a little different."

"Different how?"

"Eighty," said Gully.

Dale nearly spit out his beer. Eighty percent? Gully wanted *eighty percent* of what Dale cleared in winnings after paying his debt? His usual had been forty for newcomers, and twenty-five for long-standing associates. Dale used to get him down to fifteen back in the day. The terms *were* different.

"Can't accept higher than thirty," said Dale.

"Couldn't possibly see my way under seventy," said Gully.

"Forty is an insult but I'll take it."

"Fifty is generous, Dale. Very generous indeed."

Gully extended his hand. That, Dale knew, meant the negotiations were over. Dale took the man's hand and shook. Fifty percent. Better than eighty, sure, but steep.

"High risk loan," said Gully. "I'm sure you understand."

"How about another beer to help me along?"

"Why the hell not?"

Gully set down another beer, flashed a crooked grin, and told Dale to sit tight. Then he disappeared round back. Dale sat driving a finger through the moisture that had accumulated on the bar. He sucked at the sour taste that coated his tongue. Fifty percent. Times *had* changed.

Dale got to thinking. Gully was a last-resort kind of guy, the sort you only went to when there were no better options. Fifty percent was an insult, sure, but the truth was he *could* have gone higher. What was Dale going to do? Reject the offer? No, he knew Dale had to have a stake, and he also knew there was little chance of him recouping his loss should Dale lose—which he wasn't going to do, of course, but still. So, the question remained: Why hadn't Gully gouged him for more? He could have gotten Dale for sixty or seventy percent, set the stake terms low. He should have, in fact. Unless someone made him a better offer.

Sudden fear fell like a block of dry ice in Dale's gut. He slid off his stool and went round back of the bar. There he spied Gully on the phone, the man's words inaudible over the music. Dale slipped past and went to the bathroom, drained his aching bladder, and washed up. Alone before the mirror, he stared at his own disguised face. His mind was running the numbers, the odds tumbling like dice loosed from a hand, the pips of possibility turning over and over.

"Shit," he said.

When Dale returned to his stool, Gully was already there and sipping a beer.

"Don't you got a bar to run?" said Dale.

"Sure do," said Gully. He reached into the cooler and removed two fresh beers, set one down in front of Dale, and opened the other for himself. The beer in his hand, Dale noticed, was still a quarter full.

"Mighty kind," Dale said in the most relaxed and amicable voice he could muster. He had ten minutes, maybe less. "Don't see the stake."

"On its way," said Gully. "Think I keep that kind of cash around?"

"Used to," said Dale.

"Things change," said Gully. "You know better than anyone."

"That they do," said Dale. "And that I do. Listen to us. A couple of old timers yakking on the porch. You and me."

"Me and you," said Gully. He touched his beer bottle to Dale's, took a swig, and let out a loud blech.

Heartless, thought Dale. Cruel. The man doesn't even feel bad for what he's done, for what he's about to do. Dale looked about, saw the college yuppies had congregated at the far end of the bar. Dale sucked down his beer and stood. "The degradation of old age," he said.

"You just went," said Gully.

"Every hour on the hour these days," said Dale. "Sometimes twice. Don't touch my beer. I'll be back in a second."

"Don't forget to wash your hands," said Gully. He laughed his Sloane Gully laugh, a kind of cackle that sounded like an idiot gargling river rocks.

Dale pointed down the bar. "Looks like you got honest customers."

With obvious disdain, Gully slid from his stool, came around the bar, and made for the yuppies. Meanwhile, Dale was en route to the toilet, listening to the excited chatter of the yuppies. A decent distraction. Dale passed the bathroom and kept going to the back exit, then out into the blinding sunlight and took off at a wobbling, creaky trot across the parking lot, the beer swishing in his gut. There was a line of trees at the far end, the highway beside it, and yet another parched ditch choked with weeds. Dale plunged into the ditch, hunkered down, and waited.

He knew the risk he was taking. He ought to go, leave, forget it. But he couldn't. He had to know. And a few minutes later, when the silver Kompressor pulled into the parking lot, Dale's heart sank.

"You snake," Dale hissed under his mustache. "You lurking cottonmouth."

Lerne emerged from the silver car dressed in maroon seersucker. He stood a moment in the sun, adjusted his clothes, and checked his large, well-groomed hair in the side mirror before he disappeared into the bar.

Dale escaped via the ditch, crouched low in case Llewellyn was still in the car, and slithered away into the woods. It was a long hike back to his temporary abode. It left him plenty of time to think, plenty of time to ruminate on the sting of betrayal. Sold down river by Gully Sloane. On the one hand, he could scarcely believe it. He'd known Gully for more than three decades, knew him when Lerne was getting skinned knees in the schoolyard. That ought to stand for something, right? But the truth was simple. Lerne had made him a better offer.

The woods were going dark and purple by the time Dale found himself among familiar trees. An eerie quiet blanketed the place. Dale paused, reconsidered his approach. Acting on instinct, Dale dropped to his belly and slithered toward the culvert in which the Ford rested. From the edge of the clearing, he spied his abode in ruins, the windows broken, the doors ajar, his belongings hacked into bits and scattered in the weeds. A message had been written on the windshield in what looked like blood. *HELLO.* A glistening trail lead toward the drain pipe. It was one of the raccoons, its belly sliced open. Flies had already gathered on the dark, matted fur.

The bile rose in Dale's throat. Lerne had found his hideout. He wasn't safe there any longer. He wasn't safe anywhere.

Just then, Dale heard a noise from the other side of the culvert, the musical ringing of a phone, then a man's voice in response. Llewellyn, the lackey, emerged from the tress, a lit cigarette in hand. His other handheld the phone to his ear.

"No," said the lackey. "Not yet, anyway. Want me to stay longer?"

Don't bother, thought Dale. Careful not to make a sound, he slithered back the way he'd come, and when he was far enough away not to worry about noise, he sprang to his feet and ran.

Chapter 4

One afternoon turned into two. Two turned into five. Before Gene knew it, a week had gone by. Most afternoons he spent with James and Laura, and often just with Laura, the two of them swapping stories. Some days they sat in the back of her animal control truck, eating frugal lunches during her break, and others they spent getting a high-noon buzz in downtown bars with shots of cheap whiskey and cold beers to take off the edge. In the evenings, they rounded up James, who as Gene had predicted, did his level best to hide the fact that he was head over heels in love.

And Gene could see why. Even for someone like himself, it was hard not to get pulled into her orbit—and once there, even harder to escape. Not that he wanted to. Granted, Gene's interest in Laura wasn't romantic, but even he could admit the allure she had for anyone with two working brain cells. Laura's very existence hinted at possibilities Gene had never considered. And anyway, what *had* Gene considered possible? Take James, for example, the too-sweet boy next door, the plucky hometown homebody who never left, never would leave, and sought nothing more in life than to get married and move two blocks from his parents. For crying out loud, he might start going to church. Gene wouldn't put it past him. Closet Republican. Gene shuddered.

But hadn't Gene's possibilities been equally narrow? Broke kid from a broke family, a grifter with nothing to show. The only thing he'd ever been truly good at had been his stay at Big John's, his work with dogs. So, who was he to talk?

But Laura was different. She'd gone ten rounds with life, no gloves, and she was still standing. A graduate student. A dog cop. She seemed primed to do *anything*. Gene was content to stick around for another few days, maybe another week. He was making a new friend—a good one. The Texans hadn't come looking for him. Maybe they never would.

He was thinking about that while they sat in the back of the empty animal control truck sharing a sandwich. It was Laura's lunch hour on a slow, hot day, and they were parked downtown outside the State House where the conversation had turned to some of Gene's more ridiculous exploits.

"Fly in my beer," said Gene.

"We don't have beers."

"No one's perfect. But no, that's how you get a free beer or two. I used to bring a plastic fly to the bar, drop it in the glass when I was about halfway done. Then I would call the bartender over and complain, and nine times out of ten they just pony up and pour you another. Nobody wants a customer making a fuss about bugs."

"Imagine what you could do with a real fly."

"Tried it with a plastic roach once in the summer. They jumped then. Why they never caught on is beyond me."

"Lot of things are. For example, the point."

"Of the fake bugs?

"The free beers. The alligator hotel thing in Florida. Whatever stupidity you were up to in Texas. All of it. What's the point? It's not the money or you would have stuck with something else."

"Blunt," said Gene. He was kidding, but the truth was he felt a little sore. Laura had a way of cutting to the chase that showed him things about himself he didn't always like.

"Blame the heat," she said, and flicked a crumb from her lap. "But tell me. I genuinely want to know."

Gene thought while he chewed. He hadn't anticipated the question but drumming up an answer proved to be difficult. "Punching up," he finally said. He didn't like the knowing look in her eye, and he *definitely* didn't like the way it made him feel as if he had forgotten to get dressed that morning.

"That's a pipe dream," said Laura. "It's not about someone else or some abstract notion of justice. Be honest."

Gene found it harder by the moment to meet her gaze. He looked out at the State House, watching the politicians and clerks and lawyers and lobbyists climb the steps because it was preferable to the alternative. The alternative was, of course, admitting to himself, silently at first, that there was an uncomfortable node of truth to what she had said. And there was that word again: uncomfortable. So, he asked himself while he bit into his sandwich half, why was it, pray tell, that as uncomfortable as she sometimes made him, he still spent every available minute with her? What exactly was it he wanted? For that matter, what did *she* want? Was *wanting* even the point? That's what she had asked, after all. The point.

"The jackpot," he said. "The big payout."

"We quoting Kenny Rogers here?"

"I'm talking about doing something that flies in the face of all odds."

"Even if it means conning someone who never did anything to hurt you?"

"It look like I'm out here ripping off old ladies?"

"Rich investors in Florida," said Laura. "Tech investors in Boulder. Rich dullards with money galore. I get it. But what about Big John?"

"Big John?" said Gene. He was genuinely confused. He shoved the last bite of sandwich in his mouth and said, "I never took a thing from Big John."

"You left him in the lurch. And for what?"

Despite himself, Gene felt himself getting angry. He didn't like her line of questioning—not that afternoon, anyway—and he sure as hell didn't like what she was implying. "See my previous statement," he said.

But Laura was shaking her head, balling the sandwich wrapper into her pocket and clapping the last few crumbs from her hands. "He gave you the job," she said. "Sponsored you. He believed in you. Then you messed up and left him in the lurch. What happens to him? Does he score big, too? No one does because it doesn't happen."

"It will," said Gene, trying not to sound angry. "One day."

"Keep telling yourself that," said Laura. "All the way to jail."

Before Gene could reply, her phone alarm went off. Break over. Relieved, Gene hopped off the truck and balled up the last bit of his lunch in its wrapper. She offered to give him a lift back. He declined. Without saying as much, he knew he would see her later, just as he knew they'd spend another evening taking turns buying rounds of shots while James stewed beside them. Theirs was a fast developing friendship not unlike what he had with Big John. And he damn sure needed someone like that in his corner.

But the truth, right, he told himself as he hopped on the passing bus, was a little more complicated. He was sharp enough to know that Laura was carving up his ideas, picking them apart, turning them around and showing them to him as though he hadn't been the one to cough them up in the first place. And why was she doing that? So that he might see what she saw: That his ideas—some of them, at least—were found wanting.

But another thought occurred to him as he rode the bus toward home, one that had surfaced once or twice before, one to which he had yet to give much credence, and it was this: In teaching him his own shortcomings, she was showing him how to identify them on his own, showing him how to look deeper into himself than he had ever dared. What else would he see? What else would he find?

By the time Gene got home, dusk was stretching lengths of gold and red over the trees. The humid heat was sweltering. But despite the awful weather and the subtle dress down he'd received over lunch, Gene was in such inexplicably good spirits.

His good spirits withered a bit when he saw Rich's dilapidated truck parked in front of the house. They were likely waiting in ambush, his brother and mother, prepared once more to impress upon him the many reasons he ought to partner with Rich. Well, they could wait, Gene thought as he made his way to the barn. He'd already *been* ambushed. No reason to rush into another.

In the barn, Gene took stock. The place was orderly, freshly scrubbed. Fifty-pound bags of dog food were stacked in the far corner. The loft was cleaned and patched, the floors swept. He had to give it to Rich and Mattie. Even the truck, to Rich's credit, had been cleaned, repaired, and painted. Sure, the outside and inside were a matching shade of dull metallic gray, and sure, sometimes when he started it up music piped from the roof speaker, a warped fragment of the old ice cream tune, but all totaled, it was pretty damn impressive for a doomed venture.

If only Rich and Mattie would get it into their thick skulls that Gene was done with doomed things. He loosed the best, most well-behaved dogs from their cages and sat among them, grateful for the reprieve they provided. They politely nosed about, tails thumping, and gave little whimpers of pleasure when he pet them. There were, he was pleased to note, three different groupings of cages, one each for the three different groupings of dogs he had pointed out to Rich. Those around him were easy adoptions, for example. Smart, good-mannered pups who had been abandoned. The next group was wary, not yet fully trusting of people or each other, and had to be more thoroughly trained before anyone would even consider them for a pet. The last, well, that group was housed at the back of the barn, away from the noise and commotion up front, their cages spaced well apart. That was where the problem dogs resided, those who got too excited around other dogs, or worse, exhibited aggression or too much territoriality. Those dogs would need constant training for weeks or months before they were ready to join the second group, and even then, some of them may never lose whatever feral behaviors they'd picked up.

Gene sat among the dogs, petting and scratching and soaking up their sloppy wet kisses, grateful for their loving company. It had taken a little work on his part to convince Mattie not to name the dogs with her brand of bad nomenclature. Mister Love Face, Doctor Happy Touch, and Kissy Bottom—such were a few of her chosen titles. Besides, he'd told her, dogs already had names—true names. They'd tell anyone who listened, Big John had taught him. All a person had to do was hush.

That one, for example. A striped black and brown mutt with calm, wise eyes. From the day the dog had arrived, Gene had felt a particular kinship with him, and in the evenings, when he went to the barn to be among the animals, it was always that one who was the calmest, the gentlest, the most trusting. Now the dog sat, tail wagging patiently, until Gene was able to offer his full attention. They looked at each other for long minutes, dog and man, while Gene tried his best to blank his mind into a kind of meditative state that, like all of Big John's ridiculous training methods, wound up working. He was waiting, as he had been waiting for more than a week, for the dog to tell him with a look, with a wag of the tail or a little noise of jubilant love, who he was.

Outside, the damn cicadas were having a go at driving everyone insane with their noise. But Gene sat calm and patient looking into the dog's eyes while the dog looked into his. The light thinned and the shadows stretched across the barn floor. The other dogs began to settle back into their cages. Then the striped mutt licked its chops and blinked in a way Gene could not have described to anyone on Earth but Big John without sounding insane.

"Doc," said Gene. The name had come to him, suddenly. Like a country physician who'd seen pretty much everything and never got rattled. Bumps, bruises, wounds galore. You name it. No sweat. Doc could handle it.

The dog yawned and stretched out at Gene's side. *About time,* he seemed to say.

Gene thumped his ribs and rubbed his belly. Nice to have someone in his corner for a change, he thought.

Gene put the dogs back in their cages, all but Doc. When he got to Doc's cage, he paused, and so did the dog, the pair of them as if to say, in unison, *Is this necessary?* "All right," said Gene. "You win."

With the other dogs secured and bedded with plenty of water for the night, Gene closed up the barn and went reluctantly toward the house, Doc in tow. If Mattie and Rich wanted to gang up on him, he might as well get it over with. He could just as easily slip out to the cookhouse with Doc, get the fellow some exercise with the ball, and regale him with stories until they both got tired enough. Maybe some poetry like at Big John's. There had to be a volume of Keats somewhere in the house.

Lights were on in the house. Music trickled out of the windows, barely audible over the buzz of the air conditioners. Interesting. Gene opted to avoid the front door and headed round back. Both porches vacant. Very interesting. It was then that he noticed lights on in the cookhouse. There he found Rich seated at one of the ancient desks. His brother was pale and sweating, caked in dirt. Rich looked blankly at Doc, then at Gene.

"I saw him," Rich said as though prompted.

"Who?" said Gene.

"Hollis Lerne. He bought a sword."

"A sword? Is this real or more ghost talk?"

"He looked like a man possessed."

"So what?" said Gene. He pushed the other desk flush with his brother's, head-to-head, and pulled up another of the dusty, ancient chairs and fell into it. Doc made circuits, sniffing at every dusty, cobwebbed corner of the room. "I was hoping to avoid the spooky talk tonight," said Gene.

Rich swallowed hard, wringing his hands. His eyes, when he raised them to meet Gene's, were just the slightest bit accusatory.

"Just seen you go out to the barn," he said.

"Seen me do it most every night. So what?"

"So, you know what we got here."

"Listen," said Gene. "Do what you want but leave me out."

"But you're staying a while, right? Why not help? You could be part of something."

"I am," said Gene. "My own damn life. You should try it sometime."

Gene had meant the joke to hit lightly, but Rich winced.

"I never asked you for anything. But any time you needed help or money, who was there? All I'm asking for is a little of the same."

Gene spun in his chair. Here it came. The guilt trip, right on schedule. He felt for his brother, he really did, because Rich was right. In the past, if Gene was in trouble and called Rich for money, his brother always delivered, practically no questions asked. Now his brother was clearly spooked and asking for his assistance and Gene was telling him—what? No dice? Not quite. More like: Not interested. It was well past time Rich took control of his own life, ghosts and all.

"Once and for all," said Gene, "I didn't come home to start no business. Sorry, Rich."

He didn't like the look of crushing disappointment on Rich's face. Nor did he like the tilt of Doc's head. Everyone, thought Gene. Judge, jury, and idiot savant. He rose before his brother could offer some dozen other explanations why they ought to waste copious time and money on a doomed venture and went off toward the house. At his side, Doc trotted along, loyal but clearly not pleased with the recent proceedings.

"Takes time," Gene told the dog. "He'll get it. Sooner or later."

In the house, the kitchen phone was ringing. Stuck around it were notes in Mattie's neat script saying, "If it's the crazy, ain't nobody home."

From the floor above him, Mattie hollered. "Someone get the dang phone!"

"You sure?" Gene called back.

"Read the notes!"

"Sure," he told Doc, and picked up the phone. "Hello Central. Nobody home. How can I help you?"

"Hello, Eugene," said a familiar voice. "Or should I say Gene Temmens? We've arrived."

Gene's heart leapt into his throat. He knew the voice. Knew it all too well. The voice belonged to Loke, one of the three Texas collectors who'd driven him from Austin. And if Loke had found him, that meant Malak and Roy had, too. But how? Gene had given most everyone in Austin a fake last name, a fake backstory: Elbert Harris, son of a dirt farmer out of Rolling Hills, Nebraska. That left two or three folk tops who knew Gene's true identity, and none of them had been in contact with the collectors, much less involved in heavy sports betting. Gene swallowed hard. For better or worse, he had to know.

"Loke," he said. "Who gave you my number?"

"Give us some credit," said Malak's voice.

Big John, Gene thought. Then: No. Big John wouldn't have talked.

"Credit," said Roy. "Exactly. We're smart, see? Smarter than you gave us credit for."

"I know what you're thinking," said Loke. "The old dog man you used to work for? We didn't even have to knock on his door. Turns out there's a thing called public records and word of mouth and hot damn, wouldn't you know it, if a man puts his ear to the ground and digs, I mean really *digs,* there's no end to the nonsense he can dig up. Like your name and phone number on a certification you got to be a—what was it? Dog trainer"

"Call us romantics," said Malak. "Now we're in Columbia, just down the road. And you know what that means."

Gene considered his options and came up with—nothing. He was in no position to challenge them or call their bluff, and anyway he didn't think they were bluffing, not if they had his mother's phone number. Running? That was out. If he tried anything cute, they would retaliate.

"Now here's the question," said Malak. "Where's our money?"

Gene steeled himself. He had to toe the line, but barely, or they would fly off the handle. "Boys," he said, "you'll never believe me, but I don't got it."

"Oh, that we know," said Loke. "You lost it on bad betting."

"But you got *something,*" said Malak. "Always do."

"And we know where you live," said Roy. "Where your *family* lives. Ain't that something? Mister Elbert Harris, I mean Gene Temmens, with a family and everything. We'd hate to pay them a visit."

"So, here's what's what," Loke said in his low Texas drawl. "Let's get together and talk this out. Then you give us what's ours and we leave you alive and whole. Don't that sound fair?"

"Pay attention, now," said Malak. "We're making healthy suggestions."

"And if you skip town," said Roy, "we'll be there, at your house, having this talk with your folks. You know how we get when it comes to money."

"Take a second and think," said Loke. "Ready? Let's try it again. What you got?"

Gene's heart sank. He had fooled himself into thinking the trail had gone cold, that he was free and clear, safe. How stupid could he get? Now he was pinched, and if he didn't find something—anything—to offer and fast, things were going to escalate and fast. But what? Rich had no money. Neither did Mattie or Dale. No one in town would loan him the money, legitimately or otherwise. He turned in place, desperate, seeing little but the disheveled house, the wastebasket full of crumpled notes, the screen door, the truck in the yard, and beyond it the dogs. Then he saw Doc at his side, the dog's gaze directed at the screen door. He looked up, saw Rich coming across the yard from the cookhouse. He saw the barn in the distance, a faint silhouette in the last of the day's light. He looked again at the truck.

Then it hit him, a plan so far-fetched and risky he could scarcely believe it himself. It came in a flash, so suddenly that Gene didn't fully comprehend all the angles. But the angles, they were there, and they were, ostensibly real. And beyond that, way out past the darker shadow of the barn, he saw the potential for something *more,* some opportunity that only desperation exacerbated might afford him.

"I got something," said Gene. "But I need time to put it together."

"Tomorrow," said Loke.

"Blood from a stone, boys."

"Blood's right," said Roy.

"All I'm asking is a sporting chance. Trust me, you won't be disappointed."

"Oh, Christ," Loke fairly hissed into the phone. "We're off Senate Street in the Hilton. Friday at noon in the hotel restaurant."

"And Gene?" said Malak.

"Be on time," said Roy. Then he hung up.

Lerne was parked outside the Hilton, poring over the pictures Llewellyn had sent to his phone earlier that week: snapshots of three Texans in his very line of work. The men had arrived in town a few days ago, taken up residence in the hotel, and had occupied themselves mostly at the bar with occasional forays about town. They wore expensive tailored suits and fine leather boots and Stetson hats and almost always went about as a trio; only at night, and only after a great many powerful draughts of liquor did the one called "Roy" amble about town without his colleagues. They had come to Columbia for the youngest Temmens boy, something Llewellyn did not know. But Lerne did. He knew all of this because he had eyes and ears everywhere. In the hotel bar, for example, was a young man who owed him money on a bogus set of antique China plates he'd tried to push onto his pawn shop earlier that year. Now he was working off his debt.

Besides, he thought with a smile, the oaf who sold him the saber, Rich, was not the type to be sought by well-groomed Texas collectors. Gene, on the other hand, fit the bill and perfectly. Lerne was pleased to know he'd been dead-on about the boy. If money was involved—and it always was—Lerne would further take advantage. Already he had seeded the proper channels. Did someone need a loan? Hollis Lerne was willing to lend.

But as for the Texans, Lerne seethed. Bad enough their casual encroachment on his turf. Worse yet, one of their number, Roy, the balding, paunchy man, bore a striking resemblance to Kinsey West. Just looking at the man's picture brought back the humiliation, the rage. Lerne was beginning to realize that nothing—not his turf, not his feelings, not a goddamn thing—would truly be his until he confronted the specters of his past. Then and only then would he be free of his misgivings.

As if on cue, Llewellyn, positioned in secret within the hotel, called and delivered the news for which Lerne had hoped. Two of the Texans had just left, dressed for drinking and dancing and such. As the man spoke, Lerne saw the Texans in their ridiculous ten-gallon hats and fine-pressed suits exit the building. They got in a black rented Lincoln and drove off—right past him, in fact—without sparing so much as a glance in his direction.

"And the fat one?" Lerne said into the phone.

"Still here," said Llewellyn. "Want me to sit him down?"

In the past, Lerne would have conceded, let Llewellyn handle things. The lackey excelled at violence and intimidation. He seemed to take personally any affronts to Lerne's person and property and could be relied upon to avenge any slight tenfold. But Lerne had other, newer ideas. He wanted to try something.

"I appreciate it," said Lerne. "But I'm going to have a talk with him myself."

Through the phone, Lerne could hear the hesitation in Llewellyn's voice. "Boss?"

"Go back to the house and wait for my call. I aim to make a new friend."

There was a pause before Llewellyn asked, "You sure?"

That was the second time in a few short days his henchman's disbelief had been given voice. In the old days, Lerne never had the stomach for such a confrontation, for violence. But times were changing. Every cut he inflicted on someone else took the fear out of him, made room for more of himself. He'd proven it that very week, testing the weapons on the fat Spaniard's gift, the black Lab, tormenting the dog while it was chained in his shed. The animal, so docile at first, had grown craven and fearful, revealing its true nature. After a few days, the dog grew a pair and began to put up a fight such that Lerne, terrified to get in range, had retreated. Then, just yesterday morning, Lerne had stepped out onto his patio, his usual breakfast of donuts in hand, and saw the shed door had been forcibly opened, buckled out from the inside. A hole dug under the fence provided the means of escape. At that moment, Lerne thought with grim satisfaction, the dog was likely mauling some bewildered citizen, living its last wretched days in agony.

But more to the point, Lerne was in charge. Lerne made the rules, gave the orders. He would have to keep tabs on his employee lest the man forget his place.

"Your concern is noted," said Lerne. He hung up and produced a flask. Within was the brew, a new and heady elixir of sweet tea vodka with ground Oxycontin and a bit of Zolpidem to smooth the edges. This he nipped, medicine for mind, body, and soul. A luscious calm overtook him. He was a conduit as he stepped from the car, nothing more.

He found the Texan—the one with the paunch and the bright yellow boots—at the hotel bar, a row of empty beer bottles arrayed before him. Lerne noticed the small red veins in the man's bulbous nose, the bald pate showing under the brim of his gray Stetson. The resemblance to West was uncanny!

Already Lerne was approaching a boil.

"I hear you're looking for Gene," Lerne said as he slid into the stool beside the Texan. It took effort to keep the heat from his voice.

The Texan glanced at him, then turned back to his beer. Contempt. Lerne could feel it oozing out of the man. "Who's you?" said Roy.

"I'm his brother, blood kin. Are you the one—let's see. Roy?"

The Texan looked him up and down and sucked his teeth before nodding. "That's me," he said. "Bring what he owes?"

Lerne smiled, tingling with pleasure. Right on all counts! The Temmens boy owed the Texans—something substantial, Lerne was willing to wager. He filed it away for future reference, produced from his wallet a thousand dollars in crisp bills, and slid the money across the bar.

"A thousand," said Roy. "That's it?"

"I beg your pardon?"

"Damn right you beg. That's pathetic."

Lerne's face began to burn. No one but Kinsey West, the holdout of old, had ever treated him with such disregard. As a child, Lerne had endured constant torment from his peers—beatings, humiliation, emasculation. As an adult, he had endured worse. No matter how many houses he owned, how many whores sucked him off, how many pawn shops he bought and rehabilitated, he remained to the world at large little more than a boil, a pimple. On the outside, he maintained his smile. But inside, in the meat and bone, in the deeper, darker parts that roiled and boiled, a singular vision emerged like Excalibur held aloft by the bitch of the Lake. No one, but *no one,* would ever again disregard him. In an instant he decided on another course of action, drastic and necessary. The new way began then and there, and it sure as shit started with Lerne *not taking one lick more.*

"He's got the rest," said Lerne. A calm had overtaken him—how strange! He felt new and powerful and sure of himself.

"All of it?" Roy said with a hint of cautious skepticism.

"One lump sum. Don't ask me how."

"Hot damn. Must be scared. Where at?"

"Just a few miles, edge of town. I have my car, a fine Mercedes."

"He buy that for you?"

"He called it a gift." Lerne produced the keys and held them aloft. "It, too, will be yours."

Roy bristled. Lerne feigned profound regret, his very best impression of a man prepared to offer up a treasured possession. The key was to play it humble, let the Texan think he was in charge. Because soon, very soon, he was going to find out different.

"Let me call my associates," said Roy.

"You may," said Lerne. "But Gene was very specific. He asked for you alone, said you'd understand. And the car, that was to be for you alone. It's practically new."

Roy wobbled slightly in his stool. He was drunk, Lerne saw. All the better! The Texans gaze remained fixated on the keys.

"Thinks I'm a softy?" said Roy.

"He thinks you're fair," Lerne said in his most reassuring tone. "Spoke of you highly. My brother isn't a bad fellow. He's just, what's the term? Dim. I was also asked to pay your bar tab."

"Well," Roy said with a sour belch. To Lerne's surprise, the man's expression turned sorrowful. "Always liked the kid," he said. "We used to go drinking. He probably told you. Used to have a blast. But damn if he didn't screw up big."

Lerne perked up. His opportunity was upon him. He leaned in, put his arm around the Texan, and paused for a dramatic beat. The man smelled like hotel soap and cheap beer. An uneven day's stubble had sprouted along his jaw. "What he regrets most is the damage to friendship," said Lerne. "But he wants to make it right. Tonight. You and me, we'll go see him and then you won't have to worry."

Lerne could almost pity him. The lies he'd fed the Texan had practically moved the man to tears. Not cut out for this business, Lerne thought. Not cut out for much of anything. Nothing except cutting and they'd see to that very soon.

Finally, Roy nodded, wiped the large white boogers from the corners of his eyes. "All right," he said. "Let's go see your brother. Let's get this done with. You drive."

Lerne could hardly believe his good fortune. Never before had he been so bold, so precise. He was changing, he realized as he threw money on the bar and guided the Texan to his Kompressor. It was as if when he sharpened his blades, they sharpened him.

Once in the car, Roy opened his jacket, and showed Lerne the holstered pistol. He motioned to Lerne's shirt and said, "Let's see it."

Lerne exposed himself and endured the man's squeezes and pinches. Roy found the flask and gave it a little shake.

"What's this?" he said.

"One for the road," said Lerne. "By all means."

Roy's eyes narrowed with suspicion. "You first."

Lerne obliged with a long pull on the flask, felt the brew warm and comforting in his stomach. He passed the flask to the Texan and took delight when the man choked and sputtered after but one taste.

"Christ Jesus," said Roy. "It's gone off. Drive, skinny."

But after that the fat Texan got pliant, cozy. The brew worked on him. They passed the flask back and forth and soon Roy no longer complained about the peculiar flavor. He seemed to enjoy it. And Lerne grew ever more comfortable as they approached the city limits.

"What's that banging in the trunk?" Roy said.

"A sword," said Lerne. "Listen here. Maybe you heard about a man round these parts in your line of employ. Fellow named Hollis Lerne. "

"Can't say I have."

"This here's his town."

"Some chicken-shit Carolina boy?" Roy began to laugh. "Son, I'm from Texas. We eat Dixie up."

Lerne tightened his grip on the steering wheel. "That ain't even close to nice," he said through his teeth.

But Roy was staring at him, squinting in the passing lights of cars. "Who's that singer? Because you're the spitting image."

"Randy Travis," Lerne said with pride.

Roy squinted harder. "No," he said. "It's Meat Loaf. I'm very sure."

Bile rose in Lerne's gullet. *Meat Loaf*? He glanced at Roy and found the man's oblivious, watery gaze was fixed on the road. Smug, nasty, duplicitous. A pig waiting for the spit. Lerne took the last mile into the woods in total silence, grinding his teeth, and brought the car to a halt outside an abandoned farmhouse, an ancient and rotting domicile squatting near a pond and sheltered on three sides by dense trees.

Lerne motioned. "He's in there," he said.

Roy squinted at the building. "The light's is all off," he said with a heavy slur. His eyes, heavily lidded, struggled to remain open. The brew had hold of him. Yet Lerne felt—what? Fresh. Clean. Renewed. He took another nip from his flask and felt his courage bolstered. There was no going back. They had arrived.

Lerne said, "Y'all come here, flaunt yourselves. Don't you know?"

"Oh, Christ," said a pale and sweating Roy as he pawed at the door. "That flask. What did you give me?"

"Meat Loaf," said Lerne. He was struggling to keep his voice from coming out in a frenzied bark. "Look here. I take you out for a nice drive to a nice place. I only lied a little. I ain't Gene's brother. But you been rude this whole time. And here I been letting you sip from my flask. In my car. Don't you get it? This is my town!"

Within him the rage erupted. In one smooth movement Lerne reached under the seat where he'd stowed the stiletto and struck. Roy peered down at the handle of the knife protruding from his flank, at the spreading red stain on his shirt. Lerne extracted the blade and drove it again. Roy's eyes bulged. Lerne stepped calmly from the car, walked unhurriedly around the vehicle, and opened the passenger door. The Texan toppled into the dirt. A small matter to casually separate the man from his pistol. Lerne dangled the gun between two fingers and placed it on the roof of the car. A part of him took in what he'd done, what was before him. The blood, the agony, the sheer fucking *ecstasy* that began when the blade parted the rude Texan's flesh. None of the old squeamishness remained. The blood, the violence, the absurdity, all of it felt good and natural.

"I used to be like you," he told the wheezing, bleeding Texan. "Then I got the good news. Now look at me."

Lerne held out his hand, palm to the ground. He was shaking. Practically vibrating. All at once he began to laugh. If he had known all those years ago how easy it was, how *good* it felt, he would have stuck Kinsey West himself when he had the chance. He would have bled him up and down the block, tarried behind him while the man crawled about, gasping for air.

"Please," Roy said as he crawled about. "I got money. Just get me to a hospital."

But Lerne was no longer listening. He was flushed with adrenaline, tuned to a higher frequency. He was in awe of the man's fortitude, a gift. It inspired him. He went to the trunk, got the sword. Then he returned, holding the weapon aloft.

Roy was still on the ground, deflating. The blood kept coming out of him, drenching his shirt and jacket. "What's that?" said Roy. "You sick fuck, we'll kill you. We'll gut you like a fucking animal."

"Now you got the news, too," said Lerne.

When he was done hacking and chopping, Lerne rested, listening to the and the rush of his own blood in his ears, audible over the cicadas. In his pants, an erection so stiff it ached. He fished the Texan's ten-gallon hat from the weeds and set it atop his head. Of what had he ever been so frightened? In a way, he reasoned, he had bled as they bled, just metaphorically. He had spent years, a short lifetime, in fact, bleeding onto every surface. His parents and their bitching in the boat house. The explosion. The dog that had chewed on him. The debtors who mocked him. They'd all bled him. Columbia had bled him. They'd all taken turns sticking him until he was perforated, a crude meat lampshade. But now he had the sticking instruments. The chopping kind. And *they* would be the ones doing the bleeding.

He removed the man's cell phone and wallet, the thousand dollars he'd given him, and the stiletto where it had snagged in the man's flabby stomach. He was amazed at the simplicity, the intimacy a blade brought to such matters. If only he'd known, he thought as he dialed Llewellyn to come clean up, he might never have wasted so much time.

Gene met the collectors in the hotel restaurant. They were having omelets with potatoes and toast and two carafes of coffee sat beside their steaming mugs. He noticed they'd loosened some of their Texas garb to match the heat and humidity of South Carolina, attired now in cotton slacks and breezy linen shirts. All that remained of their Texas garb were their ten-gallon hats, points of pride among the men.

"Morning, boys," he said as he dropped into the booth beside Malak. He met their angry, red-eyed gazes with his own merry smile.

"It's afternoon," grumbled Loke. He motioned toward Doc and said, "Who's your helper?"

"My attorney," said Gene. "Roy in the shitter? Y'all look like you chewed the curtains last night."

The Texans grunted. They were very hungover, that much was apparent. But there was something else in their expression that gave him pause. He looked down at the table and noticed there was no third plate, no third mug. Odd. They were a trio, the story being that they'd grown up together in Austin and hatched a doomed plan to rip off a local gangster. Of course, they failed. And of course, the gangster found their ineptitude charming. He tied them to chairs in the basement, naked but for their socks, and brought before them a bulging burlap sack. Before the young men could so much as make a peep, the gangster upended the bag's contents over them: snakes. Dripping with serpents, the trio howled behind their gags, more so when the gangster began to dance before them, scooping up great tangled lengths of snakes and shouting at them to believe, believe! And when the gangster asked them to prove it by joining his organization and become his collectors, they agreed on the spot, swore blood oaths to the crazed man and his many reptiles. Only later did they find out the snakes had been harmless, rat snakes and garters. They admired the gangster's guile, his pluck. The man's creativity they would take for their own. In time they'd achieved such success and notoriety that upon his passing the gangster left the entirety of his criminal organization to them.

How much was fact or fiction, Gene didn't know. But he did know they rarely separated from one another's company for more than a few hours—at most for the night. Even then, come first light, they were again a trio. Rumors in Austin held that their partnership was romantic in nature. Others claimed they were fraternal triplets, though they looked nothing alike and clearly varied in age. The point was this: For Roy to be absent from such a meeting did not bode well. Gene decided to proceed more cautiously.

"Where's our money?" said Loke.

"In the business," said Gene.

Loke ceased chewing and narrowed his eyes. "Reckon you said the word business when you were supposed to say, right here."

"Business," said Malak. "Since when are you a businessman?"

"You mean some scam you're running," said Loke. "That's what you meant to say. And that is, might I add, a very stupid thing to say."

"I mean a legit business," said Gene. "I'm offering a ten percent cut of our monthly profits until I put together what I owe."

The Texans glanced at each other across the table. "You're fucking with us," said Malak.

"And even if you weren't," said Loke, "we know what would happen. In a month, ka-boom. You're gone, business is gone, money runs dry. Then we're right back where we started. No, Temmens, I don't think you meant to say 'business.'"

Gene's stomach knotted. The fact that they'd even mentioned the various possibilities meant he had them interested—a minor, but crucial, victory. But he had to go slow, lay it out with care.

"Look," he said, "I don't have it up front. Y'all knew that. But I can pay you out monthly until I do. And I *will* pay it all off."

"A hundred grand," said Loke. "Not counting interest, mind you. What kind of legit business is going to turn that around?"

"You'd be surprised," said Gene. "Let me show you."

Suddenly he had their attention. They were suspicious, sure, but when he stood up with Doc, they began to follow.

He led them to the truck and opened the back, showing them the cages he and Rich had installed, along with the work orders, receipts, carbons of the checks, and the papers from the city making the business real and official. All of it conceived, constructed, and executed in a whirlwind couple of days. Convincing Rich had been predictably easy. His brother had been only too glad for the change of heart—played on Gene's part with the perfect blend of reluctance and remorse. Rich's enthusiasm had done the rest, including convincing Mattie. The rest, however, was a different story. It had taken a monumental amount of hustle to get everything pushed through so fast, including but not limited to bribing a few city officials with the entirety of Rich's disability check, then bribing a few city clerks with his VA pay for the month. He was pretty sure Rich had been sitting on a few thousand surplus dollars, but he decided not to inquire about that. Not when the money snowballed everything into being. The rest had been elbow grease, plain and simple, borrowing much of what he'd learned from Big John and supplemented with *making it up out of thin air*.

He stood back while the collectors scrutinized it all, licking their thumbs and leafing through the paperwork like accountants on the audit. Every now and then a look of studious disbelief passed between them. Gene Temmens *legit?* They couldn't believe it. Gene could scarcely believe it.

"How does it work?" Loke finally ventured.

Gene was only too happy to oblige. What began as something Gene had been sure would crash and burn in days had miraculously exploded. The first few adopters had spread word that the dogs picked up from the Temmens brothers were the most loving, well-behaved creatures they'd ever met. Once the city folk got wind, things picked up. They had nothing better to do with their time and vast quantities of money than spoil their dogs and practice diligent negligence. But they wanted to change. It was simple enough to drive out and spend five minutes looking over a dog, scoop up the animal for transport back to the ranch, and leave the owner with a fat bill for room and board in the new and improved barn, training, supplies, and transport. The bills, no matter how ridiculous, were paid, and the owners gracious when he called them to come pick up their pooches. Hell, when it came to the city folk, it didn't seem to matter how much extra stuff got tacked onto the bill at the end.

What they were paying for, Gene explained to the astounded collectors, wasn't necessarily Gene's expertise, Rich's tender grooming, or Mattie's complimentary basket of questionable peaches that she gave to every customer. What they were paying for—what they craved above all else—was authenticity. Bring their dog to a city trainer where some dry, corporate employee with an ugly collared shirt and squeaking shoes would make them sign a bunch of paperwork under fluorescent lights? Talk to people named *Craig?* Named *Steve?* No, they wanted to load their aggressive or excitable or dopey or just plain bored dogs into their expensive luxury SUVs, drive out of the city, risk their shocks and tires on a badly beat-up dirt road in the hills, and park in front of a country house on a country estate. He was talking about folk from Heathwood and Forest Acres and Kilbourne Heights, folks from Spring Lake, Parkway Place, all those areas with big green lawns and massive houses surrounded by enormous fences, those areas with the new construction homes that looked like they'd disintegrate in a light rain. They wanted to see the renovated barn, the peach orchard, the old oaks standing guard around the perimeter. They wanted to be talked down to by a wise and crafty country boy and his batty mother. They wanted to marvel at the batty mother's peacocks who, oh Lord, were they high? Was the batty mother high? Could these country folk who hadn't gone to college train a dog? They wanted to find out! They wanted to amble about while contractors tore up the roof of the country house and restored the siding and put in the new windows on a place that, a month ago, probably should have been condemned. They wanted to be scolded for spoiling their dogs, told that *they*, and not the dogs, were *the real problems* and that good training could only go so far. They wanted to be chastised for their negligence and ignorance, dressed down in front of other customers, and then gently thanked for their patronage by the family's oldest son, a giant with a beard and crazy tattoos who looked like a homeless spelunker, and goddamn it, they wanted to hear it all in a real Southern twang. They were paying for the splendor of Dixie, the sweaty boys with the truck, their wheezing mother and her stoned peacocks, the *real goddamn deal.*

The Texans grunted. They'd all been standing in the hot noon sun, sweating while Gene talked, looking minute by minute worse for wear. But they hadn't said a word. They had listened. And that, Gene knew, was crucial.

Between Loke and Malak there passed a look of faint, incredulous hope. They smelled a prospect, Gene knew, because *he* smelled one. Of course, he didn't tell them he'd fudged the numbers, that a quarter of the receipts and carbons were forged, that the business was burning through every dollar as soon as it hit their bank account, and that it was going to be a good long while before he saw that changing. And he certainly didn't tell them how much work it all took—fifteen-hour days and not a dime to hire extra staff. He didn't—and wouldn't—tell them any of that unless it was necessary.

"Couldn't be happy with anything under forty percent," Malak finally said.

Gene had to swallow to make sure his voice didn't crack. "Ten percent," he said. "We send every rescue to get spayed and neutered and that ain't cheap, even in bulk."

"You're not in a position to bargain," Malak said as he jabbed Gene's chest with the paperwork.

"No argument there," said Gene. "But a lower monthly means longevity, less risk. Hell, maybe six months I might have enough saved up to pay you outright. That's payoff plus interest."

Loke and Malak gave him a flat stare. They could smell a con and yet everything seemed in order. Gene knew the real question was no longer if they were getting what they wanted. He'd already sold them. It boiled down to exactly how low they could go while retaining some dignity.

"Twenty," Loke finally said. "You pay out first of the month. Come up short even once and we break both legs."

"Wouldn't dream of it," said Gene.

"No joke," said Malak. "We'll break you at the kneecaps, watch you crawl around. Then we'll crack your shins and femurs. You'll never walk again. Got us?"

"Loud and clear," said Gene. He took from his back pocket the contract he had drawn up that morning at the notary's office, signed on the spot, and handed it over. He tried not to let his hand shake.

Loke scrutinized the form and snorted. "Mother of fuck," he said.

"What?" said Malak.

"It says twenty percent in the contract."

Malak snatched the paper from his colleague, stared at the print, and shook his head. "Fucking swindler."

But he, like his compatriot, wore a grudging smile, the kind that told Gene they appreciated the gutsy play. They signed and Gene took the carbons and got in the truck, promised to stop by in a week with their first payment. But there was something he had to know.

"Where is old Roy?" Gene said. "I think I could have gotten him to fifteen."

A serious frown creased Loke's face. "We don't know," he said. "But yeah, knowing Roy, you might have. Always had a soft spot for you."

"We went to bed early," said Malak. "Left him in the bar. This morning, he wasn't in his room."

"Or the bar," said Loke.

"He leave a tab?" asked Gene.

"Paid in full," said Malak. "Cash."

Gene noted the look of genuine concern on the Texans' faces. "And he didn't call? That ain't like him."

"We're going to stick around until we find out what happened to him," said Malak.

"I'll keep my eyes peeled," said Gene.

With that he bade goodbye to the Texans and started back for the ranch, shaky with relief, Doc panting on the floor between the seats. In truth, the business couldn't support a twenty percent payout for more than a month or two before it folded. But the deal stalled the Texans, bought Gene some breathing room to scrape a real plan together, a way of paying the Texans back that hopefully didn't bankrupt his brother. All he needed to do was find someone willing to loan him a hefty sum at a lower interest rate. He'd preemptively tried the banks, private investors. They took one look at his nonexistent credit, took note of his last name, and sent him packing. That left a certain kind of lender, the kind Gene was used to dealing with, and thanks to Dale's reputation, all of those had turned him down already. All but one.

Word on the street had it that Hollis Lerne was willing to lend. And Gene was game to find out.

Rich was eating lunch in the cookhouse when the call came in.

"This Gene?" said the voice on the phone.

"That's my brother," said Rich. "He's busy with dogs."

"Laura asked me to call, tell him to come on down for a pickup."

"Come down where?"

"Shelter ten, numb nuts. Where else?"

With that the voice hung up. Rich chewed his sandwich in distress. All he wanted was to enjoy his tuna salad in his new favorite place. Rich had spent several nights sanding and staining the twin desks in the cookhouse, and had done the same with their accompanying chairs, even oiling all their old joints to cut down some on the creaking. In the corner beside his and Gene's desks he'd installed a mismatched pair of filing cabinets that he had salvaged from the side of the road. Someone's detritus was someone else's something or other. He couldn't remember. But the cabinets looked, with their new coats of paint, the part. Mattie had hung some of the old photographs and posters they'd salvaged from clearing out the barn; most of them concerned the history of the estate, the old peach cannery that had hummed and hawed on the property. In one photograph dated 1882, the former-former-former owners stood arrayed before the "recently restored" front porch, dressed like in boiled shirts, stiff as boards. Lots of history on the property. Lots more to come.

Across the cookhouse were the old cooking and canning machines, no longer operational, but well-preserved. His plan was to take them apart, get rid of all the rust, and make everything look brand-spanking new—or as close as he could get it. Then there was Doc's corner complete with crate, bed, food bowl, and a basket of toys, and beside it another desk in the process of rehabilitation. Some more chairs stacked in the corner. New phones on the desk and phone lines stapled to the walls. A window air conditioner buzzing beside the door. It was his office—the first he ever had—and he loved it all the more because he shared it with his brother. All he wanted to do was finish his lunch and resume the never-ending list of chores and responsibilities that occupied his every waking moment. Plus, he'd grown to dislike the shelter pickups because if Laura wasn't there, the other employees gave him guff. Animal control had made it clear they considered what Gene and Rich were doing to be a rogue enterprise. Their cooperation was terse at best.

But as Gene was occupied with a few troublesome dogs that afternoon, and Mattie made a mess of things when sent to collect animals, it fell to Rich. At least it gave him a welcome break from the work of fixing roofs and fences, sprucing up the dilapidated house and barn, grooming the dogs and exercising them. In two weeks, they'd restored the place to a semblance of its former glory with training pens around the barn and a little corral, complete with the painted and stripped body of Gene's old Lancer, for the goat, now called Tapioca, to climb.

Still, Rich reflected as he shoved the last of his lunch in his mouth and headed off through the orchard, there was a lot left to do. Repairs, painting, general maintenance, and that was nothing compared to the orchard. In the old days Dale—never terribly handy—had tended the trees, his one point of pride as regarded home care. Every growing season, twice a week, the man would be out in the orchard, propped atop his tall ladder from dawn to dusk, separating the bad fruit from the good, pruning back branches, and flagging sick trees that required a little extra care. It gave the man great pleasure to restore an ailing sapling or to deworm an entire crop. And it had always pleased Rich to see his father in the orchard, even to glimpse the soles of the man's shoes on a ladder rung, his legs and body lost in the tree's dense foliage. It meant Dale was home and looking after his trees. It meant their family was together.

Now, Rich spied rotting fruit piled here and there beneath wild and shaggy branches. The fallen peaches drew flies and creatures less savory. It gave Rich a great fright to empty the rat traps every morning. Greater still was the thought of what Dale was doing out there alone, hunted by Hollis Lerne. Rich had meant to get away, find his father and help the man find a better, more stable shelter. Sharing lodgings at the Days Inn was out since Rich had returned home and taken up residence in the upstairs bedroom. But there had to be something Rich could do. But that was thing, he thought as he rose and grabbed his keys and headed out across the orchard. There was always something he could do—and had to do. Every minute of every day and night. Too much work, he thought as he climbed aboard the truck, and not enough hands on deck.

He drove to shelter ten and braced for a fresh scolding. The dog cops curtly told him to go on back. Rich took it as a sign of progress. The ghosts were disappointed.

Reach over that counter and punch the man, they said. Show him what for.

"Hush," said Rich.

"You tell me to hush?" said the dogcatcher. He stood and puffed his chest.

"No, sir," said Rich. "It was ghosts."

"Ghosts? Are you high?"

"No, sir, no," Rich said as he retreated. "I'm sorry, I am, goodbye."

Rich made his way between rows of dogs in cages, begging the ghosts to hush. On good days they barely made a peep, wandering off, bored and melted, to mutter about the days before the bombs. Such respite was fleeting. On bad days he couldn't so much as get out of bed before they started with the badness and kept at it, sunrise to well into the night, until Rich was driven into the bathtub to hold his tubers and beg for silence. The potatoes had been his advice from a previous therapist—something he could distract himself with; something he could focus on that would grow and thrive with very little aside from water and sunlight. The idea was for Rich to see himself not as a destroyer or as one destroyed, but as a nurturer, as someone who could grow living things, tend to them, and not bite librarians or talk to dead people. And it had worked so damn well until he bit the librarian.

But today was just such a bad day. And on such days Rich had one and only one priority: Get away from everyone before the ghosts drove him to do something terrible.

In the loading bay, he found another dog cop caging seven new dogs. The man gave him a once-over and snorted.

"You're Temmens?" he asked.

"Me and my brother," Rich said defensively.

"Right," the man said as he opened the back doors and spat. "Y'all got that ranch outside town, huh?"

"We just started," said Rich. "Is Laura here?"

"Laura is out working. Which is what I'm trying to do. But here we are, right?"

Something about the man's tone told Rich he was being mocked. Him and his brother. Their whole enterprise. The ghosts gathered, laid greedy hands upon Rich's shoulders. Put your fingers in his eyes, they said. Kick him. Ask him if his mother still works the corner. Go on. He wants it. We want it.

Rich trembled. Beads of sweat tickled his face. He could feel the pressure mounting, the terrible head of steam building in his stomach. If he bit a dog cop, the real cops would arrest him—again. They'd put him in jail—again. He couldn't afford that. The business couldn't afford that. His wayward brother was actually working, actually helping, and Rich couldn't afford to let him and Mattie and the dogs down. He had to hold his tongue and get the hell out of there and *fast*.

To Rich's relief the dog cop didn't say anything else. He led Rich to the caged dogs, let them out one at a time, and handed over the paperwork for Rich's signature. Rich signed, took up the leashes, and led the dogs out the back door. There in the sunlight he looked them over. Laura had enough authority to make the adoption process painless and practically instant, but there was a catch. Most of the dogs she could funnel out of Animal Control were damaged goods—wounded, aggressive, slated for euthanasia, and so on. Before him stood a Corgi with a bandaged paw, three mutts of terrier origin, some breed of retriever with a drooling problem, and a mottled mutt mongrel whose disproportionately tiny head and massive paws suggested a Yorkie and Great Dane mix. Finally, there was a Spaniel mix with a crazy eye turned the wrong direction, the calmest and sweetest of the bunch. Rich crouched beside that one, trying Gene's little trick of listening for the dog's true name. His brother had never explained it very well, likely because it was bullshit. Most of Gene's stories were. Unlike Rich, Gene had never left the United States. He'd never spoken another language. He'd never gone off and seen bombs dropped on a road until it turned to glass—whoops, back up, slow down. Rich didn't want to go there. Not ever. And anyway, the point was that Gene's personal mythology was just that: mythology. The Spaniel mix, however, was delighted at Rich's company and licked his fingers. The dog radiated such good feelings that the ghosts backed off.

It's a nice dog, we guess, they said. Too bad you ain't got the knack.

"Says I don't?" said Rich.

Then by all means, tell us. What's his name?

Rich dug about in the murky recesses of his damaged brain. A name rose up from his youth, a favorite childhood story.

"Chanticleer," he said.

Chati-what? asked the ghosts.

But Rich ignored them. He knew the dog with its crazy eyes was as likely to be adopted into a stable and loving home as Rich was to be rid of his ghosts and crippling PTSD. Fine. That made them excellent companions. Gene had Doc. In time, Rich might have Chanticleer. As for the other dogs, it was tough to say. Gene had told him designer breeds sold fast and were as likely to return. Mutts, on the other hand, were harder to place, but they usually took. Still, Rich thought as he pulled the truck round and started loading the dogs into cages, seven more dogs to look after pushed the ranch nearly to capacity. They were already working day and night and running on fumes as far as money. Some of the cash reserves—drawn from Rich's disability—had already disappeared. The one time Rich had broached the subject, Gene told him it was a business investment and gave him such a withering look that Rich had immediately let the subject drop. If he pushed, Gene might change his mind and leave. Rich couldn't run the business without him.

Rich was almost done loading the cages when a man appeared from behind the disposal bins and approached. He looked to be a roadie for the Grateful Dead, bearded and with blonde braids spilling from his rumpled boat hat, dressed in ragged jeans and a soiled rock and roll t-shirt. Dark sunglasses covered his eyes. A vagrant, thought Rich. Likely looking for money or drugs.

Then the vagrant spoke, waving to him. "Rich," said the man. "It's me."

"Dad?" said Rich.

"Saw the truck," said Dale. He patted its side, peering in back. The dogs took an immediate liking to the man, all happy barks and tails slapping against the bars of their cages. He worked his fingers into Chanticleer's scruff.

"This yours?" said Dale.

"Ours," said Rich. "Me and Gene. Mom's helping, too."

Dale seemed not to have heard him. He was looking over the freshly painted truck, the cages, the upholstered seats. He was in disbelief. "You actually got a business," he said. "These dogs. Where you keep them?"

"The barn," said Rich.

"Son, that's falling apart."

Rich chose his words carefully. "Not anymore. We're fixing it up. The house, too. And we got offices in the cookhouse. You should come see it."

The effect was not what Rich expected. Dale's expression vacillated between sadness and surprise, happiness and regret. He seemed poised on some precipice of rapid and constant transgression, as if anything he might say would disrupt what he or Rich were feeling. Rich reached into the cab, brought forth one of his potatoes in its jar. The tuber had already put down bright white roots and was beginning to pucker in spots on its brown skin. He handed it to his father intending to convey compassion. Dale took the jar and tuber in his old and wrinkled hands and looked at it for a moment before he raised his gaze back to the dogs in their cages.

"I was going to look for you," Rich said in hopes of changing the subject. "Where you staying?"

"Nowhere," Dale said quietly. "Lerne found my spot."

The look of consternation on his father's face deepened into a weary frown. It was the look of a hunted man, one with few alternatives to surrender. But surrender to Lerne wasn't an option. Even Rich knew that the debt was too high, too outstanding for the man to accept anything less than pain—possibly worse—as payment. There were plenty of things Rich couldn't control, but his father's safety would not be left to chance.

"If you want to help," said Rich, "come by the ranch. The orchard's out of control."

"Your mother would kill me. Then she'll go after you."

"She won't. And you can crash in the barn. Or the cookhouse. I'll fix up a spot. Or maybe take my room in the house."

Rich had never seen his father cry. Not once, he realized. His mother? Plenty of times. Gene? Here and there. Himself in a greasy motel mirror? There weren't enough fingers and toes in all of Columbia to count those incidents. But never Dale. Now, however, Rich saw tears form in his father's eyes and found he couldn't look at the man. Why did seeing his father suffer embarrass him? Why, rather than endear him to the man, did his father's watery eyes fill Rich with disgust?

"Think about it," Rich said as he closed up the truck. "We need help. You want a ride?"

Dale was pretending not to wipe his eyes as he climbed into the truck. If there was anything Dale could be counted on, it was to help his family in a crisis, even if his methods were highly suspect. Rich knew his father possessed an incredible charity of soul, a generosity seldom matched save for his propensity to divest himself of everything at a card table. If anything would get him to hazard the dangers of Mattie's wrath, it was that they needed him. The only question was how to convince Mattie to so much as let the man step foot on the property?

God above, Rich thought with a touch of panic. He was wheeling and dealing his own family. He was more like his father and brother every day.

"My oldest," Dale said as they drove from the shelter. "A successful businessman."

For a moment Dale simply beamed with pride. Then a shadow fell over his face, deepened by the dark sunglasses. He leaned in, conspiratorially, and said, "Be careful. Gene always has an angle."

"Not this time," said Rich. "Where should I drop you?"

"Let me think. Meanwhile, consider what I said. I'm serious."

"So am I. About all of it."

Dale frowned and let it go. As for Rich, he drove off, trying to slow down his racing thoughts. Dale's words had gotten under his skin. He was convinced the man was wrong about Gene. His brother was playing it straight this time—he'd told Rich as much, promised him they were in it together. And he meant it.

Oh, buddy, the ghosts said as they crowded close. Can you be so, so dumb?

Gene pulled up at the *Gold, Guns, Antiques* and gave the place a once over. Big lights on the sign, glittering scales painted on the door. Through the windows he saw long cases of cheap watches and shabby handguns, speaker cabinets with peeling felt, and guitars cloudy with dust. Junk, every bit of it.

From the back he unloaded and leashed his helpers for the day—a pack of troubled dogs he'd finally judged ready for public excursions, the most irksome of which was a stubborn border collie named Ringo, a fussy, hyperactive dog prone to herding cars. He was, like all the other dogs, considerably more even-tempered since he was fixed, but he still had enough nervous energy to give the pack an unruly edge. Doc helped temper it. The perfect mix.

The plan was simple. Hollis Lerne would have money to loan and Gene was absolutely confident he'd get a better interest rate than what he was paying out to the Texans. Gene had to borrow as much as he could from Lerne, pay back the collectors, and when the Texans were mollified and happily back in Austin, then Gene could start paying back Lerne from the business's monthly profits. Less stress on the books, zero risk of Gene getting his legs broken. The dogs were simply a way to rattle Lerne, a distraction that would let Gene negotiate a loan with stellar terms. Because if he didn't, he was good as dead. The business had enough liquid cash to cover the first two payouts to the Texans. After that? They were in uncharted water.

With that in mind, Gene rounded up his pack of dogs and led them into the shop, Doc at his side and off the leash. The clerk at the counter glared at him.

"Can't come in with them dogs," said the clerk.

"I vouch for them," said Gene. "Tell your boss I'm here."

The clerk's eyes narrowed. "He expecting you?"

Gene smiled. "He is now."

The clerk glanced once more at the dogs before he slid around the counter and went through the door in back. The surprise visit, the dogs, it was all calculated to put Lerne on his back foot, give Gene the best possible opening. Not like he'd need it. Dig as he might, there was no dirt to be found on Lerne. Sure, the man's lackey had busted up a couple of debtors, but it was nothing much beyond what, say, Sloane Gully did, and it wasn't even close to what Loke, Malak, and the strangely absent Roy did every week. Lerne didn't get involved with much else. Not even a prison record. In short, there was nothing to justify the fear in which Rich and Dale held the man. He was, in Gene's estimation, easy pickings. A loan shark, yes, but a mild one with little in the way of a history to warrant the fear with which Dale and Rich regarded him.

After a few minutes, the clerk emerged with Lerne in tow. He was dressed in a red silk shirt and tan seersucker. At the sight of the dogs, Lerne crumpled, grabbing at the counter. That, Gene knew, was the opening salvo. The rumors were true—Lerne was terrified of dogs.

"They can't be here," hissed Lerne. He was bent almost double, his legs folded under him, very near to collapse. Beside him, his pawn clerk was struggling in vain to raise him up by the arm.

"Don't give them a thought," Gene said. He let out a sharp, high whistle and the unruliest dogs immediately heeled. They sat beside him, a row of panting, tongue-drooping canines smiling from ear to ear. To Gene, to anyone who loved dogs, they looked serene. To someone terrified of dogs? They probably looked like a firing squad.

"I'd like to talk," said Gene. "In private."

"With them?" said Lerne. He was breathing hard, his eyes threatening to roll back into his skull.

"Just us," said Gene. "Maybe in the back office if you don't mind."

Gene patted Doc and gave Ringo a look that told the dog, in no uncertain terms, to behave. Then he handed the clerk the leashes and followed Lerne into the back office and shut the door.

Lerne collapsed in a desk chair, his face pale and beaded with sweat. Gene fetched a paper cup of water from the cooler and brought it to Lerne. The man sipped, looking for all the world like he might expire. It was terrible to see a man so fraught with terror that it crippled him. Worse still to see it involved dogs.

While Lerne hydrated and settled his nerves, Gene took a moment to survey the room. A large desk, filing cabinets, computers, and phones—not unlike what Rich had done in organizing the cookhouse. And not at all uncomfortable. There were comfortable chairs pushed against the far wall where a bank of monitors afforded a view from every security camera across several businesses. A true operational hub for the business of hawking someone else's garbage. Across from Lerne's desk were many pine crates, large and heavy looking and marked as special deliveries. One was open and displayed, amid much disgorged bubble wrap and shredded newsprint, an axe of medieval design.

"Pricey old thing," said Gene. He hefted it, testing its weight.

"Don't touch, please," said Lerne. He seemed much recovered and was dabbing the sweat from his face, fanning himself with his hat. Gene almost felt bad. Sweaty and shaken from a pack of domesticated dogs? Sheesh. The chump never had a chance.

"Let's cut right to it," Gene said as he replaced the weapon into its cushioned crate. "I know who you are, what you do."

Behind his desk, Lerne grinned, aimed a finger in Gene's direction. The rumors were true. The man did greatly resemble Randy Travis, but longer, ganglier. A bigger, toothier grin. "That was a pun," said Lerne.

"Unintentional," said Gene.

"I can forgive the one. And I could say the same about you. Youngest Temmens. Got you a dog business. Successful from what I'm hearing."

"Word gets round, don't it?"

Lerne spread his hands. "I like to know what's going about. Matter of business. Like the business I got with your daddy. But we'll get to that. I'm glad you got this dog business. I like to see young Southern white men make something of themselves. Ain't nearly enough of that these days."

Clever, thought Gene. Nothing like a racist jab to feel him out. "You from here?"

"Born and raised," Lerne said with a smile. "Five Points, not too far from here. Not now, of course, but as a child. Neighborhood has changed. A lot darker if you take my meaning."

Gene certainly did. Not that he wanted to get into a protracted argument about white flight, racist economic policy across the city and state, the goddamn war on drugs, and so forth. No point. It didn't matter what Lerne believed. He was trying to feel Gene out, see whether he'd join in a little good ol' boy fun.

"Horrel Hill," said Gene. "Little past it, actually."

"The old peach plantation," said Lerne.

"Cannery. Got an orchard, the old house. But we don't do much with the peaches these days."

"Kind of a rough area," said Lerne. "Can't say as I make it out that way much. But now, of course, I don't go near Five Points unless I aim to do business. Got me a place out in Huntington. A few others here and there. Nice neighborhoods. Don't have to worry about some low-life blasting music all hours of the day and night. Of course," he said offhandedly, "it's pretty quiet out where y'all at, too. Peaceful. I like that. Especially these days. Look outside. Here we are just off Byron Road and it ain't what it used to be five years ago. Right about the time you left, if I'm not mistaken. Things are changing."

"Lots of things," said Gene.

"Too many poor people these days," said Lerne. "They have my sympathies. But at some point, you got to take matters into your own hands. Take what's owed you. Wouldn't you say?"

At last, thought Gene. They'd come round to it. "Times are hard," said Gene. "Folks need help. Nothing wrong with that."

"Exactly," said Lerne. He had recovered his composure—all that he'd lost and more, Gene noted. Gene had expected the man to stay rattled for longer, but he would take what he could get.

"If we don't help one another, who will?" said Gene.

"That's all it takes," Lerne said with a smile. "And if I understand correctly, that's what you need. A little help."

"Need's a strong word."

"Is it? Banks won't play ball and you need a loan, a hefty sum. But Hollis Lerne is willing to lend."

Well, hot damn, thought Gene. The loan shark wasn't quite as gullible as he looked. Time to switch tactics and see how Lerne fielded blunt delivery.

"A hundred grand," said Gene.

Lerne whistled. "That's not a little help," he said. "It's a *lot*."

"For a fellow who lives in Huntington? That's humility."

For a split second, Lerne's smile cracked. Little payback for the earlier remarks, thought Gene. And Lerne knew it, too. All at once he relaxed, leaned forward in his chair.

"Say it's yours," he said. "What you aim to do with that kind of help?"

Gene shrugged. "Outside the banks, that kind of help don't normally come with a questionnaire."

"But say it does."

"Then I'd say make the most of it."

Lerne let out a high, easy laugh and pushed his chair back. "I can see my way to a hundred large. But let's talk terms. That kind of help, I'll need to tack on a fifteen percent interest rate."

"I can get eight from folks at Andre's. Let's call it five."

"Andre wouldn't go a hair under twenty percent."

"Would for me."

"Considering that's where your daddy and me first met, I very much doubt it. But I could see five if you're willing to do something for me."

Gene paused to consider. He was certain he'd just seen a glint in the man's eye. Lerne thought he smelled blood in the water, a desperate sucker ready to pawn his life in exchange for money. But Lerne was clueless. He was about to get gouged—and deep. Gene knew folks like Lerne. Plenty of them. They grew up poor, made a little money, and started to believe they were important, started seeing themselves as real movers and shakers, big fish in small ponds. Poor bastard could stand to learn a thing or two from the Texans. But for five percent interest, Gene would hear him out.

"Go on," said Gene.

"All my life they gave me such a fright," said Lerne. He motioned again toward the window. In the shop, the clerk was sitting cross-legged on the floor, petting the dogs. Only Doc sat apart, his eyes on the office door. "Got bit as a child," Lerne continued. "Parents never let me have pets. I been living with that and it's tiresome. I see that now. I want over it."

"Being afraid of dogs?" Gene asked.

"Precisely."

This, thought Gene, was an unexpected wrinkle. A hundred grand loan at five percent in exchange for . . . dog therapy? He was either brain damaged or drunk, but Gene wasn't complaining.

"Just to clarify," said Gene. "You want me to help you get over your fear of dogs. I get that right?"

"Very and truly," said Lerne. "I seen you come in with them dogs. I see you with that one." Lerne pointed. "What's his name?"

"Doc."

"This Doc. This little doctor! I see you love him. He obviously loves you. Look at him sitting polite. And the rest of them out there, not a one is making a fuss. I am beside myself. And I've been thinking a while now, why can't I have that? I got these businesses. I got houses. I got cars and money to lend. But I also got this fear, you see? So teach me. I want to learn. I want to be rid of the bad old feelings."

Of all the things Gene had expected to hear come out Lerne's mouth, none of that had crossed his mind. It sounded too good to be true, which meant it *was*. There was something else on the table, something hidden. But what? Gene knew he had to be cautious. He needed more intel. But the clock was ticking. The Texans were going to expect their payments on time and in full and even if he and Rich worked twenty-four hours a day every day, they would eventually fall short—sooner rather than later. Then Gene would get every bone in his body broken, some of them twice. And when the Texans tired of busting him up? Who knew where they turn next. Maybe the dogs. Maybe his family.

"And that's all?" Gene asked. "You loan me a hundred big. I help you get over your fear of dogs. That's it? That's all that's on the table?"

"That's all," said Lerne. "I see that you hesitate. That's good. Like me, you got smarts. Now look here."

Lerne rolled up his pant leg, exposed an old and faded scar. Whoever had stitched it up had done a terrible job as the scar resembled a gnarled and knotty cord of pink flesh that shone against his pale, skinny leg. He said, "That's where it got me. Right there. I'm not talking some giant pit bull. Was a bitty thing, not even half the size of your Doc. Now please understand, the scar I don't care about. We all got those. But the fear? That's a whole other story. You seen what they do to me, even nice ones like you brought. With your help it can be different—my whole life can be different! For that, I'm willing to play ball."

Lerne gazed into the shop. The fear he talked about was etched into his face. Gene could see it in the corners of his eyes and mouth, little creases that made him look older than he was. But what the man had said struck a chord in Gene. Through the glass, Lerne saw, just out of reach, something he wanted, something that countless people enjoyed without a second thought. Didn't Gene feel that way all the time? He was afraid, too. He was afraid of getting stuck in Columbia and ending up like his father, a has-been of a has-been, friendless and destitute. He was afraid his mother's lungs would fail and leave her stuck in bed, gasping, until the rest of her up and quit. He was afraid his brother really was crazy, that he really *did* have ghosts, and that one day Rich would do something far worse than bite a librarian. He was afraid when Laura made him feel small and dumb because he *was* small and dumb, and he was afraid of what it would take to *stop* being small and dumb. To *be* otherwise, like her, that took a bravery he didn't know how to conjure. More than anything, he was terrified that one day he would come home to a crumbling house and find the door unlocked and the rooms empty and nothing in the cupboards except the dried, upside-down husks of cockroaches and nothing in the sink but old water stains and rust and nothing really in any room, nothing, just empty space and dust, and the only sound would be the static in his head that told him there was nothing he could to fix *any* of that. And the noise told him something else. It told him he deserved what was coming.

Maybe, he thought while he went and fetched himself a paper cup of water, that was just how things went. Something in life bit you and the fear, like venom in the bloodstream, did its work. Maybe everyone got one chance to get it right. But maybe not. He thought of the times when he had accompanied Big John on the man's monthly trips to the prisons. There Big John had implemented a program whereby he brought in dogs for the prisoners to learn about the animals. Many prisoners attended the sessions. Many more came after simply to play with the dogs. Hardened criminals broke down after just a few sessions. Some they held fast and sobbed into the animals' fur. Others begged the dogs for forgiveness. Still others lapsed into peals of laughter at the sight of a happy dog, tail wagging, tongue lolling, and became meek and repentant. Once, very near the end of Gene's time in Austin, a recently paroled prisoner visited the shelter. He told them about the difficulties of getting a job, finding a place to live, and reconnecting with family after so many years in the slammer. He had robbed a gas station as a teenager and accidentally shot the clerk. The gun had just gone off, he told them. But it didn't matter. He believed himself beyond redemption for such a thoughtless, stupid brutality. In prison, he had tried to kill himself and make amends with the universe. Then Gene and Big John and the dogs showed up. The ex-con told them their visits with the dogs had done what years on the inside could never do. The program, the sessions with the dogs, he told them, had saved him.

Big John smiled then and said something Gene would never forget. He'd said that every dog, no matter how bad or how vicious, deserved a second chance. Why not every man, too?

So maybe, Gene thought as he gulped down his water in the back office of *Guns, Gold, Antiques,* that applied to chumps like Hollis Lerne. Maybe Gene *could* help rid this man of just such a fear. And in the process, he would help himself and his family. It was a win-win.

"For five percent interest," Gene said, "I think we can work something out. But I want to split it, put two and a half percent on my loan, two and a half on my daddy's debt. And I need the full balance up front."

Lerne turned from the window, collected himself. "Half now," he said. "Half at the end."

"No interest until I get the second half," Gene countered.

"Retroactive from day one."

Gene sighed and pretended to carefully consider the terms. In reality, there was nothing consider. He'd won, accomplished what he had set out to do. Why stop there? If Lerne was willing to come that far to meet him, he'd make the man reach a little, see how far his arm stretched.

"Retroactive on the interest," Gene said with feigned reluctance. "And two conditions. The first is that you got to cut my father's debt."

"How much?" said Lerne.

"Whole thing."

"Half."

"Half, then. And leave off the chase."

Lerne raised his hand and said, "Deal."

"Not yet," said Gene. "Second: I'll teach you how to get on with the dogs. I'll even do you one better and teach you how to train them. And if you want, you can adopt from us, no charge. But—and I want to make this absolutely clear—no harm comes to the dogs. Not now, not ever, or the deal's off. We clear?"

Lerne grinned, extended his hand. "I'm glad we could do business."

They shook. "Feeling's mutual," said Gene. And he wasn't lying. Already, Gene felt the burden lifting from his shoulders. He was close, so close to being free and clear, he could almost taste it. Honey, mana, sweetness on the tongue!

When Mattie saw her boys' truck come up the drive she noticed nothing unusual. Not until Rich emerged with a weirdo in tow, some fool dressed in beach shorts and a bad polyester shirt already dark with sweat. But she recognized the face under a soiled canvas hat, the bow-legged gait as he walked about, staring in awe at the property. It set her blood set to boiling. *Dale.*

She rose from her porch chair, oxygen tank in tow, and ambled down the steps. "You get!" she cried.

Dale started, fixed his dark sunglasses on her. She'd mash his face for such arrogance! But Rich stepped between them—arms up—before she could start clobbering. Then Gene was there, hemming her in.

"Easy," said Gene. "He wants to help."

"Help?" said Mattie. She glared at her two looming sons. "He'll gamble the dogs on cards!"

"It's fine," said Gene.

"Fine?" Mattie snarled. "*Fine?* Look at this place. Look at *me.* It ain't fine. He don't know what fine looks like."

"There's nothing to gamble," said Rich.

"Of course there ain't!" said Mattie. "He already lost it all! Dale, come out here where I can get at you!"

"We need all the help we can get," Gene said. He indicated where James, recently recruited to help, was at work painting the barn.

Mattie's spine stiffened. She took credit for hiring James, had gone on and on about how the boy needed some honest work what with the unemployment in Columbia and the place needing all the extra hands it could get. She took credit for a great many things, actually. The shampooing of all the sweet muffins, cooking the dinners in which her boys never seemed to have much interest. But she would not take credit for Dale. There was no credit to take! All the man had done was put them in the hole, again and again and again, year after shitty year, and she'd be damned if he'd do it again now that they'd gotten a little business going. She rounded on her youngest, prepared to give him what for, and found he was on the phone, something about an aggressive dog cornered at the car wash. Before she could get his attention, he was in the truck and gone and Rich had scurried off with Dale toward the orchard. They were gone, the lot of them! Scattered!

The nerve, Mattie thought, quaking with rage. Her own blood kin sassing her while she'd been working herself to the bone climbing ladders, soaping dogs, and dealing with fussy customers. And now they'd brought the man—the very man who'd put her in the poor house—back onto the land he had very nearly gambled away without *her* consent. Well, she knew what to do.

She found Rich in the barn feeding the dogs. She jabbed him in the ribs and took no small pleasure when he jumped.

"What's the *matter* with y'all?" she said.

"Mom, okay," said Rich. "I get it, but please, he's in danger."

"He is now."

"Someone cut up a raccoon. It could have been Dad. They were waiting for him."

"What raccoon? What are you talking about?"

"He was living in a car. Mom, they were waiting for him. If he had been there, he might be dead."

If it had been Gene doing the talking, Mattie would have gone right to the house, got the broom, and come back to give him *what for*. There was, by her estimate, plenty of *what for* to dish out, and Gene was, according to her ledger, overdue. But *that* one was gone in the truck and her oldest boy wasn't the sort upon which she could vent her frustrations. Too docile, Rich. Too soft. Ever since he had come back from Iraq, ever since he'd started talking to dead people, Mattie couldn't bring herself to be mad at him—leastways not with a broom or magazine. The boy wasn't right. No point in making it worse.

And anyway, Rich wasn't the sort to lie. If her oldest said Dale was in danger, she believed it. She could believe that crazed, pursuing voice that called now and again was perfectly capable of slicing up wildlife in its quest to hunt Dale. The rift between her and husband was enormous, but that didn't mean she wanted him dead.

"Mom?" said Rich.

"Hush," said Mattie. "Let me think."

"He won't be no trouble, promise."

"You can't promise for that man," said Mattie. She hated that Rich had moved her to pity. "He can stay," she said, "but not in the house. Fix him up something out here. Something with a fan. But no hot plate. And if he works up those dogs and keeps them up at night barking, tell him he won't need no Hollis Lerne to do the killing because I'll do it myself. Tell him that. And if he has to use the bathroom, tell him to go in the woods. But if he comes in the house to go number two, he better clean that toilet top to bottom and pay for his own paper, because so help me God, I know damn well who put us in this position, you understand?"

"I'll tell him."

"You stay put. *I'll* tell him."

Rich seemed prepared to protest, but the look Mattie shot him nipped that in the bud. "Go easy," said her youngest.

Mattie snorted, passing James on the way out. The boy was pleased as punch to have work, all the more if it brought him back to the place he considered his second home. They'd practically raised him, her and Dale. He was practically one of their own. And there James was, working tirelessly to make something that wasn't even his a success. Need she remind her boys that without James and her, they would be several hands down and the worse for wear? No, she did not. But would they listen to her? No, they would not. They never did.

And that, she thought while she untangled her oxygen hose from shrubbery, was the problem. Her boys didn't *listen*. There it wasn't even opening day yet and there were more sweet muffins than she could possibly pet—the barn cleared and stocked with cages, the pens and corrals occupied with animals in training. Now, strictly speaking, some of those animals weren't ready for petting (Gene's orders), and some weren't sweet muffins in the strictest sense—like Tapioca the goat, handsome astride the Lancer, bleating and farting; and like the peacocks she'd never bothered to name, high as kites on space pills and necking in the woods; or the occasional flock of geese that landed in the orchard, lured by the sweet, cloying perfume of the peaches but ultimately disappointed by the lack of bodies of water, actual perfume, or decent geese accommodations, the fuckers.

But anyway. Those pills were *good.* The latest batch was strong.

They would blunt the pain in her chest but not her wrath. Gene and Rich didn't get it. They had a responsibility to do right by all those loving animals. And her. *And her.* They had to take care of them, keep them safe. Not bring riffraff about.

All the huffing and puffing made Mattie's lungs ache. She leaned against a tree, slid a space pill into her mouth, and swallowed. Her peacocks gathered, preening in the sun. Mattie longed for the days before her lungs went bad. She wanted, sometimes, to sprint just a few yards and not feel her whole body pucker in want of oxygen. She wanted health and prosperity. She wanted things to be all right.

About the time she got her wind back, the truck returned, and Gene emerged looking worse for wear. There had been a harried look about the boy those past several days. Mattie knew it meant he was up to something, but any attempt to get it out of him ended in denial. She'd raised a damn reticent brood, Mattie had. Bunch of secret-keepers. Well, a proper swatting would fix it. She was on her way over to deliver just that when she saw the pained expression on his face, the blood on his hand.

"What happened?" asked Mattie.

"Back up," said Gene.

Gene opened the back, and after several harried attempts, coaxed a muzzled and growling black Labrador from its cage. There were marks on the dog, scabbed scars across its snout, welts on its ribs, patches of fur missing, and in the dog's eyes was a wild look of terror surpassing anything Mattie had ever seen. Her heart quivered. Someone had hurt that sweet muffin. Someone had made sport of its suffering.

Gene seemed to know it, too. She saw the rage in her youngest's eyes. He was bad sometimes, sure, but there was good in him, too. Like her, he didn't like to see animals get hurt—and certainly he didn't like whatever had happened to the black Lab. The dog thrashed about, snarling and snapping.

Someone had taken that sweet muffin to the very edge of depravity and beyond.

"Gene," she said. "Maybe you ought to leave her a while. She's mad and then some."

Gene didn't respond at first. His attention was focused on the dog. "I back off and she won't learn," he said.

"At least go take care of your hand."

"Mom, *go*," said Gene. "She's spooked enough as it is."

Mattie looked closely at her boy, then at the dog with its bared fangs, its raised hackles. Badness had come to them. That very day. She knew who to blame and she knew just where to find him.

She stomped off through the orchard and found Dale in a peach tree. He was up there with the clippers, trimming branches, and just the sight of him on the ladder gave her feelings that she didn't want, didn't ask for. Who the hell told him to dredge up the old in Mattie's heart? Who asked for it? Those feelings were dangerous, she knew. In the past, they had allowed her to forgive him again and again. They had made of her an enabler while he sank them into poverty. Did he think trimming a few trees would make things right? Did he think—what had her boys said? Living in a car with raccoons would pay his debt? Did they say dead raccoons? Did someone knife a raccoon? The pills were hitting hard and she had trouble remembering.

"What's this about a raccoon?" Mattie barked up at her husband.

Dale shut the clippers off and wiped his sweat-soaked face. "Hi, darling."

"Don't you dare darling me. I asked you a question. You respond. That's it. That's all the communication you deserve."

Mattie wheezed. All that yelling had drained her lungs of their precious air. She took a moment to collect herself, get a second wind. Then she stood up tall, glared at her husband. "Hollis Lerne cut up some raccoon you lived with. And I hope I don't need to ask if that's code for a hussy."

Dale looked—the nerve of the man—offended. "You most certainly do *not!*"

"That voice that calls here with its nastiness—that's *your* fault. The state of this place? *Your* fault. The violence I'm about to unleash? Guess."

"Honey, look—"

"I told you about that honey darling business," Mattie growled. She kicked the ladder. Hard. "You brought this on yourself. And now we got something, me and my boys, and I'm warning you. If you screw this up, I'll shoot your face off."

"Mattie, I don't want no trouble."

"Little late. You owe me a life savings and a marriage." Mattie shot him a look that she hoped looked determined and severe and *not* exasperated and oxygen-starved, then turned and collected herself, and went back to the porch. She didn't want to give her husband the opportunity for any sweet talk and she sure as hell wasn't in the mood to hear no more about a cut up raccoon. The thought of that nasty voice on the phone hacking up some innocent animal made her sick. The whole thing made her sick.

Back at the house, Gene and the dog were gone and the truck was shut up. Mattie felt crispy on the inside, scorched. The Temmens always fell far short of the mark, didn't they? Cursed, the family. Bad brains, bad hearts. But not doomed, she thought while she scanned the yard, the trees, the outlying barn.

Not while they had the ranch.

And that reminded her: she was tired of looking at the blank sign. They'd stuck that post in the ground last week right where the yard met the orchard path, right next to what had to pass for a front gate, a giant piece of signage Gene had swiped from a defunct storefront and upon which Rich was going to paint (though with precisely what *he* wouldn't disclose) the name of whatever the hell their business was becoming. Which begged the question: Had she won? Gene was still home and Rich and he were working together. There was even money, though from where and under what conditions, Mattie didn't have the patience to extract from her boys. They were there. They worked together. With her. There were dogs. New paint on the house. Renovations and repairs. There was, as if on cue, her no-good husband back and trying to win them over—win *her* over. Hadn't she been *right?*

But something felt off and Mattie had almost, *almost*, expected that. She could not yet explain the feeling, nor identify, if identify was the correct word, the minute components that allowed it to be seen by the naked human eye and smelled by the human nose, and otherwise registered by human faculties, as *off*, and . . . what was she saying?

The inside of Mattie's mouth was parched. She went into the house, got a drink of sweet tea, and stood at the window to refresh herself and ponder the day's events. But she couldn't concentrate.

The sign. The damned sign was still blank! If her boys couldn't agree on a name for the business, well, she would take the reigns—take liberties! To emphasize that point, she dug out a wooden spoon from a drawer, considered drumming it against the stove, then decided that *none* of that spoon business made a fucking lick of sense. Talk about high. She put the spoon away with a little prayer, then looked out the window. The blank sign. Her boys. They owed her *big*.

"Come on," she said to the peacocks waiting for her on the porch.

From the work shed she retrieved a bucket of paint and a brush. In the dim light of the shed she could not discern the paint color. No matter. She would make do.

Beside the sign, she set the paint and brush. Then she took James's ladder from the side of the house—not, she thought with a cackling laugh, while he was *on* it—and stole away back to the sign. She prepared her materials. She climbed the ladder. Then she set about painting the sign. The sun was behind her, low on the trees and shedding good warm light. Fact was, she thought while she worked, people had to know what they were getting, what kind of place it was they were bringing their dogs. Her boys didn't get that. But Mattie did.

When Mattie finished, she climbed down the ladder and set aside her tools. Then she stood back to better admire her work. It was good. A little wobbly in some letters, and a little drippy in others, but that was fine. What mattered was that it was real. It was true. In a world of uncertainty, the sign gave everything around them a firmness. Couldn't have asked for a better name or a better place to call home to her wayward, wily kin.

SWEET MUFFIN RANCH, it read.

Part II:
Fire

Chapter 5

Rich was in the barn loft shoring up the bale when he saw a familiar silver Mercedes Kompressor pull up at the gate. From the car emerged Hollis Lerne dressed in eggshell seersucker. On his feet he wore blood red boots, ostrich skin.

Electric fear crackled down Rich's spine. It was true that Gene had, in his own words, gotten Lerne to "lay off" Dale, though no explanation of precisely *how* he'd achieved that (and what it was going to cost them) was forthcoming. But that didn't mean Hollis Lerne wasn't dangerous. Rich hadn't forgotten how it felt to be in the man's presence, to see his fingers tighten around the saber's handle. It still made Rich's guts squirm. He crouched at the bale's edge and watched as Lerne summoned his henchman, Llewellyn, and there they stood, just before the gate, making what Rich could only assume to be small talk. He couldn't hear them from that distance. But he could hear the ghosts approaching, their interest piqued. That alone told Rich all he needed to know about Hollis Lerne.

Gene appeared from the cookhouse and started for the gate. Perhaps, Rich thought, his brother would tell the man to get off their property and never come back. Their business was concluded, was it not? But Gene shook hands with Lerne and the lackey and began to lead them toward the bar. Rich's stomach fell into his shoes. What was Gene doing?

What's it look like? said the ghosts. Showing him about.

"He's crazy."

The ghosts rattled with laughter. Look at the kettle calling the pot, they said. Pay attention now. Get you some boots like his, boy. A nice hat. Least that way you could look decent.

With a sinking heart, Rich watched his brother guide Lerne about the place. They'd done so much work in the past weeks, had an opening day during which they'd reached capacity in the span of three hours, fielded countless training appointments and adoptions from customers, made sure every single intake was spayed, neutered, dewormed, and checked by the city's low-cost vets, and still the calls wouldn't stop. Word in town was that the Temmens brothers were the best dog trainers in the whole state, but Rich knew the credit belonged to Gene. Folks were saying he could read doggy minds, rehabilitate even the most ferocious and abused pup back to domesticity, and get through to even the most negligent owners on the importance of training and care for their pets. That didn't even touch on the wilder rumors: He could train herds of goats as evidenced by Tapioca and his friend, the new arrival Banquo, a spotted buck they'd discovered tied to the gate one morning with nothing, not even a note, to explain his presence. Now the goats, fast friends, took turns headbutting each other and launching off the Lancer.

Other rumors included the following: Gene could teach possums to read. He could convince llamas to stop spitting. He had trained a herd of pot-bellied pigs to sniff out not truffles but *gold deposits.* The more ridiculous the rumor, the more Rich liked it. It was true that Gene was great with dogs—not half as good as his mentor Big John, or so his brother claimed, but great all the same—and it was also true that in the short time the business had been open, not one untoward thing had occurred—no scams, no grifted customers, no hint that Rich would wake up on day to find that Gene had vanished in the night. . Gene had taken Rich's idea, protoplasmic in its form, and gotten it to walk on four legs. They had something real, something destined to be a bigger, better success than anything Rich had dared to dream. So, what in the nine, ten, or fifteen hells was Gene doing with *Hollis-goddamn-Lerne?*

Rich crawled on his belly to the edge of the barn loft and peered over. Gene had come into the barn, Lerne in tow and visibly trembling, and was pointing out the cages, the corral, and the training stations, quickly describing his training methods.

"You don't whoop on them," Lerne was saying. "Ain't that a thing? Here I believed a dog needed, nay, *craved* it."

"They need exercise, rules, and love," Gene said firmly. "Not beatings. We correct and encourage behaviors, but we don't punish."

"I stand corrected," Lerne said with a meek little laugh. He kept a wary distance from the dogs in their cages, starting at every movement. He was terrified, Rich realized, scared out of his wits—until he looked upon the black Lab, the troubled dog Rich and Gene, through weeks of care and training, rehabilitated and brought back to the fold. For when Lerne's gaze fell upon the animal, a hint of deep and abiding hatred flashed across his eyes. Or so it looked to Rich, perched as he was some fifteen feet in the air and trying to stay hidden. And if Rich had seen it, disadvantaged as he was in perspective, Gene *must* have seen it.

But no, Rich realized. His brother was distracted by the dog's whimpering, paying little attention to the madman at his side. The dog had retreated to the back of its cage, something she hadn't done in over a week. Maybe she, the yet-nameless dog, had seen what he had seen.

"Got a shy one there," said Lerne.

"Rehab," Gene said. "Someone messed her up bad."

"That they did," said Lerne. "All those scars. She was lucky to make it, then. Sport or some such?"

"Plain old evil," said Gene. He remained crouched beside the Lab's cage a moment longer before he stood and motioned beyond the barn. "Let's get started."

While Rich watched in growing terror, Gene led Lerne to an empty training pen and delivered a primer on how to meet a dog for the first time. It took a few minutes for Rich to understand. He was teaching Lerne—teaching him to be around dogs. As for Lerne, he played the attentive pupil, perfectly behaved. But Rich knew better. The man in the pen was not the man who had purchased the saber. The Lab knew it, too. Below, she paced in her cage, tail between her legs. How could Gene be so oblivious?

Gene called Doc into the pen and bade him sit down. No sooner had the dog entered than Lerne blanched. Gene advanced with the dog a step at a time and Lerne retreated, his limbs slackening. Soon he was upright thanks solely to the fence, a limp and trembling scarecrow with big hair. From him issued a whimpering of inarticulate terror. He remained that way for several long minutes, propped on the fence, making the noise and such while Gene looked on with pity. Then Gene sent Doc out of the pen.

"Is it over?" said Lerne.

"For today," said Gene.

"I was taken away, very cold," said Lerne. "Like that day in childhood. And yet I was here."

"Still are," said Gene. He went to help the man up but Llewellyn was already there, hoisting his employer with as much dignity as the situation would allow. A few minutes passed in which Lerne, his clothes soaked with sweat, could do little more than hold fast to his henchman, drink water from a plastic bottle, and babble incoherently about some childhood encounter with what sounded to Rich like a dire wolf. When he had regained his composure, Gene led them from the pen and took him on a winding path back to the gate.

Christ on the cross, Rich thought with a shock, did Gene think he could rehabilitate the man, bring him back to goodness like some mistreated dog? And the ghosts thought *Rich* was dumb?

Only when Lerne and Llewellyn had gotten in the car and the silver Kompressor had passed beyond the gate did Rich raise his aching, trembling body from the floor of the loft and descend the ladder. In his brain, a thousand thoughts whirled and smashed together like debris caught in a tornado. By the time he'd made it all the way down, Gene had returned, and a guilty, angry look had settled on his face. "Up there the whole time?" asked his brother.

"What's he doing here?" said Rich.

"What's it look like? He's a customer," said Gene. "A paying one, mind."

"A customer?"

"I miss the memo? This obvious question day? Yes, a customer."

"This about dad's debt?"

"Some."

All at once Rich understood. The tone in Gene's voice, the anger on his face, the fact that he was dealing with the man like any other customer—the guy who had been hounding their father all over Columbia. It was absurd. Unless Dale had been right. Unless there was an angle.

"You cut a deal with him," said Rich.

"You already knew that, remember? Got him to lay off Dad?"

"That ain't what I mean. That's *Hollis Lerne*, Gene. He's not some sucker at a craps game."

"And this ain't a craps table," Gene shot back.

"What's he paying for?"

"You already know that, too. Saw it from on high. I get him accustomed to dogs, help him get over his fear. I do that and he leaves dad alone. Better, in fact. He cuts his debt."

"By how much?"

"A lot."

"A lot ain't a number."

"And this interrogation is over. Did you get dad off the hook? Didn't think so. Now can we get back to work?"

"I'm serious, Gene. That man's bad news. And you ain't telling me all of it."

Gene gestured at the loft. "Got your half," he said. And with that, he walked out of the barn.

Rich stared after his brother, his brain aching. On the one hand, Gene's explanation made sense. Gene proffered his services in return for Lerne backing off Dale and—erasing? reducing?—*something* to Dale's debt. Lerne was clearly terrified of dogs. That, at least, hadn't looked a bit like fakery. But on the other hand, it didn't add up. Dale owed Lerne a *substantial* sum, and even with a head full of ghosts Rich didn't see that sum getting blanked out after some dog training lessons. Besides, Lerne could get that help from somewhere else without reducing Dale's debt by so much as a penny. And Gene had to know that, right? If Rich knew it, he *had* to. And if Rich knew it and Gene knew it, that meant Lerne knew it as well.

And that meant Dale and the ghosts, they'd all been right. Gene had an angle, a scheme, and somehow, someway, the ranch was involved. Worse, it was clear his brother thought he was winning. It was a game to Gene. Except Lerne didn't play by the rules.

Rich debated what to do. He could chase after Gene, try to convince him that whatever scheme he'd cooked up wasn't going to work. Likelihood of success? Not good. Gene could be obstinate. He could be stubborn. Haranguing his brother had almost never been a viable tactic. So, if Gene couldn't—wouldn't—see the problem, it fell to Rich to take action. He finally had something of his own, something into which he could put himself, body and soul. And now it was in danger. He couldn't sit by and do nothing.

Ha! said the ghosts. Ho ho! You? A potato man? You ain't got the stones.

"I do," said Rich.

You versus Lerne? said the ghosts. That sucker will eat you alive.

They were right, Rich realized. He couldn't take on Lerne alone. He needed help.

Rich raced across the orchard toward the only person even half as crafty as his brother and found Dale up in one of the trees, pruning back overgrown branches. A wide circle of clippings and fallen peaches surrounded the legs of the ladder.

"Is he gone?" Dale said. "Thought I had heatstroke for a minute but there's no mistaking that car. Or those damned ugly clothes."

"You were right," said Rich. "Talk to Gene, tell him he can't deal with that man."

"He don't listen to me," said Dale. "Never did. Besides, what am I supposed to say? He already *dealt* with the man, didn't he? Got my debt cut. Got him to leave me the hell alone."

"Then you got to help me."

"Son, help you with what? What's there to help?"

Rich stared up at him in exasperation. "I should have listened. That what you need to hear? Look, all that money you owed him, all that chasing you around town and cutting up a raccoon, and he gives up so Gene can help him be friendly with dogs? I might be crazy but that don't add up. Does it?"

Dale lowered the shears. Rich could tell there were things he wanted to say, things he'd waited a very long time to say. Lerne was finally off his back. He was back at home, working on the ranch, and given enough time, he might even find a way to get back in Mattie's good graces. He didn't have to live in a car with raccoons, didn't have to find a stake, didn't have to get back in a game. He didn't have to live that old life, the one that cost him everything. And now Rich was—what? Asking him to poke the hornet's nest? Push his luck with a man who was going to gut him like a fish? Rich didn't know what he was asking. He only knew he needed help, and his father was the only one craft enough to provide it. Dale knew Lerne better than any of them. He'd know what to do.

Finally, Dale sighed. He looked down at his oldest and wiped the sweat off his face. "What do you want me to say?"

"That you'll help," said Rich. "We got to find out what Lerne's up to. And we definitely got to find out what kind of deal Gene made with him."

Dale aimed the shears toward the barn. "Have you tried asking him?"

"Dad. Maybe I'm wrong. If so, fine. I hope I am. But what if I'm not? What if it's not a raccoon he cuts up next? What if he does something to Gene? To the ranch?"

Dale took off his hat and ran a handkerchief over his sopping forehead. He looked toward the barn, then around at the trees in the orchard, as if searching for an answer in the foliage. He shook his head. It was too much to ask, Rich realized. Dale had spent months giving Lerne the slip and there was his oldest sone asking him to reverse course and pry into the man's affairs. It was dangerous. There was no way to know what Lerne would do if they were found out—no way to know what Gene would do, for that matter. And maybe after all Rich was wrong. Maybe there was nothing to uncover, no secrets to suss out, no plot to expose. Maybe Gene was right and Rich's bad brain had finally driven him over the edge. But if Rich was right?

"Meet me in the cookhouse at close," said Dale. "Don't tell nobody. Not a peep. Got me?"

"Not a word."

"For what it's worth," said Dale, "I hope you're wrong. I hope we both are."

Rich ambled off, his heart pounding. Around him the ghosts followed, curious and nattering What did Rich think he was doing? He was a timid potato man. His only accomplice was a low-down gambler whose luck had long since run out. They didn't have any evidence, any *thing* other than Rich's intuition that something was amiss. A hunch, if you will. And need they remind him that his intuition was—how to put it. Not so good. Not so reliable.

"What do you expect?" asked Rich. "Can barely hear anything over all your stupid noise."

The ghosts didn't like when he got sassy with them. They preferred him timid and pliant. On and on they nattered in his ear as he walked back to the barn. There were cars pulling up at the gate and Gene was out there to meet them. Customers. Back to work. The ghosts laughed. They said ol' potato brain would forget soon enough. Didn't he have enough work to do? Didn't he have enough to keep him occupied? Besides, they asked as he climbed again into the barn loft, what in sweet hell did Rich and Dale aim to do?

"Whatever we can," Rich said as he climbed into the loft and took up hammer and nails.

En route to Andre's card shack, his henchman at the wheel, Lerne received a call from Marco.

"Is set," said the fat Spaniard. "Two weeks from today. Early. I call before I come, we show them what they want to see."

"Well and good," said Lerne.

"Everything will be ready. You are sure of this?"

"Positive."

"We talk soon."

Lerne hung up, immensely pleased with himself. Several weeks ago, the fat Spaniard, much less the dogs, would have rattled him. He would have struggled to keep his voice level when talking about the dogs, the deal, and the enormous earning potential of their upcoming business venture. But the Lerne of the here and now was different. Changed. Better. He no longer feared or even much respected Marco for he saw the man for what he was: a trusting, simple oaf who spoke broken English and ate too many sweets. When the bastard sweated, he smelled like confectioner's sugar. It made Lerne queasy to be around him too long in the heat. But his relationship with Marco wasn't all that had changed. His armory had grown to accommodate new treasures, a variety of wonderful weapons. He had spent countless hours poring over online tutorials on how to oil and sharpen and care for them and had spared no expense in hiring trusted contractors to build a secret room off his bedroom closet in which to house his acquisitions. Then there was his progress with the dogs, the fear. Not only could he tolerate the beasts, he could walk them, feed them, and stand among their numbers, tall and with dignity. Construction was nearly complete on the kennel, their future and very temporary home. He was again master of himself. Master of them, too.

The Temmens boy believed it was due to weeks of daily sessions. Lerne knew otherwise. It had begun when he'd plunged the stiletto into Roy's flabby.

He could remember the man's face in the headlights, his hand grasping feebly at the Kompressor's tire. Such a large man made small. That's what a blade did. It brought low those who lorded false authority over others. And in doing so, it made room for those, like Lerne, those who deserved more than what life had given them.

He smiled at himself in the visor mirror, showing his good, straight teeth. His eyes were clear and brilliant. His whole body seemed taller, stronger. *He* was getting stronger.

Lerne nipped the brew and offered some to Llewellyn. The henchman declined. A growing look of confusion had been on his face of late. Lerne had been reluctant to discuss the matter with the man—he was, after all, little more than a paid employee. Well-paid, yes, but that hardly mattered. There was a difference between men like Llewellyn and men like Lerne. The former could never be rid of their old selves while the latter, once filled with fear, had relinquished their old ways to become something else. Something better. But Lerne knew it was better to have things in the open with those on his payroll and decided the time had come. "Speak your mind," he said.

Llewellyn looked at him. "About what?"

"About whatever it is you been chewing on. I got eyes, Llewellyn. And haven't we been good to one another? Haven't I paid you well? I'm asking for communication is all."

Llewellyn frowned, turned his gaze out the window. "I don't know about this dog business," he said. "They're animals, but Christ, the things they do to them."

"No worse than what you've done to people at my direction."

"I guess," said Llewellyn. But he didn't sound convinced.

"I've always treated you right," said Lerne. "Is this about money?"

Llewellyn's face tightened. The tasks Lerne assigned were arduous, not for the faint of heart. But the compensation was always considerable. Never before had the henchman shown a crisis of conscience. Lerne would have to watch him closely.

"No, boss," Llewellyn finally said. "Forget about it. There's no problem."

"Good," said Lerne. "Let's keep it that way."

After that there was no more talk. In short order they arrived at Andre's card shack. There Lerne was surprised to find among the throng two newcomers, the remaining Texas collectors in unpressed chinos and rumpled cotton button-ups, sweat-stained ten-gallon hats atop their heads. With the fat one out of the way, Lerne had almost forgotten about them, but now, yes, now, he could have some fun.

Lerne stepped from the car. He was dressed in new clothes bought that very morning: boots of glossy snakeskin, a cotton suit and red silk shirt of such impeccable weave that it felt like wearing naught but cobwebs. Atop his head was an expensive Cuban wicker hat with a blood red band above the brim. He strode in like royalty among the sweaty, anxious gamblers, meeting their wary stares, before turning to the Texans. They stood on the porch talking to Andre, the aged proprietor atop his pickle barrel. By the looks of things, they weren't getting what they wanted. Lerne strode into their midst with a grin.

"I don't believe we've been introduced," he said. "Shame on Andre for being a poor host."

Andre shot him a look but said nothing. He didn't fear Lerne—not exactly. But that, too, would change in time. Once, he had considered Andre a vital part of Columbia's economy—of *his* economy. But Andre had not kept up with the times. There was plenty of online gambling these days—had been for years. Plenty of other ways to separate suckers from their money. And Lerne had plans for Columbia, plans that included Andre. He reached out and took from the man his trademark Bowie knife, pleased at its heft. The shack's proprietor remained silent. Nor did he move to take back what was his. Ah, Andre, Lerne thought as he returned the man's knife, how things had changed. But never mind. He turned instead to the Texans and extended his hand.

"Hollis Lerne," he said.

"We know you?" said the one named Loke.

"Doesn't matter," said the one named Malak. "Don't want to know you."

Lerne ignored their petty insults. They were, after all, from Texas, a state in which shit ran in the blood. He would forgive them their first slights as a matter of Carolina courtesy.

"Friends," he said, his hand still extended, "I saw you here, new faces, and welcome you. Columbia is a fine city. What brought you to Andre's?"

The Texans had not altered their expressions. They looked down on him. Disregarded him. "We're just looking for someone," said Loke.

"Might it be young Temmens?" Lerne said with a confidential smile. "I know him as well."

Lerne expected the Texans to be impressed. How, they would wonder, had he known? Instead, they looked bored, and maybe slightly suspicious. A knot of anger began to tighten in Lerne's stomach. He would try once more with the friendly approach. After that, well, other avenues would have to be explored.

"Step aside with me," he said. "I'm sure I can help you."

They followed him to the side of the porch where, with Llewellyn's help, they could separate themselves from the crowd. There was a wrought iron table and the overhead fan provided a respite from the heat. Lerne dabbed himself with a handkerchief and invited the Texans to sit.

"I didn't catch your names," he said.

"Get to the point," said Loke. "What about Temmens?"

"Let me guess," said Malak. "Owes you, too?"

Lerne could not help but notice that they remained standing. They *saw* his hand. They were *aware* he was attempting to be polite, and yet they insisted on adding insult to injury. They were from Texas, he reminded himself, a place where people with teeth were stoned as witches.

"No," said Lerne. "Just a friend, really. I look out for him here and there. Hard to do when he gets into such trouble. And if I'm not mistaken, he owes y'all a hefty sum."

"What if he does?" said Loke.

Lerne grinned, putting on his nicest face. The plan was forming in his mind. He would massage the Texans with talk of Temmens, get them comfortable. Under pretense of an offer, he would take them someplace quiet to talk—say, the abandoned farmhouse. There, with dusk coming on, far away from the prying eyes of the city, he would ply them with the brew and good talk. They would listen to him for he was wise and getting wiser every day. And when they relaxed and let down their guard, he would plunge the stiletto into them. Then while they scratched and bled in the dirt, he would retrieve the sword from the trunk. Fitting, was it not, that they should die in the same manner, in the same place, as their fat fucking friend?

"Seeing as young Gene is my friend," said Lerne, "I'd like to discuss purchasing his debt."

"You want to buy it?" said Loke.

"Cash, of course," said Lerne. "There's a place we go, a business place, very private. I can arrange for my employee to meet us there. With money. Plenty of money. You see that I'm unarmed." He opened his jacket to display the lack of pistol or holster.

The Texans stepped away to confer. Lerne reclined in his chair. He prepared to accept their surrender. It wouldn't blunt his rage. On the contrary, it would *feed* his anger, make sweeter that approaching moment when he cut them open and showed them the awful stuff people from Texas had on the inside. Then and only then they would know, truly know, that they had been bested by—who else? Hollis Lerne. He smiled a private smile.

Amid such thoughts the Texans returned, sweat dripping from their faces. Lerne regarded them as he might packaged meat. But the pair before him didn't seem to notice. They, in turn, regard him as one would a fly on a dog turd. The one named Loke spoke first, his tone curt.

"That kind of thing impress the local hicks?" he asked.

"Pardon?" said Lerne. He leaned forward, unable to believe the scorn in the man's voice.

"Southerners," said Malak. "I swear to God every one of them is crazy."

"I think maybe we have a misunderstanding," said Lerne. "I've offered you a substantial sum of money to buy my friend's debt. That's a hell of a courtesy between folks who don't know one another."

"Got that right," said Loke. "We don't know you from Adam."

"What makes you think we'd do business with you?" said Malak.

"In other words, what Gene owes ain't for sale," said Loke. "Excuse us now."

Together the Texans returned to their rented Lincoln and drove off. Lerne watched in a rage, the muscles of his face cramping. Their refusal made no sense. Not unless Gene had already cut a deal too good to pass up. Impossible, and yet there could be no other explanation. Had Lerne underestimated Gene? Lerne began to tremble. He had thought the days of disrespect were over! He had been wrong—but only a little. He could fix it and then some. And fix it he would.

"Rude fucks," said Llewellyn.

"Very," hissed Lerne.

"That's a rental," said Llewellyn. "Want me to steal it later, drive it into the river?"

"I'll handle it," said Lerne. He flashed the lackey a look that said the conversation was over. The man took the hint and shut his trap. They returned to the car where Lerne sat in the passenger seat, seething, and put his plans in order. First, he would finalize his deal with Temmens and Marco, make sure everything went smoothly. Then he would take care of the Texans. He would pay them back in kind, tenfold. Home, he bade his henchman, then thought better of it. Something was thrashing in his chest, screaming to get out, and he knew what it wanted, what it *needed*—to quiet down. He directed Llewellyn to take him to the motel on Nates Avenue where he flashed money at the first whore who approach his Mercedes.

"Got the time?" Lerne said to the woman.

"For you, all day," she said.

"And all night," Lerne said as he unlocked the doors.

Gene was in the cookhouse on the phone with a customer when Mattie brought in the mail. At first, Gene hardly looked at the envelopes, sorting them almost automatically into bills, bills, more bills, and junk. The customer was droning in his ear about his feisty Dachshund whose penchant for ankle biting had earned it the enmity of the entire family. Gene only half listened. Mattie was supposed to take the calls, but she and Rich were swarmed with drop-offs at the gate. Meanwhile, Gene was supposed to be in the pens working the problem dogs, except he wasn't going to get there until sunset because he had five more pick-ups scheduled and James was busy exercising the resident dogs in their near-capacity pens, and after that he was on repair duty because they couldn't afford more contractor bills. If only Dale hadn't been missing the last few days, he could have fielded the calls. But what did Gene expect? That was Dale Temmens to a T. Never there when you truly needed him.

"He bites and bites and we're sick of it," the customer was saying over the phone. "Now the children have learned from his example. They bite each other. They bite my wife. Last night, my three-year-old daughter bit me. You got to help us."

"Kids are above my pay grade," said Gene. "But I can help with the dog."

"Can you come get him today?"

"Tomorrow," said Gene.

"I don't know if we got that long. My wife, she's got Ace bandages on both ankles."

But Gene had ceased listening. At the bottom of the mail pile was a letter he'd almost thrown in the junk pile save for the dozen or so forwarding stickers slapped on the front. The thing had made quite a journey, Georgia to Arkansas to Texas to South Carolina. But its origin point was what caught Gene's eye. Florida. He tore the envelope open and out dropped a check to the tune of five thousand dollars, signed by Don Lettuce. Along with the check was a note: "The first of many," it read. "Call me!" A phone number was scrawled across the bottom.

"Isolate the dog," Gene said into the phone. "Calm environment. Might isolate the kids, too. I'll call you tomorrow."

He hung up before the customer could respond and turned the check over and over in his hand, unable to detect any hint of fraud. It was real. The question remained: What was it for?

No, he thought, it had to be a hoax. Or a trap. The Alligator Hotel he and Don had cooked up before Gene left Florida, it began as a joke, the result of a long night of drinking. But one thing led to another and a few months later, Gene had successfully rounded up a troupe of brain-dead investors, skimmed heavily from their investments, and left the rest up to Don. The check would inevitably bounce. And when it did, Gene would be in yet another bad situation—this time with the bank *and* the investors. Enough was enough, he decided.

It took him less than a minute to find the hotel's website. The Don Lettuce Alligator Hotel & Resort. Five-star reviews—plenty of them. Pictures of the rooms, the grounds, the alligator pits, and—were those airboats? A brand-new dock? A gift shop? Could it all be real?

"Call me," he said aloud to Doc as he dialed his desk phone. "We'll see about that, won't we?"

From his bed in the corner, Doc gave up a reassuring sigh.

His call was answered almost immediately. "I been trying to call you," said Lettuce. "Sent you a dozen letters. Where the hell you been?"

"All over," said Gene. "Texas for a while."

"Sweet Christ, not Texas."

"Tell me about it. But I just got your letter and someone at the post office must have accidentally stuffed it with a phony check."

"Phony my ass," said Don. "That's the first. Second one is already in the mail. Third goes out next week."

It took Gene a second to catch up. "Third? Don't play with me, Don."

"You think I'd cheat you? Tell you what. Take that check—and the other two, and all the others that will be coming your way—on down to the bank and cash it. Then buy yourself a ticket out here."

"A ticket to Florida?" Gene didn't understand. Was Don offering him a job? What exactly had they agreed upon? His memories were hazy—also the result of the long night of drinking—but somewhere in the back of his tired brain there was a faint recollection about collecting a percentage when—*if*—the hotel turned a profit. He stared at the photos on his laptop, at the five-star reviews full of nothing but glowing praise. Had they accidentally created some kind of smash success?

"Help me out here, Don," said Gene. "I'd like a little peace of mind about the expenses and such. Got to make sure you're not overpaying me, you know? So do me a solid and email me over the paperwork. Receipts, statements, bills. You name it. Just for curiosity's sake. I'll call you back when I get a second to look it over. Got to run."

Gene hung up. From out in the orchard, from the barn, there came the sound of barking dogs, cars coming and going, the crunch of tires on gravel. All the usual sounds. But inside the cookhouse, there was just the buzzing of the air conditioner. Gene watched while the emails appeared in his inbox, each with digital copies of the requested information. He printed what he needed, and sat there, hard copies in hand, scrutinizing every line for some sign of falsification, for just one little number out of place, for a single fake tax write-off. But there was nothing—nothing fake, anyway. It was real. The hotel was a runaway success. Don was bringing in twice what the ranch did even with the overhead and investor pay-outs. The projections were, for lack of a better term, terrifyingly good. In the final email, Lettuce laid out the plan. The place had a slow start, but a customer's viral video of the alligators wearing hats made the place the talk of the Internet. He didn't know how the alligators acquired the hats, and he sure as shit didn't know who risked life and limb to put them on the reptiles, but the rest was history. A year, two tops, Lettuce told him, and they could look to make a franchise out of it. In the meantime, Don had set aside a suite, all expenses paid. Come down to Florida, the email concluded. Things are about to get good.

Gene looked to Doc for guidance. "Can you believe it?" he asked the dog. And after Doc stood and shook off his nap, Gene said, "Me neither." Gene looked down at the check in his hands. The first of man, Don had said. But Gene knew he was holding more than a check. He was holding the literal embodiment of his dreams, the once in a lifetime, against-all-odds gamble that no one could reasonably hope to achieve. And there it was, crisp and held between his fingers. Proof that even a dunce like him could pull the slot and hit jackpot *on his own terms.*

Gene's future, once threatened by calamity and misfortune (most of it his own making) was suddenly free and clear. His life was suddenly his own again. He'd almost forgotten how it felt. The check, the whole idea of going to Florida, opened entirely new vistas. He had to be careful. He had to consider it from all angles. And he needed advice.

"Come on if you're coming," he said. Doc scrambled up, tail wagging, and was out the door before Gene had grabbed his keys. At the gate, Gene told Rich and Mattie he was headed out for pickups, then leapt into the truck and sped into town. On the way, he texted Laura and told her to meet him for lunch. The check was folded in his shirt pocket, damp with sweat. What was he going to say? What would he do? He didn't know. But Laura would. He would lay it all out, tell her every little detail. He could trust her to tell him the truth (even when it felt like sandpaper on bare skin), and more importantly, he could trust her to keep a secret. If and when he made a decision about what the check and Don's offer meant to him, he wouldn't have to worry about someone else knowing as well.

He stopped at the pet food store and got Doc a doggy ice cream. While there, Laura texted him back, said no to lunch, but yes to coffee. Her treat. Gene objected. His treat and his insistence. See her in ten minutes. Gene called in their order, then waited for Doc to finish his cone. That gave him time to settle his stomach, which had been doing backflips for the last hour. By the time he grabbed the coffees and drove to Shelter Ten, a plan had begun to form in the back of his mind. It had scarcely made itself known to him—just hints and whispers, more a fluttering feeling behind his ribs than a concrete set of ideas. But still, it was forming, and when that happened, Gene knew better than to question the process.

He drove around back and found Laura sitting in the loading bay, a big industrial fan aimed at her back, her jumper covered in sweat.

"Sure you didn't want it hot?" Gene said as he handed Laura her iced coffee.

"It's a goddamn oven, the entire state. How do you people live in this?"

"Booze and brain damage."

"No wonder y'all still vote Republican."

"Hey," said Gene. "Don't look at me. My family never did that." He pulled up a chair for himself, then got a bowl from the truck and filled it from the hose for Doc—who was, as usual, already climbing in Laura's lap. Gene watched them play for a moment, content that Doc had good taste in friends. It meant Gene might, too. But Laura must have seen something in Gene's face because she was staring at him, eyes narrowed, a hint of a smile on her mouth.

"You did *something,*" she said.

"A while back," said Gene. He sat backwards in the chair, arms draped over the back, and drank half his iced coffee in one go. "But yeah, I did it. Now you got to hear about it."

And with that, he told her everything—every stupid detail that he had left out in the past: How he met Don, how they cooked up the plan, how Gene had been secretly worried that the angry investors would one day track him down, and so on. He spilled every bean in the jar. Then he showed her the check.

"It's real," he said as he watched her turn it over and scan it. Her eyebrows rose.

"And there's more?" she asked.

"Lots."

"What does it mean?" She handed back the check. Something in the way she did it bore special import. The check felt heavy suddenly. Different.

"Good question," said Gene. "I don't know yet. Or I'm only starting to know. I might take him up on his offer."

"Florida? You're going to Florida?"

"Maybe."

"To—what?" said Laura. "Manage an alligator hotel?" She looked at Doc while she spoke and something about that bothered Gene. He watched Doc sniff Laura's pockets, watched him do happy spins when she scratched at the base of his tail. Gene knew where she was going and he didn't like it.

"Not manage," said Gene. "Well, yes. Manage."

"In a swamp."

"A national preserve."

"A national swamp."

"It's got airboats. And air conditioning," Gene fired back. She still hadn't taken her eyes off Doc and Gene was getting increasingly uncomfortable. "But I'm just thinking about it. That's all."

"You're doing more than just thinking," said Laura. "You're plotting. You're already half out the door."

"I'm just thinking about it. The money's better than the Ranch."

"Right," she said. "The Ranch. Why are you so eager to pick and head down to Florida when you've already got going here?"

Gene drank his coffee to buy him some time. Here it comes, he thought. The very thing he had hoped to avoid. But that wasn't true, was it? He'd known Laura would ask the tough questions. He'd known she wouldn't cut him slack. That's why he'd come to her. That was the advice he sought. And boy, he was bound to get it plus some.

"Because it's not mine," he said. He was talking, he knew, from a place of feeling rather than thought and logic. Nonetheless, what he was saying made sense to him. It might even make sense to her. "Not really. I never intended to stay. You know that. They know that."

"You mean your family."

"Well, I don't mean City Council."

"But then you started a business. Poof. Like magic. I'm calling bullshit. There's a lot you ain't telling."

Gene held his fingers about an inch apart. "That's neither here nor there. This place, what we got, it doesn't feel like mine. It feels like Rich's cracked idea. I helped because I was desperate."

"A cracked idea that's working," said Laura. She fetched a treat for Doc and tossed it to him. He caught it midair, gobbled it instantly, and sat, tail wagging, ready for another.

"That doesn't make it mine."

"And an alligator hotel run by a man named after a leafy green is yours? Are you hearing what comes out of your mouth?"

"Unfortunately," Gene said with a sigh. "It's hard to explain."

"I applaud the effort."

"What's down in Florida, it's mine in a way this isn't."

Laura frowned at him. "Malarkey. You're the dog man on the Ranch. You're the one folks in town talk about. The trainer. I like your brother. He's a good guy. I like your mother, too, and I really like that she's always high. That shit she packs in the pills is grade A. But they can't do it without you."

"Why the hell not?"

The frown turned into a look of genuine frustration. "Why am I explaining this to the person who already knows the answer?"

"Fair," said Gene said. He rattled the ice in his empty cup. "I'll put it this way. Know how you bounced around different places? Did different things, met different people? And you could go back to school, right? You could pick up tomorrow and go back. They're holding your spot. And even if they weren't, you got brains. You could go somewhere else, some other graduate program. You have something out there that you can finish. Something that's yours. That's what I'm talking about. You got school. You got whatever comes after. I don't have that. What I got is a dog business I didn't want. What I got is a bunch of expectations I never asked for. I got my family back on their feet. I helped my brother do something other than grow tubers at the Days Inn. I helped my mother fix up the place. I even helped my father come home. Now what? I don't owe them. I finished up what's here. Now I have something else. I got the hat trick I always wanted—accidentally real, sure, but beggars can't be choosers, and I got it because I won."

"I hope to God this isn't a 'playing by my own rules' spiel."

"Not a bit. The rules didn't matter. What matters is I got something down in Florida that I can build and not look over my shoulder every day. And who knows how big it can get? I don't. You don't. Don sure as hell doesn't. But isn't that the point? I get the chance to be someone new. Gene before this, Gene after it." He pitched his cup into the trash and scrubbed his hands through his hair. "Anyway, I'm just thinking about it. That's all."

"A whole new person," said Laura. She shook her head. "It's not that easy. And that's not all you're thinking about, is it?"

Gene couldn't help but smile. She read him plain as day and far better than he could read himself. No wonder he was thinking what he was thinking.

"Sure," he said. "I'm thinking you could come with me."

Laura tossed Doc another treat. She shot Gene another skeptical look. "Gene," she said with incredible patience. "I like you. But we're just friends."

"Do I look stupid? I mean, stupider? I know we're friends—good friends. That's the point! You're a lot smarter than me. Plus you got a knack for finding ways to make it when the chips are down. That hotel is already making good money. With what you bring to the table? We might make a whole hell of a lot more. We might do things I can't even think of. This ain't romance. This is a job offer. A change of scenery. New direction."

Laura chewed on her bottom lip. She was intrigued, Gene knew. Intrigued and still skeptical. But hey—that was progress. "You're talking about partners?" she asked. "Would Don go for that?"

"Leave Don to me," said Gene, trying to contain his excitement. "But yeah, I think he would. In fact, I know it."

Laura tossed Doc a last treat, then checked her watch. "Break's over."

"But comrade," said Gene. "The revolution."

"I'll think about it," she said as she bent to pet Doc. "And what about him? He going with you if you split to Florida?"

"Doc goes where I go."

"I was asking him," said Laura.

Gene stood, replaced the chair, and hopped down out of the bay. "Mum's the word," he said.

"That'll cost you a few beers after work."

"Highway robbery," said Gene. "But I'll pay. I have no choice." His phone began to ring. Late for his pickups, which meant he was late for his training sessions. Check or no check, he still had work to do.

As he hopped in the truck the tangled knot of feelings settled behind his ribs. Excitement. Opportunity. A heady rush of his future expanding in front of him. Yes, reckless sense of everything was finally coming together. He had to think. He had to plan.

"Be honest," he said to Doc as they drove toward his appointment. "Did you think I had it in me?"

The dog sneezed.

"That's all right," said Gene. "Until an hour ago, me neither."

Outside the gas station, Dale sat sweating beside the ice machine. For hours his attention had been laser-focused on *Gold, Guns, Antiques* just across the street. He watched in case Lerne emerged to make a move, or in case something bizarre happened, or in case *anything* happened. But that day, as every day he had spent in observation, staring at clouds would prove more exciting.

For almost two weeks, he and Rich had spent every free moment shadowing Lerne, watching the man's various properties, his comings and goings, his daily forays. What they'd discovered was disappointing: a man of weak villainy whose trips to his pawn shop or Andre's seemed as mundane as a trip to the grocer. The oddest thing they'd yet witnessed were the various late-night forays of the silver Mercedes, its occupants hidden behind an impenetrable tint. Once, in the Datsun, they'd tailed the vehicle down to Nates Avenue, and glimpsed a woman of the night climbing into the car before it returned to the house and disappeared into the garage.

Now, sitting in the shade of the store's overhang and filching ice from the buzzing machine at his side, Dale further pondered the situation. Aside from prostitutes, Lerne's only other passion seemed to be cumbersome home deliveries consisting of massive wooden crates containing—what? Furniture, most likely. Antiques. It was, after all, his business. There was, however, the kennel he'd recently built on one of his properties, an enormous and, admittedly, well-constructed building that dwarfed some apartments. What lay inside? What was Lerne up to? Dale didn't know. No answers were forthcoming and when he had attempted to talk to Gene, figure out the nature of the boy's interactions with Lerne, interrogate the purpose for the kennel, his youngest had responded with predictable terseness. Lerne was getting over his fear of dogs. He had land and money aplenty. Who was Dale to begrudge a man a shot at something decent?

Something decent, Dale thought. Meanwhile Dale Temmens was baking in the sun, disguised as a vagabond, and subsisting on ice chips. And frankly, he'd had it. He vowed that very night to tell Rich he was done. If Lerne was up to something wicked, he would have shown his hand. Gene was a grown man. Who was Dale to tell him what he could and couldn't do? Who was Dale to preach about life choices? Anyway, he was anxious to get back to the *real work* that lay ahead. He enjoyed helping on the ranch, and he was grateful to have something to occupy that *didn't* upset his estranged wife, but that wasn't going to fix the problem—namely, that he'd lost all their savings and plunged them into poverty. No amount of pruning the peach trees was going to fix that. No, what Dale needed to do was simple. He had to raise a stake, get back into a game. He had to put his bad luck behind him and *win*. That, as far as Dale was concerned, was that.

While Dale daydreamed about regaining his lost glory, a gleaming Chevy Malibu pulled up. From the car emerged Lula, a notorious poker player known for ruthless bluffing and incredible stamina at the card table. Rumor had it she was among the very best—perhaps *the* best—in town. Other players spoke of her in hushed, almost reverent tones. But Dale knew better. Lula had grown up in the worst parts of Belleview and made a name for herself playing backwoods cards against the very best Columbia, Lexington, and surrounding cities could muster. He remembered her from his own glory days, little more than a tenacious teenage girl with a God-given talent for cards. He had played her twice, years ago, and bested her both times. She was too cautious with big pots and bad at keeping a poker face. When she won, it was through sheer pluck. But what was she doing there? If Dale's memory was accurate, she had moved across the state two years ago, right about the time Dale's luck began to decline.

"You back in town?" he said before he could stop himself.

She stopped and gave him a scathing look. "I know you?" she said.

The disguise, Dale realized. She didn't recognize him. And for the moment, he was content to keep it that way and have a little fun.

"We played cards way back," he said. "You might not remember."

Lula made a little hum in the back of her throat, the very pitch of intense disinterest. "Sure, I wouldn't," she said.

"Back to play the best?"

She snorted and said, "The best? You're looking at her."

"That's brash, miss. What about Ned Oglethorpe?"

"Weak."

"Angeline Carry?"

"She don't know clubs from spades."

"How about Dale Temmens?"

Lula turned, stared hard at his sunglasses. There was a time when his appearance at Andre's, the very mention of his name around a table, would draw nervous stares from all in attendance. If Dale Temmens sat at a table, all but the bravest players would fold. To her ears, Dale believed, a great name had just been invoked. He braced for recognition, respect. Instead, her frown gave way to an easy, knowing smile. She threw her hands up and let out a laugh that shook her frame.

"Dale Temmens?" said Lula. "He lost it a ways back. Not worth considering."

Dale's heart fell into his stomach. "He's a legend," he said.

"Maybe in your days, old timer. In mine? Good riddance."

With that she was gone into the store, a cloud of sweet perfume trailing in her wake. Dale sat, the ice chips he'd filched gone to puddles in his hand. His personal stock had not simply plummeted. It had vanished, like his fortune, and like his luck. No wonder he couldn't convince Gene of anything. No wonder he couldn't help Rich. Mattie was right. He was useless.

In despair Dale rose and made his way across the gas station. He was ready to throw in the towel and go back to pruning peach trees and swallowing the scraps of his pride when a large maroon Escalade caught his eye. The vehicle pulled up in front of Lerne's pawn shop. From the passenger side emerged none other than the owner in bright red boots, crisp beige seersucker, and dark sunglasses. Dale watched as the man entered his shop and spoke briefly with the clerk before disappearing into the back office. That part, thought Dale, was normal. What struck Dale as odd was that he'd never seen Lerne ride with anyone save his lackey, and never in anything but the silver Kompressor.

Small matter, Dale told himself. Probably something ordinary, boring. Then he noticed the license plates on the vehicle. *Charleston, South Carolina. The Palmetto State.* Odd indeed for Lerne to be riding about with folk from Charleston. Dale darted across the street, pulling his hat low over his face, to get a better look. At his approach, the driver's window slid down. A chubby hand protruded, gem-encrusted rings on every finger, a fifty-dollar bill pinched between the fingers.

"Para su desgracia," said the Spanish-looking fellow behind the wheel. His beard glimmered with oil.

Fitting, Dale thought with some bitterness. The man thought him a beggar. But as he reached for the money, something moved in the back of the vehicle, barely visible through the tinted glass. The Spaniard addressed Dale with a wave of his hand.

"Evitad cuidadosamente del perro, señor," he said. "You are in bad way. This help."

No sooner had the man spoken than Lerne appeared, as if summoned. He shook his hands at Dale and hissed, his face crinkled in disgust.

"No food, no money," Lerne said as he boarded the vehicle. "Away, hobo. Fuck off into the ether."

Dale backed away, watching while the vehicle vanished into traffic. Like Lula, Lerne hadn't recognized him—had cast him as a homeless beggar in sweat-soaked rags. Not far from the truth, Dale said as he pressed a hand to his chest. His heart had climbed out of his stomach and was hammering behind his ribs. Focus, he told himself. What had that mysterious fellow said? Dale struggled to recall what rudimentary Spanish he knew. Something about being cautious, avoiding. And perro? Perro, animal. *Dog.*

Dale's brain began to race. Slowly, tortuously, the disparate threads began to form an image. Nothing clear, mind, and nothing certain. But it was there, some hazy, blurry collage of possibilities. Bad ones at that. And if there was even a chance they resembled reality? Maybe Rich wasn't crazy after all.

And Charleston, he thought as he brought forth the burner phone Rich had given him. What the hell was in Charleston?

Chapter 6

Gene rose at five a.m. sharp, glad to find Rich was already up and out. He crept downstairs and saw Mattie in the kitchen, warbling to Doris Day, with the peacocks pecking at the back door. On the stove, something was turning black in a frying pan.

Ordinarily, Gene would have swooped in for coffee, a taste of something burnt before he procured apples and peanut butter, his breakfast of choice, and fled to the cookhouse before the day's work piled up. But this day was different, significant. He'd spent the night tossing and turning, struggling to make up his mind. Then it made itself up. He didn't owe Columbia anything. He sure as shit didn't owe his family—not after he had helped get the ranch up and running. He would go to Florida and push his luck—and the alligator hotel—as far as it would go. But to do that, he had to tie up loose ends. Laura had, as usual forced him to think about things he might have otherwise overlooked. For example, the ranch, its future, and the Texans who, should he miss a payment, were prepared to make his insides his outsides. That meant he had to wheel and deal before he left town. One more time, he told himself as he grabbed his shoes and darted out the side door. Then? Free and clear.

A yawning Doc was waiting on the porch, his favorite place to sleep when not snoring beside Gene in bed. The dog's tail gave a few stiff wags and he fell in beside Gene as they moved through the still-dark orchard.

The truck was where he had left it—backed to the barn in preparation.

Gene was ready with a story to appease his father should the man be up and mobile at that incredulous hour, but Dale, like Rich, was gone. So, too, was the Datsun. That gave Gene pause. Rich and Dale had been traipsing about of late, going off on mysterious errands they refused to explain. The few times he'd bothered to interrogate them, they'd deflected. Fair. But it didn't matter. Today was the day. Free and clear ahoy.

Gene worked quickly to load the twenty dogs Lerne had adopted into the truck. Last to be loaded was Chanticleer, the Spaniel mix with a crazy eye. That, too, gave Gene pause. Rich was fond of Chanticleer, always taking the dog for extra walks in the evening, always giving him extra treats. Gene had asked Rich if his brother wanted to adopt the dog, but Rich had said no. Chanticleer deserved a better life, a good home. What could Rich offer? He talked to ghosts, bit librarians. What if the ghosts took a dislike to the dog? What if Chanticleer took a dislike to them? In the end, Gene decided it wasn't worth the trouble arguing. And anyway, if Lerne was willing to give the dog a good home and plenty of care without any hangups, so be it. Rich had his chance.

Then, of course, there was Lerne. When they'd begun their sessions, Lerne could hardly look at the dog before collapsing into a panting heap. Within weeks, he'd learned to control a pack, guide them with ease. It was, Gene felt, a most remarkable transformation. Every time he saw the man at peace among the dogs, not a trace of the old quailing terror to be seen, he felt a genuine sense of accomplishment. What's more, he felt gratitude. He'd been given the chance to help a man earn a second lease on life and he'd landed a good home for twenty homeless dogs. Big John would be proud. And Rich would get over it.

Gene's thoughts were interrupted by the whimper of a dog. It was the black Lab, pacing in her cage. There were mornings when the dog woke him with her howls—mornings when she made the most God-awful sounds, like someone was flaying her alive. On such mornings, Gene would rise from bed and find the dog curled against the back of the cage, stricken with terror. Dale would be there, of course, and sometimes Rich, the pair rubbing the sleep from their eyes, lost as to how to comfort a dog who suffered from such terrors. The only thing that did the trick was for Gene to open the cage, let her climb into his lap. There, with her heart pounding so hard he could feel it through her ribs, through his own ribs, he would hold her and pet her until she settled down, until whatever terror had passed. Ten minutes, twenty, an hour, it didn't matter. He held her as long as it took, telling her with his hands and arms that it was all right. He was there. He had her. And in those moments, Gene felt a peace that otherwise eluded him. It always ended, of course. She had to go back to her cage and he had to get on with the day's work.

Gene opened the cage and took the dog in his arms. She licked his face and immediately he felt that her panic was different. He held her for a while, surrounded by sleeping dogs in their cages, Doc watching from the barn door. The black Lab burrowed under his arm, and when he tried to stand up, she refused to budge. It was as if she was telling him, begging him, not to go.

At last Gene put her back in her cage, refilled her water bowl and told her not to worry. Mattie would be coming by shortly with breakfast. But she wouldn't meet his eyes.

He boarded the truck, Doc between the seats, and drove to Lerne's in a funk. The Lab had been with them for some time, and while she'd made good progress, he knew she was never going to get adopted. Too skittish. Too scarred. And when Gene was gone? Who was going to calm her down? Who would go out there in the dark and sit with her and hold her and tell her what she needed to hear? Gene looked to Doc for a hint, but the dog, who sat seat-belted into the passenger seat, stared out the window, watching the gray, weird dawn roll over the trees.

"Maybe she'll come with us," he said. And when Doc didn't acknowledge him, he said, "Glad you agree."

In town, dark rain clouds blotted out the sun. The weather app on his phone had told him to expect rain in Columbia by noon, but the ozone already tickled Gene's nose. Ten, he figured. Eleven at the latest. Then the clouds would open.

When he arrived at Lerne's, the man himself was waiting on the front porch. He gave a tight little wave and rose. By the time Gene had parked and opened the back, Lerne had opened the gate to his yard and was standing there, beaming at the new arrivals. Gene opened the cages, assembled the dogs in a neat pack, and brought them to their new owner.

"My new friends," Lerne said as he petted and scratched his new adoptions. "It's a dream, this day. I never imagined."

"Your kennel waterproof?" said Gene.

Lerne looked at him and Gene saw something, an expression. Frustration.

"Everything proof. Coffee?"

"Love some." The weather, thought Gene. It made everyone edgy. Himself included.

They went, men and dogs, into the spacious yard. When Lerne had first suggested adopting so many dogs at once, Gene's hackles were raised. That was a common tactic of dog fighters, scum of the Earth who pit helpless animals against each other for sick thrills. He had recalled a day back at Big John's when Austin Animal Control had brought over a pit bull, the lone survivor of a raided dog-fighting ring. The dog was gone on rage, growling through his muzzle, hostile to every person that so much as breathed in his direction, and beyond eager to murder any dog he spied. A hopeless case. Big John's rescue was the dog's last chance.

They got the muzzled dog into the problem pen, a wide concrete yard with a stake and chain in the middle. As soon as the dog was tethered, the city boys went off with Big John to sign paperwork. Gene remained by the pen, his stomach twisting itself into knots. Without knowing why, he entered the pen and sat with his back to the dog. He heard the metallic snap of the chain going taut behind him, the furious growls, the labored breathing. And when the dog calmed down and returned to its spot, Gene got up and left. Every day for weeks he repeated the process until the dog's protests ceased. One day he inched closer and was able to touch the chain. A week later, his fingers grazed the dog's neck. Slowly, carefully, Gene took off the muzzle. The dog's cold nose traced his fingers. His ears twitched. They were on a precipice. The dog would bite him and they would start again from scratch. Or the dog would trust him and something new would begin.

All at once, the pit bull slumped to the ground and began to pant. On his face was an exhaustion the likes of which Gene could scarcely understand. It emptied him. He traced the dog's muscled flank, felt the trust in the beating of the dog's heart through his ribs. The fear was gone.

But Lerne's accommodations put Gene's mind at ease. The kennel, perched in the shade of an enormous magnolia tree, was a modern structure with all manner of conveniences that would make caring for so many dogs a breeze. Yes, Gene thought, they would have a good home here. Plenty of space, plenty of good food. Someone who loved them. Even now, Lerne was going among them, petting and greeting and dispensing treats from his pockets the way Gene had taught him. An apt pupil. And now someone, who after a lifetime of terror, had learned to love dogs. Gene turned the pack loose and they darted off to investigate their new home. While the dogs nosed about, Lerne took Gene to the back patio and fetched fresh mugs of coffee from the house. Then he produced an envelope and slid it into Gene's hand.

"Well worth the price," said Lerne. "You may count it. I won't take offense."

Gene peered into the envelope and felt his stomach take up gymnastics. Fifty thousand in cash that, when combined with the fifty Lerne had already given him, made up the sum total of Gene's debt to the Texans. Free and clear.

"Are you all right?" said Lerne. "Coffee too strong?"

"Perfect," Gene said as he shoved the envelope into his back pocket.

"You went pale of a sudden. Sit, relax. There's things I want to talk about."

"Listen," said Gene. "I only have a few minutes. Bunch of appointments lined up today."

Lerne's face stiffened. The features became rigid, locked in an almost grimace. Then, quick as it came, the look vanished, replaced by a happy grin. Lerne gestured to the dogs, pointing out Chanticleer.

"He named after the rooster?" he asked.

"Guess so," said Gene.

"I recognize that we met under strange, tense circumstances," said Lerne. "How very fitting! But today is a fine day. Months ago, I thought I would be afraid of them my whole life. Now?" He gestured happily to the dogs playing in the yard, to the kennel beneath the magnolia branches. "I have a family. Me, whose parents died when I was very young because they smoked and argued, and the boat house had too much gasoline. It was a terrible shame. Now I can be like a father to them, the dogs. The past is washed away, made clean. And it's you I thank."

Lerne took his hand and held it awkwardly above the table. Gene squeezed, shook, and waited until Lerne let go. When the man didn't, he said, "Was you that did the hard work."

This seemed to please Lerne. He released Gene's hand and stared, teary-eyed at the dogs as they romped on the lawn. As for Gene, he was ready to skedaddle. There were things to do before he left Columbia—some good, some bad. None of them easy. He gulped down his coffee and stood. "I hate to run.

Call us if you need anything. And don't worry. These dogs are going to love it here."

Lerne grinned. "They will. And for the record, your father's debt is cleared. I don't want unpleasantness. That's been the point, really."

"No one does," said Gene. "Appreciate it."

"It eats at you," said Lerne. It seemed he was talking more to himself than to Gene. "It chews and chews and chews."

"Before you know it, what's left?"

"Teeth marks," said Lerne. He flashed a big-toothed grin and sipped his coffee. "We understand one another. We are alike."

Wouldn't go that far, thought Gene. Out in the yard, Chanticleer bounded, big ears flapping, his wonky eye staring at the sky and ground alike. They'd taught him a lot of things, those dogs. He hoped they would continue to teach Lerne. But he had to focus. He was nearly at the finish line.

"Been a pleasure," he said.

"Immense," said Lerne as he walked him out.

At the gate, Gene turned and had a last glimpse of the dogs frolicking in the yard, of Chanticleer bounding among them. Then the gate was closed and Lerne was gone. Gene made for the truck. He was eager to get on the road, get to the Texans. But something nagged at him, a feeling that he had overlooked something. But what? The dogs had a gorgeous luxury kennel. Dale's debts were zeroed. And Gene had the cash to pay off the Texans once and for all. A whole new life lay ahead of him. He didn't have time to stand in Lerne's yard and ponder imaginary problems.

Once on Senate Street, Gene called Don Lettuce to make sure everything was still a-okay.

"How's business?" he said. "Still holding strong?"

"This morning," said Lettuce, "two families of tourists got into a fight about who got what room. First, they offered twice the going rate. Then, they tried to throw each other in the gator pits."

"Get a net over those."

"Way ahead of you. Wire mesh, tensile strength of eleven hundred pounds. Don't even rust. How soon can I expect you? And are you coming alone or with your friend?"

Gene grinned. As anticipated, Don Lettuce had been all too happy to welcome Laura into the fold—provided she wanted to go. She hadn't given Gene a firm answer yet, and every time he asked, she claimed she was still thinking. "Call you when I'm on the road," said Gene. "And who knows? Stock the liquor cabinet for two just in case. And throw some in for yourself."

"Any special requests?"

"Nothing peach flavored," said Gene. He hung up and turned his attention to more pressing matters. With the money Lerne had given him, he was clear of the Texans—or would be within the hour. That left one problem: He owed Lerne a hundred grand—and Lerne's payments, taken from the monthly profits of the ranch, would seriously drain the business. Even if Gene contributed a portion of his salary from the alligator hotel—a thing he fully intended to do—the ranch couldn't safely sustain the payouts, especially not if profits dipped after his departure. But there was a solution. Gene could sell his half of the business, use the money to pay off half of Lerne's loan. That would reduce the payouts per month to Lerne down to something Gene alone could cover, and the ranch could pay his salary to whoever bought the share. The business would be safe and Gene would pay off Lerne in a year, two tops. Everyone was going to win. Everyone.

Good plan, thought Gene. Just one *more* problem. The business was too new, too untested to spark bank or commercial buyers, and too small to attract private buyers. That left one kind of buyer, the kind hungry to make a dollar off Gene, the kind that felt slighted by him and perhaps believed they were owed something above and beyond simple repayment. The kind that, given the slightest provocation, would just as likely break Gene in half as take his money.

At the hotel, Gene parked and looked at Doc for reassurance. What did his father like to say at times like those? "Sabers up," he said. What a stupid phrase. Perfect, though, for someone about to do something that bordered on suicidal.

He climbed from the truck, Doc at his side, and entered through the restaurant. He slipped the waiter a twenty and a few choice words that convinced the young man to bring their breakfast extra quick, his on a plate and Doc's in a bowl. Then he paused to scrub a hand through his hair and rub his face. He was dressed to impress in a gauzy cotton shirt and chino shorts, a wide-brimmed Panama hat atop his head. He'd stolen the idea for the hat from Lerne, a marked difference from his usual topper of ratty ball caps stained with sweat. The effect was of a Southern man about town, breezy, confident, calm.

Or so he hoped.

Loke and Malak were at a table in the back, their faces drooping, their shabby linen clothes soiled with bits of food and drink. Grime was under their nails and they were drinking black coffee and pushing bits of breakfast around their plates. They looked like decrepit tourists of the lowest order, wayfarers with unshaven chins. They were still dangerous, Gene reminded himself, still able to break his legs if he pushed them the wrong way. And Roy was still missing. It meant they'd be testy, looking for a reason to lash out. And that meant he couldn't give them the smallest opening.

"They just let you bring dogs in here?" Loke said, motioning to Doc as Gene pulled up a chair.

"He keeps me honest," said Gene.

"Then he's slacking on the job," said Malak. "To what do we owe this unscheduled meeting?"

"At this unholy hour," said Loke. "Make it quick. I need a nap."

Their tones were gruff, Gene noted. But they each took scraps of bacon from their plates and fed it to Doc. The dog was working his magic, making them generous. No better time to sweeten the mood.

To that end, Gene produced two envelopes—fifty thousand in each—and placed them on the table. Loke and Malak glanced at the envelopes, then at Gene, then at each other. Their faces, normally unreadable, were completely unguarded. Surprise. Curiosity. And more than a little wary. They each took an envelope and peered inside. Their faces registered surprise. Still controlled, Gene noted. Still dangerous. But even that little bit of surprise meant the money did the trick. Gene would never get a better chance to deliver the pitch.

"Good morning," said Gene as he leaned in and stole another piece of bacon for Doc. "You're paid in full."

"Who did you rob?" said Loke.

"Give me some credit," said Gene.

"Was you, I wouldn't use that word," said Loke. "Credit."

"Riposte," said Gene.

"I fenced in school," said Loke. "Was pretty good at it."

"No shit?" said Gene.

"Total shit," said Malak. "Picture him with a fucking sword. He would take his own eyes out."

"Go take a fucking nap," said Loke.

The waiter brought Gene's breakfast, and some chopped carrots and fried eggs for Doc. The Texans relinquished their plates.

"Y'all mind if I eat while you argue?" said Gene. "Got a long day ahead of me."

"Let's hear it," said Malak. "How'd you get these early Christmas gifts?"

"Just told you," said Gene. He punctuated his speech by smacking the bottom of the ketchup bottle and dousing his home fries. "Our little ranch ain't so little anymore. Barn's full. Building three more pens this week. It's my brother's show, really. He does it all—rescues them, trains them. I just supervise. People love this hick business. It's just like I told you."

"But," said Loke." I hear a fucking *but* coming."

"But," said Gene.

"Big surprise," said Malak.

"Time for me to be moving on," said Gene. "Can't play second fiddle to my brother forever. And anyway, it's his business, you know? It's set, stable, and growing. As for me, I got something of my own down in Florida. Which is why I want to make you an offer."

Gene slid the paperwork for his half of the business across the table. Any other day, the Texans would have seen right through him, peppered him with questions until they rooted out exactly where he'd gotten the money. It was rule number one of doing what they did: Follow the cash. Rules number two through ten usually involved major impact damage to someone's musculoskeletal system, so Gene very much wanted to keep them on rule one. But the Texans, while still dangerous, were off their game. Roy had mysteriously vanished and they'd never in a million years expected Gene to come up with the full balance, much less deliver it in cold, hard *cash*. Loke and Malak were sharp, sure, but things were moving too fast for them. Time to press the advantage.

"Here's the deal," he said, "I'm willing to make you both the proud owners of half of Sweet Muffin Ranch."

"Come again?" said Loke.

"Half?" said Malak.

"My brother owns the other half and doesn't want to sell. No surprise, right? It's his baby. But like I said, I'm heading to the Sunshine State. I go, the business stays. And grows. That's what I'm offering you."

"And we'd want to buy this *why?*" said Loke.

Gene smoothed out the paperwork and walked them through it; the ranch's profit margin for the three months it had been in operation, the high income, low expenditure, and a little fiction about how Rich wanted to expand and build a second location downtown. He elaborated on the various investors that had approached them, conveniently leaving out the fact that the investors were mainly bored suburban folk who liked to drive over, take pictures with the animals, and reel off idiotic ideas on how to turn a hick business into something *real*. One thing he didn't have to dress up much was the buzz the ranch was getting. The local TV news had been out with their cameras. Magazines and newspapers were calling to set up interviews. The ranch was hot. If ever there was a time to get in on the ground floor, Gene explained, it was then and there.

Gene pushed aside his empty plate. He'd give it two, three minutes, and maybe a little more coffee before he asked the Texans for their decision. Meanwhile, he took a moment to bask in his performance. The angle, the pitch, it was his finest work to date. All that remained was to seal the deal and Gene knew he had to let them broach it.

Loke and Malak pored over the paperwork for several more minutes, drank their coffee, then shook their heads. There was a hint of a smile on Malak's face—a good sign! But Loke was glaring across the table at—nothing? Not Gene, anyway. If Roy was there, he would be the buffer between Loke and Malak, the one to even them out. But Roy was still missing and the Texans were more unpredictable than ever.

"How much?" said Malak.

"Eighty big," said Gene.

"Out of your very small mind," said Loke. He practically growled. Gene would have to be *extra* careful with him.

"A common accusation," said Gene. "Not this time, though. Got the numbers right in front of you."

"Ain't worth more than forty," said Malak.

"Boys," Gene began, but Loke slammed a fist on the table. Doc jumped. Gene jumped, too.

"That 'boys' bit," growled Loke. "Let's knock that off. You're talking to grown fucking men. Grown men whose partner has mysteriously vanished in your shit burg of a hometown. Watch your mouth."

"Noted," said Gene. He had gotten too cocky, too sure of himself. Time to switch gears, use more tact. "Gentlemen," he said, "here's what I'm getting at. Two years' time and you just made your money back plus some. Three years? Five? You're so far in the black you'll need an accountant for your accountant. And that's just the beginning. When they get a second location up and running, you'll see those numbers double. Even if Rich decides not to, so what? The place is full. No sign of slowing down. A business owned outright and operated on private land by my family. But best of all—pay attention, now—none of this requires your presence. You get to go back to Austin, sit back, and *collect*."

"All I hear is *if*," said Malak.

"*If* your brother expands," said Loke.

"*If* business keeps up," said Malak.

"Knowing you," said Loke, "this thing will go belly-up in two weeks."

"Look," said Gene. "Barring fire, flood, or act of God, the ranch ain't going anywhere, and we got insurance out on those three. What's on the table is guaranteed income. You make your money and I go off to make mine elsewhere. I'm giving you first crack. Don't want it? Okay. No harm, no foul. I figured we have history together. I'm trying to settle up, trying to make things right. I have another interested buyer. Sorry I wasted your time."

Gene reached for the paperwork. He'd barely touched it when Malak grabbed his wrist. The Texans looked first at him, then at each other. If there was one thing Gene could count on them to do it was drop trou and call in the kicker whenever the chance for more money presented itself. He'd called their bluff. Now they had to show their cards. It would look like a win in their book. And with Roy's disappearance they were only too desperate to tally something in that particular column.

"Forty-five," Malak finally said.

"Other parties have offered more," said Gene. He reached once more for the paperwork. Loke slapped his hand away.

"Fifty," growled Malak.

Gene began to reach again, then paused for a crucial, planned moment. He arranged his features into what he believed would convincingly relay genuine conflict of interest. It worked. Malak demanded a pen from a passing waiter, held the tip over the paperwork, and looked to Gene.

"Fifty," he said again.

Gene hesitated a moment more. He was there, on the very cusp of complete and total victory. All he had to do was say the word and they would sign it. So why was he hesitating? For effect? That was it, wasn't it? What the hell could be stirring behind his ribs?

"Deal," he said.

"One thing," Loke said as he signed. "If something goes wrong? If say, business tanks before the business appreciates in value?"

"If it shutters in the night before we get back our sale price?" Malak said as he signed.

"If something otherwise denies us what we have just purchased?" Loke said as he passed Gene the contract and pen. "If something like that happens? Any of those? All of those? It doesn't matter. We'll find you."

"We'll break every goddamn bone in your weaselly little body," said Malak.

"And then we'll kill you," said Loke. "Slowly. We'll take our time."

"Then we'll get to work on your brother," said Malak. "You get me?"

"And after that, dear old Mom and Dad. We'll pay them a visit at home. Very late. You listening?"

"Because let me tell you something. I refuse, *refuse* to ever get taken by Gene Temmens again. You understand us?"

"Understood," said Gene. He tried not to let what the Texans had said diminish the thrill of victory, but it did. Don't sweat it, he told himself as he signed the contract. The money he was going to make down in Florida—the money that was already coming in—would buffer things if the ranch fell through. And if it didn't? He could go back to doing what he did best.

He turned over the paperwork into Loke's waiting hand, then picked up one of the envelopes from the table. All the while, the Texans eyes remained fixed on him. He could practically feel the malice radiating from them.

"Been a pleasure," said Gene. He stood, then paused. "Mind if I ask you something?"

Loke rolled his eyes. "Shoot."

"Any sign of Roy? Any word?"

The Texans' silence told Gene everything. Wherever Roy had gone—and it was *highly* unusual for them to be separated so long—that was none of Gene's business. He left a tip on the table, slid the envelope into his breast pocket, and bid the Texans adieu. It wasn't until he was in the truck that his heart began to slow down. He'd done it. He'd actually done it. Free and clear. For good. All that remained before he could celebrate was to drop off Lerne's money, pack his meager belongings, and break the news to his family. It wasn't going to be easy. Rich, Mattie, and Dale would be upset, but in time they would get over it. And why not? Rich would be able to direct the business as he saw fit. No more listening to his younger brother. He would have something of his own, something that was well and truly *his.* It would be harder, thought Gene, to say goodbye to the dogs.

The storm broke on the way to Lerne's. Sheets of water whipped up and down the streets, slowing traffic to a crawl. With the rain came a feeling of unease. Time, Gene felt, was of the essence.

Lerne wasn't home and no one answered the door, so Gene waved at the security camera, then wrote a note on the envelope, took a picture with his phone, and pushed it through the mail slot.

Half the loan repaid, it read. *Pleasure doing business.*

He sent a matching text to Lerne, then raced back to the truck. Not that it mattered. He was soaked head to toe, water dripping from his ridiculous hat brim. He tossed the thing behind his seat, rang out his shirt on the floor, and patted Doc's flank. The dog was completely unbothered by the storm, calmly sitting in the passenger seat and watching the sheets of water run down the windshield.

A peal of thunder rolled across the city. The rain intensified, hammered on the truck. It sounded like ice picks trying to punch holes through the metal.

In the humid pink dawn, Rich hunkered in the foliage across from Lerne's house, camouflaged with leaves and branches stuck to his clothing. Dale was beside him, snoring lightly. Rich's stomach growled. Was his alliance with his father not on such tenuous grounds, he'd send the man for biscuits and sausage, a little coffee—something to keep them going. But waking Dale meant facing the man's scorn and disbelief. Despite the mystery surrounding the Escalade and the Spaniard, they'd discovered nothing of worth save that Lerne and the Spaniard made occasional forays to Charleston. Two days ago, in fact,

Rich and Dale had trailed the vehicles on the highway, and Rich had let them get too far ahead, afraid of arousing suspicion. By the time they'd gotten back to Columbia, Dale had once again declared the enterprise a fool's errand. He wanted out, done. No more scampering about in the hopes of catching Lerne and his thick Spanish friend doing much of nothing. And besides, they were behind on work at the ranch, and Mattie and Gene were steaming mad, and what the hell was it all for, anyway? Some hunch?

It had taken Rich an awful lot of begging to convince his father for just one more day of faithful service. They were close, he felt, to the heart of the thing. Charleston, the dogs—that was the key, Rich felt. So very close. If they didn't find anything that day, Rich had agreed, they would be done with it. The longer Dale slept beside him, the more time Rich could squeeze from their last day of covert surveillance. He let his stomach grumble. Better to be hungry than alone.

Rich checked his watch. It was 5:17 a.m. Moments later, the visitations began.

First Gene, arriving before the mist had cleared from the lawn. He unloaded twenty dogs from the van, Chanticleer among them. Rich's heart constricted in pain as he watched his brother, and the animals disappear into Lerne's private backyard. The pain sharpened into anger when Gene reemerged without Chanticleer. Dale had warned him. But no one, not even their father, could have expected such a betrayal.

Hell, said the ghosts. Was Rich that stupid?

For once, Rich had no retort. The ghosts were right. His brother had allowed Lerne to adopt Chanticleer. That was bad enough. But why had he done it so early and in secret?

You should listen to us more, said the ghosts. We got a bead on things.

"That so?" said Rich.

Ask us anything, the ghosts intoned. They were immensely pleased to be taken seriously.

"Where's he going?" Rich asked with trepidation, scared they would, in fact, tell him the answer. "What's he going to do?"

Easy, said the ghosts. Something he don't want you to know about.

The anger in Rich's stomach began to boil. More taunts, more jabs. He should have known better than to trust the ghosts. He was working up a head of steam when Dale jolted awake.

"What's it?" said Dale. "Were you talking to me?"

"Gene brought Lerne's dogs," said Rich. "About twenty or so."

"If he bought them, they're his."

Rich decided to say nothing. There was no point in picking a fight with his father, and besides, not all was lost. He could work up the nerve, buy Chanticleer back from Lerne. The loan shark had seemed more reasonable of late. Perhaps he would take pity on Rich.

Moments later, Llewellyn arrived in his black Cadillac. Not long after, the maroon Escalade followed suit and the Spaniard, accompanied by Lerne's lackey, proceeded to the gate. There they were met by Lerne, engaged in jovial conversation. Nothing out of the ordinary as far as Rich was concerned. He'd seen this set-up before. Until, moments later, an aged and shabby vehicle marked Craig's Produce pulled up and disgorged two grizzled men Rich had never before seen.

"Who's that?" said Rich.

"Beside him, Dale was squinting to see at such distance. "Don't know," he said. "But that ain't a fruit van. Look at the plates."

Rich could just barely make out the design on the van's back plate. *Charleston.* Another clue.

With his phone, Rich snapped what pictures he could before Lerne and the others had disappeared into the yard. Then he gathered what courage he could and crept to the van, taking close-up pictures of the license plates. When he rose to peer through the windows, he saw that window screens obscured much of his vision. Through the fabric he glimpsed the vague outlines of—what were they? Storage racks? Cages? He snapped a few pictures, praying his camera would provide the clarity his eyes could not. By then his courage had begun to falter, and the sound of approaching voices dashed what little remained. Too late to return to his hiding spot, he darted instead to the side of the house away from the gate and threw himself down around the corner just in time to see Lerne and the others emerging from the side gate, the Spaniard's lackeys leading four dogs on leashes. Rich's heart lurched. Chanticleer was among them.

The dogs were loaded into the produce van. One grizzled man went in back with the animals while the other went up front to drive. Then Lerne and his lackey in the Kompressor, and the Spaniard in his Escalade, followed the van down the drive and around the bend. As soon as the last car receded behind the trees, Rich leapt up and made a beeline toward the Datsun, calling for his father to move some ass.

"Where you going?" Dale cried after him.

"We got to follow," said Rich.

"Again? Rich, this is getting long in the tooth."

By then Rich had started the gasping engine. He waited just long enough for Dale, still complaining, to climb in through the window before he mashed the gas. The Datsun fishtailed, then straightened out as the tires bit pavement. Just as they reached town, heavy rain began to pummel the road. Rich felt the peals of thunder in his teeth, his bones.

They picked up the tail in town, straggling behind the produce van to avoid detection. Now and then Rich saw Lerne's Kompressor in the lane beside the van and the Spaniard's Escalade in the other. All three headed out of town, direct for Charleston, just as they had last time. Except this time was different, thought Rich. The van was with them and so were the dogs. All they had to do was follow the dogs.

A few miles outside Columbia the rain thickened. Sheets of water hammered the ancient car. Before long the vents stopped blowing air and the windshield fogged so that Dale had to keep wiping it with his shirt.

"Look at us," Dale complained. "A pack of idiots doing God knows what for God knows why."

"Keep wiping," said Rich. He was squinting to see anything through the haze his father was making on the glass.

"We shouldn't be doing this," Dale went on. "I'm old and you're deranged."

"They got the dogs, Dad. We have to follow the dogs."

"Just stay in your lane," said Dale. "And back up a bit. Don't want them to see us."

A few miles outside Charleston the van and its escorts took an exit ramp, turned north on a county road. A faded sign pointed the way to *Wholesome Sugar Refinery*. Rich lengthened his distance from the entourage as they turned onto another, smaller road, then another. Dense forest sprang up around them, the trees dark with moisture. Soon even the day had darkened, branches and heavy clouds blotting out the light, and the rain showing no sign of slowing.

Rich drove without the headlights, wincing every time the Datsun found a pothole, praying through his teeth that the ancient car wouldn't up and quit. Beside him, Dale leaned forward, scanning for signs of the convoy's passage. Even the ghosts, huddled in back, were quiet and watchful.

"They turned ahead," said Dale.

"You sure?"

"Go a little past. A little further. Here. Pull over."

Rich brought the car to a halt on the muddy shoulder. The dirt road, more mud and shallow pools than discernible pathway, snaked off into the trees. For a moment the only sound Rich could hear was the rhythmic drumming of rain on the car's roof and windshield, and the gurgle of water sheeting on the glass. There was something wrong, something bad about the place. Rich's throat was dry as the desert.

"What's back there?" Rich said.

"Hell if I know," said Dale. "Refinery, I guess. But an old one."

"I mean really back there. This ain't right. Why would they bring dogs here?"

Dale stared at the road and frowned. Over the course of the ride, he'd gone from put-out and fussy to wary and grave. Now he looked suddenly aged and wizened, as if the entirety of their mission had fallen onto his shoulders. It had, in a way. Something was wrong—very wrong—and if Rich knew it, Dale knew, too.

"Dad," Rich began, but Dale cut him off.

"Hush," said Dale. "Give me a minute. Let me think."

The minutes stretched out, tracked by the rain slapping the car. Rich's heart wouldn't slow down. He was sure they'd found what they were looking for, sure that they had to know what lay down the road. They had to know why Lerne had brought the dogs there. But now that they had found it, he couldn't find the courage to get out of the car.

The ghosts found this amusing. It figured, they said. Came all this way and too chicken-shit to follow through. Good old Rich!

Finally, Dale sighed. "Stay with the car," he said. "I'll take a look."

"What if someone comes by?" said Rich.

"Pretend you broke down. And listen. Don't start talking to them ghosts. Not even for a second. I need you sharp."

Rich meant to say more but couldn't form the words. He wasn't going to let his father down. Not there. Not again.

"Just stay put," said Dale. With that, he leapt from the car, slammed the door, and dashed into the woods. In no time at all he was gone from sight. Sheets of water rolled up and down the road, hammering the car. All that lay beyond the windows was reduced to muted gray smears.

The ghosts stretched, put their feet up on the seats. Go on, they chided. Crank her up and go home. Know you want to.

"I can't," said Rich. "You know I can't."

Then go after him, they said. Get out there, get wet.

"I can't!" Rich moaned. Damn it! He had already screwed up! No more listening to the ghosts, he told himself. But their voices bored into his head.

You ain't got the stomach for this, they said. We all know it. Tsk, tsk. Let your dear old daddy run headlong through the rain into who knows what, did you? What a son. Ought to be ashamed of yourself. We are.

Rich choked down a sob. They were right. He was ashamed of himself because he was a quailing nothing, a worm. Even in the Army he'd been spineless, so scared of what might happen that when something *did* happen he froze up. A part of him was still there, still on that road where the JTAC called in the bad coordinates and blasted perfectly innocent folk to carbon smithereens. Part of him had never left that place where the bombs fell. Where the ghosts got up out of the smoking rubble and started their haunting.

Go on, said the ghosts. Blubber. Cry. Weep into your stupid beard. What's it going to matter? Do you know who you're messing with? Drive away, dullard. Save yourself.

Rich locked his hands on the wheel. In the back, the ghosts guffawed. They took strength from the inclement weather and his suffering, grew more powerful as both intensified. He had to push them out of his mind. Chanticleer. He thought about Chanticleer, about the searing betrayal he felt toward Gene. Why hadn't he asked him? Why did he get to have Doc and Rich got nothing? Hadn't Rich been honest and kind to his brother? Hadn't he worked hard? But Gene didn't care about any of that, did he? All Gene cared about was himself. And Rich had done what he always did: He let his brother walk all over him.

Rich checked his watch. How had an hour elapsed since Dale's departure? He should have been back. What if he was in trouble? What if he was hurt?

Rich picked up his phone but who could he call? Gene? He wouldn't care. Mattie? She couldn't do anything stuck at the ranch. Besides, his phone had no signal. Dale's phone was probably no better off. They were cut off, alone. His father and Chanticleer could be dying in the woods and there was no one to help. No one to save them. No one but *him.*

The realization hit Rich like a punch in the face. He broke into a cold sweat. Now or never, he told himself. They needed him. Now or never. With a deep breath, Rich mustered what scraps of bravery he could and stepped into the rain.

Get a load of this, said the ghosts. They fell out through the door and oozed to their feet.

"Now or never," said Rich. He repeated it like a mantra, trying to draw strength from the words.

The ghosts doubled with laughter. Oh, this is going to be good, they said. Chickenshit found some stones? Wouldn't miss it for the world.

Rich took one step, then another. Then another after that. Before he knew it, he had reached the tree line, sloshing through mud and underbrush, sinking a boot into every possible puddle. Every step brought new pangs of fear. He kept the road on his right and more than once threw himself down onto his stomach as vehicles ambled along the way the van had gone. Then, in a shudder of terror, he saw it coming the other way, Lerne's Kompressor, and huddled behind a tree, not daring to move a muscle until it was gone.

Go on, the ghosts chided. This what you want? Or you want to run back to the car, drive home to mommy?

Yes, thought Rich. That *was* what he wanted. He wanted to turn and run back in the direction he'd come, get into the Datsun until he stopped shaking, until he could *breathe* again. But there was still no sign of Dale or Chanticleer. He had to go on.

Deeper into the woods, the ground grew spongy, riddled with pools of muddy water. Rich waded through and found on the other side an aged chain link fence. A section near the bottom had been bent back a bit, enough for him to widen and crawl under. Further on, he saw another fence and the dark outline of buildings beyond. The sounds of many voices, of car engines and tires on gravel flitted down from the compound. So too did the barking of dogs. He was nearly to the fence when he spotted Dale sitting against a tree, hands wrapped around his ankle.

"I told you to stay," Dale said as he approached.

"What happened?" said Rich.

"Twisted it," Dale said between his teeth. "Bad. How stupid can I get?"

"Can you walk?"

The muscles in Dale's jaw bunched. The answer was obvious. Rich would have to help him back to the Datsun. But he couldn't leave yet. He had to know.

"Did you see where they went?" said Rich.

Dale motioned to the buildings beyond the next fence. His face was pale, creased with fear. He'd seen something—something bad—and Rich didn't think he could bear to do the same. He'd used up whatever courage he had dredged from the depths of his soul. All that remained was to get his father up and moving. They would be back at the Datsun soon. Then on the road, then home. But no sooner had those thoughts formed than another rose, clear and cold from the muck of his brain. Chanticleer.

"I got to find him," said Rich.

"You can't," said Dale.

"I got to."

Dale seemed about to protest further, then thought otherwise. Reluctantly he nodded and said, "You get scared, you run. Don't let nobody see you. And son, be careful. Very careful."

Before he could change his mind, before fear ground him to a halt, Rich crept to the fence. Decaying brick buildings loomed beyond, their windows gaping like eye sockets, save one around which vehicles of all varieties were parked, the one from which the sounds of humans and dogs emanated. Rich pulled up the bottom of the fence, straining even with his great strength to bend the links enough to crawl under. The result was a great many cuts and scrapes along his neck and arms. He slunk close to the building, wondering how best to proceed when he saw a metal ladder providing access to the roof. Rich ascended. At the top he probed the roof to determine if it would hold his weight and found it freshly tarred and shingled. He crept forward through the downpour and found a skylight. There he wiped grime from a corner of the glass and peered into the building.

The Spaniard stood beside a makeshift ring of plywood. Near at hand were other men passing money back and forth. Lerne's dogs, Chanticleer included, were lined up. The Spaniard was talking to the men, joking, smiling. He motioned to the dogs as if proffering goods for sale, then selected Chanticleer. The Spaniel mix went into one end of the plywood ring while at the other a man held a frothing, snapping pit bull. Rich's heart shuddered. It was all he could to clear the mud from his phone and snap pictures of the proceedings below.

"Please," Rich prayed. "Don't hurt him."

In a rich and sonorous voice, the Spaniard called all in attendance to attention. He asked them to note Chanticleer's obedience, his docile nature. He gave a series of simple commands to which the dog responded perfectly. Sit, lie down, stay. Chanticleer's tail wagged and wagged. The perfect bait dog, he proclaimed. He told them a demonstration was in order. They should watch closely.

Then he let the Pit Bull go and Rich was witness to brutality and horror such as he'd not seen since the war. Every fiber of his being curdled in revulsion. It was a slaughterhouse. And he and Gene were supplying the bodies.

When the trial was over, the men cast the body of Chanticleer through a side door. Rich descended, creeping around the side of the building. There he beheld the dog laying in the mud, its wounds too numerous to count. Rich was paralyzed with terror, sick in the pit of his stomach. To his great surprise the animal stirred, whimpering, its flank heaving in labored breath. One dark eye rolled to meet Rich's gaze. There was still a chance to save him, still time.

He carried Chanticleer back under the fence. By the time he reached his father, blood had run down his hands, slicking his clothes, his arms.

Gene was out of patience and prepared to lose his flipping cool if Mattie did not produce his wallet and cease all foolishness by the count of three.

"One," he said.

"Go on, count," said Mattie. She'd had taken up a defensive stance on the landing, blocking the stairs. Worse, she was armed with a rolled-up newspaper and a daring look in her eyes. Not even Doc, waiting downstairs and watching the proceedings from a safe distance, was willing to interject.

"Two," said Gene.

"Why leave?" asked Mattie. "There ain't nothing for you in Florida."

"I told you," Gene said as he steeled himself for three. And he had. Ever since she'd come upon him packing in the afternoon, alerted by the CLOSED sign on the gate, they'd been at each other. He had patiently explained the alligator hotel. He had patiently explained that the ranch wasn't doomed—it was, in fact, safe, even if he had to send money home to prop it up. He patiently explained that he loved them all very much, his strange and fractious family, but he had decided to depart for Florida that very afternoon, yes, *that very afternoon.* He told her—thrice, in fact—that he was very, very sorry for the sudden and unexpected nature of his departure, but could she please quit hovering with her tank and a weapon so he could pack his things and get on with his life? Mattie was predictably distraught and expressed it by clubbing him with anything and everything in sight, going so far as to chase him up and down the stairs until her breath ran out and she collapsed upon the landing where, now that she had enough wind to stand, she had set herself up as a defensive bulwark, prepared for a lengthy siege. What, she wanted to know, was he thinking? What had he done? Didn't he understand he was in too deep to just pull up roots without yanking everyone out of the ground with him?

Despite the drubbing, Gene had tried his level best to keep his cool. It was going to be fine, he told her. He'd trained Rich and James to care for dogs, and more importantly, how to train the customers who caused all their dogs' problems. They had Dale to back them up, care for the orchard, help with intake, and do odds and ends. And they had Mattie! She was great with customers, great with dogs, and knew how to answer phones. What more could they ask for? He had even left detailed instructions that covered every aspect of the business in the cookhouse, along with letters to everyone meant to serve as an apology of sorts—and for Rich, contact information and monthly payout amounts for the new co-owners, Loke and Malak. He wasn't about to tell Mattie that last bit. None of her business. Not yet anyway. Would she kindly go downstairs and enjoy her day off with a space pill or two? He would call her from Florida. He was going to be fine. They all were. And when was the last time *anyone* in the family Temmens had been able to say that with sincerity?

At the time, Gene's speech seemed to do the trick. Mattie had begun to relent. Then Rich called, tried to get Gene on the phone. Gene refused. Whatever Rich had to say wasn't going to deter him, and when Gene asked his mother what precisely Rich wanted, she couldn't get a proper answer. Bad reception. But whatever his brother had said to Mattie kicked his mother into high gear. She explained he couldn't leave, that Rich had said so. Well, Gene countered, Rich said a lot of things, often to people who didn't exist. Mattie was not deterred. She went to work, throwing his clothes into the goat pen, making off with his bag, and while he'd been occupied rescuing what articles could be salvaged from Tapioca and Banquo and pulling his now sopping-wet bag from the horse trough, he discovered that she had made off with his wallet. All the while she harangued him, telling him to wait for Rich to come home, to reconsider. Think about James, about Rich, about her and the sweet muffins. They needed him, didn't he see that?

Thing was, Gene had tried to see it from her point of view. He really had. But as the hours passed, his anger and frustration had begun to boil. He was supposed to be on the road. He was supposed to be moving on with things—from Columbia—and catching I-5 all the way down to SR 90, then West across the state to his new subtropical home. Point was, he was supposed to be *gone.* But he wasn't. He was stuck, his wallet hidden somewhere, his bag sopping wet, his clothes chewed by goats. As he stood before her on the stairs, he was fast approaching a meltdown.

"Three," he said.

She made to swat him, but he was ready. He ducked the blow and wrested the newspaper from her grasp, flinging it over the stair railing.

"Why do you have to leave?" Mattie said as she gripped the banister, presenting herself as a human roadblock.

"How many times do I have to say it?" said Gene.

"Until it makes sense. We're finally back to something resembling a family and you got to up and leave. Rich wants you here. I want you here. Them dogs out there sure as hell want you."

"What about what *I* want?" said Gene. "Got to babysit Rich's ideas? Got to pick up after everyone else? Where was anyone to help me when I was down and out?"

"You never asked!"

"Didn't have to," Gene said with more heat than he intended "Already knew the answer. Now scoot. I'm going to Florida."

He didn't like the things he was saying. They were true, yes, but he didn't like the way they sounded coming out of his mouth. Like someone else was talking through him, someone meaner, dumber.

"But this is your *home,*" said Mattie.

"Home? *Home?* Have a gander."

Gene gestured about to indicate every offensive grievance; the walls that needed a new lick of paint; the stairs with their missing banister rails and patched steps, lined with a faded, ragged runner pockmarked with cigarette burns from when Mattie used to smoke; the upstairs bathroom with the crooked door that never quite shut, and the shower with hot and cold taps reversed so that, even twenty years on, a man could still accidentally scald or freeze himself before he realized his mistake; the floorboards in the hall, warped from too much humidity and threatening to give out; the rickety air conditioners jammed into bedroom windows and the old sheets and blankets used to insulate the space between the units and the frames; the ceiling with the brown water spots and the roof above that, no matter how often it was patched, sprung a new leak every April, guaranteed; the bedroom in which Gene had grown up, the pastiche of playing cards that both decorated one wall and masked the crumbling plaster that Dale had sworn, and thus failed, to fix. The list went on and on.

To all of those things Gene gestured, and to Mattie, and to himself, to every impotent minute he'd spent beneath the roof of that crumbling old house, and to every minute he'd spent with barely a dime to his name. He was gesturing at what he'd been looking at his whole life, what he'd been taking in and making part of himself whether he wanted to or not, and now he stomped in sudden fury.

"Home?" he said. "This look like it to you?"

But as soon as the words left his mouth, he regretted them. Mattie's face, normally stolid, gave way to anguish. Tears slid down her cheeks. He didn't blame her. He heard himself. He *hated* what he was saying. He hated feeling the way he felt. Some days, he hated being who he was. But it was true, wasn't it? How, Gene thought, could he make her understand? Why was it, he wanted to know, that everyone else in the family could do as they pleased, live whatever life they wanted to live, and no one expected otherwise? But not Gene. The prodigal son. The black sheep. The eternal fuck up. Why, he wanted to know, was it okay for Rich to rope him into a business he helped start out of desperation, but when he decided to move to Florida and put his time and energy into something that was all his own, something he had dreamed up, something that would *still* help his wayward family that *he and he alone* had to justify his choices?

Why couldn't they understand that? Why couldn't they let him go?

"Yes, it does," Mattie said in a choked voice. "It does look like home."

"Mom," said Gene.

"Wallet's in the toaster," she said. She wiped away the tears as soon as they fell.

The anger went out of Gene like air from a punctured balloon. He loved his mother, he truly did, but she would never understand. What he wanted wasn't what she wanted—a family, a couple of kids, a house, a steady job. Happiness. But had she ever really had it? He remembered her younger, hair bound in a kerchief, sitting at the kitchen table, smoking a cigarette and rubbing the arch of her foot. In her other hand, a glass of red table wine. She had just gotten home from work and was pointedly *not* asking where Dale was, because she knew he was at Andre's and she had exactly three hours to fix dinner, get Gene and Rich in bed, and hustle over to her next job.

Gene watched his mother shuffle downstairs. She would get over it. In time, they all would. He waited until she was in the living room, then descended to the kitchen and retrieved his wallet from the toaster. There in the kitchen, he paused. Was Mattie right? Was he doing something monumentally stupid? Something wrong?

Doc came over, nosed Gene's hand, and looked up at him with wise brown eyes.

"You'll like Florida," said Gene. "Aside from the heat."

Doc's tail gave a little wag. He rubbed against Gene's leg, indicating that, whether he agreed with the decision or not, he was in Gene's corner.

Back in the front room, Mattie collapsed into the chair beside the fireplace, dabbing sweat from her brow, sucking hard on her air. He knew she was holding it in, unwilling to break down in front of him.

Gene poured her a glass of iced tea and brought her a damp cloth. "Spike it," she said.

He found a bottle of peach brandy in a kitchen cupboard, dumped out half the tea, and refilled the glass from the brandy bottle. When he returned to the front room, Mattie looked more composed, her color even.

"When will I see you?" she asked as she took the glass and gulped down half in one swallow.

Gene took the damp cloth from her forehead, turned it inside out, and replaced it on his mother's mottled brow. "Christmas," he said Gene. He didn't need to add "maybe." She heard it in his voice and nodded.

"Call when you get there," she said.

"I will."

"You won't."

"I didn't mean what I said."

"You did. Now go." She bunched the washcloth in a fist and ran it over her sweating face. The house's window units struggled with the summer's brutal heat. It had to be eighty in the house, and it wouldn't be much cooler by the time she went to bed. He would get her better air conditioners. Good ones. Premium units. First thing.

Gene gathered his chewed-up clothes, jammed them into the still-damp bag, and went to the door. He was trying to think of something worth saying to his mother when the Datsun, covered in mud, skidded to a halt in front of the gate. It discharged two mud-covered figures—Rich and Dale, by the looks of it, the latter heaped on the former's back like a sack of potatoes. By the time Gene had gotten to the bottom of the porch, Rich had ambled over and set Dale down on the stops. One of the man's shoes was gone and his ankle was swollen and purple.

"What happened to his ankle?" said Gene.

Mattie had appeared from the house, tank in tow. "Why y'all so muddy?"

Gene was about to echo her question, ask his brother and father what the hell they'd been up to when something struck him in the chest, hard enough to knock him off his feet and send him sprawling in the mud. He stared up in disbelief as Rich hovered over him. In a flash his brother had him by his shirt, had hoisted him off the ground and was holding him aloft.

"You sold him!" Rich hollered. Gene felt his brother's fists against his chest, saw a look in Rich's eyes that could scarcely be believed. Rage. Pure, unfettered rage. And anguish.

Before he could say anything, Rich released him, and Gene fell again into the mud. He scrambled back, prepared for an onslaught. But Rich had backed off and stood with his hands over his eyes. What the hell was going on?

"Rich," Gene said as he got to his feet, hands out to ward off any incoming blows. "Talk to me. Who sold what? What happened to dad's leg?"

"Chanticleer," Rich said through his teeth. His hands balled into fists. "They killed him."

Gene's heart skipped a beat. "Killed him? Who?" He turned from Rich to Dale. "What's he talking about?"

But his father only glared up at him from the steps. "Show him the trunk," said Dale.

Before Gene could protest Rich grabbed hold of him and dragged him to the Datsun. His brother's fingers were so tight around his arm that Gene thought Rich might snap it in half. But when they reached the car, Rich let go, opened the trunk, and peeled back the raincoat. At first Gene didn't understand why Mattie cried out or Rich began to sob, for whatever it was he gazed upon was so covered in mud and muck as to be unrecognizable. Then he saw the snout, the ears, the crazy eye. He saw the blood. It was Chanticleer, his legs tucked up underneath him, muscles forever tensed. The dog's face was locked in a terrified snarl, so unlike his loving, easy-going demeanor that Gene scarcely recognized him. Gene touched the dog, the fur stiff as bristles, the body beneath his fingers cold. Beside him, Doc began to whimper.

"We tried to make it to a vet," Dale said as he limped over, aided by Mattie. "It was too late."

"Oh God," said Mattie. "The sweet muffin. Who did this?"

"Lerne," said Dale. "Who else? Goddamn it, Gene. Why didn't you listen?"

Gene felt his body grow cold. Something happened inside him—a door slammed open, a window was thrown wide. He heard himself as if at a great distance. "I didn't know," he was saying. "I had no—"

His brother's voice shattered whatever he had been thinking. "You did," Rich roared. "We told you! But you don't listen. You never do. And it's them that pay for it."

"Dog fighters," said Dale. "A whole ring. We drove fast as we could but he never had a chance."

The look in the dog's eyes, the wounds on him—Gene had seen them before. He knew what bait dogs looked like after the fact. The truth hit like a cannonball to the gut. Gene had trusted Lerne because he had well and truly believed he had helped the man get over his fear. He hadn't. Lerne wasn't afraid. He was something else. Inhuman. And hot shot Gene, the slickest of the slick, had helped him close the circle.

Gene turned and retched beside the car. His stomach crumpled and pushed out everything he had eaten that, everything he had ever *thought* about eating. Meanwhile, Dale talked.

"We got pictures," said Dale. "It ain't just him. Those other dogs are going to get the same."

Gene retched and retched. Meanwhile, his feelings caught up. They were right, his brother and father. They had *been* right. And Gene had gotten suckered. But that wasn't what ripped him up inside. It was the body of Chanticleer, the knowledge that the other dogs he had given to Lerne's care had suffered the same fate. It was the fact that he *knew* something was off about the whole thing, that he had ignored his instincts, ignored every warning flag, in favor of self-interest that hit him hardest. The nausea fled, replaced by rage, and crystallized into a decision. He spat and wiped his mouth on his sleeve. Too late for Chanticleer, he thought as covered the dog. But not for the rest of them.

"You call the cops?" said Gene.

Rich nodded. He'd sat against the car, staring off into the rain. It was blood, Gene realized—those dark stains all over his brother's hands and clothes. There were things coming, Gene knew. Feelings, thoughts, realizations—many yet to come. For now, he had to take them one at a time, be decisive, act. And all he could think of, all he could see, was a descending cloud of rage.

Gene shut the trunk. "Show me the pictures," he said. "That's step one. Then we clear out the back of the truck, get some things from the barn and basement. And then we go to work."

Rich blew a honker of snot into the dirt. He looked defeated. But not done. Not by a long shot. "What we going to do?" he said.

Gene stared hard at the trunk. Hours ago, Chanticleer had been an unlikely adoptee destined for what was supposed to be the good life. Now, beneath the raincoat, the crazy eye stared off into nothing. Son of a bitch was going to pay. Gene promised.

He helped his brother to his feet. "We're going to get our dogs."

It was early in the a.m. when Lerne stepped forth from the gas station store, a box of powdered donuts in hand. He paused to take in the vacant gas pumps and quiet streets upon which little but service vehicles—garbage trucks and the like—occupied lanes. He looked at the city stretching in either direction, at the roadside trees and the greenery set to soak up the summer sun, and decided he, too, would soak up the light before it got too hot. Finer things, Lerne believed, required finer environs.

So decided, Lerne leaned against his freshly washed car and ate his breakfast. His spirits were high, elated such that he hadn't slept all night. Simply visiting the pit and seeing the dogs lined up had almost been too much, and only with great difficulty had he restrained himself from drawing a new dagger of Persian heritage and carving the animals one by one. He'd driven back to Columbia, had a little fun with a woman of the night, gorged himself on lust. Like all the other times it wasn't enough. He always had to edge things forward with good, cold steel. And after all the mess had been cleaned up and Llewellyn sent to dispose of the remains, he'd shaved and showered and dressed in baby blue linen and ventured forth for sustenance.

He pinched a donut between his fingers, scrutinizing its exterior. The powdered sugar fairly gleamed, faintly metallic in the sunlight. All things of worth, he realized, took their cues from better things.

Sated, he retired to the cool dark of the Kompressor's interior and mixed a new batch of the brew, more potent than ever. It sang in his blood, crackled in his brain. Things once mysterious were beginning to make sense. His manipulation of the Temmens, his conquering of the dog fear, and his expansion into the Charleston underworld via Marco's dog fighting rings—so much accomplished in so short a span of time. Gracefully and with tact. He was better, stronger than ever. What had begun with the saber had grown exponentially. And his appetite with it.

A call interrupted his meditations. The ID read Charleston but it wasn't Marco. A new client? A new business prospect? Was Lerne's name already being bandied about? Spoken of in great esteem? He answered, prepared to be venerated, and received instead a voice screaming in broken English. It was the fat Spaniard after all.

"You fuck," the man screamed. "You shit, you worm!"

"What's the matter?" said Lerne.

"The dogs, the fucking animals, why you no tell me? Now the police, they lock me up! Madre de Dios, I get loose and I come and kill you, fucker."

"What police? Where?"

But Marco had hung up. In Lerne's stomach a gaseous bubble of fear burst. Had the pit been raided? Had the dogs somehow failed to live up to expectations? No, something was wrong. If the authorities had pinched Marco—and it seemed they had—they would pinch him next. He called Llewellyn, and was told that cops had swarmed the house, raided the kennel. The henchman had barely made it out unscathed.

"Did they take the dogs?" said Lerne.

"Kennel's empty," said Llewellyn. "But that wasn't the cops."

Something pricked the back of Lerne's brain. "What do you mean not the cops?"

"I mean it was empty before they got here. Cameras are blacked, locks cut. Grease on the hinges. In and out job."

"In and out," Lerne said dumbly.

"Looks like someone double-crossed you," said Llewellyn. "I'll lay low until you call."

Lerne hung up, numb with shock. Double-crossed? Surely the henchman was mistaken. The fat Spaniard wouldn't sell him down river—not that quickly and not without cause or promise of profit. There was nobody else involved in the dog scheme, nobody else who knew. Then Llewellyn's meaning became clear. The dogs were gone but nothing else had been touched. Such a contemptuous, defiant act could only come from one who felt slighted, one who felt personally touched by malice and saw fit to respond in kind. A person willing to reach into the jaws of the lion in the galling belief that the animal would not bite.

"Temmens," Lerne hissed.

In a fury, he backed from the lot and peeled into traffic, careening toward the outskirts of town. The boy was supposed to be gone to Florida or some such. Why would Temmens betray him? How did he find out? Lerne had played him to perfection. Perhaps, he thought, Llewellyn was wrong. Perhaps it wasn't Temmens. And yet, in the bubbling acid of his stomach, Lerne knew it was true. He guzzled the brew, pounded on the steering wheel.

"*Temmens!*" he roared.

At the ranch, Lerne found the ranch shuttered, the sign turned to CLOSED. He bounded from the car and hurdled the gate. A hush had settled over the place, punctured here and there by woodland noises. Lerne briefly considered retrieving the broadsword from the trunk, then decided against it. There was a chance, however remote, that the Temmens were not in fact the culprits. He had to be sure before he brandished the blade. Because once he started with the sword, there was no stopping things. Besides, he thought as he bent to touch the stiletto concealed in his boot, if it *was* the Temmens, he wouldn't need much to take care of the matter.

"Yoo-hoo, halloo," he cried as he strode through the orchard. He attempted friendly airs, plucking a peach from a low-hanging branch. After one bite he spat it into the dirt. Small white worms writhed in sour flesh. Everything about the Temmens was riddled with pestilence.

Gene alone stood before the closed doors of the barn, an antique double-barreled shotgun nestled in the crook of his arm. So, the boy would make no attempt to escape complicity? Very well. As for the shotgun, Lerne knew it to be a ploy—the boy didn't have the stones. He sauntered forward, took the brew from his jacket, and raised the flask.

"Morning," he said. "Care for a nip?"

In response came the sound of many dogs barking from within the barn. Gene said nothing.

"A fine day," Lerne said. "Good sun, warm. And I'm wondering. Is them my dogs in there?"

"Not yours," Gene said in a flat, tight voice. "Not no more."

"We had a deal, you and me. We had trust, a bond."

"That we did. No harm came to the dogs, remember? But you went and did something else."

Lerne couldn't suppress a laugh. He sauntered forward, fearless. "Boy, do you get it? This is a mistake on your part. And not the kind you want to make."

"Hell it ain't," said Gene. "Dog fights. That's a new low, even for you."

"Don't pretend you didn't know," said Lerne. "Way down deep, when you brought those dogs, you knew. You had to. Because folk like you and me, ain't a damn thing we don't notice. That's us to a T."

"No 'us,'" said Gene. "It's you. I was dumb. I didn't listen. But it was you that took them out there. Now it's you who's going to pay."

"And who sold them to me?" Lerne almost doubled with laughter. "That's good," he said. "That's rich. Them words, you think they mean something? You think what you're saying has any weight? Boy, I have to ask you: Do you think this is over? Do you think you got things wrapped up to your satisfaction? Because if you do, you didn't get the memo. Here it is: Ain't nothing over until *I* say. You get me? It's my words that count. Mine that bear weight. Now you best pack my dogs in your little animal wagon and return them to my kennel. Else I'm liable to do who knows what. Give you a taste for starters."

For emphasis, Lerne produced the stiletto, watched the boy's eyes flick nervously over the blade.

"I ain't standing here to talk," said Gene. "I'm here to make sure you get what's yours."

"And what's that?"

Gene aimed the shotgun at Lerne.

Lerne broke into coarse, unrestrained laughter. What had Gene taught him about dogs, how one could tell when an animal posed a serious threat and when it was just puffed up with fear, bluffing in the hopes that whatever scared it would leave? It was the way, wasn't it, when lesser creatures overstepped their boundaries? One had to step in and correct them. Sharp, quick, to the point. And hadn't Lerne suffered enough indignity, enough outrage? Truly, he thought as he hefted the blade, there was only so much a man could take until other instincts took over. Other, better instincts.

"Boy," Lerne said, his voice quaking with fury, "you don't understand. You haven't been listening. I want to tell you simple. When we're done, you ain't going to have a mouth. I'll cut your face off, gag you with your own lips. I'll slice you ear to ear, you and your idiot brother. And when I'm done, I'll carve y'all's names in your momma's titties, you hear me? I'll slit her open and hang her guts from the trees and strangle your daddy with them, and before he goes to the other side I'll show him my sharp things, take a little piece each time, and I'll make him eat it. I'll choke him with your momma's goddamn tubing, you hear? Then I'll go in that barn and have a sit down with every goddamn one of those dogs, you get me? I'll skin the little shits, cut them every which way. I'll burn this whole rotten city to the ground just to hunt every last dog. You listening, boy? *You picking up my fucking signal?"*

Lerne took a step forward. Across Gene's face there flashed genuine fear. Thought he had what it took, did he? Wrong, so very wrong. And it would cost him dearly.

Gene thumbed back the shotgun's hammers. Too late, thought Lerne. A bluff like all the boy's bravado.

"How much you want to bet it's not loaded?" asked Lerne. Oh, he was going to take his time with the boy. He was going to ensure young Temmens felt every cut, every nick, every scrape of the blade all the way to the bone. Lerne was going to find whole new levels of enjoyment in what he did to the boy, to the whole forsaken family.

Then Gene said, "Doesn't have to be."

For a moment, Lerne could not tell what the boy meant. But Gene lowered the gun, and as if on cue, Lerne heard the sirens, the tires crunching on gravel. He spun and beheld police cruisers in the drive, the officers already making their way through the orchard. The boy had tricked him, taken him to task. Clever, very clever. Lerne would give him that. In a matter of moments, the police would have him. But not before he gave Gene the mother of all cuts.

As Lerne pivoted, he saw movement from the corner of his eye, and heard Gene's boot scuff dirt. There followed a sound, wood cracking bone, and Lerne found himself on his back, pain ricocheting throughout his skull. As his vision cleared, he beheld Gene standing over him and holding the shotgun like a club, the boy's features twisted into a snarl such that Lerne thought he would kill him. The rage, the ugliness. Delicious! Then came the police, barking at Gene to drop the weapon, grabbing up Lerne and cuffing him. A police woman kicked aside his blade. They cuffed him and began to drag him away. He saw Gene kneeling before the barn, hands in the air.

Just before they pitched Lerne in the back of a squad car, one of the cops broke open the barrels of the shotgun, presented it for all to see. Lerne howled, thrashing in his captors' grasp. Empty, both chambers!

Chapter 7

Three days after the arrest, Gene got a call from the detective and was told to come by. He drove down first thing in the morning, eyes still crusted with the scant few hours of sleep he'd gotten. Dale accompanied him, his father now the only member of the family still speaking to him. Mattie's disgust over Lerne extended to Gene's involvement, a thing she'd been willing to overlook before the man's crimes came to light. And Rich, shaken by what he'd seen at the pit and the brutal death of Chanticleer, wouldn't so much as look at him after they'd returned from raiding Lerne's kennel. Gene couldn't blame them. Only Dale, who knew firsthand the cunning tricks Lerne employed, offered sympathy.

At the police station, Dale offered to go in with him. Gene shook his head.

"You sure?"

"What he's going to show me, you don't need to see."

"Son," Dale began, but Gene motioned for him to stop. Whatever Dale had been about to say, whatever comfort he'd been about to offer, Gene didn't deserve it. He left Dale in the truck and went into the police station with Doc. The detective was at his desk looking nonplussed. He barely glanced up when Gene knocked.

"Coffee?" said the detective.

"Please," said Gene. "Black."

"Long night I take it?"

"Could say that."

While the detective went and got coffee, Gene sat before the man's desk and stared hard at the folder sitting front and center on the blotter. His guts shriveled. He already knew what the folder contained. He didn't have to see it. But he was going to see it. Even if the detective tried to dissuade him—and he wouldn't, Gene was sure—he was going to look.

"Got something for you," the detective said when he returned. He put Gene's coffee on the desk, then settled into his chair and drummed his fingers on the folder. "Not going to be easy. Just warning you."

Easy? Gene thought. What about any of it was easy? He sank into the familiar plastic chair where for two days he and the detective had gone over the story ad nauseam, revealing every sordid detail of his involvement with Lerne, his part in opening the business, everything but his involvement with the Texans. And like his family's stories, it all checked out. The pictures Rich had taken had been enough to get Charleston police involved. The fight pit Rich had visited, along with another found on the outskirts of the city, had been raided and shut down. Within the premises, police had found copious evidence of the brutal and terrible activity, and together with Rich's pictures, had been able to identify five of the dog fighters present that rainy afternoon. Arrests had been made, and it was expected that the state would press charges. As for the family Temmens, they were in the clear. They hadn't, strictly speaking, committed any crimes.

As to what would happen to Lerne, the detective still had no answer. The man was held on a high bail thanks to his stunt at the ranch, but the only charges yet proven were trespassing and threats. His culpability in the rest was problematic. Yes, there was paperwork showing Lerne had adopted the dogs from Sweet Muffin Ranch, and yes, it was his dogs that had been involved, but they couldn't prove Lerne had been at the pit or that he'd sold the dogs to Marco, the fat Spaniard. Not yet, anyway. Plus, Lerne had an expensive lawyer. He had money, connections. Would he get off? The detective didn't think so. But neither did he think that Hollis Lerne would do any serious time.

And time was something Gene no longer had. Once the news stations picked up the story, business at the ranch ground to a halt. Folk about town didn't know what to think, weren't willing to risk their beloved pets on a place with possible ties to a maniac, criminal, and dog fighter. Even if Gene got the place up and running again, would anyone patronize them? Worse, the revenue stream to the Texans had suddenly dried up. Gene had sent the bookies every dime of what Lettuce had sent him—and would keep doing that as long as he could—but it wouldn't take the Texans long to decide he'd broken their agreement. Then he'd be right back where he started—pinched.

As for Don Lettuce, Gene called him, told him plans were on hold. The man was understandably upset, but when Gene told him of Lerne and the dogs, Lettuce was aghast. What filth, what trash, he'd declared. Soon as Gene got his situation figured out, he should let Don know. Business hadn't slowed. His offer was, for the foreseeable future, on the table.

"Appreciate the warning," Gene told the detective.

"Not for long, you won't."

Gene braced himself—not that it would do much good. He had seen the pictures Rich took. He'd seen Chanticleer with his own eyes. Didn't matter, though. Gene knew it couldn't prepare him for what was in the folder, and when the detective pushed the folder across the desk, he was proven correct. Gene thumbed through pictures of the plywood rings, the scratch lines painted on blood-stained concrete, the drains in the center of the floor clogged with fur and gore. Gene swallowed a hard lump and moved on to the next picture. A coiled hose tagged for fingerprints. Tire tracks in the mud. A mass dog grave, the bodies of the animals dusted with lye. Here and there an eye open, staring off into whatever cold darkness had swallowed up their last moments.

Gene shut the folder. He felt like he was going to puke. Of the twenty dogs he'd sold to Lerne, he and Rich had recovered ten from Lerne's kennel. One was buried in the orchard. The rest had been heaped in that hole.

The detective set the trash can down in front of Gene. "Makes you sick, don't it?"

Gene nodded, unable to speak. At his side, Doc leaned against his leg and whimpered. Gene dug his fingers into the arms of the chair. It was the only thing keeping him upright. That and the white hot anger that had not, would not abate.

"Got two dogs at home," the detective said as he collected the pictures and put them back in the folder. "Love the both of them. Someone did something like this to them, frankly, I don't know what I would do. Probably more than what you did. Now things are a little different."

Gene's grip on the chair tightened. "Different how?"

The detective sighed. "You should know. He got out on bail this morning."

Gene sat forward. The blood pounding in his ears almost blotted out the detective's words. "Out?" he asked. "Lerne?"

"Until trial."

"Got to be kidding me."

"Wish I was. We talked about this. Man's got money, a good lawyer. And the evidence on him is incomplete."

It took everything Gene had to prevent himself from hurling the chair across the room. "That man fed dogs to a murder ring and ya'll let him walk? That's how this works?"

Across the desk, the detective stared at Gene with a level gaze. "That's how the law works, unfortunately. I can't fix that. I don't make the laws. How it also works is you got involved with a known loan shark, a very shady dude. Don't play innocent. You knew who he was. You knew the risks. What did you think would happen?"

Gene scrubbed his hands over his face. What could he say? That he thought he could help? That he thought he was taking Lerne for a ride and helping his family in the process? That he hadn't paid attention, seen the warning signs? But that was the problem. He *had* seen the signs. He'd felt them. And what did he do? Did he act on it? Did he do his due diligence? No. He schemed and plotted and looked for a way out.

"What do we do?" he said.

"You do nothing," said the detective. "I keep an eye on Lerne. If he doesn't make his court dates, that changes things. But don't get your hopes up. And in the meantime, don't leave town."

Little late for that, Gene wanted to say. Instead, he glanced once more at the folder, knowing he'd see its contents every time he closed his eyes for years and years to come, then showed himself the door.

"We'll be in touch," the detective called after him.

Gene made his way down the hall and into the lobby, past the rows of folk awaiting booking, and out onto the building's steps. Early still and the sun was already hammering the pavement, glaring off the cars in the parking lot. He made it to the edge of the stairs before he vomited. After, he sat on the steps while the sweat dripped from his face. Beside him, Doc whimpered. He bent and gathered the dog to him, grateful beyond words for the feeling of him. Then he thought of Chanticleer, of the lye-dusted dogs heaped in the hole. Later, there would be plenty of time to think about them. Plenty of time to rehash everything he'd done wrong. Now, though, they still had work to do. Doc licked the sweat and tears from his face until Gene stood, spat over the railing, and began to amble down the steps. The dog trotted beside him, tail wagging, as if to say, *Get it together*. And Doc, as usual, was right.

Together they made their way to the truck where Gene climbed aboard, prepared to deliver to the bad news about Lerne. Then he froze. Dale wasn't in the passenger seat. Doc sniffed and gave a little grunt—all the warning Gene received. Two pairs of hands shot out from between the seats and dragged him into the back of the truck. A blow to the stomach took the wind out of his sails. Another slammed him to the metal floor. Curled on his side and gasping, Gene gazed up as the Texans materialized out of the close, hot darkness. At the far end of the truck, Dale was tied and gagged on the floor.

"What's the old joke?" said Loke. "If you want to find Gene Temmens, park outside a police station."

"Tell your friend to cool it," said Malak. "Or you'll be down another dog."

In the doorway, Doc was barking, ready to pounce. Gene snapped his fingers and waved him down. The dog shot him a puzzled look and inched back, still growling, until he was lying between the seats. While Loke calmly closed the door separating the cab from the truck rear, Malak pinned Gene's arms.

"Have a nice chat?" asked Loke.

"Never mentioned you," said Gene. "Not one word."

"We know," said Loke. "You don't squeal."

"That is your one redeeming feature," said Malak.

"And because it would incriminate you," said Loke.

"But one of your many *not* redeeming features is your ability to hold up a bargain," said Malak. "What did we say would happen if the business tanked before we saw our just dessert?"

"Maybe we weren't clear," said Loke. He turned to his partner, shrugged. "Maybe it's time to say it a different way."

Gene began to tell them about money from Florida, that they were going to get paid after all, but Loke produced a handkerchief and stuffed it in his mouth. Then he produced a hammer and calmly, methodically pinned Gene's hand flat against the floor with his knee. "Pick a finger," he said to Malak.

"Pinky," said Malak.

The first blow broke the finger. The second shattered bone. Behind the gag, Gene screamed.

"Pick a finger," said Loke.

"Ring," said Malak.

The hammer came down with a crunching thud. Pain exploded in Gene's hand. He screamed and writhed but Loke held him fast.

Loke raised the hammer and said, "Pick a finger."

"Pretty soon," Malak said in Gene's ear, "you won't be able to hold a leash. "Middle."

Another crunching *thud*. White flashes appeared before Gene's eyes. The pain eclipsed itself, became something larger and sharper than he imagined possible.

"No screaming," Malak said as he removed the gag, "or we'll put this back in your pie hole and do another three for good measure. Got me? Good. Next question. Do you know what we want? Why we're visiting you today?"

Gene nodded frantically. The tears were streaming down his face. He was good as dead if he didn't give them what they wanted. Except what they wanted was no longer his to give.

"Fifty grand," Gene said between gasps.

"Bingo," said Loke. "You give us back our money, we return your business and stop breaking your dainty little fingers. Simple as that."

"Lerne's got it," said Gene.

"Lerne," said Malak. "*Hollis* Lerne? Weird guy, skinny?"

"The nut you got locked up?" asked Malak.

The collectors exchanged knowing glances. Even through the haze of pain Gene saw his opportunity. He had to press the issue, had to know how it all connected.

"That's him," said Gene. "Why?"

"Little son of a bitch," said Loke. "He came to us, wanted to buy your debt."

"We told him no way," said Malak. "Figured you'd come through. And then you did."

"But here we are, back in familiar territory," Loke said as he gestured with the hammer. "Malak, would you replace the cotton? I'm tired of fingers. Pick a knee cap."

"Wait, I'll get it!" cried Gene. "I just need time!"

"Lower your voice," said Malak. "We're right here. Anyway, you're out of time." He began to stuff the handkerchief back into Gene's mouth.

"A week," Gene sputtered around the intruding cloth. "Give me a week! I'll get it, every penny, I swear it!"

The Texans paused, exchanged glances. Gene was promising the impossible. He knew it and they knew it. But working in his favor and still fresh in their minds were the envelopes of cash, the fact that he did, in fact, clear his debt, albeit briefly. Could he do it again? And really, did it matter? They had him. If he didn't come through, he knew what they would do to him. And if they couldn't get ahold of him, they'd turn to his family.

Finally, Loke leaned close, jabbed the hammer into Gene's chest. "One week," he said. "No games, no deals."

"This is your last chance," said Malak.

"Pay up in full or you're dead," said Loke.

"Deal," said Gene.

"Bad choice of words," said Loke.

"And if you try anything, and I mean *anything*," said Malak. For emphasis, Loke jabbed Dale with the hammer. Then the Texans released Gene, mopped their sweating brows, departed out the back door, and closed it gently behind them. They left behind the gag and hammer, the latter gummed with blood and bits of skin.

With some difficulty, Gene crawled over and loosed his father from his bonds.

"We got to wrap that," Dale said as soon as he was free.

Gene struggled to speak through the haze of pain. "Gauze," he said and pointed at a bin of medical supplies they kept in the truck. "Wait. Peroxide. Next shelf."

While they cleaned and wrapped Gene's bloody, broken fingers, Gene pulled open the door to the cab. Doc rushed in, licking Gene's face and whimpering like someone just got murdered. Close, thought Gene. Too close.

He kicked the hammer away and climbed into the passenger seat.

Dale fell into the driver's seat. "Where you going to get that kind of money?"

"No idea," said Gene. "Hospital."

While Dale drove, Gene tried to think through the pain. A feeling of stark dread held him. He wasn't just in trouble. He was trapped. They all were—him, Rich, Mattie, Dale—unless he found a way to pay off the Texans. But fifty grand? Where could he drum up fifty grand in a week? And if he couldn't, what else could he offer them?

What else was left?

Lerne was locked up for three days before he could get Llewellyn access to the money needed to post bail. As he waited, he came to new knowledge. He saw his life as a series of haphazard incidents populated by adversaries, each more cunning and depraved than the last. First, he'd been traumatized by a dog, chewed like a savory treat. Then he'd been orphaned, unable to so much as interest his bickering parents in prolonging their sad, nicotine-stained lives. Next, came the nude pistoleer, the man who had cemented the cowardly reputation Lerne had long railed against, and who in turn was followed by Kinsey West, the suburban holdout of old who had played him like a pawn shop fiddle. Then Dale, the vagrant patriarch of a family about as valuable as gum scraped off a sidewalk. That brought him to Gene, his newest, most cunning adversary—the one who had pushed him to the precipice of doom. It wasn't Lerne's fault if he'd acted untoward in the eyes of the law. He'd been driven to such extremes by a lifetime of abuse and disrespect.

He explained this to his lawyer. It produced no effect. The man was focused on the case and had little confidence Lerne could beat the wrap. There were too many photographs, too much linking Lerne to Marco who unlike Lerne, had an extensive criminal record. He suggested pleading guilty. Lerne might serve two years, maybe three.

"Years?" asked Lerne.

"Could be less," said the lawyer. "Depends."

"On what?"

"How bad the district attorney wants to push it. Whether Marco rolls on you. He might cut a deal, give you over for a reduced sentence. Then again, you could do the same."

Yes, Lerne thought as he sat before his lawyer, rigid in the chair. He could were it not a death sentence. If he rolled on the fat Spaniard, the man's people would hunt him to the ends of the Earth. His choices were to succumb to the authorities or turn traitor and number his days—no choice at all.

Then a new thought entered his mind. At each and every turn of his life, Lerne's enemies had taken him by the scruff and shoved his nose into his own mess. But who had allowed them such power save *Lerne himself*?

"It was me," he said.

"I didn't catch that," said the lawyer.

"I dug the hole, built the walls."

"In legal terms this is called admission of guilt."

"I did it—me. All they had to do was push."

"As your lawyer, I must recommend you stop talking."

Lerne returned to his cell and stretched out on his cot. He was in the pit, in the darkness, where feral things bit and tore. He was the worst of men—he who had not followed his heart, his truest desire.

He fell into a deep, twitching sleep, filled with dreams of snapping jaws and shining fangs. He woke bathed in sweat. The windowless cell was lit by a single flickering bulb affixed to the ceiling. The guard was standing in the doorway, explaining that Llewellyn had finally paid his bond.

"My sword," Lerne said when processing returned his clothes and hat. "And my knife."

"Held as evidence," said the guard.

"They're *mine*."

"Now they're the state's."

Lerne seethed. He dressed and emerged into the parking lot and was blinded by the sun. Gradually his eyes came into focus. He made out the Kompressor and Llewellyn standing beside it. The henchman gave a tentative wave.

"Tell me," Lerne said as soon as he got in the car. "Did they arrest Temmens?"

"I don't think so."

There is no justice, Lerne thought. The world is without a compass.

"Boss," said Llewellyn. "You all right?"

"I'm in a death pit of my own making. Drive."

"We got to talk about Marco," said Llewellyn. "He's out, too."

"I said drive. We'll talk later."

At home Lerne found little solace. All that remained of the kennel was an empty shell on a concrete slab. His gardens had been mangled, the flowers trampled, the bushes uprooted. Everywhere about his manicured lawn were the tracks of the authorities, dirt on his marble patio, gravel thrown in disarray on the drive. In the house there were more muddy prints, much general disorder. He could imagine them in their grimy boots, traipsing through his houses, touching, searching. A panic entered him.

"The other houses," said Lerne. "They get in them, too?"

"The few I been to," said Llewellyn.

"But not the armory?"

"They never found it."

Relief flooded Lerne. All those gleaming blades, his most beloved collection. He went into the secret room, among the treasures, touching lightly, and stopped before the empty places where the broadsword and the stiletto had resided. He would never retrieve those weapons, never again feel their cool confidence in his hand. But he had others, plenty of options. For instance, the well-honed kidney dagger he took from its mooring. Lerne preferred the layman's name: the bollocks dagger, so named for the two round protrusions just below the hilt that resembled swollen testicles.

"Boss, I know you said later, but we *got* to talk about Marco."

"So, talk. What do I care?"

"He said he was coming by."

"Let him in when he arrives," said Lerne.

"You serious?"

"Why not? He can't do me any worse. Not if he doesn't want me making things worse for him. It's leverage. Just let him in."

Llewellyn went away. Judging by the look on his face as he exited, he was trying very hard to mask his skepticism. Lerne cared little. Left alone among his treasures, he needed release, rejuvenation. He fondled the dagger and himself. True and terrible steel, unwavering in purpose. Why hadn't he listened? Why hadn't he taken the good lessons to heart? The weapons had never faltered, never failed him. And they never would. A climax nearly took him off his feet. A release, yes, but not enough. There was work yet to do.

He limped away to shower and dress in fine beige seersucker, baby blue boots. Then he made a new brew of methadone and lithium, a twist of bennies, a zing of spiced rum. The perfect concoction to get the heart beating at *just* the right tempo and keep it there, steady. The doorbell rang, followed by a scuffle at the door and some shouting. The fat Spaniard's voice carried through the house. Lerne met him in the living room and dismissed Llewellyn.

"You owe me," Marco was saying, red in the face. "This—who? Temken?"

"Temmens," said Lerne. "It's a family."

"A family?"

"Cockroaches," said Lerne. "They live in holes. Say what you got to say and let's have done."

Marco's face screwed up in disbelief. "Jokes? This no funny. I put a lot of money into this. The people back me, they are no pleased either. Mark words, you will pay or I make life hell."

Pay? thought Lerne. He was burdened with treachery, fighting for his life, and that man was worried about *money?* Lerne was happy to oblige. He took several large bills from his wallet and threw them into the air, very flippant.

The fat Spaniard glared. "You throw life away," he said.

Lerne doubled over laughing. Then, all at once, his laughter cut off. By God, the fat fuck was right. Life, death. At last, he understood. "I got life," he said. "Let me show you."

The fat Spaniard's cheeks turned from scarlet to purple. But he followed Lerne into the bedroom, then into the secret armory. Marco ran his gaze over the weapons, the suit of mail. He touched the English longsword and when he withdrew his hand a greasy fingerprint remained on the polished steel.

"Here it is," Lerne said in a voice thick with the heat of revelation.

"Is what? Antiques? What you talking about?"

"*This* is life and death."

Marco wiped his sweating brow, glanced around, and shook his head. "You no understand. My English is not good? I try better. This is very serious. And these toys, baubles, they will not save you. My people, they kill you. Only I protect. Now tell me what you say to police?"

But Lerne was no longer listening. It was bad enough to have the man in his home, to have the fat fucking pig sweating in his armory, pawing at his treasures. That was all *one* thing. It was *another* thing entirely for him to make threats. Lerne was sick of threats. He was sick of being pushed around. No more taking it from the common rabble: the Marcos, the Kinsey Wests, the Temmens. No more taking it from anyone. Time, in fact, to start giving back.

"There, behind the axe," said Lerne. "Money in bags. Take all you are owed."

"Where?" asked the fat Spaniard.

"Right before you."

While the fat Spaniard craned to search, Lerne slipped the fine English longsword from its mooring and rubbed the man's fingerprint from the blade. The instrument of his ascent. Only proper, then, to name the weapon, baptize it.

"I dub thee Shadowcast," Lerne said to the sword. "The malignant, the unholy."

The fat Spaniard's eyes bulged as the blade went into his belly. Lerne worked the sword a while, watching the blood gush as the fat Spaniard's face contorted. After a while the man went slack all over, falling among the weapons. Lerne wrested free the sword and began to pick through his weapons, intent on choosing the proper implement to finish the man. He didn't want him expiring quickly, not like Roy or the whores. For there before him was the release for which he'd long searched, and he wanted time, sweet time, to savor every second.

He selected the bollocks dagger and was about to resume his good work when something caught his eye. It was Roy's hat, hanging from a peg. A sign, an omen. Fortunes had aligned. He set the hat atop his head, adjusted it to a raucous tilt, and turned to receive the fat Spaniard's appraisal. The man was trying to staunch his gushing stomach.

"A priest," he said. "Please get."

"It's me," said Lerne. "I've arrived."

"The rites!"

"Get anointed," Lerne said as he bent to his work. "Suffer every bitter drop."

At the hospital, Dale waited in the lobby while they set and cast Gene's broken fingers. When his son emerged with a volleyball for a hand, Dale was on his third cup of crappy hospital coffee and wanted nothing more than to get home and in bed. But Gene was hungry—and so was Dale, for that matter—and anyway they needed to talk, Dale's insistence.

They stopped at a bar and ordered burgers and cold beers and Dale sat patiently while Gene told him about the Texans, Lerne, all the wheeling and dealing, all of it. The long and short of it was that they needed to find a way to drum up fifty grand and pay off the Texans or Gene—and by extension the rest of the family—were dead meat. That wasn't what bothered Dale the most, though. While Gene struggled to get his burger to his mouth, one thought kept ping-ponging around in Dale's skull: This was all his fault.

True, he hadn't cut any deal with any Texans. He hadn't sold half a business to a loan shark. Also true. But Dale knew damn well who had set the precedent for his youngest son. Gene had learned all his tricks from Dale, consciously or otherwise, had studied every pitfall of Dale's life and made them his own—amplified them to preposterous proportions.

None of which mattered now. They were in and deep. Time was running out. And far back in Dale's mind, a long dormant plan rose to the surface. He had considered the plan before and always dismissed it as too reckless, too risky. That was then. He had seen what Gene was up against. The Texans weren't going to grant them an extension and Lerne was out on bail. They were all out of options. Save one.

"Sit tight," he told Gene. His youngest nodded groggily. Half the burger had found its way down his chin.

Dale slipped away and called James, told him to come get Gene, and gave him the address. Then he dashed out to the truck, backed from the parking lot, and sped away toward the ranch. He found the place quiet—the dogs bedded in the barn, Rich puttering in there with them. So far so good. But the front door was locked, and Mattie glared at him when he knocked.

"You forget where you sleep?" she said through the screen door.

"Need a few things from upstairs," said Dale. "Clothes."

Mattie frowned, but the deadbolt drew back, and the door opened. Dale went straight for the stairs. He had to move quick.

"Where's Gene?" Mattie called from the bottom of the stairs.

"With James," said Dale. That, at least, was true. By then, he had already crept into the old study and found what he was looking for. For a moment he paused to take in the gravity of what he was about to do. If it went wrong, that was it. Mattie wouldn't just exile him. She would divorce his ass. She might even kill him. His sons would likely never speak to him again. He would be the architect of their doom—more than he already was. But if it worked? He could fix everything. He could save them all.

He grabbed a handful of clothes from the bedroom to keep up appearances, then practically tumbled down the stairs. Mattie was occupied in some other room. Small blessings. Dale barked out a goodbye, then dashed back to the truck and drove back across town—and farther still. When he pulled up at Andre's and strode up to the porch, no one paid him much mind. Inside, however, was another story.

The cashier did not take kindly to Dale's statement that he had no cash, no money, and was in fact prepared to throw him out until Dale produced his stake in the form of the deed to their land, the orchard, everything. Technicalities with zoning and the old cannery business, the former owner had told him. Legalities. At the time, Dale had considered it an object of curiosity, a point of interest if little significance. Now, though, it was the very thing to get them unstuck from between the rock that was the Texans and the hard place that was, well, also the Texans.

Andre himself was called over to approve. "What's this about a deed?" he asked.

"I want a big game," said Dale.

Andre sucked his teeth. "Here you come," he said, "hot off a losing streak, and expect me to stake you on a piece of paper."

"It ain't just paper," said Dale. "That's my land—all of it. Look it over. I sign it, you stake me. I win and I'll cash it out at value."

Andre snorted. "You win," he said. "Picked up stand-up comedy in your spare time, I see."

Dale bit his tongue while Andre looked over the deed. The wizened proprietor hemmed and hawed and sucked his teeth, and when he had made sufficient drama, he nodded to the cashier.

"Stake him for twenty," he said.

"Twenty?" Dale moaned. "It's worth five times that!"

"Says who? Twenty big or take a hike. And listen up. You lose tonight, you're out for good. Hope you get me loud and clear."

For emphasis, Andre patted the Bowie knife strapped to his hip.

Dale took his chips from the cashier and went out onto the game floor. He felt Andre's gaze boring into his back. Felt the eyes of the other players, too. He needed a table he could win. Big pots. Fast games. Easy cards. Then he stopped. At the table in back was Lula, her insults still fresh in Dale's mind. They were often the last thing he thought about before he fell asleep at night, and just as often the first recalled when he opened his eyes in the morning. He sauntered over to her table and took an empty seat across from her. Time to show her what a real card player was made of.

"Heard what you said about me," he said as he took the chair across from her.

Lula glanced at him and shrugged. "So what?" she asked.

"So now we find out," said Dale.

"Do we?"

"Now we play some real poker."

"Played better. Beat them, too."

"Guess we'll find out."

"Guess we will."

She waved over a dealer and while the man cut cards, she sucked her teeth and pushed a thick ringlet of hair behind her ear.

The dealer dealt. The game began.

Dale came up with an early flush and threw out some high nervous signs to keep Lula guessing. If she noticed she gave no sign. Fine by Dale. He would play the fool a while, appear to stumble, get scared. All the better if she took a few easy pots off him, felt like she was softening him up. Let her smell blood in the water. Then he would strike.

He won the first hand, lost the next two. Then he won the fourth and fifth in rapid fire fashion, small pots that hardly mattered. The pace—that was what mattered. He had to set the pace, count the cards, and stay cool, calm, collected. He let the pot swell and checked whenever he counted out a bad hand. Two more hands went to him. He was doing it, by God. He was winning! Across the table he scrutinized her face, searching for a flicker of concern, a worried crease, some tell that would instruct Dale when, where, or why she changed tactics. But as before, Lula's features registered zero concern. The literal embodiment of a poker face.

In the next game, Dale applied pressure, made rapid checks and even faster raises. By his count she had nothing better than two of a kind. He called her bluff, expecting to see her face contort as she learned what he already knew—that he was outplaying her. What she did instead was drop three of a kind. Dale reeled. Three of a kind? Where had he lost count? Had it been two sevens? Two fives? He glanced across the table and saw, for the first time, a change in Lula's expression. She was smiling at him.

Dale turned his eyes to the cards, tried to pick up the count. It was fine, he told himself. He had to be a little more careful, that was all. But then he lost the next three hands, each a sizable pot, and suddenly a cold ball of ice had found its way into his stomach. He wiped the sweat from his brow. If only his heart would slow down a little.

He took a hand, lost another. The ball of ice wouldn't melt. His heart was hammering. Across the table, something had come over his opponent. She radiated calm confidence. And the smile, that *goddamn smile,* was frozen on her face.

All at once a commotion erupted in the background, an argument, dire pleading. Dale turned and saw Gene and James, held by two burly bouncers, pleading with Andre. Reluctantly, Andre signaled for the dealer to pause the game and for Dale to come over, join them in conference.

Dale took Gene by the good arm, led him off near the door.

"What are you doing?" hissed Gene. "Andre told me what you put up as stake. Fold."

"Gene, listen—"

"We'll find a way to buy it back. Just fold."

Dale stared at his youngest in abject pain. He was prepared for his son's admonishment—expected it, even. What he was not prepared for was the stark, undisguised panic burning in the boy's eyes. He'd never seen his youngest lose his cool, go to pieces.

"Son, I was there," Dale said in an attempt to reassure his son. "I heard the Texans."

"No shit," Gene shot back. "And what do you think happens if you lose the land, the house? What if it gets sold out from under us? Do you have any idea what you've done?"

Dale's heart battered his ribs. Gene was right. Dear God, what had he done? But what *could* he do? Nothing. He was doing everything he possibly could. And he could win if his son let him focus. He called for a drink of water. The room was impossibly hot. Just breathing was becoming a struggle.

"Son," said Dale. "Listen to me. We need the money. They'll kill you. Then they'll kill the rest of us. Don't you get it? I can do this. I can win."

"Cash out," Gene pleaded. He was practically in tears. "Please, Dad. Please."

"I can't," said Dale.

"Like hell."

"He means he's under the stake," Andre said as he sidled over. "He cashes out now, he forfeits what's left. Which means the deed's mine."

Gene's eyes darted from Andre to Dale, back and forth. He seemed on the verge of screaming or crying or both.

"I can do this," said Dale.

Gene blinked. "You already have," said his youngest. He sank into a chair beside James.

Dale's face burned with shame. The boy was wrong. Dale could win. He returned to the table and his pitiful pile of chips. The water came and he drank it in two huge gulps. Hard to breathe. Hard to think. And his heart, good God, it felt like an egg too long in the microwave. Something was wrong, wasn't it? Didn't matter. At the rate they were playing, at the pace he had foolishly set, he couldn't last long. Nor could he slow it down. He didn't have the endurance anymore. Not like young Lula across the table. He had to turn it around and fast. Lady Luck, he prayed, for shit's sake, show a little love.

For three hands Dale and Lula made stale war, checking and folding, neither willing to go on the offensive. It was an opening, Dale thought. She was backing off, unsure. He counted cards and knew a two or three on the opening draw of the next hand signaled opportunity. And that's just what he got: his first card a two of clubs, his second a two of hearts. Don't give it away, he told himself. Don't look at her. Don't give her any sign. Another card each. An ace. Had his prayer been heard?

Another raise, another draw, another ace. Dale's hands trembled. He had it! If he was careful, if he played it perfectly, he could bait her into a game-breaking mistake. He raised. Lula raised. Dale paused, then raised again.

Then, without a word, Lula went all in, pushed her pile of chips into the middle of the table.

Dale stared hard at the pot. His ruse had worked. She'd taken the bait, hook, line, and sinker. She had thought his greatness gone, a remnant of days gone by, had she? Well, see here. That simply wasn't so. It was before him, his glory renewed. He pushed his chips forward, all in.

"Let's see the cards," said the dealer.

Dale turned them over. His two pairs beamed up at him. He looked across the table, saw Lula smirk. Dale's heart skipped a beat.

With casual grace Lula showed her cards. Three of a kind, queens.

Dale stared at the cards. The Queen of Hearts, that one figured. But the Queen of Diamonds? Hadn't that been discarded? Or had it been the King? Something inside his chest came loose. Noise in his ears, in his lungs. The room began to spin. A knot of pain tightened in his chest. He felt the chair give way, and the floor rushed up to meet him. The last thing he saw before the pain took hold was the cards, his Aces and twos plummeting amid the rest of the deck.

Rich sat in the cookhouse, slumped behind his desk. Beyond the door, lengthy summer light had given way to early evening shadows, and tenuous strands of purple and gold streaked through the navy dusk. It was hot in the cookhouse and Rich knew he ought to turn on the air conditioner, shut the door. But part of him just didn't care. He listened to the cicadas, loud as chainsaws. He ought to go on to the house, take a shower, go to bed. But he wasn't done thinking. Or drinking.

Earlier that evening, angry and discontented, he had taken from his secret stash a new bottle of peach brandy. Now he was deep into it. The liquor first stoked, then mellowed Rich's anger, so that his feelings tapered to a fine buzz. For hours he had been drinking and thinking about what they were *going* to do. Could they get the ranch started back up? Was there even a ranch to restart? What did any of it mean? He didn't know. And in that uncertainty, there were many emotions, too many for him to sort and catalog in so short an amount of time.

Rich sat up and groaned. The brandy was starting to bite back, make him lethargic. He tried not to look at the ghosts who, in their boredom, sat staring at him, unblinking, with their melted eyes.

You smell, they said. Get in the trough.

"That's not a people place," said Rich.

We are your doctors, said the ghosts. Get in the water.

Doctors, Rich thought with disgust. What had they ever fixed? Not him, apparently. Sure as shit not the ghosts. But they were right about one thing: He stank. Rich headed off to the barn, found the hose, and gave himself a light shower. Halfway through, he remembered that he had neglected to undress and decided to continue neglecting that step. He got himself and the surrounding vegetation good and wet. Now the outside matched the inside of his skull.

That improved nothing, said the ghosts. And we're still bored. Where are you going?

Rich drifted through the orchard, his heart a sodden lump in his chest. At Chanticleer's grave, he stopped to clear fallen fruit from the mound and tell the dog he missed him. He wouldn't mind if Chanticleer came back as a ghost. Maybe he would keep the others in line.

Fat chance, said the ghosts. And wasn't you and your brother going to make a headstone? This here's just a pile of dirt.

They were right, Rich realized. Gene had promised they would fashion a makeshift headstone to properly mark the dog's final resting place. But like everything else his brother promised, it had failed to materialize.

"Do it my damn self," said Rich as he ambled back toward the barn.

Quit crying, the ghosts said as they trailed him. It was just a dog.

"He wasn't *it,*" Rich corrected as the tears fell into his beard. "He was my friend."

What's it matter? He's dead, like us.

"He ain't like you. Y'all were an accident. The coordinates were bad."

What do you think happened to your dog, buddy? All you do is call in bad coordinates.

Rich paused. His hands were shaking. Something else was shaking inside of him. "It wasn't me. It was the JTAC."

Was it? asked the ghosts. What was your rank and designation? Who humped it with the radio? Do you even remember?

Rich fled to the barn, pulled open the doors, and ducked inside. Within, the dogs were barking and circling in their cages. From outside, he heard the goats bleating in their pen. It was the ghosts and their damned nasty talk that had upset the animals.

"Look what you did," he said as he pulled the light cord. He expected a quip, a counter from the ghosts, and when none immediately came, he made his way toward the pile of lumber they'd set aside for repairs. "Good," he said aloud. "Need a damn break anyway."

"I know you ain't talking to me," said a voice behind him.

A chill went down Rich's spine. A human voice, familiar.

He spun and beheld a figure clad in fine-pressed eggshell seersucker, a cruel-looking battle axe held at the ready, and a ten-gallon hat perched atop his head. The man's face was lost in shadow beneath the brim of the hat. But in the space between heartbeats, Rich knew who stood before him. Before he could cry out, the axe swept through the air. There was a deafening crash. Jagged bolts of pain drove into Rich's skull. Then he was face-down on the floor and hot sticky blood was pooling around his head. A pair of bright blue boots appeared in front of him. Then a fist bunched in his hair and yanked back his neck. The eyes of Hollis Lerne, burning with murderous rage, bored through him.

"Look what I did," said Lerne. "Look what I'm going to do. You get to see first-hand. Where's your brother?"

"Lub lub," Rich managed.

Lerne kicked Rich onto his back. "Never mind," he said. "I'll find him same as I found you. Crawl away if you can. I could give a fuck. I'll find you out there in the trees."

Rich watched Lerne take up some sloshing object. Burning wetness splashed Rich full in the face. The smell came in dizzying waves. Gasoline! Through a stinging blur he saw Lerne capering about, dousing the beams, the walls, the dogs barking in their cages.

Rich tried to turn over. The pain knocked him senseless. His eyes wanted to close. His brain wanted to shut down.

"Pray," said Lerne. "Weep, beg. It's all the same. No one's listening. No one except me."

With that, Lerne heaved the nearly empty can into the loft, struck a match, flung it against the wall, and was gone. Fire leapt up the beams, snaked along the floor. In their cages, the dogs were howling, trying to back away from the encroaching flames. Get up, Rich told himself. Free the dogs. Warn Mattie. Get help. But the pain in his skull had worked its way down his spine and legs. He felt the heat lick his hands and cheeks. He smelled his own singed hair and began to crawl toward the dog cages. He wouldn't abandon them! Then the ghosts were there, gathered around him. They pinned him to the barn floor, grinning in delight.

You're back with us, they said. Forever.

Rich cried out, choking on smoke. Radio static crackled through his brain. He heard the JTAC calling in the bad coordinates, heard the man's useless prayers. Then the barn roof all but vanished, replaced by blue sky striated with harsh white jet trails. Rich began to scream.

It was the war all over again. And the bombs were falling toward him.

She was the architect of great mess, Mattie was. It was supposed to be stir fry but several problems quickly arose. One was she didn't know precisely what went into a stir fry except rice and she was plumb out of that. Chopped vegetables surely made the cut, but she didn't know which ones, so she chose from what was at hand—an old onion, some broccoli, a cored pineapple. Also, wasn't there some kind of special pan involved? She didn't have that. Nor did she have anything to fry the vegetables in except canola oil, so she put it all in a cold non-stick with eggs and set the flame on high. The result was great slabs of singed egg-battered vegetables. She put some on a plate and took a tentative bite. It had all the qualities of a well-cooked shoe.

Mattie rolled her eyes over the shelves on the far wall, the cookbooks and recipe guides, all useless. She'd never had the knack. Dale had always done the cooking. His scrambled eggs? The best she ever had. His three-bean salad? Exquisite.

Mattie sighed and resumed eating her terrible meal. She wasn't one to waste food. Normally around that time, the peacocks would come a-pecking, ready to get loose with her and sit on the porch and talk about a bunch of nothing. Then they would go out to visit Tapioca and Banquo, then the dogs, and then putter about. Oh, hell, she thought, and put down her fork. She had no appetite. Not yet. But a space pill and the nightly jaunt around the ranch would change that.

She went to get the space pills and passed the double-barreled shotgun propped in the doorway. Not loaded. Heavens no. Just there, in arm's reach, in the event it was needed.

As she popped a space pill, Mattie thought fondly about the old days when she could just smoke a joint that she'd rolled herself. She and Dale used to sit in the living room, listen to records, and smoke themselves into pure love. Very often they ended the night in bed, working each other into ecstatic exhaustion.

Well, she thought as she shuffled about the house, oxygen tank in tow, those days were gone. But the records, at least, remained. She went to the stereo and looked through her favorites. Skynyrd's *Second Helping*. Dio's *Holy Diver*. Def Leppard's *Hysteria.* Bowie's *Diamond Dogs,* a particular favorite because she loved to howl along to the opening track.

A heavy thump from the front porch shook her from her reverie. She heard the front door handle jiggling.

"Rich?" she called. "That you?"

There was no response.

"Dale?"

A cold shiver of fear went down her spine. She went to the window and pushed back the curtain. A throbbing orange light blanketed the orchard. Thin gray columns of smoke rose from the barn.

All at once the face of Hollis Lerne appeared before the pane, a ghoul topped by a gray cowboy hat. Mattie screamed.

"Yoo-hoo, halloo," said Lerne.

Mattie drew back. She heard the screen wrenched open, then a grunt moments before the bloody blade of an axe cleaved through the front door. The wood splintered and trembled around the blade in a widening hole.

"Be a dear," Lerne hollered from the other side. "Open up. I'm friendly and bear presents."

Mattie stumbled back, fighting for every breath. Again, the axe blade crashed through the door. In moments the lunatic would be through. Then he would chop her to pieces. But as quickly as it had come, the fear solidified into grim resolve. Well, that was just the way, wasn't it, she told herself as she reached with trembling fingers for the shotgun. Leave it to Mattie to take care of everything. Good a time as any to teach that lunatic just who he was messing with.

"Just you and me?" Lerne piped through the hole in the door. "That's a shame. But at least we can take our time, right? Wait for the others to come home and get their own hospitality."

Mattie fetched shotgun shells from the old box on the mantle. No telling if they worked. Only one way to find out.

"I'm tired of your stupid voice," Mattie hollered as she loaded the barrels. "You want in? Come on, then!"

A final blow split the door nearly in two. Lerne's face appeared, framed by the hole. "Get your dancing shoes," he barked in shrill tones. "We going to *swing!*"

The face retracted. In its place his slender arm, grasping for the lock. Mattie closed the breach of the shotgun and cocked the hammers. Lerne's hand found the deadbolt and threw it open. Mattie's finger fumbled onto the trigger and squeezed. The recoil kicked her into the chair, knocking the air from her lungs. Howling erupted behind the door. Through the stars in her eyes Mattie saw a fine mist of blood on the jamb. She pulled herself to her feet and made it onto the porch in time to see the madman, now hatless, leaping down the steps and into his Mercedes. She fired the second barrel. The blast slammed her against the house. Fine white holes peppered the Kompressor's back glass as the vehicle sped away into the dark.

For a moment Mattie could do nothing but hold to the blasted doorway and suck hard from the tank. Her lungs, her chest, they ached. Spots of color danced before her eyes. No time, she scolded herself. There was fire to contend with, animals to rescue.

Then another thought hit her, this one more dire: *Where was her son?*

"Rich!" she hollered, hobbling down the porch and darting into the orchard. *"Rich!"*

She reached the cookhouse at a near sprint and stuck her head inside. Empty. She wheeled about, saw a curtain of flame where the barn should be. Sweet Lord, she thought. Please don't be in there. She ran as fast as her wheezing lungs would allow. Great plumes of smoke rose from the barn door, poured from the windows. Mattie paused before the conflagration, sucking hard from her tank. She would die if she went in there, of that she was certain. But if Rich was in there, it didn't matter. And the howling, terrified dogs—they needed her!

She tore a strip of her house dress, plunged it into one of the troughs in the training pen, and doused as much of her as possible with what remained of the water. She wrapped the strip around her head. Then she took one last deep breath from the tank before she pitched it into the brush and plunged into the barn.

The fire was everywhere, racing up the walls, choking the loft, creeping toward the cages wherein the dogs thrashed in terror. For a moment she was overwhelmed with the force of the blaze. The heat hammered her, stabbed her stinging eyes, crushed her withered lungs. Further in, she saw Rich shuddering on the floor, his face drenched in blood. A surge of adrenaline coursed through Mattie's body. Without a second thought, she hoisted her son to his feet, threw his massive arm over her shoulder, and started for the door. Instinct took over. She let Rich down and propped him beside the training pen. Still breathing. But still bleeding. She tore another strip from her housedress and wound it around her boy's head, watching in terror as the blood soaked through the fabric. All the while the dogs howled in the barn. She couldn't leave them to burn to death.

Rich's eyes fluttered open. He seemed to see her. His lips parted.

"Don't move," she gasped before she ducked back into the barn, rushing from cage to cage, opening the doors, trying to shoo the dogs to safety. Her new strength was ebbing, her lungs burning, and already the spots in her eyes were back, bright will-o-wisp flashes in her rapidly darkening cone of vision. Her legs began to buckle. She spun, disoriented. Where was the door? Above, a beam groaned in protest. She threw open cage doors, coughing until it felt like her head would explode, turning this way and that, struggling to see through the thickening smoke. First her lungs gave out, then her legs. She went down in a heap, gasping and choking. Somewhere beyond the crackling roar of the fire she heard the dogs barking. She'd freed them, she thought as her vision narrowed to a black cone. Most if not all.

Then something had hold of her. Mattie had sight enough to see the black Lab, its teeth clamped on her sleeve, dragging her along the floor. Go, she tried to say. Run. But there was no air, no breath. Then Rich was there, his bloody, bandaged head protruding above the smoke, his eyes glazed, and he was pulling her along, shouting something she couldn't hear. Somewhere in the chaos she lost sight of the dog. She tried to turn and look, but it was too late. There was a sudden splintering crack and a roar of fire as the barn came toppling down.

Part III: Dog Star

Chapter 8

Five days after the fire, Gene returned to the ranch in the dark of night. He strode about, armed with a flashlight and a bat, Doc at his side. This did little to assuage his fear. Lerne was still on the loose. The detective kept saying he'd get caught sooner or later, that Gene ought to be patient, that it was a matter of time. But Gene knew better. They weren't going to catch him—not before the man returned to settle the score. And as for time? They were fresh out.

At the ruined barn, Gene kicked at the rubble. It reflected the state of his family. The doctors said Mattie would recover despite the further damage done to her already tattered lungs. The burns she suffered were minor, and with a little bed rest and a lack of aggravation, she ought to be back on her feet in as little as a week. It was her story, though, which impressed them to no end. It was beyond their understanding that a woman with such advanced emphysema had relinquished her tank and forded the fire and smoke, much less nearly carried her six-foot-four, two-hundred-and-twenty-pound son out of a burning barn before returning to the blaze to free the dogs from their cages.

If only he'd been there, thought Gene. Way he figured, they'd just arrived at the hospital about the time Lerne attacked. Dale's color had been mottled, his lips blue. The whole ride over in the ambulance, he'd been gasping and grabbing at his chest. A minor heart attack. And in typical Dale fashion, he bounced back fast. Three days later, he was on his feet, sitting beside Mattie's and Rich's beds, annoying the nurses with endless questions, acting entirely ignorant of the fact that he'd nearly died in a poker shack.

All things considered, Mattie and Dale had gotten lucky. They would recover—mostly, in Dale's case, and somewhat in Mattie's. Rich was another story. Along with first degree burns on his arms, he'd suffered a chipped skull and major lacerations to the cranium; it was a few days of brain swelling and fever before he'd stabilized. From what Gene understood, he had roused himself to drag Mattie from the barn, then collapsed, comatose, which was his current condition. When he would wake—*if* he would wake—was unknown. Wait and see, the doctors told them. Wait and see.

Well, Gene thought as he prowled the grounds, he couldn't afford to wait for anything, but he sure as shit had seen. By all rights, the lunatic had won. He'd destroyed the barn along with half the trees in the orchard, and only the timely arrival of the fire department had saved the house—even though it and the land upon which it sat no longer belonged to the Temmens. Lula had bought the deed from Andre and, in what could only be described as petty, ordered them to vacate. They were broke, homeless, and wounded. Had it not been for Laura arranging temporary shelters across the city for the dogs, Gene and thirty-some dogs would be crashing on James's couch. The dogs, at least, had escaped almost unscathed. Only the black Lab, the dog Mattie swore up and down helped her escape was missing—presumed dead.

And that was it. Lerne had won. Except Gene had a nagging feeling that Lerne wasn't finished. Not yet. The way Gene saw it, they'd played each other, him and Lerne, point for point. But putting the man behind bars, threatening him with time in the slammer? That had been the last straw. Were Gene a betting man—and he was—he would wager that Lerne wasn't going anywhere, not until Gene and his kin were dead.

Unless, of course, the Texans beat him to it. Five days ago, Gene had his fingers broken. Time was up. Gene didn't have a cent of the fifty grand he owed Loke and Malak and he sure as shit couldn't scrape together that kind of cash in their current circumstances. Perhaps that was why a single, simple detail from Mattie's account of Lerne's attack stuck in his mind. She'd thought nothing of it, and when Gene had sat bolt upright and asked her to repeat it, she asked what could possibly be so damn important about a gray ten-gallon hat. Of course, Lerne *did* wear hats, just not the ten-gallon variety. The Texans wore those. One Texan in particular.

That little detail set Gene's mind racing. Gradually, he began to assemble the pieces. Something Loke and Malak had said during their demolition of his fingers: Lerne had tried to buy Gene's debt. But how the hell did Lerne *know* there was a debt to buy? And then for Roy to go missing, Roy who *never* spent more than a day away from his fraternal ball-busting brothers, and for Lerne to later show up wearing a gray ten gallon?

Now, led by the beam of his flashlight, Gene combed the porch, the lawn, the drive, scouring the ground to find what might be his one and only way out of certain death. Far from a sure thing—more like a fart in the wind. His phone was buzzing in his pocket as it had been all day. Each time he checked, it was the same numbers: Loke and Malak.

"A little more time," he said aloud.

It was then that Doc, who'd been sniffing around the sign, strode over with something held between his jaws. Gene shined the light on the object and nearly cried out in relief. Dogs, animals, the saviors of mankind. He bent and took the hat, trampled and wet with slobber but otherwise intact, and turned it over to peer under the inner sweatband.

"Just saved my ass," he said to Doc as he crushed the dog to his chest.

Doc dug his snout under Gene's armpit, wriggling happily. *Someone's got to,* he seemed to say.

Gene called Loke. The Texan picked up on the first ring.

"You're dead," said Loke. "Unless you start talking. Where are you?"

"Where else?" said Gene. "Ground zero."

"What's left of it," said Malak. "Got our money?"

"No," said Gene. "I got something else. You're really going to want to see it."

Loke sighed. "Stay put. We'll be there in fifteen."

Gene hung up, looked down at Doc, and considered how to spend what might be his last half hour on Earth. "Let's go pay respects," he said to his dog.

He went first to Chanticleer's grave mound and brushed away the ash. Next, he returned to the barn. The whole of the structure had toppled save for a few blackened uprights, a few ashen lengths of wall. About the place there lingered the heavy smell of smoke, burnt wood, and scorched earth. He walked the perimeter as he'd done several times prior, hoping he would find a clue as to what happened to the black Lab, but he knew it was useless. He prayed she hadn't suffered. But if she had, he reminded himself, it was his fault. Him and no one else.

Ten minutes later, a car came up the drive, tires crunching gravel. Gene recognized the rented Lincoln and told Doc to stay by the barn. The dog gave him an outraged look. *Going it alone?* the dog seemed to ask him. *Here? Now?*

Yes, Gene told him with a look. No telling if the Texans would even buy Gene's plan. Because one thing was certain: No more of his dogs would be hurt because of his fuck ups. Period.

Gene emerged from the orchard, stopping beside the sign. The Texans were standing beside their car and looking more disheveled than ever in rumpled cargo shorts and stained t-shirts. They were unshaven about the jowls and bloodshot in the eyes. The vehicle's headlights punched into the darkness, throwing long cones of light toward the ruined barn. Gene took a deep breath. Here it comes, he thought. The play of his career. The Texans approached.

"Where's our money?" said Loke.

"Don't got it," said Gene.

"Right," said Malak. He turned to Loke and shrugged. "What did I tell you?"

"Yeah," said Loke.

"I told you it would come to this."

"Yeah."

"But then I thought, no fucking way. He's got to be kidding. Maybe I misheard."

"Got something better," said Gene. He held his ground. Out of time. Do or die.

With that, he tossed the hat to Texans. Loke caught it, turned it over in his hand, and stared hard at the creased, crumpled crown. Then he did what Gene did. He flipped it upside down, checked under the inner sweat band, and when he had confirmed what he was holding in his hand, he tossed the hat to Malak and waited while his partner went through the same motions. Embroidered under the sweatband was a tag embroidered with the name of the hat's owner. *Roy*, it read in neat script.

"Where the fuck did you get this?" said Loke.

"Here," said Gene.

"How the hell did it get *here?*" growled Malak.

"Hollis Lerne," said Gene. "He's got Roy. Or he killed him. I'm betting on the latter."

"Killed him?" said Malak.

"*Hollis* fucking *Lerne?*" said Loke.

"Wore it the night he attacked," said Gene. "Didn't think anything of it until I remembered what y'all told me, that bit about him trying to buy my debt. Put it together with what my mother saw. And before you get any bad ideas, I got alibis. Cops already verified them. Same with my folks. We're not the enemy."

Gene couldn't see the Texans very well—too dark. But what he could read from their body language told him to tread lightly. "Where's this going?" said Loke.

"Thing is," said Gene, "I never told Lerne *who* I owed. Never told anybody. He didn't even know who I was paying off. He got to Roy, figured out I owed y'all money, and killed him."

"Why the fuck would he do that?" asked Malak. He drew his pistol. "Better have a good reason. Otherwise, sure as shit sounds like Gene Temmens trying to weasel his way out of getting his fucking head blown off."

"Do the math," said Gene. "If I'd gone to meet Roy, he would have brought me to you direct. Plus, y'all knew where I was—here—so you can verify my alibi without the cops. And you both know I'm no killer. I don't get mixed up with that kind of shit. Never did. But Lerne's a different story. Roy didn't know him."

"Roy's no idiot," said Loke. He, too, drew his pistol, and held it in a visibly shaking hand. They were on the edge. Right on the very edge.

"Right," said Gene. "He wasn't. None of y'all are. Look, I don't know how it went down. But I have an idea. Roy liked to do his own thing, right? So maybe that night he does precisely. And Lerne figures out what y'all are here for—figures he can take advantage, get my debt transferred to him, official or not. He could have gotten Roy away from the bar, maybe drugged him, told him some bullshit story, I don't know. What I do know is that Lerne was wearing the man's hat when he came here and lit the place up. It fell off his damn head when my mother shot him, and we all know that don't make a goddamn bit of sense. Roy never left his hat anywhere. You get what I'm saying? For Lerne to get hold of it means something bad happened to Roy. And between us, it ain't a stretch to imagine. Look what the lunatic did to me and mine. So, if you're asking me, yeah, I think he got to Roy. I think he killed him."

The Texans advanced without a word, kicked Gene's legs out from under him. He got to his knees and felt the pistol barrels against his head and broke out into a sweat. This was it, he realized. He would convince them or he would die.

"Why?" Loke growled. "Why would Lerne kill Roy?"

"Ask him yourself," said Gene. "Here's the deal. I'll get him, hand him over to you. If I'm right and he did it, you do what you please and we wipe the slate clean."

"How about this," said Loke. "We shoot you and go get him ourselves. Best of both worlds."

"Cops can't find him," said Gene. "Neither will you."

"And you can?" Malak said with a snort of derision. He motioned in the direction of the barn and said, "He got you, kid. You're out of your element."

"I'll get him," said Gene. "Alive. Whole. Or as close as possible."

"And if you're wrong?" said Loke.

Gene licked his dry lips. "We both know what happens. Just leave my folks alone."

The pistol barrels dug into Gene's forehead. His shoulders burned from holding up his hands, and it was all he could do not to piss his pants. His life hinged on a coin toss. They could shoot him then and there, blow his brains all over the orchard. But they still wouldn't know what happened to Roy. That was the bet he had made—that their need to know outweighed their frustration with him.

After what seemed an eternity, the Texans stepped back and holstered their pistols. In the glare of the headlights, they loomed above him as menacing silhouettes.

"Deal," said Loke. "We get Lerne, *alive,* and if we find you're telling the truth, slate's clean."

"We find out you're lying," said Malak, "or withholding information, or anything of the sort, and you're dead. No conversations, no deals. Dead."

"You got a week," said Loke.

"And then, Lerne or no Lerne," said Malak, "that, as we say in Texas, will be that."

"We'll be in touch," said Loke.

While the Texans drove off, Gene crawled into the weeds and sat shivering and sweating with terror, waiting for his stomach to quit with the somersaults. All in all, he told himself, that had gone as smoothly as possible. Of course, the Texans hadn't asked how Gene intended to find Lerne, and for that Gene was grateful because he didn't know. Lerne had a lot of houses, a lot of hiding places. Likely had a lot of vehicles, too, and money aplenty to wait out the current police search. One week to draw the lunatic out into the open. That meant Gene had to get creative. That meant he had to get to work.

When his shaking legs would finally support him, Gene rose, gathered Doc from the cookhouse, and rounded up necessities from the house. Medicines and breathing equipment for Mattie, clothes for everyone else. He went to the cellar, retrieved spare leashes, extra dog food, and some tools in case the truck broke down.

Then inspiration struck, first in the form of the bag of supplies he and Rich had used when they'd raided Lerne's kennel, then in two empty jerry cans propped by the cellar stairs. Lerne liked to play with fire? All right. Two could play.

Gene grabbed the cans and hauled them and the supplies up to the truck. The business of revenge was new to Gene. It offered him an opportunity to practice justice. It was one of his lesser virtues. But by God he was ready and willing to learn.

Mattie woke with fearsome pain in her lungs, in her bones. She was in the hospital with the hissing machines, the tubes in her nose, and the IV in her hand. Her lips were dry. She couldn't remember being so parched. And who was sitting beside the bed, just a rumpled heap of a man, but that scoundrel husband of hers, snoring like a sawmill, the soiled canvas hat tilted raucously atop his head. Ever since they'd discharged him, he'd been in that very chair, pestering the nurses, or down the hall where their oldest was refusing to wake up.

"Dale," she croaked.

He didn't stir.

"Foolsmith!"

He started upright, dazed.

"Water," said Mattie.

Dale took the pitcher and went to the sink. Ordinarily Mattie would have taken the opportunity to arm herself, take one of those magazines on the nightstand and roll it up good and tight. The better to bludgeon her husband. But the man's recent heart attack and her own frail state had forced Mattie to concede the ugly truth: they were getting old. Old*er*, anyway. A few more years and the oxygen tank might not be enough. She would be on the big machine day and night. Dale's heart wasn't getting stronger.

He brought the pitcher, poured a glass of water. He had even acquired ice. He smiled as he put the cup in her hands and despite herself Mattie felt the heat of her anger fade. Why couldn't she stay mad at him? Mattie wondered. Oh, she was mad, all right. Furious, in fact. He'd lost their home. They were homeless, penniless. And Dale was to blame, no doubt about it. What had Rich told her when she'd allowed the man to move into the barn loft? *He means well.* Mattie stared into her cup of water. Means well didn't account for diddly squat.

"Rich?" she said between pulls on the straw.

Dale shook his head. No change. Mattie couldn't suppress a cough of worry. "What about the other one?"

"Gene's off closing up the house," said Dale.

On the land you lost, Mattie almost said. But she saw a curious light in Dale's eyes and her pulse jumped.

"Fess up," she said. "What's he doing?"

"I told you."

"Dale, so *help* me."

Dale threw up his hands in surrender. Even with her laid up in bed, he was no match. That, at least, provided some small satisfaction. Her husband pulled the chair closer to the bed and spoke in hushed, conspiratorial tones.

"Way we figure it, Lerne ain't just going to go away," he said.

"Tell me something I don't know," said Mattie.

"And Gene owes those Texas boys."

"Get to the damn point."

Dale winced. For a moment, Mattie was afraid she'd induced another heart attack in the man. It would be like him, wouldn't it, to tantalize her with some crucial information before he dropped dead. And suddenly, in the midst of such musing, it hit Mattie under the ribs: they had come so close to dying, all of them. Folks lived every day with that nugget of truth lodged somewhere in the back of their brains. But to know it, to *feel* it pervading every waking second, was almost too much. She'd always thought of her family as resilient, hardy. Now she saw they could be broken like cheap pottery, and that thought *terrified* her in a way not even Lerne had managed.

"What is it?" Dale said, leaning close. "What's wrong?"

"Nothing," Mattie said, holding back the tears. She sucked hard on her oxygen and motioned for Dale to finish what he had to say.

"Point is," said Dale, "Lerne's got what Gene needs. And since the man's out there waiting to finish the job—"

"Gene's going after him," said Mattie. Proof she had raised an idiot.

Dale nodded, edging back from the bed as if he expected at any moment to dodge a blow. "He's the only one that can."

No, Mattie thought as she began to cry. Not the only one. Just like Dale didn't shoulder the blame alone. It was true he'd always been a bad influence, urging their boys to folly and ruin. He'd given Gene his knack for smooth talk, Rich his meek ways. But he'd also given them his never say die attitude, his courage—wait. Scratch that. Mattie had donated the courage. And like Dale, she had failed. She'd never tried hard enough to sway her boys from bad decisions, never laid down the law with proper authority. She had failed to find productive outlets for their talents, failed to protect them, to shelter their wayward souls.

By all accounts, they were bad parents. Her oldest was laid up with a head wound thanks to the crazy son of a bitch still at large. Her youngest was off God knew where, doing God knew what to fight the crazy son of bitch. And there they were, the mother and father of these broken, vengeful weirdos, laid up with age and frailty. What kind of parents let their children fight the family's fight alone? The bad kind. The kind Mattie didn't want to be. That, along with taking sass and lunatics hurting her dogs and the hospital's tiny juice cartons and lying in a goddamn bed all day every day and just generally getting shit-kicked by life, was enough. So, no, she again thought. Gene wasn't the only one who could go after Lerne. Not alone.

"Get my clothes," said Mattie. She threw back the covers, frowning at her own veiny legs sticking out from the flimsy gown.

Dale hesitated.

"Hop to," she barked as she swung her legs over the edge and coughed. "And find me a damn portable oxygen tank. Quick." The smallest movements were an agony. Every breath was hard fought and came with a dragging agony in her lungs. She inhaled hard on the machine and stepped down onto the cold linoleum floor.

"What do you mean clothes?" said Dale.

"Clothes, foolsmith! Fabric, finery! I can't leave like this."

"Leave?"

"Dale, if you parrot one more thing I say, Lerne won't have to kill you. Now listen. Get my clothes. Get my tank. Then I'm going down the hall to see Rich. Then we're going to help Gene."

"We are?"

Mattie slid her hand into Dale's. God give me strength, she prayed, for this man is going to die. "We're fragile," she said. "None of us will live forever. But you won't make it another day if you don't do what I told you."

"They burned up," Dale said helplessly. "Your clothes."

"Then run get some. The whole damn ward's about to see my behind."

Dale cracked a warm smile of old. "Sabers up," he said.

Mattie shooed him out the door. Alone, finally. It was taking everything she had to set aside her many, many, *many* grievances with the man, but she did it for the same reason she forgave Gene all his missteps. He was kin, and fine, she could admit it, she loved him, and anyways the whole lot of them were lost without her guidance. Lord, but she had to do *everything*.

Rather than wait for Dale to mosey about, Mattie found a spare tank in the room and hooked herself up. The little hose wasn't as good as the mask and machine, but it would have to suffice. She would see her oldest. By then, Dale should return with clothes. Then she would dress, and they would leave, her and the foolsmith, to eat a proper meal—no more mush—and get hold of Gene. Then they would come up with a plan—the only thing at which the lot of them seemed to be any good. A little family war council. Just the thing for the ailing soul.

But when she arrived at Rich's room the door was open. A nurse technician was stripping the sheets from the bed and most of the monitoring equipment had been taken away. So, too, had Rich.

"Where's my boy?" she said.

The technician paused. "Gone," he said.

"Gone where? He woke up?"

"Ma'am, he left."

"Left?"

The technician backed away in fear. It was clear what had happened. Rich had been abducted. Lerne had made off with her boy, was at that moment doing unspeakable things to him.

Armed with a water pitcher, Mattie stormed the nurses' station and unleashed her wrath upon the unsuspecting. She drove them before her, down the hall and under the desks, demanding to know the whereabouts of her oldest until security arrived, a doughy man in a too-tight shirt with a belt that hung well below his stomach. Mattie drove him under a medicine cart before returning to the desk. One of the nurses was barking codes into the phone. She let him know with a rap on the knuckles what impertinence would earn and was preparing for another round of interrogation when the head nurse appeared with a clipboard held forth in supplication.

"Ma'am, please," said the head nurse. "Nobody took him. He signed himself out. It's right here on the sheet."

Mattie peered at Rich's signature. There was no mistaking his wobbly handwriting on the bottom of a discharge form. Another nurse appeared with a bag containing Rich's clothes and keys, said he'd risen, signed out, and asked only for his wallet.

"Just his wallet?" said Mattie. "Was he alone?"

"Yes, alone," said the head nurse.

"You're sure?"

"Positive. Now will you please put down the pitcher?"

Mattie dropped her weapon, collapsing into a chair. The nursing staff emerged from their hiding places. The security guard, a long red welt across his face, scuttled away. It didn't make sense, thought Mattie. Why hadn't he told her?

"Did he say where he was going?" asked a wheezing Mattie.

The head nurse nodded and said, "Off to meet the man."

Rich left the hospital in his paper gown and stopped at the first ATM. The Army had just put money in his account. He withdrew several hundred dollars and crushed the wad of bills in his fist. The axe to the brain had opened new circuits, shut down others. For one, he no longer felt afraid of Lerne or death or even his own memories. The war seemed a passing trifle, the ghosts insignificant. What mattered was his new purpose. He would find the man who had attacked him and his family and treat him in kind. He was going to destroy Hollis Lerne.

Rich walked along the shoulder of the road and endured the honking of cars, the rude shouts of passersby. The ghosts were near, excited. They considered his present condition a wonderful turn of events.

What do you think you're doing? they asked. Because we like it. We *love* it.

"Shovels," said Rich. "Hot water."

What Rich had intended to say was altogether different. The parts of his brain that handled speech were jumbled up.

Well, the ghosts said, we hate to break it to you, but Lerne handed you your ass. He put a sizable hole in your head. They'd been there, seen it. Then they'd gone back in time to the war and gotten exploded all over again. And Rich had been with them! It was a wonderful trip, really, but they certainly wouldn't say no to more violence and brutality. Still, one thing worried them, and that was this: Rich wasn't in Lerne's league. That man would break Rich open and suck out the gooey innards. And while they weren't at all opposed to making a return trip to crazy land with Rich, they'd really rather him pursue some individual carnage first. Maybe he could, oh, they didn't know, steal a car, ram it into a crowded restaurant?

"Fresh fruits," said Rich. "Limes."

Forget tropical produce, said the ghosts. Knives, guns, that's the thing. Tell some kids they were adopted and push them into traffic. Find the elderly—any would do—and smash them against a wall until their glassy old bones turn to powder.

No, thought Rich. That wasn't what he had in mind. Warm gusts feathered his behind.

"Aid Rich," he said to the ghosts. "Where's pants?"

The ghosts paused, at a loss, and eventually pointed to a squat building in a strip mall decorated in American flags.

Rich crossed the lanes of traffic, heedless of honking horns and of speeding cars slamming on their brakes. His bare feet slapped the burning pavement. His gown blew up and showed his everythings. The ghosts trailed at a wary distance. Violence was one thing, but this kind of brazen nudity was altogether distasteful.

The store was Army surplus, devoid of customers. At the counter was a lone clerk, a gray-headed fellow reading a gun magazine. He took one look at Rich and scrubbed his hands over his face.

"Oh, sweet Christ," said the man. "Are you a Scientologist?"

"I'm not science," said Rich.

"Then can I help you, son? Can't help but notice you have a clothes problem."

The place was thick with military dress and equipment. A dummy wore a large pith helmet, nude save for several bandoleers stuffed with empty cartridge casings. Another wore a ghillie suit, hands on hips, a noticeable bulge below its waist. It looked inordinately proud of its artificial foliage. Rich approached the register and peered into the glass weapon cases. Handguns, bayonets of all varieties, knives large and small, combat batons, and nightsticks. The shelves behind the counter carried more serious ordnance: shotguns, assault rifles, flamethrowers and RPG launchers. Rich motioned, saying the first word his damaged brain could salvage.

"Spaghetti," said Rich.

"Fresh out," said the clerk. "Is there someone I can call? Maybe the police?"

Rich heard the snickering ghosts. They were in the aisles, watching, getting their sick jollies. He glared in their direction, then decided to try a different tactic. He opened his fist and the crushed wad of money fell on the glass counter. He pointed to his waist.

"Pants?" said the clerk.

Rich nodded. Behind him, the ghosts sighed in exasperation.

"Pants I can do," said the clerk. "Go down the hall and I'll bring clothes."

The dressing room was more a broom closet with a mop bucket, a toilet that gurgled, and calendars featuring women who had misplaced their shirts. A part of Rich's brain told him such women should be sexy, desirable. But Rich was in a different place and besides it had been so very long since he'd held a lover. He wasn't sure he cared much anymore. He traced their curves with a finger, struggling to find the words. Discus, grizzle, frieze. That wasn't it. But in a way, he'd gotten close. The women were just there to be ogled, used up by the eyes. There were people, whole lives behind the glossy smiles, and whatever he was touching, was gazing upon, was just the smallest part.

Getting philosophical, said the ghosts. They'd crowded into the dressing room to stare at the ladies. They tried to look cool but Rich heard the note of worry in their voices. They were right to worry. He'd changed.

The clerk knocked and fed articles of clothing through the door, one at a time. Underpants and cotton socks, combat boots, a vest with many pouches, camo pants and a black t-shirt with the phrase "Gone but not Forgotten" emblazoned on the chest. He told Rich he'd picked what he considered a solid outfit for a man recently released from a hospital. Breathable stuff what with the heat outside. He hoped he'd gotten Rich's size right.

Rich dressed and emerged to gaze at himself in the full-length mirror. With his singed beard and eyebrows, his bandaged arm and head, he looked like a man recently freed from long captivity. Very true, thought Rich. Like the ghosts, the old Rich had burned in the fire. A new Rich had taken his place. He had the combat spirit. Now he had the dress, too.

"Are you a vet?" asked the clerk. "I see your tattoos."

Rich hesitated, then flashed twelve fingers.

"Infantry, huh? I was Recon, Vietnam. While you were getting dressed, I made this up for you. Figured you'd need it."

A large duffel bag was handed to Rich, full of extra shirts and undergarments, a change of pants, and some extra socks. Into Rich's vest pocket the clerk slid a pair of mirror sunglasses. Then, while Rich watched, the clerk rang it all up, peeled off bills from Rich's wad, and cashed him out. On the man's face was honest pride, the look of a person who had taken not a cent more than he was owed despite the opportunity to do otherwise. Behind him, Rich spied a beverage cooler. He pointed, suddenly parched.

"On the house," said the clerk. "Vet to vet."

He cracked open a cold can of cola and set it in Rich's hand. Rich drank the bubbly sweetness in one long take. The sugar and caffeine hit him in a rush. His brain clicked over and began to hum.

"My talking," said Rich. "Is it better?"

"Much," said the clerk. "Welcome home, soldier."

All at once, Rich was overcome with emotion. He had entered the store practically nude and crazed and the man had treated him with incredible dignity and patience, well above and beyond the call of duty. Had the roles been reversed, Rich was not sure he would have acted in as admirable a fashion. He hugged the clerk.

"I'm sorry for all the naked," said Rich.

"Say no more," said the clerk. Though stiff in Rich's arms, the man clapped Rich on the back. "We've been there, you and me. In the shit."

"I was in Iraq. The JTAC called in bad coordinates."

"Too close to the blast?"

"A lot of folk died. Noncombatants."

That's us, said the ghosts. They clambered about, revved up at their own mention. Go on, they said. Tell him about us!

"No wonder you came in like that," the clerk said with a knowing look. "Things like that, you carry it around. Thing is, you got to know when to put it down."

"I can't," said Rich.

"Got to. Else it eats you from the inside out. Spent a lot of years walking around lousy with the things I'd seen and done. What good did it do? At some point, you got to walk away."

The ghosts pulled back, their enthusiasm drained. Let's go, they whined. This old blowhard don't know diddly.

But Rich ignored them. He was intent on the man's every word, his whole being focused on the message. He felt the old vet was telling him something crucial, something absolutely essential.

"How did you do it?" asked Rich.

"Stopped fighting," the clerk said as he jabbed a finger into his own chest. "In here, out there. Everywhere. I walked. Wasn't really *my* war—that's the trick. Oh, they sold us pretty good. Sold y'all, too. And whatever we did, good or bad, we're not there anymore. Folks can change."

"What if you can't?" said Rich. He was thinking about the need to destroy, how he couldn't rest until the lunatic was no longer a threat.

"You *have* to," said the clerk. "Sooner or later. Guess you'll know when's a good time."

The ghosts were grabbing at Rich's arm, trying to pull him to the door.

Let's go, they were saying. Hell with the old man and his bullshit. Didn't Rich have some warfare to get back to? Time was ticking. Lerne was out there.

At that moment, all Rich wanted to do was sit and listen to the man, soak up the old vet's wisdom. It seemed he'd waited years, burning with thirst, to hear the man's words like cool sweet water on his fevered brain. He felt grateful beyond words. But the ghosts had a point. There was work to do. He shook the man's hand and slung the bag of supplies over his shoulder.

"Thank you," said Rich.

"Don't mention it," said the clerk. "Before you go, want anything else? Pistol? Shotgun? I sure as hell wasn't going to sell to you when you walked in, but now that we talked, I'm reconsidering."

Rich looked toward the cases of guns, then at his bandaged hands. A gun would help. Two guns would help a *lot.* But Rich had other ideas. "Not today," he said.

"Here if you change your mind," said the clerk. "And good luck."

Rich went out into the heat. Seen through the tint of his mirrored sunglasses, the rush of traffic seemed less intimidating, the glare less bothersome. He went to the nearest gas station and purchased two large jerry cans, filled them at the pump. Then he set off down the road, unable to shake the vet's words. Rich had never been able to walk away from the war, never been able to forgive or forget. He still couldn't, not while the business of Lerne loomed. For that, he needed the anger his damaged brain was now providing, the fearlessness. He needed violence on his side. But what he didn't need, the things from which he *could* walk away, were the ghosts.

He rounded on them, the jerry cans sloshing at his side, and brought them up short. "He's right," he said.

Who is? asked the ghosts. That old man? He don't know shit.

"I don't need you. Go."

Go? said the ghosts. They stared at him in shock. What, besides the obvious, was wrong with the man?

"You're dead," said Rich. "Been that way a long while. I can't fix it."

The ghosts laughed. Fix it? they said. Why, sure he could. Think about it.

"No," said Rich.

Go back to that terrible day. Who was it, exactly, who humped it with the radio?

"I don't care," said Rich.

Hell you don't, said the ghosts. Ask yourself: Who dialed up air support? Who gave out the bad coordinates? Who sat there, whimpering and shitting himself, while the bombs fell on us? Eh, boy?"

"How come you got a Southern accent?" asked Rich. "How come you don't sound like you?"

The ghosts ignored him. What chicken-shit called in a strafe on a civilian highway? they asked. Tell us! What little shit-stain in an Army uniform doomed countless innocent people to burn to death? Don't remember the JTAC? Because *we* do. Want us to tell you, Rich, buddy? Want to know who the JTAC was?

"I already know," said Rich. "And I want you to leave. Now."

You don't get to pick what you want, the ghosts hollered. And you sure as hell don't get to walk away from us.

"Yes, I do," said Rich.

With that, he turned and resumed his stride. The ghosts gave chase, screaming their wordless, howling rage. Rich walked on, turning the vet's words over and over in his brain. He *could* just walk away from them. He *could.* They were just ghosts, just melted people, and they didn't have any control over who he was, what he did. They weren't even real. They were just parts of him, the worst, most terrible parts that he'd buried way down deep, the parts that knew who called in the bad coordinates. The parts that knew and would never forget the roar of the jet engines, the nose-dive the bombs took on the way to the ground. Rich imagined himself grabbing hold of the ghosts and dragging them, kicking and screaming, back across the years, back to the war and the highway. He imagined himself leaving them there on the hot asphalt. And when he heard the jets approaching, he turned and ran as fast as he could. He imagined the bombs detonating, the deafening thunder that shook the world from its moorings, and he kept running. He didn't turn back, not when heat from the blast crawled up his neck, not when flaming shrapnel rained down around him. He ran until his lungs burned, until his head began to pound, and when he couldn't run any farther, couldn't take another breath without collapsing, he stopped and turned and looked behind him.

He was in the woods at the edge of town. Dusk sun slanted through the trees. Birds and crickets made evensong. And Rich was alone.

He took a few minutes to catch his breath. His body, unused to such exertion, wanted nothing more than to lie down, take a nap. His head was throbbing viciously where Lerne cracked him. Rich pushed the pain aside and went on. Lerne had so many hiding places. And Rich had so much gasoline.

A mile from Lerne's house he was brought up short by the unexpected sound of a barking dog. The sound emanated from a nearby clearing that sat adjacent to the back road. Rich crept forward, staying low in the foliage, until he reached the trees. He expected to see Lerne or Llewellyn, possibly the pair together, and was surprised to see the truck—*his* truck—parked on the road's shoulder. More surprising was the dog presently barreling toward him. It was Doc, alive and well, tail wagging, tongue lolling.

A whistle brought Doc to a sudden halt. The dog looked over his shoulder and Rich followed the animal's gaze. Gene stood beside the truck, his left hand swaddled in a cast. He looked like he had seen a ghost. Rich stepped from the underbrush, crossed the road, and stood beside his brother.

"I don't forgive you," said Rich. "Not for Chanticleer, not for the dogs, none of it."

Rich had expected Gene's usual response to criticism of his character, the adoption of a bored, almost petulant look that begged the question: *You done?* Instead, his brother stood there, a look of acute pain on his face, and nodded.

"Me neither," said Gene.

"I warned you," said Rich.

"You did," Gene said in a voice so devoid of his usual cunning charm that it sounded like some other person, a stranger. "And you were right. Are right. I'm sorry, Rich. I know that don't cut it, but it's all I got at the moment. It's my fault and I'm sorry."

Rich was stunned, unable to remember what else he'd intended to say. Such a total admission of guilt was unheard of from his brother. For perhaps the first time in their lives, Rich beheld a Gene Temmens without his defenses, vulnerable. He looked miserable, angry, hurt. More than anything, he looked scared. That Rich understood. He knew what it was like to live in near-constant terror. And aside from Lerne, he wouldn't wish it on anyone.

Then Gene did something Rich would never in a million years have predicted. His brother held out his hand and looked him in the eyes. Rich recalled the last time his brother had made such a gesture—the night they'd agreed to start the business—and knew there was more to what was going on that Gene had yet told him. Lerne alone couldn't explain the haggardness he saw in his brother's features. But together, they could protect one another. Together, they stood a chance.

"One condition," Rich said he took his brother's hand. "You come clean about everything. Every last detail."

"Deal," said Gene. "Gladly."

Rich stared hard at his brother, scrutinizing his face for the smallest sign of dishonesty. To his surprise, there was none. For once in his life, Gene was on the level. His brother had sallied forth to do battle with Lerne, alone and terrified and out of his element. So had Rich. But Gene wasn't alone any longer. And neither was Rich.

"You thinking what I'm thinking?" said Rich. He prodded the jerry can with the toe of his boot.

In response, Gene showed him two cans of his own and the bag of larcenous tools. He had the shotgun, too, and a box of rubber buckshot.

"Need him alive," said Gene. "For the Texans."

"The Texans?" said Rich.

"Fill you in."

"We got time."

"No, we don't," Gene said with a worried shake of his head. "At least I don't."

"Then let's get to work," said Rich. He left his bag of clothes in the truck and hefted all four jerry cans. He felt, for the first time in a long while, a spark of hope. Dark was coming on fast and they had everything they needed. Gasoline, matches, and each other.

"What's the chance he's home?" Gene said as they locked up the truck.

"A man can dream," said Rich.

For three days Lerne lay low, healing, first at his home in Winnsboro, then, at Llewellyn's urging, in the back of an SUV, one of his many vehicles. He picked the buckshot from his arm with the bollocks dagger and a pair of tweezers and cleaned the wounds with peroxide. The brew kept the pain at bay. Antibiotic injections kept him from disease. Lucky the old woman's aim was bad. A little more on target, a little less door between them, and she would have taken his arm clean off at the elbow.

In the dark of early morning he retrieved his Mercedes Kompressor and drove it to a cow pasture at the edge of town. With the back glass shot out, the car was a dead giveaway, no matter if he used one of his many spare license plates. He no longer trusted his mechanics. He no longer trusted anyone. Out in the pasture, he doused the car in gasoline, set it ablaze, and retreated at a distance to watch. Once, it had been a treasured possession. Now it was scrap, yet another prize the Temmens had taken from him.

Time to go home, thought Lerne. Time to cut the meat.

He bade the henchman drive back to the house in Winnsboro so they might recover his possessions. There, he could make another batch of the brew, have a decent meal and a shower. Prepare for the war that had only just begun. But when they arrived, the house was gone, and all that remained was a scorched and blasted heap. Two fire trucks lingered to blast the smoking ruins with jets of water. Hissing pops emanated from the rubble. Distant police sirens drew near.

The firemen cast dubious glances in Lerne's direction. He was too overcome for words so Llewellyn covered.

"We're realtors," said Llewellyn.

"What was it going for?" asked one fireman.

"Not much," Llewellyn said as he angled the vehicle away from the remains of the house.

From a little-known garage, they transferred vehicles and changed plates. A petulant air hung over their labors, a miasma. It was the lackey, Lerne noticed. The man brooded, sullen, and Lerne was in no mood for riddles.

"Spit it out," Lerne said to his employee.

"How much you want to bet the others are going up as we speak?" asked Llewellyn.

Lerne's stomach flipped. The thought of his immaculate homes going up in smoke kicked him in the stones. He had to remind himself that the houses, the lands, they didn't matter. Emblems of his former self. He was a new man, a better person. He had plenty of money and could always make more. He had new totems, very sharp. The only worry, then, was the armory in the largest of his Columbia homes. That alone he had to save.

"And how much you want to bet it's the same damn person responsible?"

asked Llewellyn.

"Temmens," said Lerne.

"Who the fuck else?"

"He's trying to flush me out."

"I say we clean out your accounts and leave. We can get three states away before those firemen put the pieces together. And they will. Eventually. And then they'll go to the cops."

Lerne laughed. The henchman was frightened. He didn't understand. At some point, a man had to decide how much was enough. Temmens had found out about the dogs, struck a blow. Lerne retaliated, killed the oaf brother, and burned the barn with the dogs in it. Only right that the boy put Lerne's houses to the torch. There was, in fact, a rhythm to the thing, a pattern. This thing between them, they would hit it back and forth over the net of out-and-out warfare, until one or the other went too far. Then the final blow would be struck.

But Llewellyn couldn't see that. The man's perception skimmed naught but the surface. He was incapable of looking deeper.

"You're scared," Lerne said by way of explanation.

"You ain't?" asked Llewellyn.

"That's all gone. Got it all out. It was Temmens that helped, matter of fact. Now it's in him, all that fear he took out of me. And that's why I'll win."

"Win? What's to win? It's just a bunch of fires being set."

"You wouldn't understand."

"Here's what I do understand. The longer we hang around, the harder it is to avoid getting arrested."

"Is the car ready?"

Llewellyn swallowed whatever else he'd been about to say. By the look on his face, the taste wasn't pleasant.

"Ready," he said.

Lerne climbed into the back, settled under a blanket, and guzzled the brew, crushed Oxycontin, NyQuil, Amaretto liqueur, and grainy crystal meth. It went down hard and bitter, faintly cherry-flavored, and left granules to crunch between the teeth. Little pops in the brain. Beneath the blanket he caressed Shadowcast, ran his fingers up and down the cool angles of the blade. The lackey's impudence had grown intolerable. Now the man had the fear. It would warp things, obstruct the proper perspective. Soon, Lerne would have to deal with him.

They reached Columbia by seven in the morning and cruised slowly through downtown, eager to blend into traffic. Lerne directed his lackey to the house containing the armory. Behind his ribs, his heart began to hammer. The destruction of the houses was a foregone conclusion. But the armory, the weapons, the treasures—those he *had* to save.

No sirens, no firetrucks, Lerne noted as they approached his manse from the back roads. That boded well. With luck, Lerne would arrive there before the Temmens. He could plan an ambush, have it out with the boy right then and there. He imagined holding Shadowcast to the boy's throat, watching the skin pucker under the blade's tip, the boy's eyes going wide with fright. He imagined eating up all that terror, gobbling it whole out of the air, and letting it pass through his body clean and pure, transmuted into simple joy. He would put on some music and start cutting, thrilling at every arterial spurt. The boy's vital fluids would be the medium and all the world the canvas. And at the last he would lean close, peer into the expiring boy's eyes, and pry open his mouth. Then Lerne would look past the teeth filmed in blood, down into the throat, past the lungs and stomach and gonads, right to the very fading essence, and he would draw that out, a fish on a hook, and devour the boy's very soul.

The vehicle stopped short. Lerne sat upright, puzzled.

"Too late," said Llewellyn. He pointed.

Through the windshield, Lerne saw plumes of smoke rising above the trees. No, he thought. He bolted from the vehicle and stood in a haze thick with the smell of burnt wood and metal. *No!*

He ran straight for his property, slowing only when he beheld the pulverized fence and the carnage beyond. All that remained of the house was a great pile of jagged char, lengths of wall and sections of frame rising like crooked, blackened fingers. The fence, the tire tracks rutted into his lawn, such was no doubt the work of the firetrucks and police cars, for their yellow tape was strung around the entirety of the property. In an instant he was under the tape and wading into the rubble, digging at the smoking wet ruin, desperate for a sign that his treasures had survived. At first, he found only common detritus—lengths of plumbing, the corner of a solid oak door, a lone teacup, miraculously unblemished. Then he began to stumble upon them, a warped blade of a sword protruding from the rubble, its once straight edge bowed, its pommel melted into slag, sections of mail blackened but intact and jutting from beneath a length of scorched marble vanity.

Lerne wept. He raged among the ruins, grabbing at his treasures. Pain such as he'd never before experienced wracked his body. Then he saw it, a faint glimmer from the yard, partially buried under a length of collapsed fencing. He scrambled over and with a surge of strength cast aside the fence. Instantly he was confronted with deep surges of wildly fluctuating emotions. First came joy, a great ecstatic jolt, for there before him, ringed in a still-smoking grass, was the cavalry saber, untouched by flame or soot, stuck-blade down into the soil.

But then came rage arcing down his spine. For wound about the hilt of the weapon was a dog's tag and collar, very familiar, with a message scratched into the metal: *Yoo-hoo, halloo, fucker.*

The desecration was too much. In Lerne's head, some final tether snapped. What had begun with the saber came full circle. A heavy calm stole over him. He knew what he must do. And he knew exactly how to do it.

Llewellyn approached and looked around at the chaos before throwing his hands up. "He's not going to stop."

"Get the car," said Lerne. "Load those few pieces I dug out."

"Did you hear me? This guy is out for blood."

"I told you to get the car."

"And I'm telling *you*. How long before they find you—find *us?* This ain't worth a murder charge, and with all the shit I've done for you—Christ, if the cops get me, I'll get the death penalty."

"Don't you see? You already have it."

Llewellyn's face crinkled in disgust. "You have fucking lost it," he said.

"Your whole shit life is a death sentence. From the time your momma shat you out you been walking the bone road. Now, suddenly, it's too much. Pathetic."

"Fuck this. You're nuts. I quit."

Lerne stood, trembling. Had he not known it would come to that eventually? The signs had been there. But such disloyalty would not go unpunished. In a flash he sprang and drove the bollocks dagger into the henchman's ribs. Llewellyn arched at the base of his spine, tried to repulse the attack. By then Lerne had already disarmed the man, cast his pistol into the debris, and rolled him onto his back. With one hand, he threatened with the blade. With the other, he removed the car keys from the henchman's pocket. Then he produced the flask.

"Drink," he said, dribbling the mixture over the henchman's face.

Llewellyn coughed and sputtered but swallowed a goodly amount of the stuff. His eyes began to glaze and roll. He had a hand pressed to his side and blood ran between his fingers. Lerne bent close, brought the tip of the dagger near Llewellyn's eye.

"That little taste ain't it," he said. "Just a scratch. But when I'm done with Temmens, I'll find you, finish our discussion. Until then, crawl away, little worm. And think on what I said."

Lerne reared back and kicked Llewellyn in the ribs. The man howled, climbed to his feet, and staggered off across the lawn. He dribbled blood as he went. He lurched. The problem with that man, Lerne thought as he salvaged what he could from the rubble, the problem with the Temmens and every goddamn miscreant in Columbia, was that they didn't understand. Even Lerne, until that very moment, had gotten it wrong. The question was how much was enough?

Lerne lifted the flask to his lips, tasted his brew, tasted blood. The answer was simple.

There was no enough.

On the second night of the hunt, they finally came across signs of habitation. Gene was concealed in the trees at the far edge of Lerne's last house, a stately affair with massive windows, heavy drapes, and a brick driveway. Beside him, Rich was likewise hunkered down, staring at the property with a look of frustration on his face. What bothered his brother, Gene knew, was the same thing that bothered him: It looked like a set-up. He couldn't see any activity, no lights in the windows, no doors standing open—at least not from the front. And yet there was a car askew on the lawn, the mailbox crushed beneath a tire. The driver's door was open and something—blood or something that looked like blood—was slicked on the seat. Gene sighed, wishing he hadn't left Doc to guard the truck half a mile down the road.

"What's the odds?" asked Rich.

"Fifty-fifty," said Gene. "Lerne's smart enough to lay a trap."

"Maybe we're being paranoid."

"I want a look at the car. Then we can decide."

They crept to the vehicle, an expensive Acura sports model with flashy rims and wheels, leather interiors, all the accouterments money could buy. Gene risked a peek around the fender at the front of the house. Nothing, no movement, no lights. But the side gate was open—he hadn't been able to see that from the property's edge. He turned his attention back to the interior of the car. Rich dabbed a gloved finger into the liquid slicking the seat and held it up. If it wasn't blood, Gene decided, it was a damn good imitation. The keys were still in the ignition, he noticed. The check engine light was lit on the dash.

Gene paused to consider the configuration laid before them. He didn't want to rush in and make things even more dire. But how could they get worse? He and Rich had been destroying Lerne's houses while Mattie and Dale both took care of the dogs and put an ear to the street in the hopes that someone would have information about the lunatic. That last effort had proved fruitless. The man had either vanished or was laying very, very low. On top of that, Gene had only two days left to hand Lerne to the Texans and the house sitting dark and silent before him was the last of the man's hiding spots. And just as they happened to arrive, lo and behold, there's the car, the blood, the open side gate. So, yes, the whole thing looked too good to be true. But Gene didn't have a choice.

"Side gate's open," said Gene.

"I'll take it," said Rich.

"Let me. You try the front. Want the shotgun?"

Rich shook his head, a look of concern on his face. "Be careful," he said.

Gene slipped past the car, sprinting to the side gate. He peered down the side lot, saw a few dots of blood on the stone walkway, and followed it to the back patio. The sliding door leading into the house was open, a bloody handprint smeared on the glass. Gene swallowed the lump in his throat, readied the shotgun into the crook of his arm, and entered. Light fell from a doorway in the middle of the hall. More blood led in that direction, disappearing into the light. Another handprint stood out on the wall beside the light switch.

Gene was nearly to the doorway when he heard a groan, then the clink of crockery and a dribbling noise from the other side of the wall—what seemed to be the kitchen. At the other end of the hall, Rich appeared and signaled that he, too, had heard. They came at the room from separate angles and found Llewellyn seated at the table. The man was eating cereal, the act of which consisted mainly of dribbling milk down his chin and smacking the spoon around a mostly empty bowl. Blood had stained through his rumpled shirt and had dried on his hands. The man's eyes were glazed as they swept in Gene's direction.

"Shit," said Llewellyn. He dropped the spoon.

Gene raised a finger to the mouth of his black ski mask. "Where's he at?"

Llewellyn turned his bleary eyes to the window and motioned. "Somewhere."

"Here? Outside?"

Llewellyn shook his head. "Gone off. Don't know. And don't point the gun at me. You ain't going to shoot."

Gone? thought Gene. That wouldn't cut it. He motioned with the shotgun barrels and said, "Look about a quart low."

Llewellyn lifted his shirt to reveal a crude bandage applied over his ribs. "Stuck me," he slurred.

"Your employer's got some bad habits," said Rich. He was in the opposite doorway and gave the sign that meant the rest of the house was clear. Damn it. Gene had counted on finding Lerne. But there was still hope. He turned to Llewellyn.

Rich frisked the man, came away without a weapon.

"Where's Lerne?" Gene asked.

"Hell if I know," said Llewellyn.

"Hell you don't," said Rich. "He's your boss."

"I quit. And fuck him. He stuck me."

"Call the union," said Gene. "Where is he?"

"Here's an idea. Why don't you two go home and eat shit?"

It was clear from the man's flippant tone that Llewellyn wasn't afraid of Gene, not in the least. He'd expected as much. The henchman was hired muscle, the kind of person for whom hollow threats with the shotgun meant nothing. There wasn't much Gene could do. Rich, however, was a different story. His brother stood nearby, smoldering, waiting for the all-clear.

"What about Roy?" asked Gene.

"Roy," said Llewellyn. He shook his head. "That's old news."

"Tell us what happened to Roy and this all goes easier for you."

You're as crazy as he is," said Llewellyn.

"Last chance," said Gene.

"Fuck you and fuck you," said Llewellyn. He addressed first Gene, then Rich, with the end of his spoon. "I'm done with him. And you. You're all fucking nuts."

In one lightning-fast motion, Rich hoisted the man off his feet and slugged him so hard the man fairly flew into the stove. Before Llewellyn could so much as blink, Rich hit him again. The blow laid Llewellyn out. Rich stood over him, an eager light burning in his eyes. It was only then, seeing his brother looming above Lerne's former henchman, that Gene realized just how *big* Rich was. He seemed impossibly tall, barely able to fit into the suddenly cramped confines of the kitchen.

Gene set the shotgun on the counter, dug around under the sink until he located some glass cleaner. Ordinarily he would feel squeamish with such wanton violence, such brutality. But ordinarily had flown out the window. It took a certain kind of strength to get through such crises, a severity of character. He added it to his list of things to practice and splashed the henchman's face with the glass cleaner. The ammonia fumes did their work. Llewellyn started awake, coughing and sputtering. Rich grabbed him around the neck, turned his face in the direction of Gene.

"Let's try again," said Gene. "Where's Lerne?"

"I don't fucking know," said Llewellyn. He spit out of a mouthful of blue liquid. "He stabbed me and took off. He's gone in the head."

"What about Roy? Did you kill him?"

"Lerne, it was Lerne!"

"You sure?"

"Think I give a fuck about a fat Texan? But Lerne sure did. Cut him up with a sword. Disgusting."

Gene looked at his brother, saw Rich's eyes full of the same mixture of relief and shock that he himself felt. "Where's the body?" he asked.

"With the others," said Llewellyn.

For a moment, Gene wasn't sure he had heard correctly. Not until Rich began shaking the man and smacking him around. In his brother's grasp, Llewellyn, once so threatening, seemed small and insignificant. "What others?" asked Rich.

The henchman began to laugh. That was a mistake. Gene watched while Rich threw the man into the stove, pinned him down, and crushed his fingers under his combat boot heel. Llewellyn tried to break free. Rich hammered his fist into the lackey's face and ribs. There followed several long minutes of crunching bone, screaming, threats, and then, at the end, when Llewellyn finally realized Rich couldn't be cajoled or bartered with, could not be intimidated, and would not stop beating the ever-loving shit out of him until he gave the man what he wanted, there came simple pleading. It pained Gene that they'd come to that, him and Rich, such utter barbarism. But Lerne had driven them to it.

"Real last chance," Rich said in a quiet, tight voice. "What others? Where are they? Where's Roy?"

"The goddamn women," Llewellyn said through bloody teeth. "He put the fat fuck where he put them. Edge of town. In the water."

A cold sweat broke out over Gene's skin. His insides twisted. He'd thought Lerne's villainy restricted to him and his family, the dogs. It chilled him to know that others had been caught up in the man's sickness.

"How many we talking?" he asked.

"What's it matter?" asked Llewellyn. "He's—urk!"

The man's words fell away as Rich closed his hands over the man's throat. Llewellyn's face went red, then purple, then began to turn a wretched shade of blue. His legs pedaled uselessly. Gene watched in numb horror. The thought that Lerne had cut up countless others, the thought that this man had aided and abetted, made him sick. More than sick. Part of him—a large part—wanted to let Rich crush the man's throat. This was not a man who would be missed—not after what he had done. But they needed him alive. They didn't have Lerne—not yet—and Llewellyn was the next best thing. Of course, if Gene called the Texans—precisely what he should do given the circumstances—there would be pieces of Llewellyn strewn from one end of the state to the other by the time they were done. Was Gene prepared to have that kind of blood on his hands? Was he prepared to shed any blood other than Lerne's?

"Let him go," said Gene.

"You sure?" said Rich.

Gene nodded. Reluctantly, Rich released Llewellyn. The henchman fell to the floor, gasping and coughing.

"What about the Texans?" said Rich. "We need to tell them."

"We don't," Gene said as the plan came together in his mind. "But he does."

Gene pulled aside his brother, laid everything out. If they gave Llewellyn to the cops, the Texans would be able to see him, grill him, but not snuff him out. Besides, they didn't give a hoot about the man. All they cared about was finding Roy and putting Lerne out of his misery. Providing he could fulfill those desires; Gene was good as gold. All he had to do was get the necessary information out of Llewellyn and turn him over to the cops. But Rich cut to the heart of the matter.

"Why not call the Texans?" he said. "Let them take him."

Gene glanced over his shoulder to where Llewellyn was retching. Lerne was one thing, but the sad sack sprawled on the kitchen floor was just a flunky, a shit-heel. He was bad, sure. Vile. He deserved whatever Loke and Malak would do to him. But was he worth having that on Gene's and Rich's conscience? Did they really need to be an accessory to *that?*

"I can't," said Gene.

"He stood by," said Rich. "He was at the pit. He knew what they were doing and didn't lift a finger."

"That's true," said Gene. He was still staring at Llewellyn, nowhere near as sure of what he was about to say as he wanted to be. But he said it nonetheless: "We're not killers. Not like him."

Rich looked from him to Llewellyn. "Risky."

"I know," said Gene. "But I can't. And I think my plan will work."

"Think," said Rich. "Not sure."

"Nothing is."

Gene watched Rich's face while his brother deliberated. The transformation was incredible: Rich was nothing like his old self. He was practically a war machine, a hulking weapon begging to be aimed at someone, something. And that's what scared Gene. What would happen when one way or another it was all over? What Rich would be left standing? What Gene? He didn't pretend to know. But what he *did* know was this: They had to be careful.

It was tempting to take the path of least resistance, to throw up their hands and call the Texans and let Loke and Malak come and do their bloody work, but then part of that would be on them. And what mattered to Gene, even if he couldn't really say *why*, was that they minimize that part.

"All right," said Rich. "We try it your way."

Together, they returned to the kitchen. Llewellyn was on his back, mewling. His face resembled a bloody meatball with a single swollen eye darting between Gene and Rich.

"Here's what happens," said Gene. "You're going to tell me exactly where Roy and the others are buried."

"Not buried," Llewellyn gurgled. "Sunk."

"You'll tell me where. I'll know if you're lying. And if you're really sincere, we'll take you down to the hospital and leave you on the curb. You got no idea who did this to you. Some hooligans wearing masks. Dracula. I don't give two shits. After that, it's all on you. But at least you get to live. The alternative is I call Roy's friends who, I might add, very much want to meet you and take you apart piece by piece. Trust me when I say that's the worse choice. But before I call them I'll leave you alone with my brother for an hour."

For emphasis, Rich crouched down and wrapped his massive hands around Llewellyn's head. The henchman's skull seemed so small in Rich's grasp. So fragile.

Tears welled up in Llewellyn's lone working eye. "I don't want it," he said.

"Then make me believe," said Rich.

"I'm a Christian," said Llewellyn.

"Well, we ain't," said Gene. "We got dog gods, very angry."

"And you offend the pantheon," Rich growled. His knuckles went white around Llewellyn's head.

"I'll tell you," said Llewellyn.

"That ain't good enough," said Gene. "So, here's what will cut it. First, you're going to tell the cops everything you and Lerne did and take whatever sentence they drop on you. And if you get lucky and they let you out some day, you're going to give your whole life in service to animals."

"You'll serve their every need," said Rich. "Faithful, complete."

"You'll volunteer at all the dog shelters," said Gene. "You'll donate all your money. You'll be so loving and sweet and let me tell you why. We'll be watching. If you fuck up, if you fail the dogs, we'll find you. Then you and my brother are going to have the sit-down of a lifetime. Now swear."

"I promise," said Llewellyn.

"Don't believe you," said Gene. "Rich, remove his face."

"I swear!" Llewellyn cried. "Every day, on my life, oh *please!*"

The man groveled at Gene's feet. It would have moved Gene to pity had Llewellyn's crimes not been so severe. As it stood, he was fresh out of pity. Mercy, that oft overlooked virtue, would have to do.

"Sounds like we have a deal," said Gene.

Chapter 9

Gene was there to see them bring the bodies up. So was half of Columbia. The police cordoned off the area but there was no stopping the influx of onlookers and gawkers, the ambulance chasers and news crews, all abuzz over having something so overwhelmingly gruesome to report. But they were all going to get their fill of what was coming out of the swamp. And it made Gene sick.

As the morning, then the afternoon wore on, the atmosphere changed. Gradually the barricades shrank back, in some cases stolen outright. By then the crowd had swelled to encompass the field and woods about the little pond, all the way down to the abandoned farmhouse where a similar crime scene had been erected. No small number of those in attendance had brought camper chairs and coolers. It was less a celebration of gore than morbid excitement normally reserved for such looming vistas as Charleston, Atlanta, Charlotte, and the occasional shoot-out in Lexington.

Gene lingered about the fringe until he caught the ear of a young news cameraman. The kid was hardly more than a paid intern, fresh out of college, and with little effort, Gene convinced the fellow to loan him a press badge. Credentials in hand, he made his way down to the water. They'd gotten a meat wagon balanced precariously on a launch of tangled roots. Below, in the water, a scene of great horror: bodies being dragged from the muck, some of whose crude wrappings had rotted or fallen away, exposing putrid flesh.

The women, local prostitutes, were nigh unrecognizable on account of the wounds and voracious nibbling of swamp creatures. When a gray-green arm fell from a roughly bundled bit of tarp and splashed into the water, the knobby white end of the bone sticking up, all but the most hardened of the press and police ducked into the trees. Gene joined them, hunched in the weeds, drenched in sweat and heaving so hard his ribs ached. *Evil,* thought Gene. There was no other word to describe what he was seeing.

Five more bodies came up. Standing guard among the corpses were a few police with faces white as sheets. Beside them were the morgue crew, their meals down their fronts. Gene asked them about a body—big fellow, maybe wearing a fine three piece.

"Hell," said a blanched morgue worker. "That's easy. What's it for?"

"Human interest piece. My camera guys made me go first."

"Lose a bet?"

"Something like that."

The morgue worker shook his head. "Not your day, kid."

The man led Gene to one of the body bags and opened it. Gene recoiled. Everything was puffed up with water and rot, disfigured, discolored. A putrid, fetid stench rose from the bloated corpse. But it was Roy, all right. Even with the wounds Gene recognized the eyes, the jowls, and the bright yellow boots. Of the three collectors Roy had been the most jovial, the quickest wit. They'd had many a good time, Gene and Roy, cold beers on hot Texas evenings, long hours at the bar hollering over football. Time and again Gene had ribbed him about the Houston Texans, a promising but never truly successful franchise, and Roy had jabbed him about the Panthers and their almost-but-not-quite good enough seasons that effectively hobbled a generational talent at quarterback. There had been something like a friendship there, dysfunctional and dangerous, but real.

"Kind of strange he was the only guy," said the morgue worker. "Who was he, do you think?"

"A Texan," said Gene.

"Long way from home, then. Hang in there."

"Long way indeed. Thanks."

Gene made his way back to the barricades. The Texans were gathered about their rented Lincoln, faces drawn tight in preparation of the bad news.

Gene couldn't bring himself to say anything, so he simply nodded.

"Jesus H. Christ," said Loke. He was so pale Gene could see the veins in his temples.

"Positive?" said Malak. He was, like his associate, devoid of color.

Gene offered up the press badge and said, "See for yourself."

The Texans looked at the badge, then each other. Drawing silent straws. Finally, Loke took the badge and headed down toward the water's edge. When he returned, he was even paler and sweatier, and it was obvious to Gene that the man had left his breakfast back there in the weeds. Malak took his friend in his arms and then Gene was witness to something he could never have imagined: Loke and Malak crying in each other's arms. No. Not even crying. They bawled. They wailed. They had themselves a good and proper *lament,* for crying out loud, and Gene stood awkwardly by, unwilling to join in and even more unwilling to put his arms around them. Roy had been his friend, sure. But to Loke and Malak? He'd been their everything.

Gene allowed the Texans their time. And when they finally simmered down to sniffles and eye-wiping, when they blew their noses into their handkerchiefs and drank cold water from plastic bottles, then, *then* they turned to stare once more toward the pond, toward the scene where their fate and Gene's converged.

"We'll collect him from the morgue," said Loke.

"Christ," said Malak. "I've seen things but that, *that* was something else."

"And that lackey you dumped at the cops," said Loke. "What's his name?"

"Llewellyn," said Gene. "He'll confirm my story."

"He better," said Loke.

"I'm sorry about Roy," said Gene. "He was a good guy, all things considered. But we both know who did this."

"All those cuts," said Loke. He shook his head. "Like he got fed to a shredder. That sick fuck."

"Got that right," said Malak. He jammed a finger in Gene's chest. "Focus on Lerne."

"Because the deal ain't done until we have him," said Loke. He tossed the press badge back to Gene, then got behind the wheel. Moments later the Texans were gone. Gene lingered to watch a few more bodies come up out of the water. Death, darkness. Those were the thoughts that occupied his brain. He had few ideas on the afterlife, scant belief in one at all. But if there was such a thing, he hoped Roy had gotten through the door and found a spot at the bar. He hoped the man was sitting down to a cold beer and a little football on the TV. Maybe some otherworldly bartender might ask him if he was hungry from his long and treacherous journey. Knowing Roy, he'd look the man in the eye and say in his low Texas drawl, "Famished."

Gene ducked under the barricade, went on among the gawkers until he found his kin gathered around the Datsun and the truck. Doc was waiting among them, right where Gene had left him, and came up with his tail wagging between his hind legs. Gene knelt and hugged his dog. He couldn't stop thinking about the bodies, the smell. If he slipped up, he and his family would be next in line, dredged from the muck like the others.

"That bad?" asked Dale.

"Worse."

"And the Texans?"

Gene looked up at his old man and shrugged. "They want what they want. And they better get it."

"Then we better figure out how," said Mattie.

Gene scanned the faces of his family. They believed they knew what they were up against. But they hadn't seen the bodies. They didn't understand. Or did they? He looked back toward the pond. What was the point of trying to look away? No, Gene thought. Better to stare at it. Burn it into the mind. His family, they had done their best to warn him. He hadn't listened. But buddy, he sure as shit was listening now.

"Come on," he said and led his family to the truck. That morning, they'd devised a plan, haphazard but feasible. Step one involved telling Laura and James to stay elsewhere until things blew over; Laura had caught a bus back to Boston to stay with an old roommate, and James was staying in Charleston with a cousin. That, Gene hoped, would keep them safe until he gave the all clear. Step two centered around drawing Lerne out into the open, enticing the man to attack. The question was how. At the time, they hadn't come up with a solution, but on the ride over, just him and Rich in the truck, the brothers had struck gold. Now Gene drew his family close.

"Here's the skinny," said Gene. "We need Lerne and soon—about that we're all on the same page. And Rich and I know how to get him. He's off his rocker."

"Putting it mildly," said Mattie.

"But that's the thing," said Gene. "Man's got a sense of theatrics. I think he wants a spectacle. I think he cast himself as the hero."

"We give it to him," said Rich. "He burned us down but didn't kill us. It's not done. He's got to close the circle."

"What are you saying?" said Mattie.

"I'm saying we bring Lerne to where he's got to wrap things up," said Gene. "Lure him in, deliver him to the Texans, and call it a day. I'm saying it's time we go home."

With that, Gene turned and opened the back of the truck. Laid within were the antique rifles, several still in excellent condition despite their internment. It was Rich who'd remembered the weapons, recalling with perfect clarity where he'd buried them. The plan began with—and hinged upon—retrieving the family estate. And there was only one man with the skill, the pluck, the never say die, who could pull it off.

Gene turned to his father. "Here's your stake," he said.

Dale removed his sunglasses. But rather than excitement, Gene saw doubt cloud his father's eyes. "I can't," he said.

"You can," said Rich.

"I can't beat her," said Dale.

"Already did," said Gene. He held up two fingers for emphasis and said, "Twice."

"That was different," said Dale. He was shaking his head and backing away from the rifles. "I was different."

It was not the reaction Gene had expected. He had expected the man to jump at the opportunity to get into a game, get a little vengeance on the woman who had destroyed him at cards, especially on a stake which could be freely gambled without fear of loss. He'd expected the man to be overjoyed at the prospect of having someone in his corner, someone to believe in him.

But as soon as Dale raised a hand to his chest, Gene understood. What's more, he felt ashamed. That last game with Lula had almost cost Dale his life. Now Gene was asking him to once again risk it, to face an opponent he didn't believe he could defeat in an environment that had long ago written him off as a washed-up relic. He was asking his father to go, hat in hand, beg his way into a game, and possibly die trying. What the hell was wrong with him?

"Dad, I'm sorry," Gene began. "I wasn't thinking."

He reached to take his father's arm, reassure him. But it was Mattie who took Dale's arm, stopped the man's backward motion.

"Them Texans will kill Gene," she said. "Then they'll kill us."

"It's fine," said Gene. "I'll figure something out."

"What if you don't?" said Mattie. "Lerne will get the rest of us. And even if *we* get *him,* where we going to live? What about our land? The business? We going to let everyone take *everything* from us?" She jabbed a finger into Dale's ribs. "I don't care no more who got us into this mess. We're in it and there's only one way out. So, tell us, foolsmith. Can you do it?"

Dale scrubbed a hand over his face. He turned to Gene, then Rich, and finally Mattie, looking for all the world like he was ready to bolt and run or cry or both. And he very well might, Gene thought. He had before when the going got tough, when he'd gambled away the money and left Mattie to pick up a second and third job just to buy a little time. And so had Gene. Apple didn't fall far. But it could be halted in its downward trajectory. It could be raised up.

"How would I even get her into a game?" asked Dale.

"Leave it to us," Rich said with a knowing look at Gene. "We'll get Lula into that game."

"Maybe," said Dale.

"Maybe ain't good enough by half," said Mattie. "Neither are you, but you're the best we got by a damn mile. Now wipe that look off your face and say it."

Color rose in Dale's cheeks. He stared at his wife and a fire sprang up in his eyes. "I'll play," he said.

"Play is for children. I don't want you to play," said Mattie. "I want you to fix what you did. I want you to win."

Dale hefted one of the rifles and blew dirt from the barrel. A great many emotions rolled across his face, some of which Gene could only guess. Years of loss, the shame of a failed legacy, the sudden hope that maybe, just maybe, he had one last shot to take it all the way. Hard pills to swallow. Gene was only beginning to learn what it was like. Finally, there was inestimable pride and warmth as Dale regarded his boys. There passed between them the great understanding of fathers and sons, wordless and rare. The sure knowledge that whatever fighting spirit was in Dale, it was within them, too.

"Sabers up," said Gene.

"Into the sun," said Dale. He smiled the cunning smile of old.

They loaded the rifles in the Datsun, wished their parents luck, and watched them drive off between the rows of news vans. Then they were gone, and Gene was left to stand beside his brother and make sense of the great thing, so near a reconciliation, they had just witnessed. The gamble in life was not to go all in nor to sit idly and await death. It was to find the moment, the high-water mark, and ride it to the very last second. Life was force, motion. Noise and heat. It went on and on until it didn't, until a lunatic chopped you up and dumped you in a swamp, and then whatever you'd been was gone and all that was left was rotted meat and bone and a hell of a lot of work for a mortician. That was grim. But Gene didn't care. All that noise and heat had to be held onto, grasped with both hands and brought in close to the chest. All that life. Anyone who said otherwise was plumb full of shit.

And another thing, Gene thought as he closed up the truck. All could be forgiven because all could be lost. And then regained.

In the wee hours of the morning Lerne stole a Chevy Caprice and drove at leisurely speeds through empty streets until he reached a Citgo station on the edge of town, not far at all from the dirt roads that would take him to his final destination. He was far gone on chemicals and rage, coherent only in the strictest sense of the word. But he never felt sharper.

Alone at the pump, he splashed gasoline all over the vehicle and left the nozzle gurgling on the pavement. Then he went inside, his sack of salvaged treasures over one shoulder, and took the sleepy cashier by surprise.

"Oh, Jesus Christ," said the cashier.

"Almost," said Lerne. "Know who I am?"

"I think so."

"Progress," said Lerne. "Get a bag, something large, and come along."

He prodded the boy from behind the register and down the aisles, directing him in the acquisition of ingredients for his brew. In the pocket of his shirt were the last of his uppers, his potent narcotics. At the news stand, Lerne halted the boy by the scruff of his neck. The headline caught his eye. SWORD NUT'S ACCOMPLICE TELLS ALL. Below the text, a photograph of Llewellyn's damaged face. So, the Temmens had gotten to his lackey. They were clever, quick. Likely they believed it possible to turn the tables and plan an ambush. But it was *he* who would ambush *them,* seeking them in their place of power and taking it for his own. And when Lerne was done with them, he would find the henchman, wherever he went, wherever he hid, and extract the price for treason.

"What's that look like to you?" Lerne said, shaking the paper in the terrified boy's face.

"Some dude," said the boy.

"Treason made flesh. What animates it?"

"Food, water?"

"You're filth. Get behind the beer where I can see."

Lerne shoved the boy into the cooler and knelt him on the cold steel floor. Cold air blasted him. He was almost paralyzed by possibilities. He could sever the limbs or bleed him slow and watch him crawl around in his own stuff. He might take his time, make little cuts, each one larger than the next, to carefully gauge the boy's threshold for pain. What a show, he thought, as he glanced about the store. There were cameras in the corners, above the registers, out by the pumps. The boy's demise, however quick or prolonged, would be captured and archived, a warning to all who viewed it. But there were problems to consider. A customer could wander in, unawares, and summon the police. Stuck inside the store, Lerne would be cornered, trapped.

No, he decided. Better to use the boy for misdirection. He kicked the boy into the corner and held forth the flask.

"What's in it?" said the boy.

"Your whole stupid life," said Lerne. "Drink."

The boy took a swallow of the brew and bent double. He began to heave and spit.

"Now you have the medicine," said Lerne.

"I ain't sick," said the boy.

"Wrong. You been sick your whole life. You and everybody else. Drink."

With difficulty, the boy took two more swallows, each one followed by a grimace. By then, the brew had begun to work on him. His eyes began to glaze and his bottom lip hung loose and flaccid. Lerne bunched a fist in his hair and pulled him close.

"I'm taking a trip," he said. "Going to see my mother in Tennessee."

"Is it pretty?" asked the boy.

"Lovely trees. I'm leaving this very minute and I'll be there all week. Tennessee. Tell the police and anyone who will listen. But this here's for you and you alone. When it's dark and late and you're by yourself, I want you to think back on this little moment, just you and me here behind the beer, and I want you to know you came this close."

Lerne pressed Shadowcast's blade against the boy's face, felt the young man tremble. A thin red gash, the smallest of cuts, bloomed on the weeping boy's pimpled cheek.

Lerne gathered his ingredients, adding a bottle of water, a box of powdered donuts, and a pack of matches, and dashed out to the pumps. A trail of gasoline was snaking across the lot. Lerne struck a match and flung it into the approaching liquid. The fire zipped across the lot, consuming the car, the pump. The explosion threw Lerne off his feet. He rose, ears ringing, eyebrows singed, and beheld the flaming roof of the pump canopy flipping end over end as it ascended. A geyser of fire followed it, pure and terrible, to blot out the stars and moon. That was him, thought Lerne. He would rise and rise and rise.

Lerne slid away from the heat and light and headed deep into the woods. He made his way to the ranch and found the place shut up, the shades drawn. The blackened ruins of the barn drew his attention. How many of the venomous dogs had died within? Many, he bet. The buffoon, Rich, as well. He wished to get on his belly, crawl about the rubble, and feel, skin to skin, what he'd done to the place. He wanted to breathe in the burnt smell, dig out the ashen bones of the animals. He wanted to find the boy's skull and take it for a gourd.

But first, there was business at the house. A patchwork front door had been put up, boards and sheets of plywood nailed into the frame. He went round back to the big windows and there gained entry with Shadowcast.

"Yoo-hoo, halloo," he called. His voice echoed faintly through the rooms, up the stairs. He followed it and found the furniture draped with sheets, the beds made, the ceiling fans at rest. In the bathtub, a halfmoon of dry hair clung to the drain cover. A length of floss trailed from the waste basket. Had they fled? Did they really believe escape was possible? But a quick look into the closets proved otherwise. They had taken little in the way of clothes. They would return and soon. And Lerne would be waiting.

He tore the sheet from the sofa and made himself at home with his feet up on the coffee table. Such worn and aged furniture, all in different styles, different states of deterioration. What a bunch of tacky shit, Lerne thought as he ate his donuts. These Temmens—mere pretenders. Mere dirt. Their legacy, that of old glories and failed schemes, would bleed into the dirt before Lerne's fine snakeskin boots. Then he would make kindling of their shabby goods and burn the place to the ground. In five years, maybe less, no one would remember the Temmens. No one would remark on their passing. But not a soul in Columbia would ever forget the name Hollis Lerne. After he finished with the Temmens, he would rebuild what he had lost. Bigger. Grander. And woe befall any who crossed him.

He went into the kitchen and made a brew of legend, the final mead. Crushed caffeine pills and street-grade PCP went into a bottle of cough syrup. The cough syrup went into a fifth of Navy strength rum. By then the dawn light had crawled around the edges of the window shades. Lerne returned to the living room and raised a shade to let in the sun. From his salvaged treasures he selected swaths of fire-blackened mail and donned them. The weight was delicious.

He wiped a crumb of dried brew from the corner of his mouth and rolled it between his fingers. Inspiration struck. His gaze rose to the orchard, the black stubble of the barn, the cookhouse. Salt the earth, he thought. Poison the well.

Dale's plan was simple: pawn the rifles and flag, beat Lula, and win back the house. But his obstacles were many and severe. First was the fact that the weapons, veritable antiques, raised more than a few eyebrows wherever he brought them and demanded worthy compensation. So, too, did his presence. As he went from dealer to dealer, antique store to antique store, and finally to the far-flung flea markets in Lexington in search of the best possible price, folks cast one glance at the rifles (and one glance at Dale himself) before dismissing him. Their explanations, when pressed, were simple. The guns might very well be antiques, but those sorts of things had to go through the proper channels, meaning folk who specialized in historical arms if Dale wanted anything close to the asking price. Plus, it was Dale Temmens doing the asking, a man with whom few wanted to truck. His losing streak and problems with Lerne, not to mention the strange press surrounding his boys' animal ranch, had soured even the most ardent of former admirers. The result was that his price—fifty thousand in cold hard cash—was met with outright laughter.

By then it was late in the day, and Dale's hopes began to flag. They only had time for one more antique mall before business hours ended. Mattie suggested she give it a try, and before Dale could protest, she met the dealer and emerged a moment later, the clerk in tow with a pushcart. The whole time the man was loading the weapons, Mattie gave Dale a look that told him in no uncertain terms to keep his head down and stay out of it. The man wheeled the weapons into his store and Mattie leaned into the car.

"They'll try to squeeze you," said Dale. "Don't let them. Try to get fifty, but if they won't budge, don't settle for less than forty."

"What makes you think that man or anyone will even cut a check for twenty?" asked Mattie. "And they said I inhaled smoke."

"Those things are priceless."

"Says who? You ain't no antique specialist. And even if you were, they ain't exactly mint."

"I'll come with you," Dale said as he unfastened his seat belt and began to exit the Datsun.

Mattie gave his door a hard shove and glared at him. "You'll stay right here," she said. "And take a damn heart pill."

With that, she went into the store, her tank banging along behind her. Dale sat, his heart clenched uncomfortably in his chest. He took his heart pill, chased it with a handful of aspirin. It was useless, he told himself. If *he* couldn't get anything for the guns, Mattie didn't stand a chance. An old lady in whatever attire he had acquired from the Dollar Store? On a breathing machine? She looked like a first-class sucker, the kind about which a dealer could only dream.

Thus, when she returned sans cart and rifles and dragging a duffel bag in her wake, Dale was astounded.

"Stop gawking and take the damn thing," said Mattie.

Dale hauled the bag—quite heavy—into the car, then helped his wife into the seat beside him. Only when she was settled and had taken a few good hits of air and gotten some color back did he dare unzip the bag and peer within. Bound stacks of cash in various denominations were heaped in the bottom. He took one out and thumbed through it. She'd done it. Somehow, against all odds, she'd done it. That had to be a sign. Lady luck had once again cast her eye in Dale's direction.

Or had it? A quick count of the stacks told Dale they were under forty thousand. Well under.

"I could only get twelve," said Mattie.

Dale's heart sank. *Twelve thousand?* The way he'd been playing, Andre wouldn't let him so much as a look at a table for twelve. He raised his eyes to meet Mattie's gaze and thought better of voicing any complaints.

"It's all right," he told her.

"No, it isn't," she said with a wheeze. "Threw this in for the trouble."

She dug an object out of the bottom of the bag and dropped it in Dale's lap. It was a stun gun, complete with a spare set of batteries and a charger. She'd tried her best, he reminded herself. No—she'd actually come through when he'd been unable to get anyone to cough up so much as a dollar. Her best was better than his. Twelve thousand was all he was going to get. He'd find a way to make it work.

"Thank you," he said as he zipped the bag and fired up the Datsun. "I mean it. Words don't even come close."

"Damn right they don't. Now drive," said Mattie. "No mush talk until you win the damn house back."

Dale did as order and drove toward Andre's. But halfway there, Mattie pointed and told him to pull over at—of all things—a daiquiri shop. She'd been stewing in the car, building up a head of steam, and Dale expected her to unload as soon as he put the Datsun in park. Instead, she asked him how much cash he had on him.

"Cash?" said Dale. "None."

Mattie sighed, reached into the duffel bag, and removed a single crisp one-hundred dollar bill. "I need a drink," she said.

"Now?"

"Right now."

Within, there was a bar on the back wall where customers could sit and watch the daiquiri machines mix their brightly colored slushes. That or stare at the bleary TVs. Mattie led the way, wrangling the tank beside her up to the bar, and fairly dropped into a stool. Dale slid in beside her.

"A shot of bourbon," Mattie said to the bartender. "And one of those." She pointed at a machine churning a thick purple slush appropriately called "Grape Freeze."

"Mixed or separate?" asked the bartender.

"Shot first," said Mattie. "And give him a shot, too," she said, motioning to Dale. "But no frozen stuff. He's got to go work."

Dale sat in a state of remarkable confusion. Mattie had never been a big drinker—had never, as far as he knew, sauntered into a bar and ordered shots. Oh, they liked their whiskey well enough, but mostly at home with their records. That told him she had something to get off her chest and she didn't want to do it when they got to Andre's. Dale braced himself, and when the shots arrived, he waited for Mattie to take her glass in hand.

"Liquid courage?" he asked.

"Not for me," she said. "Listen up because I don't got the air to say it twice. If I could go back and do it all over again, I would leave you. Look at me. Look me in the eye. You understand what I'm telling you? You're an addict. I don't care what you call it and I don't care how you cut it. An addict is an addict. You gambled away everything we ever had. Money, clothes, jewelry, and now the house. When I think back on it, at all the times I had to work a second job, work overtime, I get sick. And when I think about all the times we could have done more, had more, felt safer if only you weren't out there gambling, I get steaming mad. Do you hear what I'm saying?"

Dale held her steely gaze and swallowed hard. In the past, he had denied his addiction, claimed Mattie didn't understand his professional calling, and had even gone so far as to accuse her of holding back his ambitions. He could have been a professional, he'd once said during one of their more explosive arguments. The kind you saw on TV. The kind that went to Vegas for the weekend to clean out chumps. The kind they wrote books about. But that had been many, many years ago, the kind of thing a much younger Dale Temmens thought made a good case. The kind of thing, he now realized, that held no water. That realization had come at a cost: his family's well-being. He'd cost them everything. And now their plan hinged on him doing what had brought tremendous harm to them all. Dale *did* understand. That was what had Mattie so steamed.

"Okay," he said. "You're right."

"I need to hear you say it," said Mattie. "If there's ever a chance we come through this, you and me, I need to hear you fess up."

"I'm an addict."

"And you're going to get help."

"I'm going to get help. I *want* to get help. I want—" and there he trailed off. What did he want? He wanted to march into Andre's and shock the world, even if he wasn't sure he could do it. He wanted to win back what he'd lost and he wanted to help his family. But most of all he wanted his wife, the woman he loved more than anything in the world—more than cards, more than himself.

"One more time," he said, tears standing in his eyes. "The very last."

"Has to be," said Mattie. "Or win or lose, that's it. I'm too old. And so are you."

Dale smiled. "Ain't that the truth."

"Good," said Mattie. "Now wipe your damn eyes and take this slug with me."

They clinked shot glasses, threw back their bourbons, and dropped the bill on the bar. The bartender raised an eyebrow but didn't complain when Mattie left him a ten-dollar tip on a ten-dollar tab. Then out the door they went, tank in tow, and drove through the dusk light to Andre's. Cars were parked in rows on three sides of the shack and the porch was thronged with nervous-looking folk who milled about, smoking, spitting, and generally doing much of nothing until one of them spotted the Datsun and pointed. As one, the crowd came to attention. Cigarettes were hastily finished and discarded into the weeds such that one of Andre's dealers was standing nearby with the hose, dousing small fires before they started.

"Is this for you?" said Mattie. She, too, was staring at the assembled throng.

For a moment, Dale was speechless. He'd never seen such a crowd, not since the glory days when he'd been unbeatable, the card king of Columbia. His boys, they'd done it. He didn't know how, but they had. Now he had to do his part.

"I think so," said Dale.

"Then don't keep them waiting," said Mattie.

Scratch that, Dale thought as he popped another heart pill. He had to win and not die in the process.

On the porch, the crowd parted, fell in on either side of them. On their faces he saw intense doubt, scorn, and skepticism. *This old loser? We came out to see this old idiot take yet another pummeling?* He returned their gazes with one of his own, as cool and confident as he could muster. He tripped on a board, almost planted himself on the ground. But Mattie's hand was there to steady him.

On the porch steps they were met by Andre himself. The man was working an apple with the blade of his knife, carving the fruit in thin, neat slices. He sized Dale up, glanced once at Mattie, and spat over the porch railing.

"Is she here?" said Dale.

"Mean the woman who ran you ragged in cards, took your house fair and square?" said Andre. "Sure is. Heard about some last grand retirement match, Dale Temmens' final game. Too bad you already had it."

"I got a stake," said Dale. He hefted the bag as proof.

"Go home," said the aged proprietor. "Take your money and your wife and get the hell off my porch."

"One game," said Dale. "Please, just one."

Andr carved a slice of apple, real slow, and slid it into his mouth. He chewed and said, "Just one. Just one. Heard that before. You even went and had a goddamn heart attack in my place of business. I told you last time what would happen, and I damn well wasn't kidding. Go home." Andre dug the tip of the knife into Dale's chest. "Because if you don't, I'm liable to run out of patience."

Dale was ready for such a response. How could he not be? He'd been hearing it in one form or another for a while, different variations on a common theme: Dale Temmens, once a great poker player, was washed up. Andre wasn't going to let him play. The man didn't make idle threats. But before he could think of a retort, Mattie pushed him aside.

"Bullshit," she said.

Andre's eyes instantly narrowed to hostile slits. He froze, the knife still poised against Dale's chest. "Come again?"

"Listen to this blowhard," said Mattie. "Man walks up with cash money and you turn him away? For what? Because he lost a bunch? Because it makes your place look bad? What are you going to do—cut him up? You ain't. You know it. I know it."

Andre's face began to mottle. "I don't believe we've met," he said.

"Because I don't change diapers," said Mattie. "You carve a man who brings cash money to your establishment and what kind of message does that send? Who is going to risk coming here? Put that knife down before you cut your own damn fingers, take my husband's money, and get him to the table. I hate empty promises. Hate stupid bluffs even more."

The apple fell from Andre's fingers. The man's face turned red, then purple. He looked like his eyes were trying to evacuate his skull by any and all means necessary. He spat chewed apple over the porch railing.

"Who the hell—?" Andre began.

"My wife," Dale broke in. "Look around. This crowd. It's like your game with Flem."

"You see this bag?" Mattie snatched up the bag, shook it about for all to see. "Win or lose, you get a cut. Always do. Now, you going to stand there and deny my husband a game or you going to make history?"

For a moment, Mattie and Andre locked stares. Finally, the man took the bad and passed it to his cashier.

"Go on," Andre growled. "Just don't die in my establishment. And win or lose, you'll never play here again."

Dale passed into the shack. Within, it was likewise crowded, every table full not with players but spectators, filling the place so that the tiny shack seemed near to bursting—all but one, the lone table in back where Lula sat, carefully arranging a massive pile of chips, her steely gaze trained on Dale. The cashier brought Dale's chips to the table. A curious energy filled the place, raising the hair on Dale's arms. There was going to be some bad poker going down, the stuff of legends.

"What's the proper thing to say?" asked Mattie.

"It's good luck," said Dale.

Mattie kissed him on the cheek. "Don't let up," she said. "And good luck."

Dale made his way to the table, stopping only to claim a glass of water, and took his seat across from Lula. He set his chips on the table in neat stacks, his heart pills and aspirin near his elbow. The bouncers came and checked his medications and the dealer set the table and began to recite the rules. Lula waved him off.

"Heard you got together a stake," she said.

"What else did you hear?" said Dale.

Lula grinned. "The last ride of Dale Temmens. A once-great's last game. Blah, blah. But then I heard you had beef with that sword nut in the paper. Word is you're going to war."

"You're no fan of him."

Lula turned and spat. "Got two pitties I rescued. What he did, he ought to die."

"No argument here."

"But that's neither here nor there tonight, is it?"

"Guess not. You heard right. War with him. And war with you. I want my land."

A wicked smile broke across the woman's face. "Then come get it," she said.

The crowd locked ranks. The dealer dealt the cards. And the game began.

The first few hands Dale gave away, playing nervously. He wanted Lula to see him sweat and struggle, get soft on a few easy pots. She grinned and Dale detected what he'd begun to suspect: She read the player, not the cards, scrutinizing her opponent for the smallest sign of indecision, the smallest hesitation, the tiniest flicker of hope or excitement. Sure, she could count cards. Everyone who was anyone could. But Lula possessed a much more valuable skill. Bluffing her would be the toughest thing he'd ever done.

An hour in he'd lost half his chips. An hour after that, he'd lost almost all of it—ten thousand gone. He threw a look over his shoulder and saw Andre on the pickle barrel, a look of grave disappointment settling onto the man's face. It was sad, Andre's look told him. To return for vengeance was one thing but Dale's display was embarrassing. Hadn't the aged proprietor told him as much? Least the man could do was go out fighting. Good, Dale thought. He wanted, needed, Andre to believe the bluff. Maybe Lula was starting to believe, too.

He took a small pot off the table when the cards went sour and gave him the only pair among them. A flicker of interest appeared in Lula's eyes. On the next hand, Dale hesitated and Lula took the bait, raised high and fast. There were cracks in her armor after all. She grazed the cards until she either saw hesitation or the game picked up speed. At last, Dale understood her style. Time to start hitting back. And that's when Dale started counting, saw the pairs and flushes and aces coming well before the dealer dealt and gobbled up three fat pots in a row. All the while he kept watch on Lula, trying to get a bead on her nervous ticks, her signs of weakness. But there was nothing, no sweating, no signs, no errant pauses other than to push a stray curl of hair behind her ear. There Dale was sweating through his shirt, chewing through aspirin, and the woman across the table hadn't so much as broken a sweat. She was less like a woman in the grips of a life-or-death card game and more like a woman out for a leisurely stroll.

A knot of pain tightened in Dale's chest. The lights seemed too bright, the room too hot. He gulped water, called for more. He had to concentrate, stay focused. He'd seen her perk up and then—what happened? Where had he lost her? He had to shake her, had to hurt her, make her understand she wasn't out of his reach, but his back ached, his eyes burned. And in his chest, the pain. He glanced at the clock adorned in snake skins. Four hours into the game. The weariness began to set in.

Dale folded two hands back-to-back, lost a third, then won the next five in a row. On the last, he raised the pot as high as he dared, knowing there were only two combinations that could beat his hand, and saw for the first time the smallest wrinkle of concern at the corner of Lula's mouth. It was an almost imperceptible crease in her otherwise flawless skin, but it was there nonetheless. Was that her weakness? The fast raise, the adrenaline rush of the big pot?

They called and Dale took the hand. Still, there was that wrinkle. He had to know, had to set it up. To that effect, Dale gave up the next two hands, won the two after that, and drew out the fourth into a back and forth raise until the pot had swollen to just under what he'd arrived holding, some eleven grand in various colored chips. He had this, a flush. But without so much as a flicker of concern she dropped a royal on the table and cleaned him out.

As one the shack let out a collective groan. Dale felt the collective disappointment, the frustration. *What was he doing?* they were wondering. Losing, that's what. The knot in his chest tightened. Dale began to tremble. His left arm was beginning to tingle. What had he been thinking? He couldn't beat her. She was too good, too fast. And he was too old, too frail. Lady luck hadn't returned to him. She'd long ago flown the coop, leaving a goose egg in his shoe. He was going to die at that table. There or on the end of Andre's knife.

Then Mattie's voice rang out, sharp and high, and broke through the noise of the spectators and the clamor of many bodies squeezed into such tight confines. It hit Dale like a bullhorn, rousing him.

"She ain't the best, damn it," said Mattie. "*You* are. Now quit fooling around before my tank gives out."

Dale looked back and saw his wife's pinched face among the crowd. Her gaze met his and held it. The knot in his chest loosened. She believed in him, he realized. They all did, his kin. And they needed him as never before.

Dale turned back to the table and his paltry eleven hundred in chips. Across the table, Lula wore a dismissive grin. And why not? She'd earned it, kicked his ass last game and had been kicking his ass all night aside from a few lucky pots. But luck, Lady or otherwise, wasn't going to see him through. No, Dale told himself, it didn't boil down to luck or bad hearts or any of that shit. He was tired of getting his ass kicked. He was tired of losing. And he damn sure was tired of failing his family. To hell with the chips, he decided as he scarfed another heart pill and drained his glass of water. And to hell with the woman on the other side.

"Put my deed on the table," said Dale.

Lula worked her fingers over her stacks of chips and said, "What if I don't?"

"You'll never say you beat the best."

"I already did."

"Not when it counts for everything."

She balled up a chip in a fist then dropped it. Dale had her. There was no denying the truth of his words, not for card players such as they. And so, with a snort of anger, she produced the deed, signed and ready, and laid it in the center of the table.

Now, Dale told himself. Now as never before: It was time to play some goddamn cards.

The game rode hard upon Dale, and across the table Lula's face once again became an unreadable mask. The first ten hands went back and forth, lightning quick, and each time Dale barely had enough chips to stay at the table. He had to draw it out, frustrate her desire to play off the fast, high raises. If he didn't read her out in the next few hands, he'd have to drop back to counting cards and deliver the game into the hands of pure numbers. But nothing about the cards was pure numbers. Reading the player didn't just mean deciphering the opponent. It meant deciphering oneself, knowing why he played, why he lost, why he triumphed. Then and only then could a player play purely, moving from hand to hand with naught but victory in his sight.

On the next hand he watched her closely. The first card produced no raise, nor did the second. Dale stared at his hand, felt his heart flutter. There was one thing he hadn't tried and he would never get another shot. He raised half his chips. She looked up, blinked, and returned to staring at her cards. If she raised, he had her. If not, he was back to square one, hovering on the edge of defeat.

Then, with the smallest hesitation, she met his raise and upped it two thousand.

Dale felt the thread of the game go suddenly taut. His one and only chance had arrived. With both hands he pressed his entire stack of chips, five thousand seven hundred, into the middle of the table. A gasp rose from the assembled crowd.

Lula stiffened. A new wariness crept into her eyes as her gaze roved from Dale to the cards. Come on, Dale urged her silently. Do it, so help me God, this last time, do it.

Lula stared at him, bearing down with all her powers of scrutiny. Was he bluffing? That's what it all boiled down to, Dale knew. Did he have it? *Could* he have it? She glanced once at the dealer's deck, and in that instant Dale was given to know two things. The first was that up until that moment, she'd been counting cards, invisibly and without flaw. The second was that she'd gotten distracted and lost count. He finally had her on equal ground. He held her stare, summoned every bit of will and control to keep his face blank and his hands at rest on the table. Life or death. Who had the guts for so much life or death?

Lula looked one last time at her cards. Then she went all in.

"Show it," said the dealer.

Lula turned over her hand, a straight flush on clubs, five through nine. She glowed, triumphant, and shot Dale a look that told him the game was hers. It had *always* been hers.

Then Dale turned over his. A straight flush in hearts, six through ten.

A stunned silence blanketed the room. Lula's jaw fell open. Then a roar burst from the crowd as they shot to their feet, hands aloft, unable to believe what they'd just witnessed. Dale hadn't been bluffing. He'd won. By God, he'd *won!*

Gamblers rushed the table and congratulated him, slapping him on the back. Men and women, old and young alike, looked upon him with awe. Amazing, they told him. Best goddamn game they'd ever seen. Pictures were taken, hands shaken, and much ado was made at the table until Andre's bouncer herded the crowd out onto the porch. Only Lula remained unmoved, still seated across the table, and glaring at Dale in disgust.

Dale understood. He'd carried that same disgust for years. And as much as he wanted to revel in victory, he couldn't. Not when it was the last game he would ever play.

From his pocket, Dale produced his personal deck of cards—keepsakes all those many years. Their edges were worn, the faces nearly unreadable so often had he handled them. Like precious baubles, treasures. But Mattie was right. If he didn't quit then and there—as ahead as he was ever going to get—he'd walk out that door only to lose everything. But if he couldn't keep playing, another generation could.

He went round and stood before Lula. "Listen here," Dale said with all the kindness and respect he could muster for the best opponent he'd ever faced. "You were this close. And one day, you'll be where I'm standing. But don't let it get away. Hear me? Don't let it eat up everything else."

With that, Dale relinquished his cards into Lula's hands. The import of the gesture was not lost. The woman's anger melted. She held the pack of cards, then stood and shook Dale's hand. In her grip he felt the bitterness of defeat, yes, but also the tempering touch of humility. She'd lost to the best? Big deal. One day soon she'd take the crown.

Then Lula was gone into the crowd, out the door, and into the humid night. As for Dale, he made his way to the cashier and waited while the man doled out his forty-two thousand dollars in cold hard cash. Andre appeared, sans knife, and took Dale's hand; within it he placed an apple, whole and untouched.

"Finest thing I ever seen," the aged proprietor said in a voice unusually thick with emotion. "Next time—"

"No next time," said Dale. "That was it. The end."

"Sure," said Andre. He grinned. Dale was too tired, too proud to respond. He squeezed the apple as if it were Andre's hand and tried to arrange his face into something approaching the genuine pleasure and gratitude he felt. But tears were streaming down his face and people were still congratulating him, singing his praises, leaning close to take selfies while he blinked in the flash. He peered through the crowd, struggling to find the face he sought. He was spent, exhausted. He needed a shower, a meal, and twelve hours of sleep. But first, he held the bag, now full of his earnings, to his chest and turned about until a hand took his arm, until that same hand guided him to the door. He looked down and beheld his good lady wife. She stood before him with tears in her eyes and a sweet smile on her face the likes of which he'd often dreamed and prayed to see once more.

"Let's go home," said Dale. He placed the deed in his wife's hand.

She smiled. "Come here, fool."

"Nowhere else," he said as he took her in his arms. "Not ever again."

Gene led his family home, discovering the broken back window, the raised shade in the living room, and the drape thrown off the sofa. While Mattie and Dale waited in the truck, Gene, Rich, and Doc made a thorough search of the house. Whoever had broken in was gone. But if it was Hollis Lerne, Gene prayed he would return.

He helped unload their belongings from the Datsun and the truck and got Mattie and Dale settled in the house. Then, with the afternoon shadows getting long, Gene called together a final council of war. The plan was simple. Lerne's hiding places had been destroyed, his lackey jailed and questioned, and Lerne's very name besmirched by scandal and criminal activities. If he didn't get himself caught by the police—and Gene was absolutely confident the man would not—he would return to the ranch for his vengeance.

To ensure minimal collateral damage, Mattie and Dale would stay in the house with the doors and windows locked. Gene and Rich would patrol the property. There was a special knock used to identify each other and they would all keep in contact via hand radios. The first person to spot Lerne would light it up over the radio, and Gene and Rich—and *only* Gene and Rich—would engage and subdue the man. Then they'd call the Texans. But one thing mattered above all others: No cops.

"What if he gets you?" asked Dale.

"He won't," said Gene. "And if the cops nab Lerne, I'm dead. It's got to be the Texans."

"How do you know these Texas boys are going to keep their word?" asked Mattie.

Gene paused. In the past, Loke and Malak had always been true to their word and Gene didn't think this time would be different, not after Gene had helped them recover Roy. And if they didn't, well, Gene had nothing left to barter, nowhere to go. He could defend himself, sure. But even with Rich at his side, would that be enough?

Gene wrote Loke's number beside the phone, reviewed the plan one last time. The whole thing was rickety, riddled with holes. What if Lerne brought help? What if he stole another car, rammed the place? What if he waited, dragged it out over weeks or months? Loke and Malak wouldn't wait that long.

Outside, he and Rich soaked everything—the house, the trees, the whole damn orchard—in case the lunatic tried another fire. Not a long shot considering the fireworks Lerne had caused at the nearby gas station. The man's story about visiting his mother was little comfort to Gene, not the least because the woman was long deceased. The Tennessee story was a ruse to draw away the authorities, open up Gene and his family to another attack. No, Gene thought as he doused the porch, the windows, the patchwork front door. Lerne wouldn't wait. It was going to be soon. It had to be.

It was late afternoon when they'd finished their watering business. Gene decided it was time to check the cookhouse and make ready their gear. The lock on the cookhouse door was intact. They went in, brushed the dust from the blotters, and sat at their desks. Between them, they had the shotgun full of rubber buckshot and the stun gun. Since Rich was more experienced with firearms, Gene would take the latter. But at that moment, he didn't want to think about weapons, Lerne, or the whole nasty business arrayed before them. What he wanted, come to think of it, was to sit back and share a quiet evening with his brother, maybe get into the peach brandy with him. Doc in his bed in the corner, with the door open and the dusk sun slanting in through the doorway, the peach fragrance blowing in from the orchard—the whole shebang. He'd never taken the time to appreciate such moments when they were within easy reach. He'd never lingered on the simple details, the rustic reduction equipment rusting in the corner, or the branches, the leaves, just beyond the window. Instead, he had always been staring off into the future, thinking about the next move, the next way to slip the noose that had been threatening to close around his neck since he'd left Austin. A month ago, it was life in the Everglades, him and Laura and Don Lettuce trailblazing the boutique alligator hotel industry. Now? A shiver passed through him despite the heat. He dug Rich's last bottle of brandy from its hidey-hole and pulled the cork.

"To the dead," he said.

"Them poor women," said Rich.

"And Roy. And the Lab most of all."

They took one swallow each, passing the bottle across the desks, before Gene replaced the cork. He needed it, that pleasant ball of fire, to steady his nerves.

"Scared?" asked Rich.

"Very," said Gene. "You?"

Rich shook his head. "That's done with."

Not for the first time Gene wondered if his older brother's metamorphosis was for the best. The man was no longer scared of his own shadow. But he didn't smile much either. There was no compromise, thought Gene. He'd gone from coward to warrior with one blow to the head. Was the old Rich still in there, buried under brain trauma? Or was the old Rich, like the Rich he'd known before the war, dead and gone? Gene didn't know. And he couldn't bring himself to ask. Rich hadn't forgiven him. That was understandable. Gene hadn't forgiven himself.

A noise from the doorway caught Gene's attention. Doc was nibbling something, dirt or crumbs or some such. Gene snapped his fingers and the dog looked up with a guilty expression and licked his chops.

"About that time," said Rich. He was checking the shotgun, removing the shells, blowing down the chambers, and reloading the weapon, all with cold, mechanical efficiency. "Where you want to start?"

"The barn," said Gene. "Then the orchard. Then rinse, repeat."

His brother looked up from the shotgun. His beard had been trimmed close to his jaw. It made him look younger, more like the Rich Gene had grown up with. But that was an illusion, wasn't it? Neither one of them were kids anymore. They were something else.

"Sure you're ready?" his brother asked.

"As I'll ever be." He meant it, too. Gene wasn't a fighter. He wasn't a warrior like Rich. If they got hold of Lerne and it came to blows—and Gene was sure it would—he wouldn't stand a chance without Rich and Doc at his side.

The brothers Temmens set off on patrol. Despite the remnants of dusk, a pale slice of moon shone above the trees. Here and there, pinpricks of stars winked through the branches. Gene walked with the stun gun in hand, poised, alert. It was mere formality. Getting close enough to Lerne to use the thing would be suicide, especially if Lerne was armed, as Gene believed he would be. But together with Rich and a healthy dose of rubber buckshot, they could put the man down long enough for the Texans to come collect. Or so he hoped.

The barn was as they'd left it—a blackened ruin that yet stank of smoke, burnt wood, scorched roof shingles—with one exception. Nearby, Chanticleer's grave mound had been dug up, and the carcass thrown onto the rubble.

"Son of a bitch," said Rich. He gathered the dog's body, returning it to the grave.

Gene worked dirt over the remains with the stock of the shotgun. By the time he was finished, it was too dark to see much without the flashlights. "We'll do it proper later," he said.

"The son of a bitch," Rich said again.

"Stay focused."

"I'll kill him."

"Can't do that."

"Then I'll hurt him," Rich said with a terrible light burning in his eyes. "I'll break every goddamn bone in his body. And they can have what's left."

Gene said nothing. The dogs, Chanticleer, the pit, the barn, and the black Lab, they haunted him every night, waking him from sleep, sweating and exhausted. He wasn't complaining. If anything, he deserved it. He turned to look at Doc. The dog had long been his compass, a trusted companion by which to gauge his decisions. But Doc was no longer by his side. Gene whistled.

"What is it?" asked Rich.

"Doc," Gene called. He whistled again. When had the dog wandered off? They'd left the cookhouse, yes, gone through the trees, yes, and—the barn. Gene whistled again and strode to the edge of the barn rubble. A choked bark sounded in response. Gene shone the flashlight toward the sound, saw Doc poised at the edge of the rubble. He was wobbling toward the light, eyes glazed.

"Doc," said Gene. "Come here."

The dog's ears pricked. He turned in Gene's direction, took two wobbly steps, and collapsed, panting hard.

"Rich," said Gene, darting between the trees.

"I see," said Rich. He was already running, the shotgun held against his chest.

Gene reached the dog first and dropped to his knees. Doc was licking his chops and whimpering, but there was no wound Gene could see. What, then? Gene plucked a granule of some substance from the ground beside Doc's snout, sniffed it. A familiar odor pricked his nose, pungent medicine and distilled spirits.

"Oh Christ," he said, sudden panic slamming him in the chest. "Got to make him throw up."

"What is it?" said Rich.

"Poison. Hold his legs."

Rich set the shotgun against a blackened length of barn wall and knelt beside the dog while Gene set the flashlight on the ground, and opened the dog's jaws. Please, he prayed, let it not be too much, too late.

No sooner had Rich taken hold of the dog's paws than Doc stiffened and growled. In that instant the rubble behind Rich erupted. A dark form arose, clad in ashen armor. There was a flash and a cry of sudden pain. Gene saw the tip of a sword protruding from Rich's side before his brother toppled into the dirt.

Gene scrambled back. He watched, paralyzed with fear, as the blade retracted from Rich's flesh. Into the beam of the flashlight stepped Hollis Lerne, his ash-streaked face crinkled in confusion as he stared down at Rich's writhing form.

"I burnt you," said Lerne. "You're dead."

The lunatic's voice jolted Gene to action. He sprung to his feet and went for the shotgun, but Lerne was too quick. The sword blade grazed Gene's arm, parting flesh. A second swipe nearly rent Gene in two. He scrambled back along the barn wall, ducking wild swings. He had to get Lerne away from Rich and Doc, find a way to get to the shotgun.

A moment later an opportunity presented itself. One of Lerne's slashes embedded the sword's blade into a standing barn beam. Before the man could free the weapon, Gene flung himself into Lerne, expecting to take him to the ground. Instead, he was swung about as Lerne pivoted and drove him against the wall. Gene pulled free, but not before Lerne grabbed something from his belt and drove it home. A shock of pain, cold as ice, punched through Gene's side. He fell away clutching the wound and felt hot wetness trickle between his fingers. In Lerne's hand he saw a dagger, long and pointed, slick with blood.

"First you," Lerne said as he wrenched free the sword. "Then I finish the oaf. Then I'll saunter up to the house and catch up with your folks. Got so much to discuss, them and I. Can you imagine? But watch it now. You're leaking."

Lerne regarded Gene with cruel pleasure and approached. Gene fell and lay sprawled, gasping through the pain in his side, scrambling to get away as Lerne's boots crunched in the debris behind him. He heard the man's rasping breath, very near hysterical laughter, and the metallic jingle of the armor. Panic seized him. It was too late. Lerne was above him, the sword raised, the blade flashing silver in the moonlight.

There was a bark—a gnashing, metallic sound. Lerne jerked to a halt. Between Lerne's legs, Doc had seized a length of mail and was pulling the man back. Lerne spun about, grunting and writhing, until he delivered a serious kick into the dog's ribs. A second kick lifted Doc into the air. Gene heard the yelp, the crack of bone, and rage unlike any other flooded his battered body. He'd promised: No more dogs. Gene dug his arms into the rubble, wrapped his hands around a loose length of blackened beam, and pulled himself to his feet. Just as Lerne righted himself, Gene swung with all his might.

The beam smashed Lerne in the stomach, bending him double. With a roar, Gene pulled back and swung again, clipping Lerne in the face. The blow sent the man spinning. A spray of liquid arced, putrid and stinking. The man was vomiting.

Gene pulled back for a third swing and barely ducked a sudden swipe of the sword. Somehow, Lerne had found his footing and recovered. A series of jabs with the blade pushed Gene back as he struggled with the weight of the beam. The stab wound in his side had gone cold as ice, sapping his rage, his strength. If he didn't clean Lerne's clock and soon, he was dead. He had to bait out a big swing, get the man off his feet, and close in with the stun gun. To that end he feigned a misstep, crying out in very real pain. He prayed it was enough.

Lerne took the bait, lunged forward, and swung the sword. Gene was crouched, ready. He gathered everything he had, every last bit of strength, and swung the beam into Lerne's knees.

There was a crunch of bone, a howl of pain. Lerne staggered but didn't fall. Gene had already skirted aside, snatching the shotgun from the rubble. He spun to face his enemy, cocked both hammers, and fired.

The blast took Lerne off his feet, parted him from his weapon. He sailed through the air and came down with a crash. Gene limped over, sure the man was down for the count. But Lerne was already turning over on his stomach, reaching for his sword. Mother of God. What would it *take?* He freed the stun gun from his belt and collided with Lerne just as the man had risen to his knees. The pair of them rolled into the rubble, Lerne drumming with his mailed fists and screaming a kind of incoherent banshee wail while Gene struggled to get a clear shot at the man's unarmored neck. A blow caught Gene in the ribs, very near the stab wound. Another caught him in the groin. The pain was otherworldly, vibrant swaths of color. Adrenaline alone kept him conscious. But the blow had left Lerne exposed.

Gene jabbed with the stun gun. The shock threw him clear, scrambling his sight. When his eyes finally refocused, he saw Lerne lying prone a few feet away. The man was on his back, limbs rigid in crude approximation of a belly-up beetle. His frame twitched. A pale white foam issued from his mouth.

Voices began to register; lights flashing in the dark. Gene rolled over and saw Dale and Mattie bearing down with flashlights, calling for their boys. Gene dragged himself upright, one hand pressed against his side, and made it to Rich just as his parents emerged from the orchard. His brother was conscious, doubled in pain. Gene tore strips of his shirt, balled them against Rich's wound.

"One of you get him to the hospital," Gene managed to say. "The other take Doc."

"What about you?" asked Dale.

"I got to stay. Did you call them?"

"You're *bleeding,*" said Dale.

"They're on their way," said Mattie. She was already hoisting Rich over her shoulder and heading back through the orchard. "Dale, get the dog!"

Gene found Doc whimpering in the rubble and knelt beside him. The dog's tail thumped at his approach. A fog of pain was in the dog's eyes. Gene shoved a finger down his throat, massaged his belly, but the poison had dulled the gag reflex. Gene lay beside him and stroked his neck. He'd been unbelievably brave, he told the dog, fearless. It was going to be okay. They would get him to the vet and fix him up. All he asked was the dog be patient, hold on a little longer.

The dog regarded him calmly, lovingly. *Gave it our best,* he seemed to say.

Dale returned and wrapped Doc in a blanket. "You're hurt," he said to Gene.

"Rich is hurt worse. So is Doc. I'll call the ambulance. Go."

With a last anguished look, Dale turned and fled into the darkness with Doc in his arms. Gene heard their vehicle tearing off down the drive. Then the quiet rushed back in, broken by Lerne's gurgling.

Rich. Doc. The rage took hold. Gene limped over to inspect Lerne. The electricity had mistreated him. His limbs remained poised in the air and his face was warped, the lips curled back on fine white teeth.

"What did my dog eat?" He knelt beside Lerne and began to hit him with his cast hand, hard as he could, in the face. "What was it?" He'd *promised.* "Was it poison?"

In a break between blows, Lerne's eyes found his, staring in unblinking hatred. "That dog wasn't afraid," he said through blood-filmed teeth. "But you were."

Gene hit him again. His strength was ebbing. "What was in that stuff?"

Lerne's fingers flexed. "Give my sword," he said.

Fuck the fist, thought Gene. He knelt, jammed the taser into Lerne's neck, and gave him everything the little device could give. The lunatic went rigid, a human two by four, and spat white foam several feet into the air. He had it coming. All that and then some. Two more shocks. Three. Any more and the man might die—and then what? Gene would die. His family would die. The Texans. Gene set aside the weapon and began to tend to his wound.

He'd just gotten his side wrapped up with a wad of torn shirt when the rented Lincoln pulled up in the drive. From it emerged the Texans, divested of the dilapidation into which they'd fallen. They were dressed for business in fine pressed suits, shiny new boots, and stiff ten-gallon hats. Toward Gene they directed looks of surprise. Toward Lerne they directed heavy, dark stares.

"There's your man," said Gene. He motioned.

In the rubble, Lerne began to cough and stir as if he sensed the approaching danger.

Without further ado, the Texans strode carefully into the rubble and stood over Lerne. Loke bent at the waist and spoke, his tone barely held in check.

"Remember us?" asked Loke.

"Remember Roy?" asked Malak.

"Bet you do," said Loke.

Malak hiked up his pants and knelt beside Lerne. "Let's go over things once more," he said.

"And pay attention," said Loke. "It's the most important question in your very dumb life."

"Did you kill our friend Roy?" asked Malak.

Lerne broke into coarse laughter the likes of which Gene had never before heard. It was loud and high-pitched, a sound that rose out of him from some dark, horrible swamp of blood and madness.

"Roy's dead," Lerne said through big, whooping breaks between the laughter.

"Did you kill him?" asked Loke.

"Yes!" Lerne gurgled back. "Yes, I killed that fat fuck! Bled him all over my goddamn boots!"

"Why?" asked Malak. "We didn't even know you."

Lerne's laughter faded. The smile vanished. He stared back at the Texans, and as he spoke, foam flew from his lips and spittle dribbled down his chin.

"It's *mine,*" he said. "Every goddamn drop, every clod. This place is *me,* you stupid fucks. The air, the water. The trees, the dirt. I'm everywhere. Even in *you,* way down deep. One of these days I'll crawl out your mouth and pick up a knife and cut your fucking head off. You hear me, you Texas fucks? I'm here until the end of time, right up until everything burns away and there ain't no sun or moon or sky. But not me. I'll still be here. Waiting for someone else to bleed."

Gene spat. Madness. The ravings of a doomed and dying lunatic.

As for the Texans, that sufficed. They borrowed the stun gun, gave Lerne another jolt. Then they stripped the man of his armor and loaded them separately—the gear into the backseat and the lunatic dumped like some disgraced animal into the trunk of their car. The last Gene saw of Lerne was a scant glimpse of the man's eyes that, though set in a face gone rigid on electricity, burned with unmistakable hatred. He seemed to look through Gene, staring straight off into the trees and the dark and far, far beyond. All-seeing, impossibly powerful, that gaze. Then the trunk shut.

The Texans helped Gene to his feet and got into their car. Loke's window slid down and cold air conditioning blasted Gene's face.

"We're square?" asked Gene.

"Square," Loke said and motioned to Gene's side. "Get yourself looked at."

"And don't ever, *ever* come back to Austin," said Malak.

The Texans drove away. Gene imagined he'd heard something from their trunk, a scream or laugh or wild animal cry. Or maybe it had come from the trees. A chill slid down his spine. By then things were getting fuzzy. He was out of sorts from pain and blood loss. He called an ambulance and limped off toward the gate to prop himself on the sign. "Doc," he called. "I'm sorry. Doc?"

When the ambulance arrived, he was laid out, talking to himself, seeing things. He thought Doc was there, riding with him to the hospital.

"I thought you'd gone," said Gene.

The dog licked his face, his tears.

"We're almost there," he told Doc, taking the dog's paw in hand. "Almost."

In the trunk, Lerne had visions. Gleaming Shadowcast appeared, beckoning. He was swimming up a birth canal lined with spears and wicked scimitars and had about him the audible clank of a man encased in fine, polished armor. He wanted to emerge and lick the brine of war from his fingers, figure out which way the sun. If only his chest and neck didn't hurt where the current had entered. The shotgun blast had broken a few ribs, of that he was certain. But Lerne didn't care. All he needed was out from that trunk, and then his sword. He'd go right back to the ranch and cut every last one of them open. He'd root around in their innards to find what they'd swallowed to make them so fucking brave. He wanted it, if for nothing other than a trophy.

The car bumped to a halt and the trunk opened. A harsh light shone in his eyes. Beyond, the looming figures of the two very angry Texans. Lerne felt curdling within him a raw and primal hatred. Thirst gnawed at his throat, his brain. He wanted his brew, his medicine, and as he reached to take the flask from his belt, one of the men snatched it and gave a sniff.

"Sweet Christ," said Loke. "What's in it?"

"Whatever it is," said Malak, "it's gone off."

"Hey, old son," said Loke. "You drink this?"

The Texans drizzled him with the brew. Lerne lapped at it, needing its strength.

They lifted him from the car and Lerne saw they were in the woods, someplace unfamiliar. He was dragged by his heels, groaning in his captors' grasps. He'd put all their heads on pikes, put the dogs' heads next to them. Then he'd burn the place and salt the earth. He reached for his weapons but they weren't there. The realities of his situation were coming into focus. What had happened? How had he failed? He'd placed his trust in the sword, cast out all fear, and claimed his turf. There was nothing else, he thought in desperation, nothing more he could do! Tell him, he prayed to Shadowcast. Tell him where he'd strayed!

At last, the journey was complete. Lerne was bound to a tree, arms and legs splayed, his neck tightly restrained. The light shone in his eyes. The Texans hovered nearby.

"All that talk back there," said Loke. "It got us thinking."

"Inspired, you might say," said Malak.

To Lerne's horror, they brought forth Shadowcast, passing it between them to test the heft. To see their hands fondle his weapon, to see them defile it with their touches, was an outrage. The bile rose. With it, the tears.

Loke leaned close, his breath warm on Lerne's cheek. "Now you're starting to get it," he said.

"What was that bullshit before?" asked Malak. "I'm here and some such?"

"Lord, but you do go on," said Loke.

"Think of it like this," said Malak. "It's you doing this to you."

"Take it a step further," said Loke. "It's always been you."

"Anyway," said Malak, "we owe you. And Roy, he owes you double."

They brought forth clamps, rubber tubing, plastic rain ponchos, and bags for their boots. Lerne sagged against the tree, a bitter, familiar taste on his tongue. Fear. It had returned at the last to taunt him, to drive him away from self-possession. But Lerne would not back down. He swallowed the fear and leaned toward the Texans, feeling the blood rushing hot into his face.

"Your friend died on his back," he said. "In the mud. Mewling like a kitten. But I didn't listen. I kept cutting."

They struck him in the face again and again. Lerne felt the blood run from his nose, his split lips. He spat a blood-slick tooth into the dirt, then another. "First I used the knife," he said between blows.

They kicked him, slammed the back of his head against the tree. One of his eyes, it wouldn't come into focus. But the other went right on staring, watching the Texans writhe in their rage.

"But the man wouldn't quit," Lerne said through swollen lips. "I laid in with the sword."

Terrible pain took hold of his tongue. He saw the Texans pull back and discard something, some little piece of meat, and he choked on his own blood. He tried to form words and couldn't. Nothing pressed against the back of his teeth. They gagged him and what was left of his tongue probed the fabric, searching for purchase. He wanted to tell them what it felt like, his hand wrapped around the stiletto as the point sank into Roy's paunch. He wanted to describe the feeling of the broadsword as it parted flesh, exposing throbbing muscle and glistening organs. He wanted to describe the look on Roy's face—intense pain and disbelief—and how the man had been too absorbed in his own dismantling to scream. But Malak wound duct tape around his face and neck.

"Who's he remind you of?" asked Loke.

"A famous person," said Malak. "Merle Haggard?"

"Meat Loaf," said Loke.

"What's it matter?" said Malak. "Do the honors."

Loke closed both hands around the sword's handle. "Going to make a lot of mess," he said. "But we got time, right?"

"Don't fly out until morning," said Malak. "Got time."

"Time for us," said Loke. "Time for Roy."

"Our closest friend," Malak said and kicked Lerne in the ribs. "Hey, old son. Are you listening? Do you know what this is for?"

"This is for Roy," said Loke.

Lerne saw the flash, heard the hum of the sword cutting through the air. There followed a bloom of hot pain in his arm. He followed the flashlight beam to where his wrist ended in stump, a trickle of blood escaping past the knotted tubing. Behind the rag, Lerne screamed.

Loke passed the sword, kicked the wriggling hand into the weeds, and tightened the rubber tubing above the stump. Malak reared back to strike.

What was a man who followed his heart, Lerne wondered as the blade descended, but the best of all men?

Chapter 10

By day four, Rich was fed up with the hospital. For one, the food was bad, and the nurses were insistent that he consume not one, not two, but *five* small containers of frozen juice concentrate every day, all the most hideous flavors. Cranberry Tropical paint thinner and the like. It was to help prevent the possibility of a urinary infection, they said, on account of his nicked bladder. But what with the copious antibiotics they'd been pumping into him, Rich was little concerned. He was also bored stiff. Lying about in a bed gave him too much time to think, and what occupied most of his thoughts was the battle that had landed him in the paper-thin gown. To him, the greater pain was not the wound but the humiliation of once again getting blindsided by Lerne. *Twice*. He chalked the first time up to his old meek ways. But the second? That was plain foolishness.

As a result, he landed back in the hospital—the same he'd previously occupied—with his same behind frequented by cool breezes every time he stood up and his nicked bladder full of bitter juice concentrate. Rich wanted pants. He wanted to go home. Finally, he called the nurses and asked to see the doctor. He had, of course, already seen the doctor—several times—but those visits had been obscured by pain medication. He wanted answers, damn it. He wanted *out*.

The man in the next bed was in for a spleen removal. He discovered through Rich's tattoos his veteran status and wanted to share.

"I'm a vet, too," said the man. "Third Armored. I saw some shit in Iraq."

"Bet you did," said Rich.

"Normally don't talk about it."

"No reason to buck the trend," said Rich. He had things of his own to think through. Last thing he needed was the man's war talk.

Only the man wouldn't stop. He unspooled at length about Tiger platoon's march down the main street in Fallujah and the 82nd Airborne's hijinks in that doomed city. He told the stories in tones of abstract horror, as if it had all happened to someone else. Rich understood. He knew that a man could experience events so traumatic that they resisted all attempts at reenactment through language. It had been like that when he'd been lifted out of the combat zone, stayed that way for years. To even think about discussing what had happened over there had once been enough to put him in a cold sweat.

But lying in the hospital bed, listening to the vet beside him ramble on, Rich found he could think back on that war with less difficulty. It would always be with him, sure, but the more recent war with Lerne had left deeper scars. Because that's what it had been, he realized. A weird, off-kilter war.

If only it hadn't cost so much, Rich thought as he mashed the nurse call button. The barn, their business, Chanticleer. Doc, too. According to Gene, when Dale had arrived at the vet, Doc was in bad shape, unconscious and barely breathing. The veterinarian later said one of the broken ribs had punctured something and the poison—Lerne's brew, they were to learn—had put the dog into shock. He'd bled to death before they could get him into surgery.

At that moment the doctor entered, a woman about Rich's age with graying hair and crisp slacks. She scanned a laptop screen, glanced at Rich as if for confirmation, and sat on the edge of his bed.

"You don't remember me, do you?" she asked.

"I was pretty high a few days ago," said Rich.

"No," said the doctor. "A few weeks ago." She tapped the side of her head. "Some nut chipped you with an axe. Now you're back for—a fence railing?"

"I tripped."

"Major piece of fence to penetrate four inches into your abdomen. And no splinters. Very clean entry. What an odd fence."

"We take our fencing pretty serious."

"You'd have to. You'd also have to travel at some serious velocity to get it that far into your body. Were you traveling very fast? Possibly by zeppelin?"

"Can I go home?"

The doctor eyed him critically. She didn't believe a lick of it, but that didn't matter. All Rich had to do was stick to the story he and Gene had cooked up. No one could know Lerne had attacked the ranch a second time, just as no one could know the man's final fate. For all intents and purposes, the man had in fact ventured to Tennessee to see his long-deceased parents. Then, inexplicably, he vanished. The detective called every now again to tell Gene that they were still looking, still keeping an eye out, but the trail was colder by the day. The doctor gave Rich's side a series of pokes and prods, checked his vitals, and listened to his heart. Finally, she ceased her examination and asked, "Are you going to be back in a week, punctured by a rogue rain gutter?"

"I hope not," said Rich.

"Me too. But I have to question the decisions of a man who has run afoul of so many common materials."

"I'll try to be more careful."

The doctor sat on the edge of his bed. She set aside the clipboard and laptop and looked Rich dead in the eyes. "Mister Temmens," she said, "let me ask you something. And I'm serious now—don't answer right away. Are you *okay?"*

Rich couldn't think of what to say. Truth was, it had been a long time since the honest answer had been anything other than *absolutely not.* What precisely did okay feel like? Was it *not hungry?* Was it *got enough sleep?* He didn't think so. If he had to guess, it was something along the lines of being at peace, at rest, which he most certainly was not. His body was healing, yes, and he no longer talked to ghosts but Rich did not feel at peace.

"Will you have one of the nurses call my brother?" asked Rich.

The doctor cast him one final look of doubt. Then she left. Rich stared after her, embarrassed. All the while, the vet in the next bed had not ceased his stories. He was talking still when the doctor left and Rich dressed, and he kept on talking when the nurses came in their blue surgical scrubs and puffy masks and wheeled the man off for OR prep. Rich heard the man's voice receding down the hall, a shrill echo tottering on collapse.

At the desk, Rich signed himself out and collected his belongings. With the help of a retractable cane, he made his way to the front in time to see Gene pull up.

"What the hell you doing?" his brother said as he leapt from the truck. "Supposed to let me come up to get you."

"Had to get out," said Rich.

Rich had to be practically loaded into the passenger seat, secured with the seat belt. The drive home proved challenging. Every bump in the road spread waves of pain throughout his body. By the time they pulled up at the ranch, he was drenched in sweat and his jaw ached from clenching his teeth.

"Where's Mom and Dad?" he asked between gulps of air.

"In town to pick up the dogs," said Gene. "Figured you could do without the fuss."

"Good call."

"Let's get you in bed."

"I been in bed," he gobbled a pain pill and grabbed his cane." Right now, I need to walk."

With his brother at his side, Rich began a slow circuit of the property. In the orchard, the trimmed trees were laden with ripe, fragrant fruit—last of the season. Where the barn once stood there were thick fresh wooden beams rising from the ground. Above, he saw the ribs of a roof and the square frame of a bale. All of it much larger than the old structure. And were those rooms being laid out? Frames for walls?

"You're rebuilding," said Rich.

"Need a place for the dogs," said Gene. "Mattie thinks we should re-open, use what's left of Dale's winnings and the insurance payout."

Rich strode up to a beam, put his free hand on the hewn wood. He looked back at his brother. "What do you think?"

Gene chewed his lower lip. "I think it's going to take an awful lot of work. Got to convince people to give us another shot, put the scandal behind us. Money wise, well, the Texans signed back my half of the business and we never declared bankruptcy. But truth is, I don't know. It's risky as hell."

"But possible," said Rich.

Gene nodded. "Possible."

"What about Florida? The alligator hotel?"

At that moment the phone in the cookhouse began to ring. Gene made to go. "You be all right a minute?"

Rich waved him off. "Answer it."

Alone beside the new barn, Rich lingered to take it all in. Much bigger than the old one. Plenty of room. Risky. But possible.

He turned, prepared to make his way to the house, and found himself face to face with two matching grave markers, side by side. They were carved wood, plain but for the names engraved on them. *Chanticleer,* read the one. *Doc,* read the other. *Beloved friend,* it said on both.

Rich told himself not to cry, but the tears came anyway. He was filled with a dull and awful ache that defied articulation, a pain both quiet and severe. He hoped the dogs, like the ghosts, were happy wherever they were, and if they weren't anywhere, well, at least they didn't hurt anymore. He didn't know if anyone could ask for more.

Gene's voice broke through the quiet, calling his name. Rich saw his brother step from the cookhouse, the phone held against his chest.

"Mom asks if there's anything you want?" he hollered.

Rich wiped his eyes, shook his head, and started for the house. On the way he plucked a low-hanging peach and took a bite. The flesh was sweet, sun-ripened. Juice dribbled down his chin.

Gene was in the cookhouse, watching the peacocks taunt the goats through the fence, when his desk phone rang. It was Laura calling from Boston.

"Tried your cell," she said.

"Lost it," said Gene. "How's Boston?"

"Fewer strays. How's Columbia?"

"Hot," said Gene. "But tolerable." They were, in a sense, talking in code. He couldn't tell her everything—not what happened to Lerne, in particular—but he had already told her enough to put her worries to bed. No harm had come to her or James as the result of his strange war with Lerne. That, at least, was a win in his ledger.

"Figured you want to hear it from the horse's mouth," she said.

"Let me guess," said Gene. "Staying put. Going back to school."

"Who gave you a crystal ball?"

"It's what I would do."

"You still going to Florida?"

Gene laughed, mirthless. He had already talked to Don, told him he was going to stay put a while. Had family business to attend. How long? Gene didn't know. It all seemed so remote. Not just Florida, but the life before the fire, before Lerne. He lay awake most nights turning over in his mind the events of the last few months, failing time and again to fully make sense of it. Nor could he make sense of *who* he had been. Who was that Gene Temmens who almost got himself and his family killed? Who was the idiot responsible for the two graves in the orchard? He looked at Doc's bed, still in the corner, and shuddered.

"That's on hold," he said. "I'm sorry about everything."

"So am I. Wasn't a bad plan, you know? You and me in Florida. I think you were right. Could have been amazing. But so can what's there in front of you."

Gene stared through the open door at the skeleton of the barn. He wanted to believe Laura. He wanted her to be right. But every time he looked at the emerging structure, his heart began to pound. Pools of sweat formed under his armpits. Who had he been? Who was he *going* to be?

"How are the dogs?" Laura asked when Gene didn't respond.

"Good," Gene said with a dry mouth. "The money Don sends is keeping them in the good life. Barn should be done in another month. After that? We'll see."

"Guess so," said Laura. "If you get bored in the winter, visit me in Boston. James, too."

"We'll freeze to death."

"Thank God someone invented coats. I'll let you get back to brooding. As for me, I have to study. Lots to catch up."

"I'll think about it," said Gene. "Boston, I mean. To visit."

"Good," said Laura. "Think about the rest, too."

"Hold on. Florida, the alligator hotel, all of it. I meant it. I just wanted to tell you I was sincere. But I'm glad to know you."

Laura gave an approving snort. "Stay warm, Gene Temmens."

Gene hung up and sat staring at the barn. His side was aching where Lerne had stuck him, but if he took a pain pill then, he'd be groggy all evening. The pain wasn't even that bad—yet. Sometimes he liked the pain. Kept him sharp. Helped him remember.

He looked again at Doc's bed. Another shudder. He needed some space. He needed to get out.

He took the truck and drove into town, determined to air out his feelings. No better place than the closest watering hole—the very same bar that he, James, and Laura had closed when he had arrived back in Columbia with his head up his own ass.

He went in, slapped down his money, and drank a double whiskey before coming up for air. Next was a whiskey neat, ice on the side. He had to slow it down what with the wound and the pain killers. At least, he told himself as he sipped his second drink, it wasn't the peach brandy. As he drank, he became privy to a nearby conversation between two men. One was very clearly a tourist with a thick Yankee accent and clothes ill-suited for the heat. The other Gene recognized from Andre's, a lesser card shark known for taking rubes in Shanghai poker. The card shark was greasing up the tourist, yakking about this and that attraction, and barely touching his drink. The tourist, meanwhile, was drunk—and getting drunker. Then Gene saw it, the smallest movement—well executed unless one knew what to look for.

A minute later, the card shark angled himself toward the bathrooms. Halfway there, he changed course. Gene sighed. It wasn't any of his business. Let it go. But if he did, he would feel like shit the rest of the night. "Be right back," he told the bartender.

Outside, Gene caught up to the card shark as he was getting in his car. "Made it easy," he said.

"Come again?"

"Give me the kid's wallet."

The man sucked his teeth and drummed his fingers on the roof of his car. "I know you," he said. "Dale Temmens's boy. Ain't seen your old man in a while."

"And you won't," said Gene. "I ain't going to ask again. Give me the wallet."

The man grinned. "Say I don't. What then?"

"What happens," said Gene said, "is I take a drive over to Andre's, let everyone know what you been up to. Think Andre is going to welcome a thief into his shack? I sure wouldn't. Was me, I'd ban that person for life. Then I would tell every other back-room rounder, make it so you can't get into a game anywhere between here and Charleston. Heck, if I was Andre, I might wonder whether you had stolen from *me,* and who knows what might turn up? That's what happens. Or—and pay attention, now, because I'm feeling generous—you give me the wallet and go the fuck home. Then I go the fuck home. We forget we ever had this conversation. How's that sound?"

The man resumed sucking his teeth, but the smile was gone from his face. "Just like your daddy," he said, and handed over the wallet. "A winner."

Back in the bar, Gene bumped into the tourist, then produced the wallet and slapped it on the bar. "Think you dropped this," he said. He didn't wait to see the tourist's reaction. He didn't really care. What had he expected—that he would feel good for doing, God help him, *the right thing?* What *was* the right thing?

His brave interjection had made his side ache something awful. Time for a pain pill. For bed. For staring at the ceiling all night. A light rain peppered the windshield on the drive home. The heat broke, gave way to a rare, cool breeze. It smelled like the woods—pine and old oak and ash trees—and like a city washed clean by funky, gray rain. It made the pain in his side worse. By the time he pulled up at the ranch, he was clenching his teeth and pouring sweat. Into the cookhouse he went for his pills. He washed them down with a swig of peach brandy—why not? Even with the pills, he wouldn't sleep. He made it as far as the porch before coming to a halt. The lights were on in the living room. The music was still going. He heard Mattie's voice from the front and Dale's response from the back. All they seemed to want, his strangely loving parents, was each other, their boys, and the animals. They, at least, had come through it all with some measure of peace. What, he wanted to ask them, tethered them? Why did he feel so adrift?

But Gene knew the answer. What had happened to them—to the dogs, the ranch, all of it—it wasn't their fault. It wasn't Rich's, either. It was his and Lerne's, and the lunatic was gone. That left Gene. He wouldn't deny it, wouldn't shirk it. Not anymore. He just wanted to know how to live with it.

Gene stood on the porch, holding his aching side. Just the thought of going into the house, the thought of dealing with his parents, made him. He looked up at the trees, the night sky, now clear. At the stars winking above the leaves. Cool enough to sleep in the cookhouse. He scrounged a blanket from the back of the truck and was halfway to the cookhouse, consigned to sleeping at his desk, when a low, mournful howl broke from the trees at the edge of the property.

Gene stopped in his tracks, heart pounding. Had he imagined the sound, familiar and threaded with pain?

Gene swung one leg over the fence, then the other. Curtains of Spanish moss tickled his face, low-hanging branches scratching his neck. He plodded forward, feeling his way through the darkness. The howl sounded again, close, just ahead. His heart pounded in his chest. A path of scorched earth lay before him, the trees bare where the fire had grazed their branches. A rustling in the brush. Gene froze. From the darkness in front of him there emerged a familiar shape. It was her, the black Lab, the fur unevenly grown back over puckered skin. The dog's eyes shone in the dark, bright with fear. Gene took a step closer, and the Lab bared its fangs and growled.

Gene felt the fear inside of him, a surging rush of terror that threatened to pull him under. He couldn't do it. He couldn't face the dog. Whatever bond he'd had with her was gone. When Lerne had burned the barn, where was Gene? Where was he when the other dogs were sent to slaughter?

Gene fell to his knees. The blanket fell from his hands. She knew the truth, the things he could not face until that moment. He was not a good man. He was small and selfish and scared, and he could not make things right. She was scared because she'd been mistaken. She had trusted him. And what had it gotten her?

Well, she was right, Gene told her wordlessly. He'd failed her. He hadn't been there when she'd needed him. He hadn't kept his promise. But this time would be different. This time he wasn't going to leave her.

Gene reached out. He asked the dog to forgive him. They were scared, he told her, but if they tried, maybe they could get past it. Because look, behind all their pain and terror, way down deep in a place that nothing could ever touch—did she see it? There was a light—the dog star—unwavering in the dark.

His fingers grazed her snout and the last of the dog's resistance melted. She fell crying and scratching in the dirt, and Gene took her fire-ravaged body in his arms and gathered her close, breathing in her musty dog smell, touching her wounds. He held fast to her, whispering the good sayings of the heart that only dogs could understand.

"It's me," he said. "I'm here, right here. Always."

Acknowledgements

A lot of fantastic people helped make this book possible. Thanks to Daniel Wallace, Malike Abduh, Martha Otis, Elizabeth Parks, Timika Dione, Maya Dean, Jeanette Tryon, Zita Hüsing, Jonathan Clark, Greg Byrd, and the many writing mentors I've had over the years: This book wouldn't have been possible without your guidance and support.

Matt Blasi's short fiction and essays have been widely published in *The Superstition Review, A Cappella Zoo, Arroyo Literary Review,* and *Gargoyle Magazine* to name a few, and his scholarly work has appeared in *postScriptum* and *The Southern Quarterly*. He earned his B.A. from the University of Florida, his M.F.A. from Rutgers University Camden, and his Ph.D. from Louisiana State University. He lives and teaches in Shreveport, LA.

Printed in the USA
CPSIA information can be obtained
at www.ICGtesting.com
JSHW031640161123
52103JS00005B/25

9 781958 901434